The Key, the Door, and the Kingdom

Emily-Jane Hills Orford

The Key, the Door and the Kingdom ©2025, Emily-Jane Hills Orford

Tell-Tale Publishing Group
Swartz Creek, MI 48473

Tell-Tale Publishing Group supports the right to free expression and the value of copyright. The purpose of copyright is to encourage writers and artists to produce the creative works that enrich our culture. The scanning, uploading, and distribution of this book without permission is a theft of the author's intellectual property. If you would like permission to use material from the book (other than for review purposes), please contact: permissions@tell-talepublishing.com. Thank you for your support of the author's rights.

Printed in the United States of America

Chapter One

"*Help!*" She flailed her arms this way and that. Her legs kicked as if she were orchestrating the fine art of Kung fu. Forces she didn't recognize pounced on her from every direction. She fought on, tossing her body this way and that. Her legs and arms became entangled in fabric. Her clothing? The long gown was cumbersome at the best of times, but for fighting, and for riding a horse for that matter, the skirt restricted movement. Even the wide drape of the arms caused her to become further entangled.

"*Help!*"

"*Anne.*" *A calm voice called out. Reassuring hands gripped her shoulders gently. She felt a sense of calm descend upon her. The opposing forces faded. Disappeared. Her body relaxed. Her breathing calmed. Her eyes fluttered open.*

"*Granny?*"

"*You had a dream, granddaughter of mine. Like the last one.*"

"*They almost got me this time, Granny. How can I stop them?*"

"*Keep practising your defense moves, Anne. You will need them. Sooner than you realize.*"

"*Yes, Granny,*" *she murmured softly as her eyes fell shut again and she drifted into a more peaceful sleep.*

Chapter Two

Granny was a good storyteller. Since Mom had to work all hours of the day and night to keep a roof over their heads and food on the table (or so she claimed), Granny was Anne's principal caregiver. Every night, and sometimes during the day, too, Granny would sit and tell Anne, even at the age of seventeen, the most fantastic stories. She didn't read them in a book. They weren't stories of the Hans Christian Andersen collection, though they were equally as good. They weren't the "Alice in Wonderland" tales either, though Anne often felt like she was falling through a time warp or a dimension shift whenever her mind wandered into Granny's tales of a door, a key and a hidden kingdom. They were so real.

"Is she telling you another fantasy?" Mom asked, scorn evident in her tired, angry voice. "Visions and make-believe. Nothing from the real world. Life is tough, Anne. Always tough. And hard work. You won't find any fairy tale endings in this world."

"There are no fairy tale endings in the world I speak of either, child," Granny scolded her daughter for her coarse comments. "Life in every world, in every time and in every dimension is hard work. It doesn't hurt to have a little fantasy woven in for good measure and to help us manage the hard work along the way."

Mom wasn't about to give up the argument. "She's seventeen, Granny. A little old for your fairy tales."

"Is that true?" Granny then turned to Anne who shook her head. "There, you see?" She pointed to the girl. "Anne doesn't think she's too old. And neither am I for that matter. I came from that world. To save your skin, Eveline! To give you a better life!

A safer life! I left behind the love of my life to save yours. And this is the thanks you give me."

"I might have been better off staying in your fairy tale world," Mom snapped. "My one visit wasn't long enough to assure me that it was real. Other than the real prince in shining armor, there wasn't much there for me. Or was it merely a dream? Another one of your fantasies. At least had I stayed, I wouldn't have to slave day and night cleaning up other people's messes." She didn't wait for a response. None came. The door to our tiny apartment slammed shut behind her as she stormed out into the cold, dark night to clean office buildings. That was her night job. In the day, she cleaned people's houses.

Granny and Anne sat in silence. Anne was deep in thought. It's true. At seventeen, Anne was at the age when most girls were flirting with boyfriends and avoiding the daily regimen of homework. However, Anne was homeschooled, mostly by Granny. So, the girl was cocooned from the rest of the world. She knew her letters. She knew her history. She knew her math and science better than most girls her age. She knew how to fight: with hands, feet, sword, knife, even a bow and arrow. Unfortunately, what she didn't know was how to socialize, how to make friends, how to be a friend. Anne had Granny. She was her world. She was all the girl needed. Even if it was rather childish for a seventeen-year-old to sit on her bed listening to Granny tell stories, Anne wouldn't change it for the world.

"Is it all true, Granny?" Anne broke the silence. "Is it really all true?"

"Yes, Anne. It's all true. And it's almost time for you to venture through the door and see for yourself. Your mother, my daughter, Eveline, never believed me. She never had the urge to explore, to discover the truth behind my stories. Then you came along and she had to work so hard." Granny let out a deep sigh, shaking her head sadly. "I wish…" Her voice trailed off. "I won't be around forever, Anne. I've told you before and I'll tell you again. There's a box in my closet. It contains my journals, instructions to the door, which you already know about since we visited there many times, and, of course, the key. It's the key you wear around your neck on the gold chain. The one I insist you carry with you always. Once you find the right door, only you can turn the key. Your mother might have turned it once, but both worlds spoiled her, taking away her innocence and her ability to believe. And, as time moved on, she found it easier to stay hidden here. In this time. In the twenty-first century. My poor, dear, Princess Eveline." She paused, shaking her head sadly. Glancing up, she gave her granddaughter a half-hearted smile. "You believe, don't you, Anne?"

Anne nodded and smiled weakly. "Yes, Granny. I believe." She didn't like where this conversation was going. Granny didn't often talk about her end. She hadn't been well for some time, now. And she refused to seek medical attention. Anne was worried. She didn't want to lose Granny. Not now. Not ever.

"Is it really true, Granny? Is there really another kingdom? One where you were Queen?"

"Yes, Anne. It's all true." Granny stood up slowly and made her way down the hall. "Wait here while I fetch something from my room."

"What is it, Granny?" Anne called out, but Granny was already halfway down the short hall, her footsteps mere patters on the cold wood floor.

The apartment wasn't much, but at least there were three bedrooms. If one could call them that. Anne's room was little more than a broom closet. In fact, her mother claimed that was what it was meant to be. The girl's bed was no more than a thick mattress on the floor, squeezed in between the two opposing walls. The chair where Granny sat half straddled the division between the girl's room and the hall. There was no door for privacy, merely a curtain that she pulled across. Not the dwelling fit for a princess. If that's what she was.

The light in her room was dim, with only a small floor lamp to illuminate the space. There were no electrical outlets, so a chord draped out the opening and along the hall to the nearest outlet. Anne was accustomed to working in the dim light. If she felt the need for a brighter ambiance, she worked at the kitchen table, where the overhead light beamed from directly above. It wasn't much better. All the lights in the apartment were low wattage. Her mother was insistent on keeping the hydro costs to a minimum. Lights had to be turned out when not in use and low wattage bulbs were in each socket.

While she waited for her grandmother to return, she slithered over closer to her light and pulled out the key, still on the chain secured around her neck. She leaned into the light and studied the key, as she often did when things were quiet and she had nothing urgent that required her attention.

She had done some research on antique cast iron keys like this one. It was made of cast iron, probably forged by hand in a blacksmith shop. It was crudely made, but solid. And small, which was a good thing, as that made it light weight and easy to conceal under her clothing. The shaft was short and hollow with a round edge. There were scratch marks along its length that suggested friction from frequent use. The end was slightly bent as if at some point it had been bent in an effort to make it work in the keyhole. The bow, which she held gingerly between her thumb and forefinger, was elaborately decorated. If held vertically, the bow had the appearance of a heart, with multiple lines of thin iron interweaving within its shape. And, in the center of the heart, was a tiny, shiny red gem, that was firmly molded in place. It was a very pretty key, a work of art in itself.

Anne hadn't yet tried the key. There hadn't been the need or the opportunity. At times, she wondered if it really was functional. Or, rather, a decorative item to wear around her neck. She wanted to keep it in plain view, to proudly display it. She had tried that once, only to be severely reprimanded by Granny, who insisted the key be hidden at all times. *It is for your eyes and your purposes only. It must be safeguarded at all cost,* she had stated quite firmly.

Hearing Granny's footsteps making their way back, Anne tucked the key underneath her blouse and sat back on the mattress, waiting expectantly. She listened to her grandmother's movement, concerned about how the older woman was moving slower each day. Sadly, Anne realised Granny's body was wearing out, but at least her mind was as sharp as ever. Granny was not as spry as she once had been. She was once tall, too, but the years had caused her to hunch over more intensely, making her posture and her poise that of a hunchback. Everything about her reflected her age, from her withered skin to the thinning hairline of what was once thick black locks. Anne was tall, too, and her hair was thick and long, but not black like her grandmother's. It wasn't even a dark brown like her mother's. Anne's hair was more of a sandy blonde, perhaps inherited from her father? She didn't know; she didn't know who her father was; at least not yet. Nothing about Anne reflected her grandmother, except her sparkling eyes and bright smile, one that shone with pleasure at every moment when her grandmother shared her stories.

Anne looked up as her grandmother entered the room carrying a thick book, one of the historical encyclopedia's she bought after having saved her meagre earnings from taking in sewing. She purchased it years ago. She handed the heavy book to her granddaughter and then returned to her seat, letting out a pained huff as she settled into her chair.

"Turn to page thirty-five," she instructed.

Anne did as she was told. At first, the page appeared blank. Then words and images fluttered across the white pages. The girl jumped, the book almost sliding off her lap.

Granny appeared not to notice. "Read."

"In the years leading up to King Arthur's reign, the country now known as England had many ruling kings, battling amongst themselves and amongst the Picts from the north and the Saxons from the east. There was much magic in the land during these unsettled years. At least, that's what the legends claim. Legends swirled around the famed stone circles like Stonehenge. In the land now known as Cornwall, three kings battled for their control over the land and its people. King Uther Pendragon, who was believed to be the father of King Arthur; King Gorlois, who was believed to be the husband of the beautiful woman, Igraine, who gave birth to King Arthur; and King Ceawlin of Wessex who frequently invaded the Cornish lands. History doesn't record much of these three kings, other than their mythical connection to the legendary magician, Merlin. Very little is known of King Ceawlin, other than the fact that he married a woman who disappeared mysteriously just as she was about to give birth to their only child, only to return years later with a grown daughter."

Anne gasped. "King Ceawlin is your husband?" She glanced at her grandmother, who nodded in response. "My grandfather?" The older woman nodded again. "And Mother did return with you?"

A third nod. "Once. And that was how you came to be. Some visiting prince, who flattered my young daughter."

"You don't know who? My father?"

"I know. It's all in my journal. When the time is right, you will read it."

"If Mother went there with you, why does she insist that it's all fantasy?"

"Because she chooses to forget." Granny sounded so terribly sad. "We had to leave quickly. Like the first time when I escaped to give birth to your mother. There's danger everywhere in that realm. Only Arthur was able to set things straight. For a short time, at least."

Anne flipped through the pages that followed the passage she had finished reading. "Why are all the pages blank?"

"Because that history hasn't been written yet, Anne. You must return to take your place in history. Your grandfather is still alive. Still king. He's waiting for you. But he's getting old like me. He can't wait forever."

"Is that why you kept me sequestered all these years? To hide me from the outside world of 2019?"

"And to make sure the magic of the past didn't trace you to this time and place." Granny spoke quietly. "You see, child, this realm through the secret door is not another dimension, but rather another time. And whatever you do in that time will alter the time line forever."

A loud banging on the outer door startled the two, ending their conversation. Granny recovered first. "You must go. Fetch the sacred chest from my closet. You know where it is. It has all you need. My journals. The ring."

"What ring?" she asked. She knew about the journals, knew the importance of the key that hung around her neck. But this was the first time she had heard anything about a ring.

"Never mind that." Granny waved a finger to stop further questions. "Place it on the middle finger of your right hand. You will learn its purpose when the time is right. When you reach the other side. Now you must hurry and do what I say."

"But Granny," Anne started, but was instantly hushed.

"Now," she spoke in a sharp whisper. "It is time. Your mother won't be coming home. Not tonight. Not here." She reached over and pulled the girl into a fierce hug. Setting her back, she wiped a finger gently over Anne's cheeks. "No time for tears, Anne. Remember what I said. Take the ring from my chest and place it on the middle finger of your right hand and keep it there always. You have the key around your neck?"

Anne nodded, a sniffle escaping her throat. This was it. This was what Granny had warned her about for so many years. It was really happening. Too soon. "But Granny," she croaked out another protest as tears leaked from the corners of her eyes.

"She is in there," came a gruff voice from the hall. "Get her. Before she can escape."

"You have heard the voices." Anne nodded. "You have had the dreams." She nodded again. "It is time. No more tears, dear granddaughter of mine." Granny again scolded the girl gently as she reached out to pull Anne into another hug. A tight one. Full of love. Probably their last hug. Granny continued, "Keep the ring and the key with you at all times."

"But Granny." Anne didn't relinquish her grip on Granny. She wanted the hug to last forever. "What about Mother?"

"She's…" Granny didn't finish. Not immediately. "There must have been an accident. And now they come for you. I knew it would happen. I just didn't know when. I can't allow them to catch you. It is time you took your destiny into your own hands." Another pounding on the door jolted the two. "There isn't time. There is money in the chest. In case you need it. Gather only what you feel you can carry. You'll be on the run. And you must move quickly and with stealth. Like I taught you." She unwrapped the girl's arms and gripped her firmly by the shoulders. "Go. Now. Before it's too late. Slip out the fire escape and into Mrs. Snelling's window. She always keeps it open. Rest there until it's safe to sneak out the back, through the alley." Granny had befriended, with reservation, the kindly old neighbor next door, taking in some sewing projects and caring for the woman's apartment whenever she was away. "You know what to do after that."

Anne nodded. They had been through the escape procedure countless times. The girl had never understood why. She thought she was safe. Here. With her mother and her grandmother. Safe forever.

More pounding. "Open up. Police."

"Go. It is not the police. It is worse. Our enemies from the sixth century have found us." It was obvious that their safe lives had been shattered.

"Granny." Anne bit back a sob. She didn't want to leave. This was the only home she'd ever known. Granny was her lifeline.

"Now."

Snuffling back a sob, Anne nodded. She quickly wrapped her grandmother in her arms. She sensed she would never see her again. Grabbing her backpack, she shoved a few treasures inside, as well as a change of clothes. At Granny's insistence, the bag had always been within grasp, next to her bed, ready for a quick get-away. It contained a water bottle, a flashlight, a long cord of strong rope (Anne was never sure what that was for), and a utility, do-it-all, knife. There were other items, too. Things Granny had added over the years. Things she insisted her granddaughter would need when the time came. The bag was already full to bursting. Now, her last-minute additions covered the top, barely leaving room for Granny's chest, which she would retrieve on her way out. She grabbed her outdoor jacket and slipped down the hall as Granny made her way slowly to the door.

"Coming," Granny called out. "Give an old girl a minute, why don't you."

She was buying the girl some time. Anne entered Granny's room and fumbled through the closet until she found the chest. She knew it was the one Granny wanted her to take. A quick look inside confirmed that it contained what Granny promised. She slipped the ring on the middle finger of her right hand as instructed, then closed the lid, securing it shut before shoving it in her backpack. She zipped the sack closed and slung it over her shoulder. She heard the lock flick on the front door. Dashing the remaining steps down the hall, she slid the lower part of the large window high enough to squeeze through, allowing one foot to feel the metal surface of the fire escape before pushing the rest of her body through. She paused. The sounds inside were muted, but she could hear the door opening.

"Where is she? Where is the girl? She belongs to me."

"Now wait a minute, young man." Granny was arguing using her disciplinary voice. "You can't just barge in on an old lady and start making demands. I have no idea what you're talking about, for one thing. What do you mean by a girl? There is no one here but me. And my daughter when she's not working."

Anne didn't wait to hear more. She slid the window back down and made her way cautiously to the neighbor's. As Granny promised, the window was unlatched and open enough to push upwards and slip inside. Mrs. Snelling was away for a few days, allowing Granny access to care for the birds that chattered in their cages in the main room. The sound was soothing. As she slid the window back down, as far as it would go, since it never was kept firmly shut, she heard a barrage of noise from the apartment she had vacated only moments before.

"Where is she?" The man's voice was louder and more vicious than before. More banging. A woman's scream.

"Granny. Oh Granny." Anne slunk down to the floor below the window ledge and allowed her tears to trickle down her cheeks. She didn't dare move, didn't dare make a sound, didn't dare put on any lights. She knew her way around this apartment as if it were her own, the layout being the same only in reverse. She would hibernate beneath the window until it was safe to escape the building. To leave behind the only life and the only family she had ever known.

Chapter Three

Anne didn't know how long she crouched underneath the window in the neighbor's apartment. She wasn't sure, but she must have dozed off briefly. It wasn't something she wanted to do again. Her safety was at risk and she must honor her grandmother's teachings and follow the journey that would inevitably lead her away from all she knew and all she held dear in the world. Her legs were cramping and she felt an urge to relieve herself, but she didn't dare move. There continued to be noise next door. There was also noise in the hallway. And, as if she willed it, the morning finally dawned with sunlight streaming through the grimy, streaked wIndow. More noise was heard in the street below and people in the apartment above were starting to move about.

It was time.

She glanced around the room, taking in its contents. Mrs. Snelling obviously used this room for storage. Good thing, too. The girl's eyes latched on immediately to the object she sought: a strong wedge of wood, a broken beam perhaps, to position above the lower part of the window to prevent it from being slid open by a thief. Or, in her case, an abductor. She couldn't latch the window as it didn't close all the way. If she were going to make her escape, her best route was through the building and not down the fire escape where everyone would be able to see her. Besides, the trailing metal steps ended a good full storey above ground. It would be a hard fall.

No. There was a better way. But she had to make sure that no one entered through the window while she made her escape. Granny had taught her to be extra cautious, extra observant. She levered herself into a standing position and tiptoed over to the desired object. It wasn't heavy and it appeared to be adequate in length to prevent anyone from opening the window wide enough to squeeze through. As she had done. They could break the window, of course, but that would make more noise and attract unwanted attention. At least, that's the way Anne reasoned.

Although she tried to be quiet, in this room full of junk, she was bound to knock something over. Unfortunately, it was a large stack of books which crumpled on her feet, causing a thump and a squeak as the pain ripped through her foot and up her leg. Her exclamation was met with similar noise from next door. They were coming. She had to move fast. Wedging the beam into place, she was satisfied that she had bought herself a few minutes to orchestra an escape.

The dumb waiter. It was in the kitchen. When she was younger, she and Granny would visit Mrs. Snelling and, while the older ladies enjoyed a cup of tea, Anne would play with the birds and explore the mirror-reflective apartment, searching for similarities and differences to their own. One of the differences was the dumb waiter. Upon opening what she thought was a cupboard door, she was surprised to find a cavernous hole, big enough to climb into and hide. Only, when she tried, she slipped down a long tunnel and landed with a thud in the basement. Granny had been distraught, concerned that Anne had hurt herself, or worse. She was fine. But she did receive quite the scolding.

"Our building was once an old house," Granny explained. "A mansion, really. There's all kinds of hidey-holes and nooks and crannies. The dumb waiter was installed to assist the staff in carrying large objects from one floor to the next."

"Like an elevator?" Anne asked.

Granny nodded. "In a way, yes. They never did block it off. They really should have boarded over the opening. At one point, Mrs. Snelling thought she might make it into another storage cupboard. A fine idea which didn't come to fruition."

"What happened to the cart or carriage or whatever they called it to pulley up and down?"

Granny merely shrugged.

That was Anne's escape plan. And that was the reason for the rope. The girl was sure that Granny had this all planned out. Probably as far back as the day Anne discovered the dumb waiter. She couldn't very well slide down as she had when she was younger. For one thing, Anne was bigger now. For another, it might really injure her and, worse, the noise of her landing in the basement would alert her would-be abductors (or assassins, she didn't know which).

The girl made her way quickly and with as much stealth as she could muster into the kitchen. She opened the door that revealed the dumb waiter, slowly, hoping fervently that it didn't creak and give her location away. She already heard footsteps on the fire escape and someone trying to open the window. Other footsteps and grunting could be heard on the other side of the door to the outer hall. She had to be quick.

Digging into her bag, she dragged out the rope and quickly refastened the bag, making sure she hadn't dislodged anything. She didn't want to leave anything behind. Especially Granny's chest. Satisfied that all the contents were secure, the girl looked around for traces of her presence.

My coat! The voice inside her head screamed so loud, she almost jumped for fear that it could be heard by the intruders. Anne glanced around. She had left it in the other room. Dare she? There wasn't time. She knew there was a closet nearby. Mrs. Snelling must have coats. She'd have to borrow one. It might make for a better disguise. Knowing that the older woman probably wore a size much larger than Anne, she quickly adjusted the bag firmly on her back, fastening it around her waist for good measure, then tiptoed to the closet and opened the door slowly in case it creaked.

Thankfully, it didn't. She was in luck. Mrs. Snelling's old winter coat hung in plain view. She grabbed it and tossed it over her shoulders, allowing her arms to slide into the sleeves. She reached for a scarf and a hat, satisfied that she would blend in well enough, looking, as she was sure she did, like a bag lady. For good measure, she picked up the woman's shopping bag, worn and holey from good use. It was full of paper towel, so she left it as is It made the bag look bulky and it wasn't too heavy or cumbersome. Satisfied that her bag lady image was complete, she closed the closet and returned to the dumb waiter.

It was time to go. The sounds beyond the apartment were getting ominously closer. It was now or never. She made quick work tying the rope to the pulley knob and testing it for strength. Satisfied, she wrapped the rope around her waist, and, thankful for Granny's lessons in rock climbing, slung her legs, one at a time, over the ledge. She made sure to pull the door shut behind her before sliding down into the cavernous dark that would end in the basement. As she slid, a crash of broken glass and a bang of a broken door indicated that her hideaway had been invaded.

"Her coat's here," a scruffy voice called out. "Find her."

Anne didn't wait to listen further. She slid down the shute, bracing her descent with her feet half walking, half slithering against the sides. It was pitch black when her feet felt a solid surface and stopped her descent. She was in the basement. Tugging at the rope, it slithered off the pulley, landing at her feet. She wound it up quickly and tucked it inside Mrs. Snelling's shopping bag, digging it to the bottom underneath the rolls of paper towel. She pulled a couple out and dropped them on the floor. She really didn't need them all; just enough to cover the rope. Gingerly, she felt her way out of the base of the dumb waiter. She knew this basement well, having spent hours as a child exploring its hidden crevices. Granny had encouraged it. Anne now understood why.

She found the door that led to the back alley. Opening it slowly, she peaked outside. It was quiet. An alley cat yelped and scampered away. There were garbage bins and dumpsters and plenty of trash. A lump stirred off to her left making the girl jump.

"Here, you! What are you doing in my spot?" Another bagperson, someone who made their home on the streets. "This is my spot. Move along."

Anne didn't need further encouragement. She slipped past the street person, tripping over another one on the way. "Hey! Watch yourself." She was greeted with grunts and groans.

Reaching the corner of the building, she peaked around cautiously. Looking up, she saw two men on the fire escape scanning the alley below. She couldn't go that way. Even in her scruffy garb, they would notice her right away. She sneaked back, careful to avoid the sleeping mounds tucked in between the dumpsters. There was a gate at the far end, one that led beyond the alley to the back of the building behind hers. She found it, inched it open and slipped through, pulling it shut behind her. Just in time.

"Nothing but bums here," a man grumbled, his voice getting closer.

"Ouch!" One of the street people complained. "Leave me alone. Can't you see I'm trying to sleep."

"Was there a girl here?" a voice demanded.

The only answers he received were, "Go away!"

"This is our home."

"Leave us alone."

Anne didn't wait to hear more. There were other street people sleeping on this side of the gate. She made her way carefully around them and inched along the side of the building until she reached the street. Looking up and down, she moved toward a group of young people jostling their way down the street.

"Hey look!" One yelped. "It's a bag lady."

"Oh! Yuck! She smells!" And they ran off giggling and chattering.

It didn't matter. They had provided cover until they reached the corner. She looked around, trying to appear inconspicuous. All she saw were throngs of people going in every direction as they made their way to their morning destination. She slid in behind a group of businessmen and followed them to the next corner. The throng thickened and pushed its way down the steps into the subway. She allowed the movement to pull her forward, away from her home. Away from the danger that threatened. Away from the loved ones that were no more.

Slipping her hands into Mrs. Snelling's pocket, she felt around. Knowing the woman always had coins jiggling in her pockets, the girl hoped to find a subway token that was still valid. She was in luck. She made her way to the turnstile and followed the lineup in front of her, slipping the token in its slot before pushing the bar forward and making her way to the subway.

Anne was on her way.

She had to get to the airport. It was the most efficient way to get out of the country; to make her way to the legendary land where Granny's stories originated. At least, it was the only way she knew of, unless she wanted to stowaway in a cargo ship and be tossed around at sea for weeks. She didn't like that option. Not one bit. All she knew for sure was that she had to find Granny's door. It could be anywhere, really. Granny never was specific about its location. But first things first: she had to find a safe, quiet place to examine the contents of Granny's chest. A safe place where Granny had taken her many times over the years, always uttering the words, *Remember this place, dear. Remember how to get here.*

She found the train that would take her to Union Station, the hub of Toronto's subway system. It was conveniently located across the street from the Fairmont Royal York Hotel, the place she explored with Granny in detail. There was a floor where no one stepped foot. It was safe. Secure. A get-away, hide-away for when the time came. Like now. Just in case.

"You never know when you might have to hide," Granny instructed. "Room 1312. A floor that doesn't exist. Not really. So, no one will ever find you there. At least, we can hope they can't find you in a room that doesn't exist on a floor that doesn't exist."

There was no thirteenth floor. Not at the Fairmont Royal York. Not at any hotel, or even any high-rise building. No one wanted to step on it for superstitious reasons. Well, there was a thirteenth floor, but it was avoided, left vacant, empty, because skipping the floor number and naming the thirteenth floor as the fourteenth floor didn't change anything, it was still the thirteenth floor.

All the instructions scattered across the years jumbled through her head as the girl moved with the crowd and squeezed in at the far end of the subway car. She gripped the nearest pole, hanging tight to keep her balance while the train pushed forward through the tunnels. She didn't want to fall over and draw attention to herself. She had to blend in. Become invisible. She was on her way. Without a trace. Or so she hoped.

A voice came over the intercom at each approaching stop. Anne listened intently, waiting. "Union Station," the electronic voice finally announced. It appeared that the remaining passengers were all disembarking at Union Station. There was a rush of humanity as the flow moved out the doors and onto the platform. Anne allowed herself to be engulfed in the crowd, allowed the flow to move her up the elevators to street level, allowed the crowd, now dwindling, to lead her outside onto the busy York Street.

She blinked as the sunlight crashed into her eyes. As her vision focussed, she took note of her surroundings, particularly of the people around her. Everyone appeared suspicious. She pulled Mrs. Snelling's coat more tightly around her and made her way to the curb. Weaving through the parade of taxis lined up in the hopes of picking up a fare, she skirted traffic and trotted across the road, adding a little limp to her stride to keep up the appearance of being old, fragile and a little helpless. She used the side entrance and walked into the hotel as guests arrived and left with hardly a sideways' glance in her direction.

Anne knew the layout of the hotel. Granny had brought her here several times, going over the routine should the day arrive, as it had now, that she needed to vanish.

"Don't go into the main lobby," Granny had warned. "Too many possible hindrances. Take the stairs down to the subway level and find the elevators."

It was as if Granny's voice was inside the girl's head, telling her, yet again, how to access the thirteenth floor without raising suspicion.

"Hey! You!" A concierge called out. "What are you doing in here?"

The man in uniform marched up to Anne. She froze. What would she do if she were kicked out of the hotel? Denied further access?

The concierge walked right past the girl. Not waiting to see who the culprit was, she took off toward the central staircase that led up to the lobby level and veered off to the right where two rows of elevators waited, each one with the door wide open in invitation. She couldn't take any elevator. Only the one at the end, which was conveniently marked, "Out of Service". She ripped off the warning sign and walked inside. She knew what to do. There was a code to activate her access to the non-existent floor. The code was activated by pressing the floor buttons on the panel in a specific order. She pressed the first number in the code. Nothing happened. She pressed the second number and breathed a sigh of relief when the doors whooshed shut.

Voices of exclamation were approaching. Hands banged on the doors, willing them to open. The doors didn't budge. Neither did the elevator.

Anne took a deep breath and continued with the next code. She pressed the third key, then the fourth and, finally, the elevator began its ascent.

She could hear voices, fading as the elevator rose.

"That elevator isn't safe."

"It's marked 'Out of Service'."

"It'll break down before she can…"

The remaining words vanished. Anne leaned back against the rail and counted the floors as they passed. "One. Two. Three." Finally, "Thirteen." The elevator shuddered to a stop and the doors opened. Barely. Enough to position her hands between the two opposing doors and shove them further apart. It wasn't easy. The doors were stuck. The 'Out of Service' notice must have really meant something. That, and the fact that the elevator had stopped a good two feet shy of the intended floor.

"Oh!" Anne groaned. The outer doors, the ones that opened to the hall on the thirteenth floor, were shut tight. Try as she would, she couldn't squeeze her hands between the sealed positioning of the doors. The elevator doors were only open enough for the girl to squeeze through. Pinned between these doors and reaching up to work the other set of doors, it didn't take long for her arms to ache.

"There has to be a better way." She slithered out of the opening and shrugged out of Mrs. Snelling's coat. It was hot in the elevator, and she doubted she'd need the coat again. Her disguise had been uncovered anyway, so she would have to come up with another plan should she try to leave the hotel unnoticed. Which she would have to do sometime.

She unbuckled the clasp that held her backpack securely in place and slipped it off her shoulders. She now understood the reasoning behind Granny's insistence that she carry a handy set of tools. She could hear Granny's voice, "You never know when you'll need a screwdriver or a set of pliers. Best to be prepared than at a loss should you find yourself in a pickle."

Anne chuckled. Granny was always coming up with funny phrases like 'in a pickle'. She had to admit, though, she was in a pickle now. If she didn't get out of this elevator and onto the thirteenth floor, she may well find herself wasting away forever until the hotel techies found a way to reclaim this elevator and her remains along with it. Not a pleasant thought.

She pulled out the large, flat headed screwdriver. Slapping it in the palm of one hand, she stood up and slithered back between the elevator doors. "Hopefully this works," she muttered to herself as she weaseled the flat head of the screwdriver between the closed doors and started prying and wiggling the device around. She added a few swear words for good measure. Good thing Granny wasn't here now, or she would have heard an earful of scolding for using such fowl language.

Something snapped. The doors moved. Apart. Ever so slightly.

"The swearing must have worked." Anne let out a deep breath. She hadn't realized she was holding her breath. Or had she?

She wiggled the screwdriver around at the base of the doors, then tucked it in her jeans' pocket and started using her hands, which now fit into the opening, and pushed with all her strength until the doors opened enough for her to squeeze through. Sliding back into the elevator, Anne repacked her backpack, making sure everything was in place. She picked up Mrs. Snelling's old coat and shoved it through the opening.

"Just in case," she muttered again to herself. She shoved her bag through, took one last look around the elevator compartment to make sure she'd left nothing behind, and pulled herself up to the floor level and through the final opening. She had barely made it through when both sets of doors slammed shut and the elevator could be heard making its descent to the main floor. Not the usual descent. This one was rather fast, increasing in velocity by the minute. She grabbed her belongings and slid back on the bare wood floor just as a huge explosion erupted from thirteen floors below. Dust snuck through the cracks of the door, making the girl cough. The elevator had crashed. Obviously into a crumpled mess.

"That should buy me some time," she said as she stood up and brushed the dust from her clothes. She looked around, taking in her surroundings. She had been in the hotel before. She knew the layout of each floor. This was nothing like any of the other floors. None of the lush adornments that identified the hotel as posh.

No carpets, thick, colorful or otherwise. Merely bare wood floors covered in dust and dirt. Cobwebs marked each corner and crevice.

The walls lacked trims and paint and wallpaper. In some places, there were holes and missing slabs of plaster board, the supporting beams lay bare.

No lights. No light fixtures. No furnishings.

No windows to allow outside light to filter in.

No identifying boundaries from one space to the next. It was all open.

Except.

Anne stood up and gathered her belongings. She made her way to the end of the elevator corridor, such as it was, and turned left. She followed the path that would mark the halls in the floors above and below her. Counting her paces. She knew how many paces it would take to reach room 1312. Room 12 on each floor was the same number of steps from the elevator. This floor should be no different. Even without the other rooms cordoned off and marked with a door and a number.

And she found the room. The only space walled in. With a door. With a number: 1312. All around this room, this door, this number, was open space. Extremely dark open space.

Dropping her possessions, Anne fumbled with the key around her neck, slipping it out from beneath her shirt. Leaning in, she was able to make the key fit into the keyhole, an elaborate, brass keyhole, one suited for the key she held. She turned the key; the locked clicked, and the key slipped out, landing in Anne's hand.

With a creaking and a grinding, the door opened. Not the way she expected it to open. It didn't swing inwards, like a normal door to a hotel room. It slid open, disappearing into the wall to her left. In the manner of the old-fashioned pocket doors. Only this time it really did vanish, even though it stopped abruptly with a resounding clonk. Bright sunlight soaked the girl's face, blinding her.

She blinked. Once. Twice.

And gave her head a good shake.

This belied all semblance of reason. It made no sense. There were no lights on the thirteenth floor. No windows to let in the sunlight. In fact, there was nothing bright and illuminating about the floor at all. Just darkness, dust and dirt.

It begged the question, why. Why was there sunlight cascading through the open doorway?

Anne remained rooted where she stood at the entrance to what should be room 1312. Her eyes adjusted to the glare and she gaped, mouth wide open, at the vision before her.

Luscious greens marked a narrow path. Birds flittered about the branches of shrubs and tall trees that created an arch above the path. Even the smell was intoxicating.

"Enter, Princess Anne." A man's voice, soft, rich, seductive, called her forward. Grabbing her backpack and Mrs. Snelling's old coat, she tentatively took one step. Then two. And finally walked through the doorway. A rumbling behind her made her jump. She looked back. The door was sliding closed behind her. Just as voices erupted from down the hall.

"There's nothing on this floor, sir."

"She's here. I know she is. Find her."

The door slammed shut and all but vanished, because what appeared before Anne now continued behind her for as far as the eye could see.

"What?" she gasped, pivoting around, doing a full circle, taking it all in. "What?" She didn't finish.

"Princess Anne." A tall man stepped out from the shadows behind a large tree. "Welcome home." With the light emitting from behind the figure, all Anne could make out was a shadow. It was tall, that much she ascertained. And it appeared to be wearing a long, flowing robe that stretched out to the ground like a floor-length curtain.

The girl made the motion of pointing to her chest. "Are you talking to me? I'm not a princess."

The man chuckled softly and took a step toward her, one hand outstretched, the other holding firmly to a tall stick, a walking stick or a talisman, Anne couldn't be sure. "Oh! But you are," he claimed. "Your family didn't reveal your noble status. Trying to keep you safe. It didn't work for long. You are no longer safe in that time and place. But you will be safe here. For now." He continued to walk toward the girl, coming to a stop and giving her a respectful bow. "Welcome home, Princess Anne. Granddaughter of King Ceawlin of Wessex and his wife, Queen Rosalind."

"My grandparents," Anne whispered, more to herself than to the man standing before her. But he heard. And he nodded.

"Come." He beckoned. "There isn't much time. I must prepare you."

"Prepare me for what?" Anne, or Princess Anne as the man called her (the new name would take some getting used to), took a step backwards. "And where am I exactly? And who are you?"

"Many questions. I will answer only one for now. I am Merlin."

Anne gasped. "Merlin?"

Chapter Four

Anne. No, she had to start thinking of herself as Princess Anne. The now princess shook her head in disbelief. Nothing made sense. First, she was in a posh hotel in downtown Toronto. Next, she stepped through a door into a forest glade of sorts. The lush greenery engulfed her, like the giant dome of the Cinesphere at Ontario Place, only with the natural habitat one might find at the Humber Arboretum or in High Park. An oasis in downtown Toronto? It was possible. But on the thirteenth floor of a posh hotel? Not likely.

"Come, Princess," Merlin urged her forward. "Foul and ungodly forces approach. We must get you to a safe place and prepare you for what's to come." He quirked an eyebrow, studying her closely from head to toe. "And dress you appropriately."

Anne stomped her foot in frustration. She didn't know where she was, when she was, or even who she was and here this man, who claimed to be the great magician of King Arthur's time, criticizing her wardrobe. "And what's wrong with what I'm wearing?" she snapped, placing hands on her hips in a show of defiance.

Merlin broke out into laughter and shook his head. "Just like your mother. Is Princess Evelyn with you? Or your grandmother?"

"No," Anne bit her lower lip. She wasn't going to cry. Not in front of Merlin, if that's who he really was. "They're both…" She didn't finish. She didn't have to.

Merlin nodded his head in understanding. "Then, we have no time to waste. Ungodly forces are closer than I thought possible. As for your," he waved his hands dramatically in her direction, "clothing, if you could call it that. It might be suitable for the twenty-first century from whence you came. But you are now in the sixth century."

"The what?" the princess gasped. "The sixth century? And next you're going to tell me we're in jolly ole England."

Merlin chuckled again. "Well, I am not so sure of the 'jolly' part. And it was not called England in the sixth century. The country, the island as you know it, was divided into many domains, including Wales, which is where we are. Carmarthen to be exact. On Ynus Enlli, just off the coast of Wales. I am taking you to my secret cave. From whence we can make plans to get you safely to your grandfather in Wessex."

"He still lives?"

"Barely. He is old. Very old for this era. And getting weaker by the day. So, time must not be wasted." He waved the girl forward. Again. Pivoted and started walking up the steep incline as the path narrowed and disappeared into the overgrowth. "No time to waste."

The princess, no longer just Anne, trotted forward. She had to keep up. There was no other option. She didn't know where she was. Not exactly. Other than what Merlin had identified as Wales. She could be anywhere. Wales was a big place. And she'd never been to Wales, in her time or in this time. Whatever time it was. And she had to find out his objection with her wardrobe.

The receding figure continued is fast pace forward. The light dimmed as the lush greenery became thicker, and the arched effect of the tall branches closed in on her. It was like a tunnel. A magical tunnel, or sorts, through the forest, created by a canopy of the lush branches of large, majestic trees which swung skyward until they arched in regal elegance over the narrow path. She glanced behind her and noticed that the path she had left behind was disappearing, the forest filling in her footpath. There was no going back. Not now.

She picked up her pace and managed to catch up, barely, just as Merlin seemed to vanish in thin air. All she could see was a rock wall blocking her path. She stopped abruptly. "Merlin?" she called out.

A hand reached through the wall and, before Anne could utter a scream, the hand latched onto her arm and pulled her through the rock wall. If that's what it was. She was beginning to doubt herself. Nothing she saw, nothing she felt, nothing she was experiencing made any sense at all.

Her eyes were clamped shut, her mouth still open for the scream that never came. Slowly, she opened her eyes and glanced around her. She appeared to be inside a cave of sorts. It was very bright, with flaming sconces projecting from the wall at even intervals.

"My tomb," Merlin explained. "Everyone believes I am dead. But wizards never die. It is better they think what they do. I can move about the world much more easily without people trying to find me and ask me to intervene for them. My magic is not for everyone's whim and desire. I have been resting in this place, where others believe I have been buried, for many years. Thinking. Honing my skills. Waiting." He glanced at Anne. "Waiting for the return of Camelot's fame and power."

Anne stepped cautiously into the heart of the cavernous chamber, allowing her eyes to roam around the perimeter, taking it all in. There wasn't much to see other than flickering light and the shadows it created. A hearth sat in the center. Lit. Warm. Comforting. Inviting.

Merlin propped his walking stick, or whatever he called it, against the stone wall and crouched on a rug near the hearth. He pointed to another rug. "Sit," he ordered. "We have much to discuss. Much to prepare. And not much time."

Anne sat opposite Merlin. Cross-legged.

Anne struggled to get comfortable on the hard rock surface. The rug didn't offer much comfort and the cold of the natural floor beneath soaked through the weave and made its mark on Anne's rear end. She shivered and inched closer to the hearth. She shrugged off the knapsack and pulled it tight beside her, then wrapped the old coat around her shoulders for extra warmth.

Merlin cleared his throat as if he were struggling to find the correct way to address this apparition from far in the future. "Young ladies of your position should not be seen parading around in such..." he sputtered and waved his hands dramatically, before finishing with the only word he could conjure up, "attire."

"And why not?"

"Like I said, this is the sixth century. For one thing, you will soon freeze to death in that outfit." He had a point. Anne was already shivering, despite the old coat. As if noticing her discomfort, the wizard waved his hands over the hearth. The flames roared more intensely, giving Anne the much-desired heat she needed to control her shivering. "Better?" She nodded.

"Now. To the task at hand. You are here for a reason. More than merely saving your life. Which, I might add," he held up his hand, palm facing Anne to ward any objection, "would be obliterated in seconds had you remained in your time and place. Or worse. That is what happened to both your mother and your grandmother. These ungodly, foul forces will stop at nothing to prevent the future you are meant to create. Or re-create, however you want to look at it."

Anne looked confused. "I don't understand."

"And stop talking with contractions."

"Huh?"

"And stop using twenty-first century idioms."

"What?"

"Each word must be drawn out to its fullest. Instead of saying, *I don't*, you must say, *I do not.* And that word, what was it?" he snapped his fingers, trying to recall. Anne helped him.

"Huh?"

"Yes. That is it. *Huh.* What does it mean?"

Anne shrugged in response. "I guess it means I don't understand."

"Then say it, without the *don't.*"

"I do not understand." She spat out each word with embellished articulation.

"Much better. You will understand. Suffice it to say, you are safer here with me, than you would be back in your time. Your plans of escape would not have worked. The contemptibly foul forces that followed you would have caught up. And they still might. But we have the advantage."

"We do?"

"Yes. You have me. Who they believe to be long dead! And I have you. Whom they cannot reach. Not here anyway. As a team, we shall succeed."

The wizard waved his hand over the flame again and a pot of steaming broth, or something with equally intoxicating odors, appeared, sizzling and bubbling over the flame.

"What the? How the?" Anne couldn't finish her questions. Her stomach retaliating with a resounding growl. She suddenly realized she hadn't eaten. In hours. Many hours. Long before her mother walked out the door and never returned.

Merlin smiled. "First. You eat. I do not need nourishment. As an immortal, I can eat or not as the need should present itself."

Confusion rippled across Anne's face. She didn't argue, though. Not when a stone bowl was filled with the sumptuous concoction and handed to her.

"Eat."

She studied the bowl. Taking a deep breath, she inhaled the steamy aroma. Then she looked at Merlin. Her brow crinkled. "How?"

Merlin chuckled. "Yes. Of course. You have been raised to eat with elegance. With utensils." He handed the girl a stone knife.

She accepted it, hesitantly. "How do I scoop up the broth with this?" She juggled the bowl in one hand and the knife in the other.

With a disgruntled grunt, Merlin wiggled his hands again and produced a chunk of bread. "With this, Princess." And he handed her the bread.

She put down the knife at her side, cradled the bowl in her lap and took the bread. She broke off a chunk and dipped it in the broth, immediately soaking up the concoction. She wiped the sides of the bowl with more chunks of bread and, before she realized it, the bread was gone, the bowl was empty and her stomach felt satisfied, if not full.

"Thank you." She nodded at Merlin, stifling a yawn. She hadn't slept in a long time either. The soothing warmth and fulfilling nourishment were making her drowsy.

"Sleep," Merlin instructed. "We shall talk in your dreams. And, when you wake, refreshed, we shall venture forth."

She bit back a smile at the wizard's words. He did talk funny. But, she realized, her words must sound funny to him as well. She didn't need much encouragement to close her eyes. Anne curled up in a ball beside the hearth and drifted off. Into dreamland. Merlin talking and leading her on a journey that both frightened and excited her.

Chapter Five

It didn't take her long to recognize the location. Well, not exactly. She still didn't know where it was. But it was the same location, the same scenery and the same events that had plagued her dreams and nightmares for years.

"Camelot," a voice whispered next to her ear. Anne jumped. That part wasn't from her recurring dreams. She moved her head sideways and glanced at the man who spoke. Merlin.

"Camelot, Princess," he repeated. "Or, at least what is left of it."

She took a step forward. Cautiously. She remembered this part of her dream. Where she stepped too far forward and plummeted down a steep embankment. She wouldn't make that mistake again. At least, she hoped she wouldn't, although it happened every time she dreamed this same dream.

"Careful, Princess," Merlin's voice echoed the warning that replayed in her memories.

She stopped. Looked. Studied the scene before her. Ruins. Stones scattered at random in what might have been a grand building or fort or some sort of architectural wonder. The scattering formed a circle. "The round table," she muttered, more to herself than to Merlin.

"Yes. The round table was very real. The intent was to achieve the highest form of equality amongst men."

"And what about women?" She kept her eyes riveted on the scene before her, looking for something. Anything. She wasn't convinced this was Camelot. Or was she? There was a certain draw to the place. An energy she couldn't explain.

"Women are the magic that holds the weave of equality in its tight web." Merlin was speaking in riddles.

Anne shook her head.. "So, what you're saying is that women were the background and not part of the circle of power."

"Stop speaking with contractions," Merlin scolded the girl. "You have too many twenty-first century morals. You have to place your mind and your soul into the sixth century. The place where your body now resides."

"So you say." Anne still wasn't convinced. She was having a hard time accepting the power of magic and believing that it was real. Time travel? Time and space? Yes, Granny had taught her a few spells. Nothing too intense. Like making an object disappear and reappear. Or making the annoying landlord lose his voice when he was chastising them on being late with the rent. Again. For royalty, they always seemed to be desperately short of money.

There was movement off to the left, what she assumed must be the south based on the height and direction of the sun, which appeared to be setting.

"They come." Merlin took hold of Anne's arm and pulled her back to the cover of the tree line behind them.

"Who?"

"Shush! Be quiet and watch. You will learn more from observation than you will from conversation."

Anne chuckled softly. "Is that your words of wisdom for the day?"

Her voice was no more than a whisper, but, regardless, it earned her another resounding "Shush!"

After a quick glance at the wizard, she returned her attention to the figures approaching the ruins.

"Saxons," Merlin grumbled. He raised his walking stick and twirled it like a baton, allowing it to complete its circular trajectory three times before coming to a complete stop with the top pointing toward the figures. The round globe-shaped top sparkled and sizzled and then voices emitted from it. Anne

jumped but said nothing. Somehow, Merlin had managed to amplify the conversation so they could listen.

"She is here. With Merlin." The voice was gruff. Anne was sure they were speaking a language other than English. She didn't comprehend why she was able to understand them. If they were Saxon, they'd be speaking in their own language, wouldn't they? Anne thought so. Granny had taught her a few phrases in Saxon, or Old English, a Germanic language that evolved into the English spoken in later centuries. She didn't know enough to carry on or even follow a complete conversation in Saxon. There was magic in the air. Merlin's magic.

"I thought he was dead." The second voice.

"We all did."

"Deal with it. Deal with her. And with him."

"I doubt I can do much with the wizard. If he is alive when he should be dead, then there is nothing that can kill him."

"You are a wizard, too, Abrecan. Born of the witch, Morgawse. You have her power and what she stole from Merlin. That should be enough."

"It was not enough the first time, my King."

"Well it had better be enough this time. I will not have my throne challenged from a weak little girl conjured up by Merlin."

The 'weak little girl' comment made Anne bristle with anger. Before she could utter any explicatives and discontent, Merlin disconnected the amplification. The riders were finished. Or so it appeared. They moved their mounts in opposite directions, retracing the path they had used to enter the sacred ruins of Camelot.

"How dare they?" Anne spat, once sure that the threat had disappeared. "I am no 'weak little girl'. I'll show them."

"No more contractions," Merlin repeated his scolding.

"Contractions be damned. I'll say what I want to say. When I want to say it. And how I want to say it."

"And no swearing. You have an attitude, I can see that. But you are a princess. Soon to be a queen."

"And the first order of business will be to find those two rogues and give them a piece of my mind."

"The time will come. But not now." And Merlin led her further into the forest.

Chapter Six

The next thing Anne knew, she was waking up on the hard, stone floor of the cave. The hearth continued to burn bright and warm. And Merlin sat on the opposite side.

She yawned and stretched her arms above her head. Then pushed herself into a sitting position. Her stomach rumbled in protest. She was hungry. Again. She looked at Merlin expectantly.

He returned her look and merely shook his head. "Make your own. It is time to start testing your skills and preparing you for your future."

Crossing her arms, she glared at the man for a few minutes. He didn't budge. It was as if he were in a trance. Or meditation. His eyes were focused on the flame in the hearth, the flame that consistently burned at the same intensity, while, at the same time, it didn't really burn anything at all. Like the gas fireplaces Anne had seen in Home Hardware. Burning without burning. It was an ancient concept and perhaps not as magical as it first appeared.

Taking advantage of the wizard's mesmerisation of the hearth, Anne lifted her right hand and dangled it over the flame. She didn't speak. She didn't have to. All she needed was her hands. And her thoughts. She focused her gaze on the flames and waved her hand in a circular motion above it. With a snap of the fingers, she pulled back, just as the flame shot to a greater height. Merlin jumped. Not significantly. Merely enough for Anne to take satisfaction that she had managed to get his attention.

"So, you do have the power?"

Anne shrugged. "I suppose. Whatever that means. Granny taught me a few things."

"What else can you do?"

"Well, I can make some porridge for breakfast. Do you want some?"

Merlin hesitated, apparently unsure of what she was suggesting, then reluctantly nodded. Anne reached into her bag and pulled out a Ziploc full of oats. She noticed a pot on the shelf behind her and claimed that, along with the ladle that was resting inside the pot. Adding some water and the oats, she hovered the pot over the flames, using the ladle to stir it while it cooked.

Merlin snorted. A half laugh, really. "I thought you might have used a bit of magic."

"Why?" The girl quirked an eyebrow but kept her focus on the task at hand. "There are times when I can do perfectly well without magic. So, why waste the power?"

"Power does not disappear with overuse," Merlin explained. "In fact, it magnifies. The more you use it, the stronger it gets."

"Very well." Anne snapped her fingers again. She hadn't given full disclosure on her magic abilities, not wanting to reveal everything to someone she had only just met. Even if he did claim to be Merlin. Removing the pot from the heat, she gave it one last stir. Another snap of her fingers and she had two wooden bowls in which to divide the concoction. Once the porridge was dished out, she snapped again, and a jar appeared in her hand. She dribbled its thick, dark brown contents over the otherwise bland cooked oats. "Maple syrup," she explained. "Only available in certain parts of North America."

Merlin accepted his bowl and took a tentative taste of the contents. He nodded in approval. "You will have to find a way to make this maple syrup available here. In this time. And," he shook his head to ward off her protest, "without the advantage of magic."

"But you said..." she didn't finish her thought. No use arguing with the master of arguments. And the master of magic. They ate the porridge in silence, each deep in their own thoughts.

Chapter Seven

Anne couldn't tell if it was day or night. Inside the cave, sealed as it was, she had no way to judge the time by natural light. The only lighting was the hearth and the flaming wall sconces, all of which cast eerie shadows in many shapes, sizes and in multiple directions.

They finished the porridge, typically a breakfast dish, one eaten after a long night's sleep. Anne had slept, and dreamt, but was it day or night?

"Morning," Merlin muttered, answering her unasked question. "It is morning. Early. Time to get to work."

Anne didn't bother to ask how Merlin knew what she was thinking. There was no point. Merlin had the powers to know everything. Or so she assumed.

"Not everything."

"Now there you go again." Anne shook her head, stifling a soft chuckle. "Didn't your mother tell you it was impolite to eavesdrop on someone else's private thoughts?"

Merlin sported a smile, of sorts. "No. And you must refrain from talking with contractions."

"Contractions! Contractions! Contractions! Is that all you think about?" Anne stood. "I need to relieve myself." One eyebrow arched, she was challenging him. She knew it; she was doing it on purpose. "Is that a satisfactory way to mention that I need to take a piss."

Merlin cringed but nodded. "Outside. I will show you the way." He walked to the wall, the one through which they had slid the previous day. At least, she thought it was the previous day. "Like this." He held one hand toward the wall's surface and placed his palm on its smooth surface. There was a slight sizzle, and he walked through. Anne followed and thumped resoundingly when her nose crashed against a hard surface. "Use your hand," Merlin's voice came from the other side.

She placed her hand, palm forward, on the surface, as she had witnessed Merlin do mere moments before. There was a soft sizzling sound. It was as if a sliding door had whooshed out of the way, allowing her to pass. She did. Without running into a hard, stone wall. She rubbed her nose. It hurt, but not that much.

"You have the power. Now you must learn how and when to use it." Merlin was already walking down the tunnels. "This way. First things first. One must always care for body needs before tackling the tasks and trials of the day." Sunlight beckoned from ahead and the two stepped into the fresh air. "Over there. In the trees. There is a gentle waterfall that provides fresh water for drinking and bathing."

Anne followed Merlin's motions, looking back only once to assure herself that he wasn't following. As if listening to her thoughts, again, a voice echoed inside her head. "I know when it is best not to snoop." She smiled to herself as she slipped through the shrubs and stumpy trees that crowded the steep incline. Satisfied she was alone; she went about her business. She moved further into the shrubbery and found the waterfall. She held out her hands to accept the wet relief. It was cold. Extremely cold. As expected, since it must have come from deep within the rock face above her. She shuddered but continued to use it to wash her hands and face. It would do. For now.

Refreshed, she made her way back to the clearing that marked the entrance to the cave. Only, it wasn't there. "Merlin," she called out. She was frantic. Alone. In unknown territory. And she had left her belongings inside the cave. "Merlin," she called a little louder. She twisted and rotated in a circular motion. She didn't think she had made a wrong turn. She was good at finding her way. Was this another one of Merlin's tricks? A test?

She was in panic mode. Her heart rate accelerated and her breathing came in a quick succession of short gasps. Tears streaked down her cheeks. "Merlin." She was screaming now. "Don't do this to me."

"Stop with the contractions!" The voice came from inside her head.

"DO NOT DO THIS TO ME!" She spat the words with rapid staccato bursts.

"Much better. Now stop panicking. You cannot help yourself, or anyone else for that matter, if you panic. Look around you." She did, through eyes still wet with unshed tears. "You see. All is as you left it." It was. Her eyes did a circular evaluation, completing its trajectory at the spot where the opening to the cave should be. And it was as it should be, with Merlin standing at the entrance, his staff in hand. As if nothing had happened to suggest otherwise.

"You ass!" Anne spat. "Why did you do that?"

"To test your reflexes, Princess," Merlin explained simply. "And they obviously need testing. And strengthening. You must not believe what you see. When things look different, or out of sorts, close your eyes and breathe deeply and slowly. Let your mind see what really is before you."

"You could have warned me." Anne pouted. Her heart rate was slowing to its normal pace. Her breathing settled and the tears dried on her cheeks.

"Then you would have foreknowledge. You must learn to be prepared for the unexpected. We shall try again later. We have things to discuss. Things you need to know. I am sure you have some questions about your dream."

"I'll say." Noticing Merlin's scowl, she instantly corrected herself. "I will say."

"Much better." He pointed to the cave. "Lead the way inside, Princess. Open the portals and return to the hearth."

Merlin vanished. Anne blinked her eyes in rapid succession. This man, this wizard, magician, immortal entity, however he was recognized or identified, he was trying her patience. As well as her sense of what was real and what was not. She was beginning to wonder if all of this were a dream, including the dream that was a dream. Very complicated. Very confusing.

"Come along, Princess. I am waiting." The voice rang out from deep within the cave.

Anne stepped toward the entrance. It was time to show the wizard what she already knew. She had made some mistakes, misjudged some circumstances, but she knew more than she let on. She stood at the entrance. Closed her eyes. And allowed her mind to take her back to the hearth. When she opened them, she was content to feel the warmth of the hearth before her. And a very surprised wizard sitting on the opposite side of the hearth. She was feeling a little smug. She had watched him intently over the short period of time they'd been together. Always a quick study, she had picked up on a few of his tricks and added them to her own little arsenal of magical tricks, things her grandmother had taught her.

They stared at each other in silence. Merlin's eyebrows arched upwards, studying intently the barely visible smirk on Anne's face.

He broke the silence. "Well. Well." Clearing his throat, he added, "It appears you know more than you let on. Sit." He pointed to the rug on which she slept the night before. "Now for your questions."

"You said that was Camelot." She didn't wait to launch into her demands. She wanted to know everything. To understand. Merlin nodded his response and she continued, still fidgeting on the rug that offered little comfort from the cold rock surface beneath it.

"What happened? Where is King Arthur? And the Knights of the Round Table?"

"The Saxons happened," Merlin was quick to answer. "They defeated Arthur. He died in battle. The knights, those who survived, are scattered across the land. Hiding, mostly. Waiting for deliverance. Waiting for the one and only ruler who can restore the order of Camelot." He paused. Lifted his eyes to meet hers. "They are waiting for you, Princess. Some are extremely old. Ancient. Many have died. Allowing their legacy to be carried by a son or a grandson. But they all wait for you, nonetheless."

"Me?" One hand went to her chest as if to motion herself as the target.

Merlin nodded. "Yes, you."

"Why me?"

"You are the daughter of King Arthur. There are other children, your half-siblings. But you are the one who will rule as Queen and restore the order of Camelot."

She coughed. A nervous cough. A cough of disbelief. She shook her head as if to remove the cobwebs that were affecting her comprehension. "No. I am not a queen. King Arthur is not my father. How can that be?"

"When your mother and grandmother returned to this land seventeen years ago, they planned to stay. Things were peaceful. More peaceful than they had been when your grandmother escaped with her unborn child, your mother. Arthur had been crowned king and was building Camelot. His knights were loyal and keeping order in the land. The Saxons were still a threat, but a distant one. Arthur came to visit your grandfather. Your mother met him and the two fell in love. When she discovered she was carrying you, she did not know what to do. Arthur was already married to Guinevere, who never did conceive. Realizing your mother and her unborn child, you, were not safe, your grandmother did what she thought best and took you all away to the future. To hide."

"But how did those riders know that I had returned? And why do they want me?"

"They found the portal to the future, the one you came through, and they tracked you. Your grandmother trained you well and you managed to escape. Back to your allotted time. The sixth century. You entered this time near my cave, which is where the portal exists. At least, one of many portals. You were fortunate to come through this portal rather than one of the portals currently guarded by the Saxons."

"But what do they want with me?"

Merlin cleared his throat. A sign of discomfort on his part. "They desire to have you wed the Saxon king and unify Arthur's Camelot with their invading force."

"What! Never! Why would I want to marry someone I have never met? And a bully at that." She shifted away, as if to push away from the very thought of such an alliance. "No. No. I want to go back. I want to return to my time. In the future. I want to be with Granny and Mother."

"That can never be. Never again. It has been written."

"Well then re-write it," she pleaded.

Merlin sat in silence, allowing the princess time to settle down. When she didn't appear to be calming, he said, "We all do what we have to do in this life. Right now, you have a responsibility to your people. The people of Camelot. And you have a responsibility to honor those who sacrificed so much to keep you alive, well and safe for so long."

Anne felt a suffocating sense of fate settling upon her shoulders. She considered his words, considered all her grandmother had taught her. Against her will, the responsibility he spoke of, kept her from voicing the denial she clung to. It was all sinking in. She had no control over her fate, she realized. The wheels of time were moving her forward. "Very well," she acquiesced softly. "What must I do?"

"Rally our forces, for starters. To do that, we must get you safely to your grandfather before the Saxons track you here." Noticing the surprised look on the girl's face, he added, "Yes.

Even here you are not safe. Not for long. You need a fighting force to defend you and all the magic in the world would not be enough without that. The Saxons have their magic, too. They have a very powerful wizard, Abrecan. He was the one who managed to open another portal to the future and find you. It was his men who invaded your home in the future. His men killed your mother and your grandmother."

"Abrecan?"

"It means storm, Princess. And, believe me, Abrecan is very good at creating havoc and storms wherever he goes. King Penda has a substantial and very powerful fighting force. He rules much of the land and is more threatening than any of the other Saxon kings and their domains combined. Time is of the essence. We must move." He nodded to a chamber that suddenly materialized behind her. "You will find a suitable wardrobe in there. We will have to burn your clothes from the future." He held up a hand to ward off the girl's protest. "We can't allow the history-makers of the future to find traces of your presence here in the past. We must forever erase our movements. To do so is our strongest defense."

"How will we make our journey?" Anne asked. "The same way we entered the cave?"

"No," Merlin shook his head, a shadow of discomfort creeping across his face. A look he quickly shut down. "Abrecan can trace the magic signatures. He will follow us more quickly and efficiently if we use magic. No. We will ride. Horses await just outside."

"The way we came in?"

"No. I have many passages inside my mountainous domain. As we speak, Abrecan approaches the main entrance. The one through which you entered." He paused as if to listen. "Go. Change. Quickly." He waved a hand in the general direction behind Anne. She was startled by the sudden flash of light. She wasn't used to all this magic. Not without warning. Granny always warned her when she was doing something with magic. Merlin merely forged ahead. Like he was doing now.

"In there," he pointed. "It is private enough."

Chapter Eight

Anne pushed herself off the ground, groaning as her legs protested the sudden movement after being cushioned on a cold, hard surface. She turned and walked into the newly created space. Once again, she was amazed. It appeared to be a bedchamber, complete with a comfortable-looking bed with thick, richly colored coverings. Oh, how she wished she could have slept in that bed the previous night instead of on the hard floor. She was about to protest but thought better of it. Merlin was right. Time was of the essence. And danger was lurking ever closer.

She found several long robes, of sorts, draped over the end of the bed. She held each one up for inspection, one at a time. "And how do you expect me to ride a horse in this get-up?" she called out. There was no answer. She studied the garments, trying to determine which layer to done first. Layered tunics. Granny insisted she learn the rudiments of life in the sixth century. Now she understood why.

Wracking her brain, she recalled. "Layers," she spoke in a whisper. It was reassuring, soothing to hear her own voice. "But what about undergarments?" She didn't see anything that looked like underwear. And how was she expected to ride a horse without leggings of some sort? Bare legs gripping the horse's sides for who knew how long? She didn't think so.

"Hurry it up, Princess," Merlin called from the other room.

She didn't have time to ponder. Merlin insisted on burning her entire wardrobe. He didn't specify when to burn it. She would wear the outfit over top of the clothes she was wearing now. Her jeans would protect her legs during the long ride. And she assumed it would be a long ride. The rest of her twenty-first century wardrobe would help keep her moderately warm, the jeans offering some leg protection. After shivering most of the previous night, she was acclimatizing herself to the new environment. No one would see it. The long robes would assure that her futuristic clothes were hidden.

She picked up the soft, white robe, assuming it was the first layer to adorn, and pulled it over her head. She pushed her arms through the long, loose sleeves and shuffled the garment at the shoulders where it was snagging with her twenty-first century attire. Satisfied that it had settled over her body, she picked up the long cord and wrapped it around the waist, tying it snugly and pulling the upper layers until the bottom no longer dragged on the floor. Next, she lifted the heavier, deep red, garment with the split sleeves and gold embroidery. Fingering the elegant decorations, she realized that most of the adornment was metal appliqué. No wonder it was so heavy.

She slipped it over top and felt its weight as soon as it rested on her shoulders. She grabbed the ends of the sleeves of the underdress and pushed her arms through the heavier sleeves. Even the split didn't help much, as the underdress's sleeves caught and snagged up to her elbows. She had to fuss considerably to get things in order. No wonder noblewomen had so many handmaidens, she fumed.

She noticed a thick leather belt and several heavy, gold broaches. She used the largest broach to fasten the tunic at the top. Then she wrapped the thick belt around her waist, satisfied to see that there was a sheath for a sword and a smaller one to tuck in a knife. She had her knife in the backpack, a treasure Granny had bequeathed to her years ago. There were stories attached to the knife. Granny claimed it came from her life in this era and it had seen many battles and shed the blood of her enemies.

Satisfied that the belt was secure, she picked up the remaining broaches. Not sure where to attach them, she fastened one on each shoulder and the last one she positioned just below the larger one that held the tunic closed at the top. One last item. A large cloak, white, made of soft furs, probably ermine. The creature had been hunted for its furs, which were dark in the warmer months, but turned into an elegant white in the cold winter months for added camouflage. She picked up the robe, it was lighter than she expected as she threw it over her shoulders. Satisfied, she pulled back her shoulders, lifted her head high and marched regally out of the room (if you could call it that).

Chapter Nine

Merlin looked up as she entered. He started to chuckle, then muffled it in a cough. "You need the broaches to fasten the cloak in place." He stood up and marched over to the girl. "May I?" She nodded. He unfastened the various broaches, taking the larger two, which really weren't needed on the heavy red robe, and positioned them on the cloak to hold the top closed around her neck, snug with the soft fur encasing her upper body. The broaches on the shoulders, he left. "These are fine for now. If you wish to have the cloak pulled back from your neck, but still secure on the shoulders, you use these. Now you are ready." He stood back to investigate. "At least, you look the part of a princess. Even if you are still wearing the dreadful outfit underneath it all." He waved a hand to stop her protest. "Come. We still have things to prepare."

That's when Anne noticed the pile on the ground between where she stood and the hearth, which still glowed warm but not as intensely. As her eyes focussed, she realized it was the entire contents of her backpack. He had dumped everything on the ground. It looked as if he was preparing to burn most of it.

"What are you doing?" she asked, though she already knew the answer. This man, this wizard, was really trying her patience. "Those are my things. All I have left of . . . You have no right." She noticed her knife lying to one side. She snatched it up and placed it in the sheath on her belt. Then she started rummaging through the remaining contents of her backpack. "Where's the backpack?"

"Already burned it," Merlin stated with a bland tone of voice. "As I will do with most of the remaining items on the floor. Go through things quickly and carefully. Keep only what you can carry and what you think might fit in this era."

Anne crouched down as best she could in the long robes of the era. She wasn't used to wearing dresses, having always preferred the comfort and ease of mobility offered by long pants, particularly jeans. This sixth-century wardrobe was not to her liking. Not at all.

The outfit draped around her ankles like a growing puddle of foamy water. Where the fabric made way to cover her belongings, she shoved it away. She reached for the small flashlight. "This could come in handy," she noted as she flicked the switch, satisfied to see a glow emanate from within. "As long as the battery holds. Once that's dead, it won't be much use."

Merlin reached for it. "It won't burn. It certainly doesn't fit in this era. And, as you pointed out, it only has a limited source of magic. Better to send it back to the twenty-first century."

"You can do that?" Anne glanced up in time to see the wizard's head nod. She resumed the task at hand, sifting through her belongings. There were edible items, food squished in its plastic coverings and cookies crumbled into a powdery mess. Very unappetising. She tossed it into the fire, not waiting for Merlin's verdict.

She sorted the items of clothing, knowing full well, now, that they were unsuitable for this era. She tossed them into the hearth, not wanting Merlin to handle items she had once worn. The thought made her shudder. As much as she disliked her new wardrobe, it was warm, even if it wasn't terribly functional.

All that remained was her notebook, a pen, a few tools that might come in handy, some personal toiletries that wouldn't last more than a month (she would have to find out what women did in this era), and her cell phone. Merlin reached for the flat, rectangular object before Anne could object.

"What is this?" he asked, turning the object over in his hand, studying it from all angles.

"A cell phone. Or smartphone. Depends on who you ask."

"I am asking you. What does it do?"

"It's a means of communicating with others in the twenty-first century and a way to keep up-to-date on what's happening in the world around you. You can also take pictures with it, use it as a source of light, and there are some games you can play on the device."

"This twenty-first century piece of magic is probably traceable."

"Like your magic. Or so you told me."

"And it is of no use or value in this era."

Anne let out a deep sigh. Purging was difficult at the best of times, but this exercise was obliterating her entire life. Her past (from the future). And, the only family and life she ever knew. "You are right, Merlin. Send it back to my future, my past."

He set it beside the flashlight. Noticing some tools in the remaining pile, he motioned for her to hand them over as well. "Not typical implements of this era. And they will not burn. I shall send these back as well."

Anne merely nodded. She clutched her notebook to her chest, refusing to relinquish it. "I cannot burn this, Merlin. It has my memories and some pictures of my family. It is my memory keeper."

"Is not your mind the best memory keeper?" he challenged.

"Yes. I suppose so." Anne held her book closer. Reluctantly, she loosened the hold on her book. Flipping through the pages, she found what she wanted. A photograph taken the previous year, the only one ever taken, of herself with both her mother and Granny. As she studied it, tears welled in her eyes and dripped onto the picture, washing away the image. "No!" she cried.

"Time has already changed the future, Princess," Merlin spoke quietly, his voice soothing. He took the book and the photograph (what was left of it) and tossed it into the flames. Standing up, he waved his hands, opening a portal, barely large enough to toss the futuristic items. Anne's past removed, deleted, Merlin handed her a leather satchel. "Place the remaining items in this and sling it across your shoulder."

Anne took the satchel and, placing it on the ground in front of her, she opened the top. "Granny's chest," she exclaimed at the object that already sat at the bottom of the satchel. "How did you know?" She shook her head. Of course, he would know. He knew everything, didn't he?

With a reluctant sigh, Anne placed the other items on top of the precious chest. She hadn't found the time, yet, to study its contents in detail. Granny's journal was in there. She wanted to read that. She wanted answers to so many questions and she hoped that Granny's journal would serve the purpose.

She stood up once the remaining items had been tucked away. With a sweep of his staff, the hearth flames sizzled and went out, the entire hearth slowly vanishing as the smoke from the flames evaporated.

"What is it with that walking stick thing you always carry?" Anne asked. She had been pondering its use for some time, but, with so many other things to discuss, to understand, she hadn't managed to formulate the question.

Merlin visibly grimaced at the question. "It is not a stick," he snapped, his voice taking on a coarseness Anne hadn't yet heard. "It is a staff. It channels my powers."

"It is the magic, then," Anne concluded. "And not you."

"I am most definitely the magic," the wizard countered. "My staff merely channels my magic. Like I said."

"And the ball on top?"

Merlin shook his head in disbelief at the questions being parried his way. "It is not a ball. It is an orb. Where do you come up with these bizarre connotations?"

"Orb. Right. So, what does this orb do?"

"You have seen it glow." Anne nodded. "It intensifies and projects my magic. It is a special crystal. One of a kind." The wizard stood. "Now. We must leave."

Merlin placed the palm of his hand on a wall behind Anne, close to where she had changed into her period outfit. Another space opened. Before she could study it intently, Merlin motioned for her to follow. She stepped into another room, chamber, whatever you might call it. Void of warmth and decoration, its circular shape enveloped a large stone in the center from which protruded a sword.

"Only King Arthur's true heir, one of pure soul and kind heart, the one who will restore the power and importance of Camelot, only that person can retrieve the sword from this stone. And only then will all things in this world be put back into order."

"Excalibur," the girl whispered in awe. The magical sword of a mythical king and the fantastic empire that he built, Camelot.

Chapter Ten

Merlin nodded, understanding her thoughts. He motioned her again. "Pull out the sword, Princess Anne. It was meant for you. The last ruling person to hold this powerful weapon was your father, King Arthur. You have the ring." She nodded in response, a little startled at his mention of the ring. "Twist it so the gem is inside your palm and wrap your hand around the hilt, allowing the gem to connect. It will channel your energies, your powers and the sword will respond." He paused briefly while Anne did as instructed. "Pull it now and then we must make haste. For unholy powers approach ever closer."

"She is in there. Behind the wall." Voices inside her head. As it had been before. When ungodly forces approach. She could hear more than she wanted to hear. It was a defense mechanism. A power for which she praised whatever gods were looking over her.

"Abrecan. Break the barrier. Use your magic, wizard." More voices. More noises.

Anne approached the stone and reached for the sword. She grasped the pummel and slid her hand reverently down to the hilt, tightening her grip. She took a deep breath and focussed her energies on the task at hand. And pulled. Prepared for considerable resistance, Anne used her muscles to tug hard. The stone released its grip on the sword easily, her back a few steps as Excalibur creaked and scraped to freedom. It glowed and glistened. Gathering her balance, she pulled it toward her, tip pointed upward. She brought the guard cross to her lips and kissed it, sealing an unspoken vow to protect its power and use it only for good.

The sword shimmered in response. The earth rumbled in protest as the foul forces erupted mere feet away from where she stood admiring her father's famous sword. The rock crumbled and smoldered into oblivion, vanishing as if it was never there.

Anne glanced beyond the sword, studying Merlin. His hands were raised, staff glowing heavenward. And he was chanting. She couldn't make out what was being said, but the earth at her feet grumbled more ferociously and she had to brace herself to prevent toppling over.

"Sheath the sword. We must make haste." Another wall opened and a breath of cold air entered the chamber. It was dark beyond. Night. And there was a thick fog that blocked the exit like a solid wall. "Come." Merlin moved toward it without hesitation, his trusty staff marking the path as he walked. Sheathing the sword, Anne pulled her robe tightly around her, only allowing a small opening so that she could rest her left hand on the sword's pummel. It comforted her. Made her feel safe. She was anything but safe.

Anne followed Merlin through the dense wall of fog. It was endless. As she moved into it, the fog seemed to engulf her entire being. Closing her eyes, she used her mind to visualize Merlin's presence. Speech wasn't necessary. She could sense his position. And that of the horses. How did the horses know where to wait for them? *You need to ask?* Merlin's voice invaded her thoughts. She muffled a chuckled and moved toward Merlin, who was holding the reins of two fine steeds, both black.

What? No graceful white stallion for the returning princess? She spoke into his mind.

Black is both graceful and noble, Princess. And it blends well with the night. Which you do not in that white robe.

Ah. But you chose it for me, did you not?

She was speaking like a sixth-century princess. So soon. It wasn't that long ago she was mumbling her words, jumbling them together and using countlesscontractions. No more.

You do know how to ride. It was part question, part statement. He didn't await a response, merely leading her to the horse with the white blaze dribbling down his face. Or was it a she? *It is a mare. Very agile and swift. Her name is Black Passion. Blackie for short.*

Blackie. Anne reached a hand to gently move the forelock out of the mare's eyes. *A fine name for a fine horse.* Blackie nuzzled the girl. *Sorry, no treats, girl. I will find you some. Soon, I hope.* She glanced toward Merlin. The fog was still blindingly thick. *Yes I can ride. And wield a sword. Granny made sure I was well prepared.* They continued to communicate through their minds. Silence was essential.

Then up you get, Princess. And we shall ride like the wind.

In this fog?

The horses know the way. They have their own kind of magic.

The wizard slung his staff across his back and into a sheath strapped from shoulder to waist. Anne watched and marveled at how the sheathed staff appeared so much shorter, ending at Merlin's waist. She blinked and shook her head. More of his magic, she reasoned. Merlin, oblivious to the princess's observations and now with both hands free, assisted Anne onto Blackie's back. The saddle was crude, but sufficient. She was thankful she kept her jeans. It wouldn't take long for this type of saddle to cut through her bare skin. She wondered how much protection her jeans would provide. No time to ponder. An explosion from where they had been only moments before rocked the earth.

"Ride." Merlin called out. His voice no longer a mind voice. It echoed and ricocheted against the fog barriers. Anne didn't need any more incentive. As she nudged Blackie forward, another explosion rocked the ground beneath them.

They rode at a neck-breaking pace for what seemed like eternity. Finally, the fog thinned. Merlin pulled up his mount, allowing the horses to walk casually, to cool off. They were panting heavily.

"What just happened back there?" Anne asked as she shuffled her position in the saddle.

"Not comfortable?" Merlin chuckled.

"I think I will ride bareback from now on. These contraptions are bone-jarring at best." She shuffled some more. "Now, tell me what happened."

"I blew them up. And my cave. Not to worry. I have other caves where I can hide and study my powers."

"Blew them all up? Even Abrecan?"

"I suspect Abrecan has managed to escape. He does have his powers, after all. But the others are buried and dead in the rubble. Abrecan will have to regroup before he can follow us. Unfortunately, he knows where we are headed. So, we shall have to keep a steady pace all night and well into the day tomorrow if we want to make it safely to your grandfather's castle."

"Tomorrow? I shall see my grandfather tomorrow?"

"Yes, Princess. Tomorrow. If all goes well."

Chapter Eleven

The gentle plod of the horses' hooves was soothing. Hypnotic. In spite of her discomfort and growing saddle sores, Anne found herself dozing in the saddle. She couldn't understand why she was so tired. She had lost track of the time. Day or night. It was dark. The thick fog seemingly intensified with every step. The air was heavy, too. Like a hot, muggy summer's day in downtown Toronto. She was warm underneath all the layers of clothing. The warmth, the stuffiness and the lack of light was like a drug. And the quiet. The two riders hadn't mind talked or spoken aloud in a long time. Other than the horses plodding along, occasionally letting out a snort, there was no sound. She was lulled to complacency as if she were in a black hole. But did they even have black holes in the sixth century? The question popped into Anne's head out of nowhere, causing her to smile.

Merlin's voice made her start. For a moment, Anne felt as if she were slipping out of the saddle. A hand grabbed her arm and set her to rights as she tugged at her eyelids to regain full consciousness.

"Did you say something?" she asked, stifling a yawn.

"We will stop up ahead. Allow the horses to drink in the stream. We can stretch our legs and enjoy a sip of the spring water as well. It is clear, fresh, cold and perfectly safe to drink."

"If you say so." Anne yawned again.

Merlin snapped his fingers and suddenly she felt wide awake. "Time to wake up, Princess."

"You did that to me, didn't you? You put me to sleep."

Merlin didn't answer right away. When he did, she wasn't sure if she accepted his reasoning. "You were complaining about the uncomfortable saddle." It was a brief answer. Not enough to satisfy her.

"You had no right."

He cut her off. "You were tired. It will be a hard ride after this brief rest. There is danger nearby."

"There is always danger nearby." She sighed heavily, her exhaustion more mental than physical. "What kind of world has danger around every corner?"

"Your world. My world. It is not so different in the future, is it?"

Why did he have to be so right? With all the terrorists and wars and murderers of the twenty-first century, there really wasn't a safe haven there either. "Okay. I get your point."

Merlin pulled up his horse and dismounted. Blackie stopped beside Merlin's horse. Anne attempted swinging her leg over the horse's back to dismount and failed miserably. The pain and the stiffness were too acute. Merlin dropped the reins, allowing his horse the freedom to move closer to the stream, where he drank heartily. The wizard reached up to assist Anne. She leaned forward into his arms, just as he grasped his hands around her waist. As he helped her slide down to the ground, Anne's legs tingled with the returning circulation. When her feet met the ground, her legs sagged. Merlin helped steady her until she was able to maintain her position without assistance. She took a few steps forward, shaking her legs and feet as she walked. There was still tingling, but no pain.

"You used your magic," she scolded Merlin gently. "I thought it was not safe to use our magic."

"A little bit will not leave a trace."

"Now you tell me. First the sleeping spell and then the pain killers. What next?"

"Drink. I shall remove the saddles. We ride bareback from here on."

"Now that is something I can agree upon." Anne followed her horse to the stream and crouched down to scoop up some of the refreshing liquid. Satisfied, she reached into her bag, already missing the more useful backpack that held so much more. She fumbled around in the bag in frustration. Standing up, she marched over to Merlin who was removing the saddle from his mount.

"Where is my water bottle? I want to fill it with this fresh spring water."

"If you mean that long, tube-shaped item, I left it in your pack to burn."

Anne felt like screaming. She barely held her emotions in check. "Let me guess," she stormed with a quiet vengeance evident in her voice. "You decided it was not suitable for this era."

"Yes. There is a water bag hanging from the saddle horn. Fill that and sling it over your shoulder. I really do not believe it is necessary, because this next ride will be fast and furious and you will be at your grandfather's castle long before you realize that you are thirsty. Besides, there will be no time to stop for a drink. We may have to fight."

"Fight? You mean as in swords and knives and bloodshed and death? The real thing?"

"Yes, Princess." He dumped the saddle on the ground and briskly shouldered past the girl to unsaddle Blackie. "Either you kill them, or they will kill you. And believe me, they will not stop to think about it first. You did say you knew how to use the sword."

"I do know how to fence," Anne responded. "But not to the death. I have never killed anyone."

"Hmm. Well! There is always a first time." He fussed with Blackie's saddle while Anne fidgeted, pacing in circles, her hand resting on the pummel of the sword as if it would garner some comfort.

"You still have the key?" Merlin spoke so suddenly that Anne jumped.

"I wish you would not do that," she grumbled, one hand on her chest as if to calm her racing heart.

"What?"

"Make me jump."

Merlin made no comment. Instead he repeated his question. "You do have the key?"

"You mean the one that opened the door to this god-forsaken time and place?" Merlin nodded but said nothing. "Yes," she said, wondering if there was another magical door for her to open.

"And the ring?"

"Yes." She fiddled with the heavy gold band that rested on the middle finger of her right hand. It was warm, the warmth emanating through her skin and tingling its way up her arms. There was magic in the ring. Magic in the key. And magic in the sword. She was fully armed.

"The key will help you find and open many doors. Some good. Some not so good. It is up to you to make choices, to choose wisely." Merlin continued by explaining the importance of the ring. "The ring identifies who you are. But, more important, it helps protect you. If," he held up a finger as if to emphasize his point, "if you know how to garner and manipulate its magic. You witnessed its potential power when you extracted Excalibur from the stone. Like the key, the ring is only a guide. You must choose wisely. Do not waste your powers frivolously. Keep the ring on your hand and the key on a chain around your neck at all times. Do not allow anyone else to claim either. Without these talismans, you are very expendable." He pointed to the sword. "And Excalibur, your strongest weapon. Only you have the power to wield and manipulate that sword. But, you need the ring. Your grandmother told you to wear it on the middle finger of your right hand, am I right?" Anne nodded. "Now you know why. "You already know how it connects to the sword. When you wrap your hand around the hilt, the gem connects to a tiny opening in the base of the hilt. Once the sword is in your hand, as long as it connects to the ring, no one can knock it out of your hand. And the combined magic of the ring and the sword gives you a power no one else can ever match."

"Not even you?" Anne asked, moving toward her horse's head and rubbing a hand over Blackie's muzzle affectionately.

Merlin chuckled softly. "Not even me. Though I must confess, I hope you never find a reason to wield it against me. I hope you will, in time, learn to trust me fully. I am probably your one and only true friend in this world."

"Hmm!" Anne wasn't so sure. And she didn't like the idea Merlin had once again been trespassing on her innermost thoughts. "What about Abrecan? Can he overpower me when I wield Excalibur?"

"No. You are invincible when you have the key, the ring and the sword."

Anne said nothing more. She was becoming increasingly more uncomfortable with all that was happening. Although Merlin's assurances that she was invincible as long as Excalibur was within her power, she didn't like the idea of killing. It wasn't in her nature to kill. Granny had made sure she was well prepared for anything, but fighting someone to the death had not been part of her training. And this man, this wizard, Merlin, was he really on her side? How could she be sure?

Because, at the moment, Princess, you have no other choice, he spoke inside her head.

"Stop listening to my private thoughts," she snapped in response.

He dumped Blackie's saddle on the ground next to the other one and waved his hands over the pile. It went poof and vanished.

"I thought you said no magic."

Merlin led Blackie to the girl. "Mount up." He helped her onto Blackie's bare back then swung himself onto his horse.

"You were serious about bareback?" the princess exclaimed, a teasing tone in her voice.

"You said something about them being uncomfortable," came the grumbled response.

She nudged Blackie forward, following Merlin's mount, a smirk fighting to gain control of her expression. "I guess it was uncomfortable for you as well."

The wizard grunted in response. "Too cumbersome for the ride we must take." He allowed his horse to make its way across the stream and climb the bank on the opposite side. Without pause, he added, "Now we ride as if the fires of hell are on our tails." He didn't wait for Anne's response, nudging his horse into a full gallop.

Anne didn't even try to respond. She had no choice but to follow. She grasped her legs around Blackie's sides and leaned forward. "Off we go, Blackie," she whispered close to the horse's ears. Blackie needed no further urging.

The gurgling stream behind them, the horses climbed a slight incline and then the fog that had plagued them since their escape evaporated, leaving behind a clear blue sky and the sun beaming down on them.

Midday. Anne spoke inside her head.

Chapter Twelve

The ride was fast and vigorous. At least, now that the fog had dissipated, Anne could see where they were and where they were going. Not that it meant anything to her. It all appeared strange and foreign. Vast, vacant land. Steep hills, hidden valleys, fast-running streams. They galloped over and through it all.

The voices of their pursuers invaded Anne's mind, getting louder by the minute. They were close. Dangerously close. And, without the fog as a shield of protection, they were just as visible as the world around them.

They galloped to the top of the next rise and Merlin pulled up abruptly. He nodded ahead. "We must pass through this valley in order to reach your grandfather's castle at Gloucester."

"Is there a problem?" Anne inquired. She wasn't familiar with the lay of the land, so she had no choice but to trust Merlin's navigational skills.

"Yes," he pointed straight ahead, about half-way across the valley they needed to traverse. "There. Abrecan and his Saxon troops."

Letting out a strangled-sounding gasp, Anne realized that the inevitable was about to happen. "I thought they were behind us. Chasing us."

"They are," Merlin stated blandly. "And they are before us. We are surrounded by unholy forces of pure evil."

"Can we use our magic now?" she asked, hoping for a means to escape battle and realizing there were few options available.

Merlin shook his head. "Not the way you suggest. Abrecan would just counter our magic with his own. No. We must fight. Prepare for battle, Princess." He pulled out a long sword Anne hadn't realized he was carrying. Merlin was full of surprises. She thought the staff was his only weapon. Obviously, she had yet to witness the many powers of this man.

She hesitated briefly, then reached under her cloak and pulled out Excalibur, allowing the gem on her ring to connect with the hilt, and relishing the tingling sensation that raced through her hand and up her arm. Reverently, the girl brought the hilt to her lips, sword tip pointing upward, and kissed it. "Hey Ho! Away we go!" She raised her sword high and nudged Blackie into a gallop, leading the charge, such as it was, down the hill at a breakneck speed.

The wizard was startled into action, clearly surprised when the princess charged ahead as she did. "Hey Ho?" Merlin grumbled and shook his head. He didn't pause to ponder the princess's choice of words. *Your charge words need refinement.* He spoke into her head as he raised his sword and charged after her.

Whatever. Anne laughed in spite of herself. In spite of the situation. There were a lot of words and expressions from her time in the future that would confuse more than Merlin in the days to come.

Excalibur glistened as the sun caught its finely polished steel blade. It had been well maintained, cared for with love and reverence. Anne was determined to do the same. She had always cared for her possessions, things that mattered. And Excalibur definitely mattered. It had been her father's prized weapon. And now it was hers.

The Saxon force heard her battle cry. One man stood in the center of the melee of heavily armed, mounted men and their accompanying foot soldiers. The man held up a staff, much like Merlin's. It was Abrecan. It had to be him. Who else would bear a staff with an orb that emitted flashes of electrical forces, randomly shooting beams in all directions? As if there was no control in its projection. Anne was convinced that Merlin's orb was more powerful, more focussed and the wizard maintained more control. But, perhaps, she was becoming attached to the man and her biases were affecting her judgement. Whatever the case might be, Abrecan was the force to be reckoned with. But she had to penetrate the mobs that clustered around him first.

Blackie charged right for the center. Excalibur took control of the girl's arm and started weaving a path of destruction in its wake. Anne didn't have time to grimace as one man after another fell to a bloody mess at her horse's feet. There was no escape: it was either fight or die, and she certainly didn't like the second option. Heads severed, limbs chopped off – the blood splattered everywhere. No sooner was one Saxon felled, then the sword was swinging at another, dropping this man as well.

One Saxon managed to grab Blackie's reins. He dodged and ducked to avoid the onslaught of Excalibur, using the horse's head as a shield. Dropping the reins on Blackie's neck, Anne pulled her knife from its sheath. Now she was doubly armed. She made a quick assessment of the man's movements, back and forth beneath Blackie's head. The man merely laughed, confident that he could foil the actions of a girl. He muttered something in his guttural language, which Anne interpreted as a taunt. So wrapped up in himself, he miscalculated. As he chuckled with malicious delight, Anne lifted her right leg to plaster his face when he expectedly appeared on the horse's right side. Stunned, the arrogant soldier stumbled back, dropping Blackie's reins. Anne, and more accurately Excalibur, didn't pause, taking advantage of his disadvantage to sever his head.

"There. Take that." Blackie snorted in agreement. There was little time to congratulate her success, as she confronted another wild Saxon. This one grabbed her left leg as she was dismembering the cocky one. Without thinking, Anne lifted her left hand and plunged the knife into the man's right eye, before Excalibur had a chance to make a trajectory movement in her defense. She was in the groove now, or so she might have claimed in her past in the future. The splattering human appendages and gallons of blood no longer affected her. She plunged on, the power of the sword, the magic of Excalibur, leading her forward. With unsteady confidence and a weak sense of power, she made her way to the center of the melee, making her way to the true enemy: Abrecan.

The battle, if that's what it was, ended almost as soon as it began. With Abrecan standing his ground, behind the two remaining Saxon's. Big burly beasts. That's how Anne assessed them. Tall, at least six foot two, with thick chests, long, unruly hair and thick, unkempt facial hair with long beards that dribbled off their chins.

Anne pulled Blackie to a halt before the evil wizard and his minions. Excalibur, dripping with Saxon blood, lowered its point to target Abrecan. The wizard's staff quivered. But so did Merlin's, as Anne caught a glimpse of him hovering nearby, still firmly mounted on his steed, but now both sword and staff poised and ready for action.

"So, this is the Princess," Abrecan broke the silence with a caustic comment, his mouth crinkling into a sneer, the orb on his staff sparkling with renewed force. "A woman cannot rule." He spat at his feet. "And a woman will not rule. Not as long as I live and breathe."

"We can always remedy that problem," Merlin retorted, allowing the orb on his staff to sizzle its response.

Anne bit back a grin and held her ground. And her mouth. Oh! She could tell this wizard a few things. Women were just as effective at ruling as men. In fact, she believed they could be even more powerful, more efficient, because they were more caring. More of everything that mattered. *Hold your thoughts, Princess.* She heard Merlin's voice in her head. She didn't need his urging. Anne was already evolving into a powerful, effective ruler. She raised her chin and looked down on the dismal enemy before her. "Really!" she half-queried, half-jested. "Is that a dare, wizard? Abrecan, is it not?" Receiving no acknowledgement, she continued. "We shall see. I believe I have already proven myself on the battlefield."

"That was Excalibur's power. Not yours," Abrecan spat his retort, more spittle dribbling from his mouth.

"You are frothing, dear wizard," Anne couldn't help herself. She had to throw some taunts his way. And she was good at taunting.

The wizard chose to ignore the taunt. He raised his staff above his shoulder and pointed it maliciously in Anne's direction. The orb at the top sizzled threateningly. Merlin raised his staff in response, aiming his orb at Abrecan's. Anne raised Excalibur above her head and gave Blackie a nudge. As the two wizards sizzled their orbs, the electrical charge snapping and bristling with intensity, Anne moved toward Abrecan. The sword glistened. She wasn't sure if Excalibur was moving her forward, or if she made the conscious decision. It didn't matter. With the sword in control, she should have nothing to fear. At least, she hoped that was the case.

The Saxons standing around Abrecan raised their arms. Anne shuddered, suspecting they were preparing to fight. Then she realized they were covering their faces, blocking the intense light from the opposing orbs and the threatening Excalibur. She laughed softly. The big brutes were scared. Of a little girl. Well, she wasn't actually little, but compared to these big brutes, she certainly felt small. And insignificant. The feeling was quickly being replaced by a surge of control, of power, as Excalibur sent its charges throughout her entire body. She felt the tingling. She knew it was the sword giving her the courage. She felt invincible.

As the Saxons fell to their knees, the path opened between her and Abrecan. Just as Blackie came to a stop in front of the wizard, the sizzling stopped and he vanished along with his Saxons. But his voice continued to penetrate the valley.

"You may have won this battle, Princess, but you have not won the war. We shall meet again." The last words faded away, as did the Saxon bodies that had fallen to Anne's and Merlin's weapons. Lowering the sword, the girl pivoted Blackie around in a full circle, her eyes studying the horizon at all angles. Searching. Nothing. No one. All that remained was Merlin and his still sizzling staff. And herself, of course. Both mounted on their trusty horses.

Merlin didn't blink an eye in astonishment. Anne was startled by the sudden change of events, but perhaps she shouldn't be. Ever since she had entered this era, things had happened that really weren't normal. If there ever was such a thing as normal.

Anne lowered Excalibur. The sun caught its shine and glistened. "What the…?" she didn't finish her thought. The sword shone. Clean. Unblemished. As if it had never seen battle. As if it hadn't been bloodied mere moments before. Every last drop of blood that had dropped from its sharp edges vanished, soaking into the ground at her feet.

Merlin ignored the girl's outburst. "We must make haste, Princess." He lowered his staff and urged his horse forward.

"So you keep telling me, Merlin."

As Merlin urged his horse into a trot, he passed the girl and muttered, barely loud enough to be heard, "You will also notice that you have no blood on your white robe. Magic, Princess. Magic. And very powerful magic at that."

Startled, she looked down. Indeed, the white robe was as clean as it had been in the cave when she first put it on. She studied Excalibur again and, with a shake of her head, proceeded to sheath the sword. Would she ever get used to all this magic?

Probably not. Merlin's voice rang in her head. She thought she heard him chuckle as well.

Anne nudged Blackie into a gallop, catching up to Merlin in a few strides. Once she was beside the wizard, she nodded to the outcropping ahead. "Someone watches us from above."

"A lot of people are watching us, Princess." Merlin sheathed his staff and his sword, then nudged his horse into a gallop and allowed the two horses to match the other's stride as they galloped across the remaining stretch of the valley before climbing the gentle slope at the opposite end from where they had entered. "But you have nothing to fear with the lad above. He is watching for us. He will let the others know we are near."

"The others? What others?"

"Sir Galahad and his men, Princess."

"Sir Galahad from King Arthur's round table? Sir Galahad, the famed knight who searched for the Holy Grail?"

"And found it," Merlin added. "Yes. That is the one."

"You said my father was dead. Killed in battle. I thought his knights were gone as well." Anne was desperate for information. She wanted to know her father. But, since he was already dead, she could only rely on third-person accounts of his deeds.

"Sadly, King Arthur is dead, as you say. Most of his knights were killed in battle. Some died of old age. Sir Galahad, son of Lancelot and Elaine of Corbenic, was one of the younger knights to join Arthur's Round Table. He was on his quest at the time of your father's last battle. When he returned with the Holy Grail, Arthur's court was in disarray and the Saxons were running the famous king's knights and followers to ground. Galahad chose to pledge his allegiance to your grandfather, as one of the few kings with the power to hold back the Saxons."

They reached the summit, and Merlin pulled his horse up short, pointing ahead. "There they are now."

Anne looked ahead and gasped. Now this was a force to be reckoned with. Not at all like the unruly rag-tag bunch of Saxons that had confronted them in the valley. There must be hundreds of foot soldiers and almost as many fighting men on horseback.

At the front of the troop, was a well-armored rider, who, upon seeing the two appear over the ledge, motioned the armed force to remain where they were as he galloped forward to greet Merlin and Anne.

"Sir Galahad," Merlin greeted the knight when he came to a stop a nose breath from their two mounts.

"Merlin." The armored man bowed his head in reverence to the famed wizard. "We thought you dead."

"And here I am alive."

Galahad sidled his horse closer to Blackie. "And you must be King Arthur's daughter." He bowed his head even deeper, but not before Anne caught the depth of intensity in the man's blue eyes. Not before they captured hers with a glimmer of something she didn't recognize. Hope? Passion? She wasn't sure which. "My princess," he paid her homage. "Your grandfather awaits."

"And why were you not here to help us with the Saxons?" Anne demanded before she could bite back the words.

"We only just arrived, Princess. And you already had things well under control."

"I sent him a message last night," Merlin explained.

Galahad chuckled. "If you could call it that." Winking at the princess, at least Anne believed she detected a wink, he added, "Merlin has a habit of invading one's peaceful dreams to get his message across."

"I have noticed."

Nodding in acknowledgement, Galahad motioned forward. "May I have the pleasure of escorting my fair princess to see her grandfather. My liege lord, King Ceawlin of Wessex, is anxious to meet his only heir."

"Very well, kind sir." Anne smiled brightly, her eyes picking up the pleasure that washed across her face. She did notice Merlin's slight roll of the eyes. It didn't matter. With a fine looking and gallant knight at her side, what else did she need? "Lead on. Is it far?"

"Just over the next rise, Princess." The knight nudged his horse forward and Anne allowed Blackie to keep a steady pace, matching stride for stride. Merlin fell in behind the two and for once, to Anne's relief, was silent, both in and outside the mind. The mounted men parted to allow the trio to pass then closed ranks behind them.

"Tell me about my grandfather," Anne insisted, her voice taking on a sultry tone. "How long have you known him? Is he as ill as Merlin claims? Why did he allow my grandmother to leave? And then my mother as well?"

"The last two questions you will have to ask your grandfather," Galahad chuckled softly, a deep throated chuckle, almost as if he had merely cleared his throat. "As for the other questions. I have known King Ceawlin most of my life. I was sent to his court at a young age and served under him until King Arthur, your father, paraded into our lives and promised a land and a life free of the Saxon menace. His dream, King Arthur's dream was convincing and, for awhile, he kept his promise. He also promised fair and equal voice for all knights of his round table. And that, too, was a promise he kept as long as he could. Sadly, both the round table and Camelot are gone, mere ruins, and the Saxon menace has returned. But not for long, now that King Arthur's heir, you," he tilted his head in Anne's direction, "has returned. And she bears none other than the famous Excalibur. You have the power, Princess. The men, the knights of past and present, will rally to your cause."

Anne pondered his words as they plodded up the final hill that stood between her and her only living relative. Breaking the silence, she repeated her second question. "And my grandfather? How is he?"

"Better for knowing you are coming to see him." The knight allowed a few moments to pass before completing his answer. "He is old, Princess. He has his good days and his not-so-good days. Today is a good day. He was bright and cheery and full of energy when I left him a few hours ago. You will see for yourself soon enough."

They reached the top of the rise. Galahad pointed ahead. "Gloucester Castle, Princess. Home of the kings and queens of Wessex. Home of King Ceawlin of Wessex. And, now, home of his granddaughter, Princess Anne of Wessex, daughter of King Arthur."

Horns could be heard from the plateau below. Their arrival did not go unnoticed. They were being heralded, invited to the grand fortress, such as it was. Anne wasn't terribly impressed. She had studied the Middle Ages and she knew what castles of that era looked like. At least, she thought she did. This one fell far short of her expectations. At first glance, it looked like a rag-tag army encampment, with tents and fire pits and lean-to buildings in a helter-skelter array with no semblance of order and no logical pathways to allow passage amongst the dwellings. She pulled her eyes away from the distressing scene and focused on the distance, where a stone structure, not particularly tall or grand, stood as sentinel over the hodgepodge surrounding it. There was a tower with flags flying briskly in the breeze, a drawbridge that presumably dropped over a moat and a considerably taller wall than Anne would have thought at first glance. All made of stone, of course. All very solid, sound, giving the aura of stability and power. Invincible? Possibly, depending on the force attacking. If the ragtag bunch of Saxons she and Merlin had just abolished in a flash was any indication of the threat level, perhaps there wasn't much to worry about.

Do not jump to conclusions. Merlin's voice warned inside her head. *Nothing is ever as invincible and safe as it seems. I repeat: nothing.*

Chapter Thirteen

Sir Galahad motioned for his men to disperse, allowing only a few mounted men to accompany them into the compound. He led the way, with Anne and Merlin following close behind. The passages between huts, if that's what they were, was narrow at best. They didn't talk. It was best to move forward swiftly, efficiently and quietly. Anne held her breath as best she could to mask the mixture of distasteful smells: human waste, animal waste, unclean bodies and unrecognizable foods cooking on makeshift contraptions over small fires. It was enough to make a person gag. She dared not. She focused her eyes straight ahead, keeping her head high as she listened to Blackie's gentle plodding and the slurping as her hooves, one after the other, sucked in and out of the deep mud and whatever else had been dumped in their path.

The residents of this part of the compound stopped their tasks and watched the progress. No one shouted, jeered or cheered. All eyes, solemn, sad, dejected, merely watched. Was she welcome here? Did the people who stared care if she even existed? Did they resent her? With her fine clothes and fine horse, looking healthy and well fed?

Once past the first line of residents, the path became clearer. There were still ramshackle dwellings, but these had some resemblance of order.

The military compound, Merlin spoke in her ear, obviously not wishing to be heard by anyone around them. *The others were migrants. Refugees, I guess you called them in the twenty-first century. Displaced from their homes by the Saxons and seeking refuge with the King of Wessex.*

And you call that a refuge? Anne wanted to snort in disgust, but that was an expression very difficult to do effectively inside her head. *I do not even call that living.*

They have no other choice. Were things any different for refugees in the twenty-first century? With homes razed to the ground, livestock confiscated, and crops burned, they have nothing. Only hope.

I cannot accept that as hope. Anne desperately wanted to turn Blackie around and go back. To assure the poor families, especially the children, that she would do all she could do, within her power, to make things better for them. To make sure they were warm, safe and well fed. Unfortunately, other than her magic, she had nothing to help her attain these goals. Yet. Perhaps her grandfather would give her the means.

You cannot save everyone, Princess. It was uncanny the way Merlin understood what she was thinking before she even thought it.

The group carried on, reaching the end of the military base, such as it was, and approached the moat. The drawbridge was being lowered as they came closer. They had been recognized and deemed safe to enter. Sir Galahad announced himself anyway.

"Sir Galahad returning with Merlin the Magnificent and Princess Anne, daughter of King Arthur, granddaughter of King Ceawlin. Request permission to enter."

"Enter. In the name of the King," a voice called down from the battlements above and the horses followed Galahad's lead as his horse plodded across the drawbridge and into the courtyard of Gloucester Castle.

It wasn't a large courtyard, if you could even call it that. Just an open space surrounded by walls and structures that resembled dwellings. Anne noticed that there were precious few windows. She imagined there was very little light indoors. It must be a dreary existence living within these confines. She desperately hoped she didn't have to stay in this castle for long. It had the makings of a prison more than a luxurious dwelling for royalty. And, it was almost as dreary and smelly as the living areas outside the castle walls.

Do these people not know how to keep things clean and sanitized? No wonder people did not live long in the sixth century.

Very true, Princess. Something else perhaps you can remedy.

Boys ran out to grab the horses' reins. The men dismounted. Sir Galahad made his way to help Anne, but she had already slid off Blackie's back with ease, not being hindered by the saddle.

"You rode bareback," the knight observed, eyebrows lifted in surprise. "I would have thought…" He didn't finish his sentence.

"Sir Galahad," a voice interrupted, calling from what appeared to be the main entrance to the castle itself. "The king awaits. He is anxious to meet his granddaughter. Stop dallying and bring her inside."

The knight motioned toward the set of steps. "Shall we, Princess?" he asked.

Merlin shouldered his way past the two, not waiting for an invitation. He was, after all, Merlin the Magnificent and he needed no escort nor a welcoming tribute. He was given one anyway. He trotted up the steps like a young man, his cloak billowing behind him. As he marched through the grand entrance, a page called out his introduction, "Merlin the Magnificent."

Anne coughed softly to muffle a giggle that gurgled in her throat. She continued to be amazed at all around her. Only days before she had been sharing stories about this era with her grandmother, in a cozy apartment in downtown Toronto, a place that didn't even exist in the sixth century. Today, she had fought a battle with the famed Excalibur and she had ridden into a castle like a princess.

She nodded regally to her escort. "Lead the way, brave knight." Galahad blushed slightly, clearing his throat to maintain his own composure.

The two marched up the steps, not as hastily as Merlin had done moments before, and entered the castle, to the page's voice bellowing, "Princess Anne of Wessex and Sir Galahad, Knight of the Round Table."

Questions popped into the girl's head, but she didn't have time to ask them. Hopefully she'd have the opportunity later. She paused inside the entrance, blinking her eyes, trying to adjust them to the dimly lit room. There was a large hearth at the far end that burned brightly. Torches sat in the wall sconces all around the room and great candelabras were evenly spaced along a grand table that stretched the length of the room. There was light, but, without windows, or, at least none she could see, the candlelight did little to brighten the space.

"Granddaughter," a voice bellowed from across the room, somewhere close to the hearth. "Granddaughter. Come forward. I must see you. I have waited a long time for this day." With a lowered voice, he uttered a command, "Go fetch Rosalind. My Queen. Bring her at once."

Grandmother? She's here? I thought she was…. She wasn't able to finish her thoughts.

She is here. She heard Merlin's voice offer a spartan explanation. *She came through the portal a few years ago and stayed. Even when you thought she was with you, she was also here with her husband. I am sure you have lots of questions. Save them. There will be time later. Go meet your grandfather and be joyful to see your grandmother again.*

She didn't need any further urging. Anne almost trotted around the long table in her rush to reach the hearth.

"Granddaughter. My Anne." The king reached up his hands, which the girl took gently in hers. She orchestrated the best curtsy she could muster and then reached forward to plant a kiss on her grandfather's cheek. The wrinkles sagged from his eyes to his chin; the skin was dry and brittle, thin and fragile like tissue paper. But the eyes were blue, a deep, intense blue, and the grasp of his hands, also wrinkled and withered with age, was firm and warm. He was wrapped well in rugs and robes, from his chin down to his toes, but his frail form was evident underneath the coverings. He was old and he showed his age, his health obviously taking its toll. He wasn't well. It was as if she had only arrived in time. Before he died.

"Anne."

The voice, so familiar, was like music to her ears. Anne dropped her grandfather's hands and glanced in the direction of the voice. "Granny?" she half whispered. Realizing she was in a formal setting, she corrected herself, saying in a firmer, slightly louder voice, "Grandmother." But then all protocol was thrust aside as she skirted around her grandfather's chair and ran into her grandmother's arms. "I thought…"

"Shh! Shh!" The queen consoled her granddaughter, as tears started drenching the shoulder where Anne's head now lay.

"What about Mother?" Anne sniffled into her grandmother's shoulder.

The queen kept a warm grasp of the girl, not wanting to let go, for either of their sakes. "Shh! Shh!" she shushed again gently. "Save the questions. For now, let us be happy and celebrate. We have so much to celebrate. Do you not agree?" She gently pushed Anne away, holding her granddaughter's shoulders affectionately, studying the young woman who now stood before her. Every bit the princess. Taking one hand, Rosalind gently wiped away Anne's tears. "Now. Come. Sit with your grandfather and I. Warm yourself by the fire."

Granny, or Grandmother, appeared younger than she had when they last sat together in Anne's bedroom sharing stories. The warmth in her hands and the strength exchanged in the embrace were evident, not only of her vivid personality and her passion for life, but also of the dignified position she held at court, as Queen Rosalind of Wessex.

Anne nodded her head, confusion rippling through her mind as she allowed the queen to lead her back to the hearth. She took a seat in the chair facing her grandfather and Grandmother took the vacant seat next to her husband. Merlin hovered nearby, his presence felt but not heard.

The king was the first to break the awkward silence that engulfed the space around them. "You look just like your grandmother did when I first met her. Only your hair is different. Lighter. Much like your father's hair." His voice was soft, like velvet, but firm and fully in control. He spoke loud enough for the ears of the small family gathering by the hearth. The room was full, knights and their ladies, all chattering softly in various corners of the room, but all keeping a respectful distance. Even Galahad had disappeared as soon as he had completed his task of escorting the princess.

Perhaps that was all it had been for him, Anne thought, trying hard to keep her thoughts guarded, away from Merlin's prying ears.

No such luck. *You have not seen the last of Sir Galahad, Princess. Not yet.*

Anne unfastened her outer robe and shoved it back. The warmth of the fire was more than sufficient to keep her warm.

King Ceawlin continued to study his granddaughter. "The color of your eyes and your smile..That is my Rosalind, all right." He reached for his wife's hand, which she took willingly and grasped with a fondness only apparent between two people who had pledged their lives to each other and carried the flame within their hearts to the end. The king glanced at Rosalind and then at Anne. "And now my family is complete." He cleared his throat. "Well, almost complete." His quick correction made a subtle reference to Anne's mother who wasn't with them. There was something she didn't know about her mother. Something that made her grandfather uncomfortable. She couldn't ask now. It was another question to save for later, to save for Grandmother to explain. And hopefully she would. Anne's life had been filled with secrets. It was time she had all the answers. Not just some of them.

"Your grandmother claims you make a fine horsewoman. Do you like to ride?" the king asked. "I understand Merlin has bequeathed you with one of his treasured mares."

The princess was startled. She hadn't realized Blackie was one of Merlin's horses. And a gift at that. She recovered quickly, answering, "Yes, Grandfather." Anne flashed a warm smile at her grandparents. "I do like to ride. And Blackie, that's what I call her. Merlin says her name is Black Passion. Blackie has such a gentle soul. We connected right away." Catching her grandmother's eye, she realized she was talking too much. Something she often did when she was nervous. She shouldn't be nervous, though. These were her grandparents. And she knew her grandmother. At least, she thought she did. She couldn't fathom how Grandmother, as she would have to call her now as it was more formal, had managed to come back from the dead (and she was sure the men who had invaded the apartment moments after Anne's escape had killed her grandmother). And somehow, miraculously, she had made it to her husband's court in the sixth century before Anne's arrival. It was complicated. More questions. She was itching to have some answers. And Grandfather appeared more interested in her riding skills.

"I understand you rode bareback. Not very becoming of a princess."

"Yes, Grandfather." She felt chastised. But the thought of another minute in that uncomfortable contraption known as a saddle, was unthinkable. "The saddle was uncomfortable. Not suited for a long, hard ride," she confessed, shuffling uneasily in her seat. Built from solid slabs of wood, with a high back and winged arms, the chair in which she sat offered no comfort at all.

Much like the saddle. Did this era not know how to make cushions? To make things comfortable? The cumbersome sheath holding Excalibur and the sack of precious possessions still slung over her shoulder, didn't add much to the comfort.

Grandmother noticed the girl's discomfort. "I fear our granddaughter is exhausted from her journey, my husband. Perhaps we should allow her some time to rest and freshen up. Then we can feast and be merry over a grand meal."

The king hesitated, as if he didn't want to end the family gathering just when it was beginning. "I have waited so many years for this moment, Granddaughter of mine. A few more hours will not hurt these old bones." He snapped his fingers, and a woman dressed in plain robes, presumably a lady's maid, materialised from the shadows behind the king's chair. "Escort the princess to her rooms."

"Yes, your majesty," the maid curtseyed and motioned for Anne to follow.

Standing up, Anne repositioned her bag, which was slipping from her shoulder, adjusted her sword scabbard, which had been pushed awkwardly to the front when she sat, and bent over to give her grandfather another kiss on the cheek. She was about to do the same with Grandmother, but she was waved away. "I shall join you in a few minutes, dear Anne," she half-whispered. "As soon as I see to your grandfather. He could well use a rest as well."

Anne nodded, backed up slightly and gave a slight curtsey before following the maid out of the hall.

Chapter Fourteen

My name is Grace, Princess," the maid informed Anne as she led the way out of the grand hall and up a lengthy stretch of stone stairs. Upon reaching a landing of sorts, the girls turned and mounted another set of steps. "Almost there, Princess," Grace huffed. "It is a long climb, but you are safest at the top of the tower. That is what the king wants – to keep you safe."

"From what? From whom?" Anne asked between huffs of her own. The steps were steep and she was tired from the long ride, the battle, and pretty much everything that had happened to her since she arrived in the sixth century. "I would have thought this castle impenetrable."

Grace chuckled softly, a sad chuckle. "Nothing is impenetrable, Princess. Look what happened to Camelot."

No more was said. They reached the top landing, only identifiable as such due to the lack of more stairs leading upwards. Grace opened a door and motioned Anne inside. It was a cozy room, complete with its own hearth, already lit with a warm, inviting fire. Fur rugs covered the floor, adding to the comfort. There was a tiny window at one end, covered with thick leaded glass, that, due to its density, barely allowed any light in. It didn't matter. The sun had long since disappeared behind the clouds, and it was threatening to rain. There was a bed covered with more animal furs. And a tub sat close to the hearth.

"Oh my!" Anne exclaimed, noticing the steam rising from the tub. She made her way across the soft fur floor coverings and stood with her hands outstretched over the rising steam. She couldn't remember the last time she had a good soak. It felt like it had been days. Could it really have been a mere couple of days? The water didn't look all that clean, not compared to the clear liquid that poured out of the taps with ease in the twenty-first century. But it was warm. It was wet. And it was definitely what she needed.

"We thought you might like a soak, Princess." Grace closed the door, making her way silently across the threshold. "It is best to keep the door closed at all times, Princess. Keeps the warmth inside."

Anne noticed the draft that had penetrated the room when they entered was being eliminated by the warmth of the fire and the steam rising from the hot water in the tub. She didn't need any urging. She slipped the bag off her shoulder and tossed it onto the bed, along with her outer robe before starting to unclasp the belt that held the sword and knife.

"Here. Let me help, Princess. I have been assigned as your personal maid."

Anne wasn't used to being helped. She had always dressed herself, cared for her belongings, kept her room in order. She studied the girl beside her, obviously so eager to please. She hadn't had the chance to really look at her until now, the exit from the main floor being one of uncertain haste. Mounting the lengthy line of steps had only allowed Anne the opportunity to see the lower end and the backside of the maid. That is, only when she managed to steal her eyes away from the steep incline she mounted.

Grace was about Anne's height. But, where Anne had long, intensely blond hair, like her father, Grace had very pale, blonde hair. The eager eyes that studied the princess were a deep blue, resonating care and compassion. At least, that's what Anne sensed. She was usually a good judge of character. She hoped it was still the case.

You can trust Grace, Princess. Merlin's voice in her head. Again. *For now.*

You can leave me alone, Merlin. Anne chastised him.

Smiling her warmest smile, Anne reached out and took Grace's hands. "I would like to be friends. I would like that very much. But I must confess, I am not used to having people help me dress. And bathe. And take care of things that I can take care of myself. So, please do not be offended it I choose to do something on my own."

Grace returned the smile and squeezed the hands she now held. "Very well, Princess. I shall be here should you need me. Just tell me what you would like me to do."

"First of all, I need a safe place for my sword and knife. One that is easily accessible, whether I am in the bath or lying in bed."

"Perhaps if you were to slide it underneath the bedding, it would be concealed, yet easily accessible?"

"Good idea." Anne finished unfastening her belt and gingerly held the weapons before her face, reverence evident in her expression. *Excalibur. You did well today. For me. I thank you.* She didn't speak out loud, only within her head. For Excalibur, not for anyone or anything else.

The sword warmed to her touch and her words, causing the girl to smile as she carefully tucked it under the bed coverings. She shoved her bag underneath the bed as well, something to look through and study later. Standing up again, she gave in to Grace's hands to assist in disrobing, too tired to fuss with the many layers, too anxious to soak in the tub before the warmth evaporated.

Once the outer layers were removed, Grace choked on a gasp. "What is that you wear?"

Anne looked down at her jeans, filthy and barely covering her twenty-first century undergarments. "Something Merlin cooked up for me," she muttered the first idea that popped into her head. "We had a long ride to undertake, and I needed something to protect my legs from chaffing."

Grace nodded, a pretense at comprehension. As Anne slid out of her only remaining clothes from the future, the maid reached to take them from her. "I will have these cleaned, Princess?" It was half statement, half question.

Anne held onto the garments and made her decision instantaneously. "No. There is not much left." She tossed them into the fire. "Better they burn, would you not agree?"

"Yes, Princess."

Rid of her soiled clothes, Anne approached the tub and climbed over the steep rise of the tub. She slid down to the bottom with ease, allowing the moist warmth to soak through her skin, soothing her weary muscles as she cleansed her soiled skin.

She soaked for some time, not wanting to escape the engulfing warmth. She must have dozed off, too. Grace had to urge her out. Holding a large wrap suspended from one outstretched hand to the other, she said, "You must get out of the tub, Princess. You will turn into a prune if you soak much longer."

Anne chuckled. "My grandmother used to say that to me." With a deep sigh, she pushed herself into a standing position and climbed out of the water that really was no longer as warm and inviting as it had been initially. Grace wrapped a large drying robe around the dripping wet princess and motioned for her to sit by the hearth. Picking up what appeared to be a wooden comb, Grace moved behind Anne and began the task of untangling the now damp mop of hair.

A knock on the door didn't stop Grace's long, gentle strokes as she gradually eased the knots free. Anne called out, "Come in."

She almost jumped up with pleasure when her grandmother stepped into the room, but Grace, with a hand gently placed on Anne's shoulder, kept her seated.

The queen signaled with her hand for Anne to remain where she was. After shutting the door behind her, Rosalind walked across the rugs to her granddaughter, bent down to plant a kiss on the girl's cheek.

"And now we can talk," Rosalind took the only other seat in the room and pulled it close to her granddaughter and close to the warmth of the fire.

Anne flashed her eyes at Grace, wondering if they could speak while the maid was still in the room. "Oh. You can trust Grace. I am sure Merlin has already said the same thing." Anne didn't have to answer. Her eyes gave it away. Rosalind chuckled. "Merlin does have a way of communicating with us, does he not? Now, Grace here is your half-sister and totally trustworthy. Is that not right, Grace?"

"Half-sister?" Anne gasped. She shuffled in her seat to study Grace again. "Really?"

"Yes, Princess," Grace smiled down at her before gently turning Anne's head forward again so she could continue with the task of combing Anne's hair.

"Same father," Rosalind explained. "Very common in this era. Very common in many eras, actually." She muttered the last part barely under her breath, almost as if speaking with disgust for the actions of the opposite sex.

"You do not regret your position?" Anne asked abrasively before she could stop herself. "You do not resent me?"

"Technically, you are base born as well," Rosalind answered before Grace had the chance to say anything. "And technically, you are a little older than Grace, making your claim to Arthur's throne stronger. That, and being the granddaughter of the king of Wessex, adds to your claim."

"Claim to what? I did not expect any of this. I did not want to live in the fairy tales you shared with me from the time I was a little girl." Anne wasn't sure she wanted this life. She had been quite happy in the twenty-first century. Or so she thought.

"We cannot expect to always get what we want, my dear Anne," Grandmother tried to console the girl, keeping her voice diplomatically soft, gentle and firm, all at the same time. "We are born into this world for a reason, and we must follow the course our life leads. Your course, your journey, is one of leadership. You are a leader, Anne. Like your father and your grandfather. I could sense that in you from the time you took your first steps. You have the ability to lead with grace, dignity and the compassion to care for the little people, those who toil day and night to barely survive." She nodded at the girl knowingly. "You saw those poor people at the outer regions, beyond the castle walls. They need you, Anne. They look at your grandfather, and they will soon look at you, with hope. Lead well, child. Learn what you can from your grandfather while you can. He is very ill. I am surprised he is still with us. But that is your grandfather. My husband." She let out a passionate sigh. "Always thinking of others first. He really wanted to meet you before he crossed over."

"You mean, before he dies," Anne was blunt in her choice of words. "Talking about death, I thought you were dead. I thought I heard those men kill you as I hid in the neighbor's apartment. I thought Mother was dead, too."

"She is. I am." The queen smiled sadly. "Let me explain." She reached for her granddaughter's hands and, taking them in hers, stroked the backs with her thumbs. Gently. Soothingly. "The men did kill me. And they killed your mother as well. I am here from an earlier time in your life. You remember that time when our mother was out of work and stayed home for weeks?"

"And you went away for a time," Anne finished. Realization dawned in her eyes. "That was about ten years ago. But how?" She didn't finish her question. She didn't have to. Merlin's magic.

"I am only here for a short time, Anne. Until my husband crosses over. Then I will return to your twenty-first century life and finish preparing you for this day." She noticed Anne's confusion. Grace had finished combing the princess's hair and had taken a seat, cross-legged on the floor rugs at the princess's feet, close enough to absorb some of the warmth from the fire.

The queen went on before Anne could protest. "You will be fine without me. Without your grandfather. You have Merlin and Sir Galahad and Grace. And your future is pretty much mapped out for you. You are ready for this challenge. But first, you must know a few things. What I cannot share in the short time we have together, the others will help. First, keep Excalibur with you at all times. Even tonight when you attend the banquet. You will need it tonight."

"I will? Why? I thought we were secure in the castle."

"You are never secure. In the castle or in the wilderness beyond. If you remember that simple fact, you will manage to keep yourself safe. For a very long time, at least." She paused to allow her words to sink in. Satisfied, she continued, "For now, this tower is your safe place. Your haven. It is the place where you can come to seek escape or just to hide."

"Like Rapunzel?" Anne asked half joking. "I do not think my hair is long enough to allow me to climb down the outer walls and escape."

Grace looked confused. Rosalind explained. "An old fairy tale I once told Anne." Grace merely nodded. The queen continued, "Perhaps you will not need to escape through the window, Anne." She stood up and made her way to the hearth. Reaching just beyond Anne's left shoulder, she pointed to a stone. "Remember this stone, Anne. It is your key to the escape route. And wear the key around your neck at all times. You do still hve to key, do you not?"

Anne fingered the chain around her neck, the one she had refused to take off when she stepped into the bath. Dangling the key in front of her, she gave her grandmother a warm smile. "Always."

"Good. Now watch." The queen pushed the stone. An opening appeared just behind the hearth. Not very big, just enough for a thin girl like Anne to squeeze through. Her grandmother was thin, too. She motioned the girls to follow and then slipped through the opening.

Anne stood up and wrapped the robe more tightly around her, reluctant to leave the soothing warmth beside the fire. She was dry, now. Even her hair. A blast of cooler air escaped the opening and shivered its way underneath the girl's robe.

"Quickly, girls," the queen urged. "We do not have much time before the dinner. We must not be late for the grand entrance your grandfather plans for this evening's festivities. He wants to put you on display, Anne. You are his only heir."

Anne chose not to argue, in spite of her misgivings about taking on such a big responsibility. She knew little about this era, except what she had read in history books and from the stories her grandmother shared, stories she once believed were mere fairy tales. The girls slipped through the opening, into a space barely large enough for one person, let alone three.

"You must close it behind you. Always. Before you descend the stairs. It will take pursuers longer to catch up to you if they can't immediately discover the secret passage." Grace, being the last one to enter the space, reached behind her and pulled the opening barrier toward her, in effect closing the opening. The light from the room behind was shut out as well and the ladies were plunged into thick darkness. "Your eyes will adjust," Rosalind assured them. "It is best to move about without light, so no one can see glimmers shimmering through cracks in the walls as you descend."

Grandmother was right. Anne's eyes adjusted to the darkness. She could make out the figure of her grandmother in front of her and she could feel Grace squeezed in tight behind. Shadows suggested shapes that resembled steps carved into the outer perimeter of the tower wall. "Come, girls. And be careful. The steps are steep, narrow and sometimes slippery. Keep one hand on the outer wall to feel your way. Use your other senses to guide your path."

The queen led the way; the girls followed close behind. The steps were treacherous as her grandmother warned, but, taken slowly and with the balance of one hand firmly placed on the outer wall, the girls managed a safe descent. When they reached the bottom, both Anne and Grace let out a sigh of relief.

"Feel along the wall, Anne." She did as instructed. "Can you feel the door?"

"Yes."

"Can you find the keyhole?"

Anne slid her hands around the recession that suggested a door or entry point to another space or dimension. Her hands stopped when she felt the cut-out incision that suggested a keyhole. "I think so, Grandmother."

"Good. Your key will fit in there. This is not the time to test it. We must return to your chambers and prepare for the feast. At least now you know where to go when you need to escape. Take Grace with you. She will always be in as much danger as you are. People know who she is, Anne. She is your younger sister. Half-sister. Keep her close. You two need each other."

"Yes, Grandmother," Anne agreed.

"Yes, my Queen." Grace could be heard rustling her skirts as she managed a curtsy. Not that anyone could see it. The space was as dark as it had been up top. But they could hear and sense it. Her voice, however, hinted at a masked tension. Anne heard it. She wondered if her grandmother had as well. The tone gave her a sense of unease, chills racing up and down her spine. Who was this Grace? And why did everyone think she was trustworthy? Anne was really beginning to wonder if there was anyone she could truly trust.

"Now." Rosalind resumed her instructions as if nothing were amiss. "Back up the stairs. Before we are missed."

The girls followed the queen up the steep steps, barely managing to keep up with the older woman who appeared much more fit than they were. Anne and Grace were huffing considerably by the time they reached the top.

"Shh!" The queen hushed them to silence. They stood, crammed in the space, next to the opening into Anne's chambers. And listened. Chills rippled up and down Anne's spine. Someone was in her room.

"It is safe to come out, ladies." Merlin. Wouldn't you know it! Always the dramatist. Always capable of sneaking up on a person.

Letting out pent up sighs of relief, the ladies filed out of the hidden room.

"Merlin!" Rosalind almost snapped. "You will give this old lady a weak heart if you continue sneaking up on me like this."

"I was merely securing the chambers, something which you ladies should consider doing in the future," he scolded in return. "There may not be a lock, but there are other ways to prevent an unwanted person from entering a chamber. And now, if you will excuse me, I shall return to my own chambers and prepare for this evening. My Queen." He held out an arm in invitation. "Would you like me to escort you down to your chambers."

Mollified, Rosalind slipped her hand through Merlin's arms and waved to the girls as the two paraded out of Anne's chambers. "Lock the door behind us, ladies," Merlin called out an order over his shoulder.

"And do not take too long," Grandmother added.

Grace quickly moved to lock the door. Turning back to her charge, she gave a look of remorse. "I was remiss, Princess. I should have locked the door."

Anne waved aside the girl's confession. "We shall both be more vigilant from now on. Let us prepare for this evening, shall we?"

Chapter Fifteen

Anne was amazed at the multiple layers of robes. The embroidery on the outer robe was exquisite. With it draped over her shoulders, Anne ran a finger tenderly over the lines of stitches. "I could never sew this well," she half whispered.

Grace heard her, though, and remarked, "I did some of it myself. My mother is the head seamstress in the castle. She and my grandmother make items of clothing into works of art."

"Indeed it is," Anne agreed. "And you helped?"

Grace nodded, preening slightly, obviously pleased with the compliments. She pointed to the bold image of an eagle perched across Anne's right shoulder like an emblem of rank and privilege. "I embroidered the eagle." She wasn't hesitant to soak up the praise.

The princess studied the fine work intently, running a finger along the even lines of stitches. "Very nicely done." Reaching for the girl who was her half-sister and her maid, she pulled Grace into a hug. "Thank you. I really do hope we can be friends as well as sisters. I have always wanted a sister."

The two stood back, moisture threatening to seep from their eyes. Studying the princess, Grace said, "I have always wanted a sister, too. And a friend." She took in a deep breath and, with the back of her hand, wiped away the renegade tears that slithered down her cheeks. "Now," she crouched down and reached underneath the mattress, fussing restlessly as if she were trying to hide her true feelings. Were the tears genuine? Anne couldn't help but wonder. Anne's tears were sincere. She knew that much. But Grace's? She didn't have time to ponder further.

Grace pulled out the revered sword and handed it to the princess, all business in her actions. "Fasten your sword belt and let us secure Excalibur underneath the outer robe so that it is accessible but not visible."

The girls finished their preparations. As Anne made her way to the door, she paused, waiting for her sister. Grace was fussing with her own sword belt and sheathing a sword. "You know how to fight?" she asked, barely masking the tone of surprise in her voice.

"I am good with a needle and a sword, Princess." Grace finished sheathing the sword, lifting the skirt to expose her leg strapped with a long-bladed knife below the knee. "I am always prepared to fight. You never know what you will meet out there." She dropped the skirt, hiding the knife and donned a robe which covered her sword. Motioning to the door, she said, "Shall we, Princess?"

Anne nodded and led the way out of the chambers. They reached the bottom of the stairs in time to greet her grandparents with a hug. The king leaned heavily on his wife, but managed to straighten his shoulders as he led the way into the grand hall. Anne walked a few steps behind with Grace following amongst the other personal attendants.

"May I have the honor, Princess?" The voice caused Anne to jump as Sir Galahad stepped out of the shadows just as she was about to enter the grand hall. He held up his left arm in invitation. Recovering from the start he gave her, she graced him with a smile and tucked her right hand through his arm.

"Sir Galahad," she gently scolded. "You should know better than to make a girl jump." Was she flirting with this knight? With her isolated upbringing, she hadn't experienced the interactions young girls usually have with boys. She wasn't sure if she felt something for Sir Galahad. It was too early to tell. But it was entertaining to flirt a little. Especially when she made the knight blush.

He returned her smile. "Yes, Princess." He feigned a voice that suggested he was chastised, when he wasn't. Not really. And the two paraded into the grand hall as the page announced, "All rise for King Ceawlin of Wessex and his wife, Queen Rosalind. And his granddaughter, Princess Anne."

The couple marched together, matching stride for stride. Anne had to admit that it felt good. It felt right. She was content, comfortable, standing next to the noble knight. He might be older than her, perhaps a decade or so, she couldn't be sure. But age melted away as their linked arms and the comfortable gate made everything in the world seem so right.

That is, until they entered the hall and took their places next to the king and queen. The king sat with a deep huff, as if all his energy had been exerted in the simple task of making it from his chambers to the grand hall. Rosalind sat next to him and Sir Galahad held out a chair on the other side of the king for Anne. Then, it was as if the doors to hell exploded. A noise at the far end of the hall alerted everyone's attention, stunning the gathered knights and their ladies. As if in a rippling effect, benches at the far end started toppling over as men scrambled to their feet, reaching for weapons only moments before the intruding force severed limbs and heads. The women screamed and ran for cover. Only, there wasn't any. Only more invaders.

"Saxons!" Sir Galahad half snarled as he whispered in Anne's ear, disgust evident in his voice. "You must find refuge. You and your grandparents."

He spoke too late, as Saxon forces quickly had the room encased in its iron grip. Then Abrecan entered at the far end with all the pomp and fanfare befitting a nobleman. He was followed by a burly beast of a man, obviously someone of rank and honor, given his slightly more noble attire. Abrecan stopped at the far end of the table, stomped his staff and proclaimed, "All hail, King Penda, Saxon king of Mercia."

Penda. He is bad. Very bad. Merlin spoke inside Anne's head.

Where are you? Anne responded in kind. *We need you here. Now!*

No, Princess. You have your sister, your knight and Excalibur. You will prevail. And make a name for yourself in the process. After today, no one will dare march into your court uninvited.

But, Merlin. Where are you?

Preparing to help Rosalind return to the twenty-first century where she will help you with your final days of training. Right now, you need to focus on the enemy. Penda's a growing force amongst the Saxon kings and overlords. He wants you and your lands. To expand his territory. And to lay claim to the dream your father started with Camelot. Now fight, Princess. Fight as you have never fought before.

But Merlin. He was gone. As if he pressed the off button on a cell phone and disconnected. Only, cell phones didn't exist in this era. She would have to stop making these comparisons.

The Saxons stomped their feet in response and echoed his proclamation, "All hail, King Penda." The noise intensified, the stomping rattled the furnishings and the high-pitched shouts caused the candelabras and the lit flames on each candle to quiver threateningly. The cups and plates set along the long tables rattled across the surface, many clattering to the floor.

"Seize the girl!" Abrecan pointed at Anne, putting an end to the chanting accolades.

Before anyone could move in, Anne was on the table, robe thrown back and Excalibur out of its sheath. She wrapped her hand firmly around the hilt allowing the gem of her ring to connect and sizzle with power. The sword glistened and shone, sparkling full of energy. The enemy stepped back in awe, afraid. They had heard what she had done earlier in the day. Unsure, they backed further away, muttering amongst themselves in a language Anne couldn't understand.

Abrecan wasn't moved by her display of power. Even as she raised Excalibur high above her head and proclaimed, "To arms. For me. For the King of Wessex. For the daughter of King Arthur. For Camelot."

Her call to arms rallied what few men had managed to keep arms and limbs and head intact. Abrecan and the noble Saxon at his heels only stepped closer. The wicked wizard moved his staff so that it no longer pointed at Anne and, with a few mixed words of a chant, sent a beastly charge directly at the king, who had not yet managed to stand in his defense.

"No!" Anne shrieked, realizing what was happening. It was too late. She glanced briefly over her shoulder, long enough to see her grandfather slumped over his end of the table, a ghastly hole sizzling through his head.

Her grandmother gave her a nod of understanding. She appeared unravelled by the events, as if she'd been there before. She merely mouthed, "Do not give in, granddaughter. You are now Queen Anne." Raising her voice, she called out in a commanding voice, "All hail, Queen Anne of Wessex. Queen Anne of Camelot. Long live the Queen."

Her men, Anne's men, echoed Rosalind's chant. It unsettled the Saxons, long enough for Rosalind to make a hasty exit and long enough for Anne to wield Excalibur in the direction of the Saxon menace. Fighting, one at a time, she slashed heads and speared chests, making her way to the far end of the table. She poised a kick or two, some hitting rather delicate locations. She was glad she had kept her twenty-first century leather boots. The soft slippers Grace had offered would never provide the pointed kick like these boots did.

Abrecan and the Saxon king had not moved. King Penda had the look of a man unsure of what to do next, unsure of this female fighting force that was making its way toward him, wreaking havoc to his men in the process. And, yes, there was another woman fighting at Anne's back. Grace hadn't needed much urging to take her place next to the sister who was now queen.

"I have your back, Queen Anne," she proclaimed on more than one occasion. "Fight on. Sir Galahad has rallied the men to clean up."

Anne wasn't the only leader receiving instructions. She was now close enough to hear Abrecan snarl at the Saxon king. "Get your men in order. Tackle the girl yourself, if you have to."

The girls felt the table rumble as Penda followed his wizard's commands, and jumped onto the table in one giant leap, sending everything that hadn't already been tossed aside, shattering to the floor. Anne and Grace managed to keep their balance. Barely. Grace's shriek caused Anne to pause. She glanced over her shoulder, just long enough to see her sister tossed over the shoulder of a scraggly Saxon beast. Anne bit back a grin when she realized that her sister had not given into the fight. The girl had her knife poised, gripped in both hands as the sword had dropped into the floor rushes. Grace worked fast and the grunt that followed satisfied Anne that her sister could take care of herself. The Saxon beast crumbled to the floor. Grace pulled the knife from the man's back, grabbed her sword and was back in action.

The distraction placed Anne in a precarious situation. She loosened her grip on Excalibur while she focused her attention on her sister. Long enough for the Saxon king to get close enough to grab her free arm. Startled into action, she snarled at the predator.

"Unhand me, Saxon beast," she spat.

Penda laughed. A deep, hearty laugh. "And if I do not?" He spoke in a language she understood, but with a strong accent.

She started to raise Excalibur, but Penda already had a grip on her sword arm as well. It was a fierce grip. She struggled to release herself, to no avail. He merely laughed, pulling her toward him. "Drop the sword, Queen Anne. You and the sword are now mine." He forced his lips onto hers. It was all Anne could do not to gag. He pulled back with a hearty laugh. "I shall enjoy having you warm my bed, lass. That is before I remove your head."

"See if you can, Saxon. I dare you." He responded by quickly plastering his lips on hers. Again.

She pulled herself together while he was distracted, squirming herself into position. And then she lifted her knee, sharply, right on target.

The king crumbled into a fetal position, letting Anne loose as he uttered a few choice words in a language Anne didn't recognize. Stepping back, Anne didn't wait for him to recover. She spat on him, raising Excalibur until the tip was pointed at the Saxon king's neck. "Ugh! You beast. You stink. How dare you lay hands, or lips, for that matter, on my person. You shall pay for this offence." With her other hand, she pulled out her knife and plunged it into the Penda's back.

"You may stink now, but not as much as you will stink in hell for eternity." She pulled the knife out as the Saxon king collapsed into a heap at her feet. The other Saxons, those still standing, stepped back staring, stunned. "Anyone else?" she held up the knife, allowing the Saxon's blood to drip unchecked on the table. The drama had its impact on the enemy warriors. One Saxon dared to challenge her. Before he could meet her in a match, she raised Excalibur, the sword moving with its own magical power as it was plunged it into the man's chest. As he leaned into the wound, she extracted the sword and brought in a full swing, severing the man's head. Her practise sessions with the fencing master had not prepared her for real life battles. She hadn't realized she was this strong. It must be the power of the sword. The power of Excalibur.

"Anyone else?" She was in control, the power of her victories sizzling through her veins. With confidence, she walked the length of the table, stepping over the fallen Saxon king with no sign of remorse. Abrecan remained at his perch at the end of the table. "And you, Abrecan? What say you?"

He spat at her. "You have not won yet, Queen Anne." Each punctuated word emitted spittle which flew at her as he spoke. He raised his staff and pointed at the king. "He and I will return. King Penda is not dead yet. But you will be. And soon."

Anne raised Excalibur in a sweeping motion, intent to behead the wizard who threatened her, the one who had annihilated all that she held dear. He, in return, held up his staff, muttered a few words in an unrecognizable language, and vanished in a puff of smoke. Without a moment to think, Anne kept the sword poised and pivoted to bring it down on King Penda, intent to remove his head. Before the sword made contact, the Saxon king vanished.

"Like I said, Queen Anne. You have not seen the last of me or King Penda. I would be careful, if I were you." The voice shuddered through the room, echoing at every corner, flickering the flames in the hearth and what few candles remain lit.

She would not allow his threats to unnerve her. She would not and she could not. She had a job to do. One that she had been raised for. One that she had been thrust into. It wasn't her choice to rule as queen in the sixth century. It wasn't her choice to reclaim the power of her father's court at Camelot. But rule and reclaim the realm, she would do. And, in the process, she would drive out the Saxon menace for good.

The room was ominously quiet, like a black hole after an explosive event. The battle had been full of raucous grunts, clashing weapons and scattered paraphernalia. Glancing around at the remaining Saxons, Anne noted the shocked expressions of those who still stood, still held their weapons before them as if to defend what little they had left. She noticed their uneasiness. They were nervous. They had been abandoned by their leaders and they knew it. They also knew that they couldn't expect much compassion from their captors.

"Grab him!" Sir Galahad made a dash from the far end of the room where he had fought valiantly to keep the mad force from entering the private chambers of the castle. Had they managed to infiltrate the rooms beyond the grand hall, who knew what havoc they could have caused. And, they might have discovered secrets better kept from the Saxons.

Everyone's eyes followed the direction of Galahad's pointed sword. The Saxons jumped into action, making a hasty retreat toward the door to the courtyard, the one through which they had bullied their way inside. They formed a protective human shield around the man, or boy, that Galahad had singled out, raising their weapons again in defense.

Sir Galahad made a sweeping motion with his sword. Aided by some of his men, the Saxon shield, such as it was, quickly fell. During the melee, the boy disappeared into the courtyard, but Galahad was hot on his heels. It didn't take long for the seasoned knight to corral the boy and bring him back triumphantly.

He approached Anne, sword lowered and his free hand gripped firm on the scruff of the boy's neck. "My Queen," he bowed graciously. "May I present Prince Peada, son of King Penda. And, should Penda really be dead, Peada would be King of Mercia."

"Peada." Anne sheathed Excalibur and the knife. Both were clean, miraculously. She wasn't sure how it happened. Perhaps she would ask Merlin about it. On second thought, perhaps she would merely accept it. "Welcome to my court. You do realize that you are my prisoner."

"Abrecan will rescue me," the boy spat, trying to look as fierce as the mob of seasoned Saxon warriors that now lay on the ground.

Remove the ring. Merlin's voice rang through her head. *Quickly. Before Abrecan can lock onto it and make the boy vanish.*

Anne didn't question. She saw the ring glistening on the boy's left hand. She reached for the hand before the boy could respond and yanked off the ring, tossing it quickly into the nearest burning hearth where it sizzled and let out a series of pops and sparks like firecrackers exploding before their time.

"Now you really are my prisoner." Anne stepped back, a smug expression of satisfaction on her face. "It is gone. I hope it took some of the hot flames with it."

"You will pay for this," the boy whined.

"Is that the best you can think of to say?" the girl taunted.

Peada pushed his shoulders back and tried to appear strong and powerful. It failed. He was much smaller than the other Saxons. Even his hair was a different shade. Almost a reddish color, more like the Picts of the north than the Saxons of the south.

"Tell me, Peada. If your father already has a wife, which he must if he has a son. Then, why does he want me for a wife?"

"My mother is dead. Taking you as his wife would secure the kingdom and increase his domain. As if you did not already know." His voice was decidedly snappy.

"Hmm! I see." Anne jumped off the table. She caught Galahad's eye. "Do we have somewhere secure to keep this prisoner? And the other Saxons, what do you suggest we do with them?"

Her knight didn't have to answer. Her men did it for him. "Kill them! Kill them! Kill them!"

"I shall take care of the young prince, my Queen." He grabbed the boy's arm and started dragging him away. In a voice barely loud enough for Anne's ears alone, he added, "I would suggest you allow the men to do as they will with the other Saxons. It is the way things are done."

Clearly unsettled with the suggestion, Anne agreed with reluctance. "Very well. Give the command." Wanting to distance herself from the carnage, she walked around the table, stepping over fallen men in the process. Her eyes fell on the slouched figure at the head of the long table. Her grandfather. She had barely met him and now he was gone. Taken from her. Those Saxons would pay. She gritted her teeth and approached.

Grace appeared at her side, taking a gentle hold of the queen's arm. "My Queen," she half whispered. "You should leave the clean up for the men."

"But my grandfather," Anne choked back a sob. It wouldn't do for the new princess, now a queen, to be caught sobbing. Death happened. And so many lives were lost in this battle. The sorrow would quickly spread throughout the castle and beyond. "And Grandmother." She glanced around, suddenly aware of absence. "Where is she? Is she?" She didn't finish.

Merlin's voice entered her head. *She escaped at the beginning of the battle, my Queen. She is safely settled in your time in the future.*

Her grandparents gone; her mother gone. Anne felt very much alone. She sniffled, resisting the urge to wipe her nose with a sleeve. *We must see to Grandfather's burial, Merlin. I do not know how these things are done in the sixth century.*

I will see to it, my Queen. His voice offered little reassurance. He would see that the dead, all the dead, received their proper fanfare to cross over to the life beyond death, if there were such a thing.

Lifting her head high, she breathed a silent prayer for her grandfather's soul and gave in to Grace's nudging to leave the grand hall. "Grace."

The girl glanced sideways. "My Queen." She bowed her head slightly.

"Come. We have much to discuss."

Grace followed Anne from the grand hall. When they were half-way up the long climb to Anne's chambers, the princess, now queen, satisfied that no one else could hear, asked, "So how and when did you learn to fight like that?"

Grace replied simply. "I am my father's daughter. As are you." The answer was simple enough.

Chapter Sixteen

The girls completed the long climb with a huff. After the battle and the stairs, they were winded.

"We should check to be sure no one is lurking somewhere in the room," Grace suggested.

"You know this space better than I do," Anne pointed out.

Grace grabbed a torch off one of the sconces on the wall outside the chamber and studied every shadowed corner on the small landing, as well as down the circular stairs they had just climbed. Nothing.

She slowly opened the chamber door. It was the only room on this floor, being at the top of the tower. As the door opened, she waved the torch slowly before her, checking the shadows as she entered. There was still some light from the smoldering fire in the hearth, but otherwise the room was ominously dark. Grace moved beyond the door and, pulling it toward her, checked the shadows behind the door. Nothing.

Anne was right on Grace's heels, both moving cautiously, studying the dark corners and hidden recesses with each step they took. Grace continued to swing the torch around in a circular motion, lighting the wall sconces in the room as she continued her search. Nothing.

"I will check behind the fireplace," Anne suggested.

"Wait." Grace held up her hand as she made a hasty step toward the far end of the bed. She reached down and grabbed a lump that she had noticed in the shadows. Standing up straight, she held her prize by the scruff of his neck. A boy. Not very young, perhaps in his early teens. "It is Sir Galahad's baby brother." She put a strong emphasis on the 'baby' part.

"I am not a baby. I am David. It is true that I am Galahad's younger brother. But I am no baby," he repeated his point, piercing Grace with a glare as she continued to hold him inches above the ground. "Put me down, or I will…"

"Or you will what?" Grace held her prize as she positioned her face within a nose breath of the boy's.

"I will tell my brother, that is what I will do. I am going to be a brave and valiant knight like him some day. That is why he sent me up here. To guard the queen's chambers while everyone was otherwise distracted with the battle. Good thing, too. I managed to scare off a couple of Saxons before they could make it to the top step."

"And how would a little mite like you do that?" Grace chuckled. Anne had to bite back a smile. It was obvious that the two had previous encounters such as this. She decided to stand quietly and observe the proceedings.

"I scared them, I did," David insisted. "I might be short, but I am strong and I know my way around this castle as well as you do. Now put me down. Please Grace. Put me down."

In response, Grace released her grip and the boy crumbled to the ground in a heap. Once he had recovered himself, he continued his account. "I heard them marching up the stairs. They are not quiet, those big oafs."

The girls nodded in agreement. "Go on," Grace insisted, arms crossed as if she really didn't believe the account.

"Well. They made it to the second level and that is when I started tossing things down upon them and making all kinds of weird noises, like this." To demonstrate, he hooted an owl-like call that, as it echoed through the chambers, definitely would make one pause. "You see?" The boy noticed the queen's nod of approval.

"Go on," Grace repeated.

"It scared them, it did. They stopped in their tracks and I heard them talking in their guttural language. As they started to turn around, I sent Mildred scurrying down the stairs."

"Mildred?" Anne found her voice and asked for clarification.

"The cat," Grace explained. "Continue."

"The cat sure spooked them. When it heard me sloshing water into pails as I proceeded to empty the washtub, another chore assigned to me, the cat shrieked away. That's when I had my idea. While the cat was charging down the stairs, shrieking, I lifted the top buckets I had filled and made my way to the top landing. While the Saxons were spooked by the cat, I emptied one bucket, then the other, on their heads, stepping back into the shadows so I would not be seen. The sodden wet Saxon at the top of the stairs lost his footing and tumbled down the stairs, in the process knocking the other Saxon, who was also sodden. It was funny to watch." The boy paused to chuckle. "Did not kill them, sadly. But they were well spooked. And wet. Very wet. After regaining their footing, they ran the rest of the way down the stairs, slipping on the steps that were soaked. To rejoin the battle, I guess."

"I thought the stairs appeared rather wet." Grace had to bite back a smile. It wouldn't do for the young boy to think he had garnered some of her respect and, perhaps even, some admiration. "Now I understand why. Good work. Now proceed with emptying the rest of the tub. But not on the stairs. And the slop pail needs dumping as well. Then you may bring the queen some fresh water."

Grumbling and muttering under his breath, "Why do I always get the dirty jobs?" he went about the assigned tasks. Opening the solitary window, he proceeded to fill bucket after bucket with water from the tub, carrying it over to the window where he dumped it.

Anne observed this procedure with concern. "What if there is someone below?" She had to ask. She had read stories of innocent people walking the streets of London as late as the eighteenth century who were doused by the slop contents from the overhanging windows above. One of the reasons buildings were constructed with the upper floors hanging over the streets below.

Grace shook her head. "Not to worry, my Queen. All that is below the window is the mote."

"Is that where everyone dumps their slops and dirty water?"

Grace nodded. "Did you not notice the stench as you paraded over the drawbridge?"

Anne nodded, wrinkling her nose at the memory. "And where do we obtain the water that we drink and wash with?" she asked. She had noticed the tub water hadn't been as clean as she was accustomed. Dirty as she was at the time, she hadn't considered complaining. But she was concerned. She knew the diseases that could easily be spread from contaminated water. Not just skin diseases, but intestinal ones as well. And some of them could be quite deadly.

"We have a well in the courtyard," Grace answered, not appearing at all concerned by Anne's barrage of questions.

"Is it clean?"

"Clean enough."

Anne wasn't convinced. This was definitely a major concern and she was determined to make it top priority on her 'to-do' list. David completed emptying the tub and pushed it into the corner out of the way. He picked up the slop pail and dumped it out the window as well, before returning the pail to its position under the table next to the bed. Closing the window, he picked up the buckets and made his way to the door. "I shall return, ladies," he called out with mock gallantry before exiting the chamber, pulling the door shut behind him.

Anne wasn't finished grilling her half-sister. "And how did you get all this warm water up here?" she asked.

"David and the other lads." Grace was busy at the hearth, poking the flames back into action. "We heated the water over the kitchen hearths, then brought it up, two pails at a time."

"That must have taken a long time," Anne noted. "There must be an easier way."

Grace chuckled. "Other than magic, my Queen, I doubt there is."

"Hmm!" Anne sat on the bed and watched Grace for a few minutes. So many things were different. She had been royally, no pun intended, spoiled in the twenty-first century. All those things that she took for granted, like running water. Clean water. Warm water. With a shake of her head, she allowed her eyes to roam the room, taking in every nook and cranny. It was cozy. But how safe was it, really. Being so high above the ground, if a fire broke out on the main level, she'd be trapped. Except for her secret escape. As long as it wasn't impacted by a fire as well. She shuddered at the thought.

There wasn't time to dwell on the 'what if' disaster scenarios. She was in this time, in this era, in these chambers and now she was Queen of Wessex, and Queen of Camelot. She had to get a grip on her situation. First things first. She unbuckled the sword belt and carefully laid it, with Excalibur and her knife still sheathed, on the bed. Reaching underneath the mattress, she pulled out her bag, relieved to find it where she had left it. She riffled through the contents until her hands reached the bottom and made contact with Grandmother's treasured chest. She lifted it out of the bag and set it on the bed next to her while she pushed the bag and its remaining contents back underneath the bed. Time to read her grandmother's journal. Time to understand all that she could. Hopefully the journal would reveal what she needed, and wanted, to know.

Grace finished tending the hearth and took a seat next to Anne. "What is this?" she asked, curiously.

"Grandmother's chest. And, inside it, her journal, with my answers."

"You could also talk to my mother," Grace suggested. "She was a friend of your mother's while she was here last time. When King Arthur returned after trying to make things up with that horrid Guinevere, he was upset to find your mother gone. That's when he took advantage of my mother. And, hence, the result..." she patted her chest, "me."

"He was quite the womanizer, our father, was he not?" Anne gritted her teeth at the thought.

"Womanizer? What is that?"

"A man who takes advantage of a woman. Many different women, for that matter," Anne explained as simply as she could.

Grace was silent for a few minutes, pondering the explanation. "I do not think that was the case. He was king, after all. Women wanted to be with him. They wanted to have his children."

"Really?" Anne was perplexed. "But why?"

The other girl merely shrugged her shoulders. "In the hopes that one day their child would rule as king or queen."

It was Anne's turn to sit quietly and ponder. She shifted in her sitting position to face Grace directly, to study her fully. "Grace. Tell me honestly. Did you or your mother ever hope that you would someday be queen?"

The question was met with silence. It was a silence that spoke volumes. It set a series of uneasy thoughts swirling around inside her head. Her grandmother had insisted that she could trust Grace. Merlin had said she could trust Grace. Grace had fought valiantly at her side. But, in reality, could she trust Grace? Could she trust anyone?

You are learning, Queen Anne. Trust no one save yourself.
Thanks, Merlin.

Breaking the pregnant silence, Anne asked softly, "Do you still feel that way, Grace? Do you resent my return and my right to be queen? Speak honestly. Please."

"No, my Queen." Grace spoke with a voice as soft as the queen's. "Not now that I see the dangers you will face on a daily basis. Not now that I see you will never find the honor of friendship and love and know that it is true."

The queen shuddered at the response. "I think I will be alone, now." She was dismissing her half-sister.

"As you wish, my Queen." Grace stood up and made her way to the far end of the room. "I will make myself comfortable in the corner here." She indicated a pile of coverings that suggested another makeshift bed.

"No, Grace." Anne stood up as well, taking on an air of regal dominance. "I want to be completely alone. Have David leave the water outside the door and post guards at the foot of the stairs. I will be fine." She forced a smile. "Please leave."

"But, my Queen," Grace tried to argue.

"Now."

The girl nodded in response, visibly chastised. She let herself out of the room, closing the door softly behind her. Anne followed and made sure the door was firmly shut. There was no lock, no visible means to secure the door from the inside. Something else she would have to rectify, and soon. Glancing around the room, the only item that appeared heavy enough to ensure that the door remained closed while she slept was the tub. It would have to do. David had moved it across the room. So could she.

It wasn't as easy as the boy had made it appear, but she finally managed to drag the tub across the floor and position it lengthwise against the door in such a way that no one would be able to push it open from the outside and force their way into her chambers. She wanted to feel secure while she slept.

Standing back, she brushed her hands on the side of her robe and studied the barricade. It would have to do. She made a quick survey of the room. Other than the secret passage behind the fireplace and the one tiny window, there were no other entry points. Her eyes fell on Excalibur where she had placed it on the bed. It was important to keep the sword handy, the knife, too. She marched across to the bed, an exercise of a mere four paces, and picked up her sword belt, unsheathing Excalibur and laying it carefully across the front of the hearth, within reach in an emergency. She removed the knife and tucked it inside the top of her boot, smiling as she recalled the looks of horror when the firm leather and thick soles made contact with some Saxon's delicate parts of the anatomy. Granny, now Grandmother, had made sure that she was trained in defensive moves and combat, not merely with sword and knife, but also with hands and feet. She was a real fighting machine and she had proved herself this day. If only she could have saved her grandfather. There was so much she wanted to learn from him. And now it was too late.

Anne wandered over to the window. It remained slightly ajar from David's earlier dumping routine. She leaned over the ledge and glanced down. It was too dark to see anything, the sun having set long ago and the cloud cover blocking any moonlight from shining like a floodlight on the lands below. She knew she was up high, but not high enough to escape the stench of the mote below. If it was used as a sewer by everyone both within and outside of the castle walls, it was a dangerous source of more than noxious odors. Her studies had provided her with considerable knowledge of water-transmitted diseases. She knew for a fact that, if she didn't change the way in which her people flushed away their body wastes, then the Saxons wouldn't have to fight to obliterate them off the face of this earth. Disease would quickly wipe them all out.

So much to address. Tomorrow. Clean water and proper sanitation were top of her list. Followed by feeding the large number of people camped outside the castle. Pulling the window firmly shut, she latched it. Not because she was afraid of an intruder crawling through the window, small that it was, not to mention a very long, steep climb from ground level. No, she wanted to lock out the horrors of the mote below and the starving population beyond.

Picking up her grandmother's journal, she pulled a wrap around her shoulders and maAnne a lasting connection with the one she loved the most. The glowing hearth and the flaming wall sconces cast weary shadows, but there was enough light to read. Barely.

Reverently, Anne lifted the front cover and took in the first words that caught her eye. Her grandmother's elegant script lavishly covered the inside cover lining. *The words you will find within these pages are fondly transcribed for my precious granddaughter, Anne, granddaughter and heir to the kingdom of Wessex, daughter and heir to the kingdom of Camelot. If you are reading this, dear granddaughter, then my time on this earth, both in the past and in the future, has come to its end.*

Had she read those words before leaving the twenty-first century, Anne would have been forced to agree with her mother that Grandmother lived in a world of fantasies.

Chapter Seventeen

The gentle crackling from the hearth was the only sound. The castle was quiet, both inside and out. Eerily quiet. It didn't matter. Anne was too engrossed in her reading to notice the almost total lack of sound.

My dear granddaughter, the journal began. *If you are reading this, then we have parted ways for the final time. We will not meet again. Not in this world. Not in any era of this world. You are now on your own and must carve your own path in life. Take care. Remember what I always told you, keep your friends close and your enemies closer and trust no one but yourself. And Merlin. You can always trust Merlin. As long as you are on the right path, the path that leads for a fair and just life for all the people in your kingdom, then Merlin will be on your side. Deviate from that path and Merlin can and will be your worst enemy.*

Anne shuddered. She didn't like the thought of Merlin as her enemy. It was bad enough to have that Saxon wizard, Abrecan, as her mortal enemy. And he wasn't half as powerful as Merlin. She paused briefly to glance at the flames. They were dying, slowly. She picked up the poker that lay next to the hearth, fortunately within reach so she didn't have to leave her cozy position, wrapped in her covers. She gave the fire a little poke here and there and smiled as she watched the embers sparkle and light a reluctant log that had slid to the back of the hearth. Hoping the renewed flame would last a little longer, Anne replaced the poker and settled back into her seat to resume her reading.

Re-reading the last paragraph, Anne paused on the line that read: *keep your friends close and your enemies closer.* She bit back a smile, recalling the day when she and Granny had decided to throw caution to the wind and borrow some movies from the local library. Mom had been disgusted when she returned home from a day of cleaning to find that we had wasted the day slogging through the Godfather movies.

In memory, Anne imitated Michael Corleone's voice and vocalized her grandmother's quote, "Keep your friends close and your enemies closer." Chastised by her mother, Anne had diligently returned the remaining movies to the library. They had only managed to watch the Godfather set. Anne loved that line. She had discussed its meaning with her grandmother to great extent.

"You know, Anne." She could hear her grandmother's voice repeating those words from only a few years ago. *"People have expressed this belief for generations. This saying has been researched in great detail and many believe that it evolved from something said in about 500 BC by the great Chinese general and military strategist, Sun-Tzu. He actually said, 'Know your enemy and know yourself and you will always be victorious.' The meaning is the same. You really have only one person you can trust in this world: yourself."*

Michael Corleone couldn't have explained it better himself. Grandmother had a way of making Anne understand. Sun-Tzu may have said something along this line in 500 BC, but Grandmother, in sixth century England, would not know of Sun-Tzu. History and the internet, the expansive information highway of the twenty-first century, were a long way off. But Grandmother must have been one of the many, over the course of time, to share this wisdom.

Anne tucked the information to the back of her mind, knowing that Grandmother's sage advice would help her out in the days and years to come. She picked up where she left off.

You have probably met some of the unholy powers of this world, including some troublesome Saxons and their meddlesome wizard, Abrecan, Morgawse's son. You will remember the tales of King Arthur's court that we shared when you were younger. Morgawse, or Morgan le Fay, was Arthur's half-sister, who, with minimal magical powers, vied for the dominance of Merlin and his powers. She bewitched Arthur, lay with him and bore a son, Abrecan. When Arthur learned of Morgawse's deceit, he banned her from the kingdom. Not a good move on his part, as he neglected 'to keep his enemies closer'. Abrecan grew up learning Morgawse's magic. He became more powerful than his mother, eventually defeating and killing her. Yes, wizards and witches can be killed, if they are of lesser power than the wizard or witch fighting against them. After his mother's death, or murder if you will, Abrecan joined the Saxons of Mercia. He served Penda's grandfather, King Creoda of Mercia, for many years. He helped Creoda establish Tamworth as the Mercian royal fortress. (You need to study its fortifications before planning your attack, which you must do as soon as possible.)

Attack? Anne gasped. She had been successful during the evening raid, but to plan an attack on the enemy's fortress? She didn't like the idea of fighting. Two battles in one day were quite enough. On the other hand, if she didn't strike back, and soon, King Penda, under Abrecan's bewitched ministrations, would recover and retaliate, probably demanding the return of his son. Something else to think about more intently in the morning. She resumed reading.

When King Creoda was killed in battle, his son, Pybba became king. He was just as fierce, ruthless and manipulative as his father. After his death, Penda was named king. Just a little ancestry info on the Saxon royals of Mercia.

Now, back to Abrecan and how this all fits into your ancestry and your future. I knew Abrecan when we both were children. And it is here that my story begins, which will lead to your story. I was kept prisoner by the Saxons, while my poor mother was used by King Creoda, in all manner of unspeakable ways. It was my dear husband's father, King Cynric of Wessex, who defeated and killed King Creoda, sending Pybba and his son, Penda, on the run for their lives. They fought back and reclaimed Tamworth Castle, but not before King Cynric rescued the imprisoned women and children, including myself, and freed all the slaves from Tamworth Castle. I must have been about seven at the time. My remaining growing-up years were spent in the Wessex court at Gloucester Castle, alongside of Ceawlin, whom I married as soon as I was twelve, which was the standard marrying age in the sixth century.

The sound of pounding on the door jolted Anne awake. She almost slid out of the chair onto the floor. The journal already lay there at her feet and the hearth was stone cold. She must have fallen asleep. She had finished reading the journal. She knew she had. The last words her grandmother wrote were forever engraved in her mind.

Once you have read this once, destroy it immediately. And destroy any photographs or pictures you have saved. What little I have shared with you in this journal is all you need to carry on with your life as a queen in the sixth century. What you didn't learn, like how I managed to access the portal to the future and transport myself and my daughter, then you, back and forth between two eras, is irrelevant at this point. Merlin will explain if and when the need arises. Suffice to say, that you are of this time and place, Queen of Wessex and Queen of Camelot, and so much more. Burn this, before anyone else has the opportunity to read it. Burn it until it is no more than ashes in the hearth.

Anne didn't want to burn the journal. It was the last remaining link to her grandmother, and, to some extent, her mother as well. It hadn't provided the answers she had hoped it would. It had been an interesting read and it did give her some background on the world she had been thrown into. She could hide the journal and the photos. But to what purpose. She had never disobeyed her grandmother and she wasn't about to disobey her now. If

Grandmother was insistent that the journal and photos were destroyed, then she must do so, quickly.

The pounding on the door intensified. "My Queen." It was Grace. "The door will not open. Are you all right?"

She sounded frantic. "Yes, Grace," Anne called out in response. "I am quite fine. I will unblock the door in a minute."

She tossed off her wraps and knelt by the hearth. There remained a few smoldering coals, enough to set the fire ablaze. Grandmother had taught her the skills she needed, even the art of starting a good, roaring fire. Tearing the first couple of pages from the journal, Anne crumpled them and tossed them into the hearth. She grabbed one of the logs set beside the hearth and lay it on top of the glowing coals and crumpled pages that were already starting to blaze. Tearing up the remaining pages of the journal, Anne proceeded to toss them in, one bunch at a time. She sniffled, but she didn't stop. There was no time for tears. Grace should never read this journal. Even if she did know the secret behind the fireplace, the portal she presumed was to another era, the one at the bottom of the stairs shown to both Grace and herself, was only one of many secrets. Anne wasn't willing to share more. Not yet. Perhaps never. Grace, Anne's half-sister, had as much claim to the royal title of Camelot as she did. She was powerful in her own right, but was she sincere when she pledged her loyalty to Queen Anne?

The knocking resumed. "My Queen. Please open. There are lords and knights waiting to meet with you. It is time to arise and address the problems of the day."

Anne bristled. "Coming." She tossed the remaining journal into the hearth, which was burning with a bright vengeance as it licked up the pages and cover. With a final glance at the photographs, taken on a rare outing to Ontario Place with both her grandmother and her mother, Anne bit her lower lip and tossed them into the flames. She watched. Briefly. Satisfied that there was nothing left but ashes, she pushed herself to her feet and moved toward the barricaded door.

She stopped abruptly. Grandmother had written more. She had left instructions for Anne to destroy all that she had carried with her from the future. That included her private toiletry items and food packs. She scurried to the bed where she had left her bag the night before, lying open, its contents partially strewn across the covers. As she pulled out the packs of food, her stomach grumbled. She couldn't remember the last time she ate. Probably not since she broke the fast with Merlin in his cave. How long ago was that?

The knocking on the door was annoying. There was banging and shoving. Grace was trying to enter the queen's private sanctuary. Anne shoved the last remaining bag of oatmeal into her pocket. For later. She would discard the packaging once the contents were consumed. She picked up the last of her granola bars. Without pause, hunger taking root, she ripped off the packaging and shoved it into her mouth – whole. Not a good thing to do with a granola bar, as it was something that required considerable chewing. Time was of the essence, so Anne frantically chewed while she retrieved the remaining items from the twenty-first century and tossed them into the flames. She hesitated briefly with the toothbrush and toothpaste. When would she ever have this luxury again? Could she hide it? Use it until there was no toothpaste remaining in the tube? She could try, but if someone did discover it, who knew what mischief they would cause. Best to follow Grandmother's instructions to the letter.

The flames sizzled and sparked violently with the toothpaste tube. The fire was hot enough, though, and managed to melt the packaging and the contents. The food packaging was next, Anne scrambling to consume as much as she could before it was gone forever. She swallowed large mouthfuls at a time, almost gagging in the process. She hadn't eaten. She was hungry. Who knew what garbage they'd try to make her eat? This was perhaps the last safe food she'd consume in a long time. If ever.

One last item. One solitary chocolate bar. It wasn't likely she'd ever taste chocolate again. If her history lessons were right, chocolate wasn't introduced to this world for at least another thousand years. Breaking open the end, she stuffed the broken bits into her mouth and let them melt on her tongue. She closed her eyes and savored the moment, before tossing the last packaging into the flames.

The knocking was intensifying. "My Queen. You must open up. Please." Grace was showing signs of distress. For what, Anne couldn't ascertain. She still didn't know how much she could trust her half-sister.

Grabbing her water bag, the one Merlin had provided, she took a long swig of water. It wasn't as cold and refreshing as it had been when she filled it, but at least it was clean and safe. She trickled some on her hands and washed her face as best she could before re-corking the water bag and placing it next to the other bag, that was now pretty much empty. Her past, from the future, obliterated.

Chapter Eighteen

More pounding on the door. "My Queen." No time to waste. Anne checked the hearth to make sure everything was burnt beyond recognition. Satisfied, she made haste to unbarricade the door. She tugged and shoved until the washtub was no longer obstructing the entry and pulled open the door.

Grace paraded into the room, carrying a bucket of water, presumably for cleaning purposes. It didn't look, or smell for that matter, appealing, but it was wet. It would have to suffice. For now.

"Why did you have the washtub across the door?" Grace asked over her shoulder as she emptied the contents of the bucket into a bowl on the table next to the bed. "And you are still dressed in your clothes from last night. Did you not sleep?" She glanced around the room, taking in the unruffled bedding and the glowing flame in the hearth. "And you started your own fire."

"I sat by the fire and slept," Anne gave a sparse answer. She didn't have to explain herself to Grace. Or to anyone else for that matter. Walking over to the wash basin, she studied the water that Grace had brought for her to wash. She grimaced at the flakes of who-knew-what floating around the surface. She wasn't going to wash in this sludge. It was a good thing she had done a cursory wash with the contents of her water bag.

"What is this muck?" she growled, frozen in place, staring at the disgusting contents of the wash bowl. "Do you call this water?"

"It is from the well, my Queen," Grace confessed, sounding chastised, shocked at the complaints. "Everyone uses it. To wash. To cook. Even to drink."

"And is everyone sick?" Anne asked pointedly, stepping back and pivoting so she could study her half-sister. "Are there skin ailments amongst the castle dwellers? Stomach sickness?"

Grace nodded. Pulling up her sleeve, she revealed black marks that blotted her skin. "We all have them, my Queen. And some are quite sick. They toss whatever they consume. It is the black death."

"It is the poisoned, filthy water!" Anne retrieved the wash basin and took it to the hearth, tossing the contents on the flames. The fire sizzled and grumbled. "Even the fire does not like it. This is what is causing your skin to turn black and the people to throw up. This water should not be used. Ever."

"But where will we get the water we need?" Grace asked.

"That is the first thing we must address." She shoved the water basin into her half-sister's chest, not viciously, not enough to cause harm. "Never again, Grace. I never want to see this disgusting stuff again. If I had not been so tired and filthy myself, I would not have trusted the bath you prepared yesterday." She could feel her skin crawling with disgust as she recalled stepping into the washtub the day before. "If you cannot find me fresh clean water, then do not even bother bringing me any."

"Yes, my Queen." Grace humbly set the wash basin aside and proceeded to move about the room, fetching clean garments for the queen. "Here. Let me help you change into something clean." Grace held out another set of robes. "You will feel better after you have changed and had something to break the fast."

"Perhaps." Anne was being deliberately non-committal in her responses. "Tell me who awaits my presence." She took on the air of importance, setting up a wall, a shell really, that prevented her from enjoying some of the close camaraderie the two girls had started to share the day before. It wouldn't serve her well to become too close to Grace. Or anyone else for that matter.

"Well. Sir Galahad, for one," Grace blushed. Anne noticed. Her sister had a crush on the older knight of their father's famous round table. Oh dear! Another possible conflict. Did Anne feel the same way about this knight? It wouldn't do for the two sisters to clash over the same man.

"And. Who else?"

Grace continued to list off some names that meant nothing to Anne. Hopefully, she would be able to sort out everybody. And in short order. If she was to rule effectively, she had to know her people.

"They all wait for your presence so they can give the late King of Wessex a proper burial," Grace continued to chatter.

"Do we not wait the prescribed three days for mourning?" Anne asked, marginally shocked at the urgency of the ritual.

Grace startled, unsettled by her half-sister's lack of knowledge regarding burial customs. "The body must be burned as soon as possible, my Queen," she spoke quietly. "The evil humors that invade a body after death must not be allowed to spread."

"In other words, the body will rot quickly if we do not proceed with haste." Anne was considerably blunter in her assessment.

She didn't wait for a response. Dressed in fresh robes, Excalibur and her trusty knife fastened to her side, Anne was ready to meet the court. With a smile, she glanced at her half-sister. "Thank you, Grace." They exchanged smiles as Grace dipped a curtsy in reply. "Stay beside me and help me sort out the identity of all who will greet me. And what might be required of me at this burial ritual."

"I will, my Queen. As will Sir Galahad." She motioned toward the door. "Shall we?" Anne followed her half-sister out of the chamber and down the long, swirling length of stairs to the main floor and the grand hall.

Chapter Nineteen

Sir Galahad met the ladies at the foot of the stairs. He bowed to Anne, "My Queen," he acknowledged her position.

David stepped out of the shadows carrying a plush cushion on which sat the crown. He bowed his head before pivoting toward his older brother.

The knight lifted the crown from the cushion and gingerly placed it on Anne's head. "We do not have an official ceremony for the crowning of a king or queen. The one who inherits the position merely takes the crown and wears it." Anne felt shivers trickled down her spine. She really was queen. She watched as the knight took a step back and bowed again. "You are now Queen Anne of Wessex and Camelot."

Anne's legs wobbled beneath her as she sensed the intense gravity of her new rank and privilege. She was expected to reign supreme, to know what to do in a crisis, to lead a people to prosperity and so much more. Was she up to the task? Could she do it?

You can and you will do this, Queen Anne. Merlin spoke inside her head as he stepped through the passageway to greet the newly crowned leader. He bowed. Lifting his head, Anne noticed a twinkle in the wizard's eyes. "My Queen," he acknowledged.

"I cannot do this alone." The queen glanced around at the few assembled. "Merlin. Sir Galahad. Grace. David." She nodded at each in turn as she spoke their names. "I will need you by my side at all times. To guide me. To counsel me. Merlin and Sir Galahad, you have great wisdom and experience behind you. I will need you two the most. Please. Never leave me."

"My Queen," Sir Galahad was the first to respond. "I am forever your servant." He tipped his head and then motioned toward the passageway that led to the great hall. "Shall we, Queen Anne? Your lords and knights await you."

"Lead the way, my Queen," Merlin insisted

Anne lifted her head high and stepped proudly through the passageway, Merlin and Sir Galahad behind her, Grace and David bringing up the rear. The room, which had smoldered with anxious voices of concern, suddenly fell quiet. And then there was a roar as benches moved back and the men and women stood to greet their new queen, bowing and curtseying with grace.

"All hail Queen Anne. Queen of Wessex and Camelot."

One faint voice echoed from the rear, "Queen Anne of all of Anglia. Queen of a new realm, England."

Queen Anne of England! She liked the sound of that. Perhaps her new Camelot would find its place on the Thames, a much better location than her father's choice for his Camelot.

As the cacophony died, Anne maintained her position, standing behind the chair her grandfather had occupied the night before. When she spoke, it was with a clear firm voice. Her grandmother had coached her on public speaking. Unnecessary, as the talent came naturally.

"My lords and ladies, knights of my late father, King Arthur's round table. You have served both my father and my grandfather well. We have much to discuss. But before we can proceed, there is a very solemn remembrance which we must embrace, to honor the late King Ceawlin of Wessex, my grandfather." She glanced at Merlin, who nodded in response, as if he were in tune with her thoughts. He usually was, Anne was certain of it. "Lead the way, Merlin." As he marched forward, down the long length of the grand hall, the men and women of the court parted, bowing their heads in respect as Anne marched serenely behind him.

It was a solemn procession that marched out of the castle, through the courtyard and into the wide expanse beyond: Merlin with his crisply billowing robes fluttering in his wake, his trusty staff marking each footstep; Anne in colorful robes and the crown on her head that sparkled on each embedded stone, some clear, others merely colorful. The clear stones captured the sun's rays. Those living beyond the castle walls understood the serenity of the parade and fell in line behind the royal procession and the people of the court. They marched beyond the final set of dwellings until they were close to the tree line. The sun had risen to its mid-day height and there wasn't a cloud to be seen. The air was still brisk, as one would expect on a spring day, but the sun's rays were quickly warming the atmosphere.

A large pyre was waiting in the open space, a body placed on top of the mound of kindling, personal possessions scattered around the base, items of significance to the recently deceased. The body was wrapped in fine robes; the hands folded above the chest. A crown sat on the head, not the royal crown that Anne now wore, but a crown of sorts to identify the royal person lying on the pyre. Boys stood in a circle around the pyre, grasping torches already ablaze awaiting the task of lighting the kindling, of sending the king on his final journey. Other torches were set in the ground securely, lit and ready for people to claim, to make their own personal tribute to the deceased.

"You must light it first, my Queen." Merlin reached for the closest flaming torch and took it from the boy before handing it to Anne. "Say some private words, say something for the gathering, your loyal subjects. Then set the mound aflame. The others will add their words and assist in the lighting."

Accepting the torch with a slight nod, Anne approached the pyre at a slow, regal pace. She paused when her toes touched the closest scattering of kindle. Looking up at her grandfather, lying in his final resting place, she searched her mind for the right words to say, to share with the crowd behind her which must now stand in the hundreds. "Grandfather," she whispered. These words were private; intent on making one last connection with a man she barely knew. She desperately wanted to make a good first impression to her people and speaking privately to the still body of her grandfather was an attempt to calm her nerves and hopefully find the right words to share aloud. "I hardly knew you, but I heard about you from Grandmother. I know of your heroic exploits. I know how much love you and Grandmother shared. May you both rest in peace together. For eternity. And I can only hope that what I do from this day forward will make you proud to call me Granddaughter." She ducked her head, a final bow. An eerie void of silence enveloped her, as if all those gathered held their breath, waiting, watching.

Finally, raising the torch high above her head, she spoke in a clear crisp voice, the words rippling from deep within as if she had practised them for days. "O Great Spirit, Mother and Father to us all, we ask for your blessings on this ceremony of thanksgiving for a kind and caring king, honoring and blessing the late King Ceawlin of Wessex, my grandfather." She spoke the words of the pagan burial ritual. Not knowing whether or not her grandfather had chosen to be baptised into the Christian faith, and knowing that most of the people gathered around the pyre were undoubtedly pagan, she chose these words to garner both their respect and, hopefully, support for the days and years to come.

Her voice carried across the large expanse of solemn observers. "We stand at a gateway, a portal to the life beyond the one we have on this earth. There will come a time when we all must make this journey, to walk bravely through the final portal, the gateway. King Ceawlin of Wessex has already left his earthly body and stepped through the gateway. King Ceawlin of Wessex is now immersed in the shining light of the unity that is both Mother and Father to all of us. We feel pain in the loss of our loved one, but it is also a pain in the realization that we cannot yet cross this threshold to join our loved one. Give us the strength and courage to continue our own journey until such time as we can join our beloved King Ceawlin of Wessex, when it is our time to pass through the gateway and into the light." Many of the words she spoke were embedded deep in her memories. They came to her freely, as if someone was speaking inside her head, telling her what to say. Grandmother? Perhaps. It didn't matter how the words came to her. All that mattered was how she presented them to the people. Her people now.

She slowly lowered the torch, allowing the flame to catch the kindling nearest. She walked slowly around the pyre, repeating the action, allowing the flames to catch and crackle, surrounding the body of the once loved king. Merlin had chosen another torch and followed in her wake, copying her actions. Sir Galahad followed as did others and it wasn't long until the entire pyre was roaring with great intensity. Completing her circle, Anne threw her torch into the blaze and proceeded to make her path through the gathering back to the castle.

Chapter Twenty

Returning to the grand hall, Anne made her way to the far end, with as much dignity as she could muster after saying her final farewell to the grandfather she had only just met. She had no more family. They were all gone: Grandmother, Mother and now Grandfather. She was alone. It was a sobering thought.

As the others returned to the hall, Anne took took the seat her grandfather had claimed the previous day. She motioned for everyone else to sit, or stand, whatever was practical given the crowded confines of the room. The tables had been removed or shoved to the sides of the hall, to allow more space. Good thing, too, as it appeared as if the entire country had come to seek her audience. How would she ever manage to remember all the who is who and each individual demand?

I am here. Merlin's voice had never sounded so much more reassuring.

Thank you. She returned the message through her mind talk.

As Grace set a cup of some liquid sustenance and a chunk of crusty bread next to her, Sir Galahad knelt before Anne, offering a public display of his loyalty to the new queen. "Queen Anne. Queen of Wessex and Camelot. Accept me as your humble servant and a loyal knight of your round table."

Anne nodded, pushing aside the offerings of food and drink. "You must eat, my Queen," Grace whispered in Anne's ear.

"Later," Anne whispered in response. Returning her attention to Sir Galahad, she stood and unsheathed Excalibur, touching the flat blade reverently on the right shoulder, then she gently raised the sword over the knight's head, laying it reverently on his left shoulder. The task complete, she lifted Excalibur to her lips and sanctioned her action by kissing the hilt. With a firm voice, she commanded, "Rise, Sir Galahad. My most honorable knight of the round table of Camelot. Rise and continue to be recognized as Sir Galahad of Queen Anne's court."

Nice display, Queen, even though this form of accolade has never been seen before. You have started a new display of acceptance and mutual respect. Well played.

Galahad rose, nodded to the queen before taking his place by her side. Another knight marched forward and knelt before the queen. Anne remained standing; Excalibur poised.

"Sir Roderick of Dumnonii," Sir Galahad announced in a clear voice.

Dumnonii is what you know as Cornwall, Merlin explained in her head.

"My Queen," Sir Roderick knelt and bowed his head in respect and repeated his peer's request. "Queen Anne. Queen of Wessex and Camelot. Accept me as your humble servant and a loyal knight of your round table." The knight was tall and muscular. His dark eyes took in the young queen with an intense mixture of respect and curious admiration. It unnerved Anne, who had little experience with young men and their roaming eyes. Just the other day, she had felt something fluttering in her chest when meeting Sir Galahad for the first time. Now, again, her heart jittered slightly. She brought it under control, not wanting or allowing another knight to unnerve her sense of stability. With the same reverence she had bestowed on Galahad, Anne repeated the accolade. She touched the flat blade of Excalibur reverently on the right shoulder, then she gently raised the sword over the knight's head, laying it with equal reverence on his left shoulder. The task complete, she lifted Excalibur to her lips and sanctioned her action by kissing the hilt. With a firm voice, she commanded, "Rise, Sir Roderick. My most honorable knight of the round table of Camelot. Rise and continue to be recognized as Sir Roderick of Queen Anne's court."

"Thank you, my Queen. I come with an army at my back to help you scourge the Saxon menace." Sir Roderick took his place next to Sir Galahad.

The day continued in the same manner. One knight after another pledged allegiance to Queen Anne, each one claiming to have an army at their back to help scourge the land of the Saxons.

At the end of the procession of knights and the repetitive accolades, Anne's legs wobbled with fatigue, but she wouldn't give in. There was more to address. "My honorable knights," she addressed the assembly. "I am honored to have your pledge of support. However, we must also address some serious issues that have plagued our people for too long. Hunger and disease. We cannot fight with a sick and hungry army. You have honored me with great numbers of fighting men, but how do we feed them and their families who follow them? How to we keep them all well? The Saxons have burned our crops, stolen our livestock and poisoned our water. If we plunder their lands the way they plundered ours, it will all be destroyed. Wasted. We must strategize and conquer with respect for the land and its people, to preserve the food that Mother Earth provides so that we can eat. So that we may remain healthy and strong. So that we can survive."

There were murmurings around the room. It was as if everyone assembled expected the queen to charge out of the castle, full tilt, with this marvellous army at her back. She had other ideas. She wanted to preserve what she conquered and salvage the food of the land along the way.

Sir Roderick stepped forward. "If I might suggest, my Queen." Anne nodded. Sir Roderick unsheathed his sword, holding up his hand to ward off the other swords that suddenly unsheathed in defense of the queen. "I mean no harm, my Queen." With the tip of his sword, Sir Roderick started tracing what appeared to be a map on the dirt surface of the floor. "We are here, my Queen," he pointed. "This is Wessex." He pointed again. "And this is the Saxon stronghold of Tamworth Castle. There is plenty of fertile land, livestock, wildlife and clean water. It is just ours for the taking."

"We cannot and will not be like the Saxons and destroy the people who work the land. We are not plunderers." Anne was adamant in her insistence. "These people who work the land are only loyal to the leaders who care for them. They work for their own survival, not for the dominance of a country. If we show them mercy, they will be forever loyal to us. They will respect us and provide for us for many years to come."

"I agree," Merlin took the initiative to speak. "Your new queen is already demonstrating a profound concern for her people. All of her people. This is admirable. Now, it is up to us to come up with ways to assist her. My Queen. What do you need done first?"

Anne nodded at Merlin, a signal of appreciation and respect. Allowing her eyes to slowly circumnavigate the room, she let the moment of silence following Merlin's little speech sink in. "First of all, I want the well in the courtyard sealed. No one is to use that water for any purpose." There was a collective gasp that filtered through the room. The queen continued as if she hadn't heard it. "It is like a poison. People are already getting sick: skin sores, stomach ailments."

"But, my Queen," Sir Galahad spoke up before anyone else could. He was shaken by the queen's command. "What will our people drink? What will they use for cleaning and cooking?"

Anne held up her hand to stop any further protests. "I will explain my plans, but first the immediate concern is to stop the use of this poisoned water. I want ditches dug to drain the muck from the mote. It breeds insects that spread disease. Not only that, it stinks. The Romans who occupied our lands had more advanced methods for providing safe water and disposing of bad water."

"But the mote provides a barrier to protect us against invaders." One of the younger knights in the gathering offered his voice to the argument.

"And look how much good it did us yesterday," Anne retorted, her voice sounding a little harsher than she had intended it to. She softened her tone. "The Saxons invaded our inner sanctum with no hindrance from the mote. If we plan to keep the mote, we must find a healthier means of managing the water. The castle should have channels dug, like the Romans did, to remove the waste from the castle, and far from the mote."

"Why?" Anne wasn't sure who asked that pointed one-word question. It came from somewhere in the far back of the grand hall.

"We cannot be successful as a people or as a fighting force, if we are not healthy. Disease is our worst enemy. Not the Saxons. Though they do come in a close second place in that department." A few chuckles filtered through the room. "As well, we need to have a well-fed fighting force and a well-fed population to back and support that fighting force. I understand that the Saxons destroyed much of our farmland and crops. We must replant and start over, not sit idly and wait for hunger to take us one by one. The first step to our success is to feed the general population. I cannot sit here and eat a fine meal when there are so many people beyond the castle walls who are starving."

"And how do you propose to accomplish that?" Another voice from the back. "We can barely feed ourselves."

There were a number of nods and grunts in agreement. Anne would not back down. "Build large bonfires, evenly spaced amongst the gathered peoples beyond the castle walls," the queen instructed. "I need large caldrons for each bonfire. Clean caldrons. And several volunteers to accompany me to the nearest spring to carry back clean water. While some of you will remain here to orchestrate the covering of the well and digging the trenches to remove the fowl water in the mote, me and my followers will bring back sufficient water for the day. Clean water. And we will start a stew. One that everyone may contribute to and everyone may partake of its contents. A few young men may like to take on the task of hunting for game. Do not go alone. And be well armed." She glanced around the room. "Any questions?"

There was considerable shuffling of feet and grumbling complaints, but no one spoke up in confrontation. "Then, let it be done." She nodded to her companions on either side of her and turned to leave the audience. Noticing David hanging around, she spoke to him directly, "Have my horse readied."

"May I come with you, my Queen," he asked in an anxious, young boy's voice.

Anne hesitated, then nodded. "Very well. And make sure we have a cart readied with buckets to fill with water."

She pivoted to face Sir Galahad. "I had best check in with my prisoner. Where is he? And how does our Saxon prince fare this new day?"

Chapter Twenty-One

Sir Galahad led the queen through the back halls and down several stone steps into the dark depth of the castle. He grabbed two torches to light the path, handing one to Anne. The dampness soaked through her cloak and to the very marrow of her bones, causing her to shiver.

"Must we keep him imprisoned down here, Sir Galahad?" she asked as she struggled to keep pace, with head held high in grace and dignity, even though the enclosed space caused her to shudder with disgust. "He is, after all, a prince. Does he not deserve better treatment than this?"

"Perhaps." The knight didn't pause in his progress through the dark, damp tunnels. "I had no alternative last night. The men were ripe for killing all the remaining Saxons. I thought he might be safer down here, where my most trusted men could guard him, keep him confined and keep the others out."

He stopped at the end of the corridor. Two men, obviously Sir Galahad's men, stood at attention. "Lads," he greeted them as if they were no older than his brother, David. "Your queen." He nodded toward Anne. The men bowed, showing their respect, but kept their attention on their lord and master. "How fares the prisoner?" Galahad asked.

"As well as can be expected, Sire." Only one man took the initiative to answer. "He howled most of the night and screamed obscenities about the injustice of his quarters. Other than that, all appears well."

"Has he been fed?" Anne asked. "Provided with fresh water to wash?"

"Yes, my Queen," the same man answered, while the other one fiddled with the keys in the lock. The door swung open.

Galahad entered first, pushing his torch forward to light the dim, tiny cell. Anne followed on his heels. "Prince Peada," Galahad commanded of the prone figured cuddled into a tight ball in the corner. "Rise and greet your queen."

Grunts, groans and muffled explicatives exploded in a tongue Anne didn't recognize, but the bundle unraveled and the boy prince, now looking no better than a common urchin, stood up, blinking at the sudden blaze of light from the knight's torch.

"Come to gloat, have you, Queen Anne?" he spat on the ground, nearly hitting the knight's feet.

"Watch your tongue and your actions, young man," Galahad warned. "You may be a prince in your lands, but you are merely a prisoner here."

"I am more than a prince in my lands." Peada snapped to attention and met the glare of light to penetrate his gaze on the knight. "These are my lands, too. All of it. For I am the son of King Arthur of the round table."

Anne jumped at the revelation. It wasn't something she expected her prisoner to reveal. Was it another ploy to undermine her position? "What!" she exclaimed. "Another half-sibling? I thought you were King Penda's son."

"I am the son of his wife, Queen Sunniva." He squinted as he turned his gaze to focus on Anne. "She was captured by our father, King Arthur, and used. I was the result. My father would have killed my mother and myself, had not the kind wizard, Abrecan, intervened. I owe my life to Abrecan."

"You owe him nothing." Merlin appeared in the cell doorway, there being no more room in the cell for another person. "If Abrecan saved your life, it was to serve his purpose, not yours. He is, after all, King Arthur's son as well." Noticing the boy's startled look at Merlin's remark, the wizard continued. "Oh, yes! Abrecan has much more claim to Camelot's throne than you. He is quite a bit older, wouldn't you agree?"

"That may well be the case, Merlin." The boy spat out Merlin's name. He was not allowing random comments to cut through his weakening shield of defense. "But the fact remains, King Arthur was my father and it stands to reason that I should be his heir, King Peada of Camelot."

"You do think very highly of yourself, Prince," Merlin retorted, using the subtleness of tone to dampen his disgust. "King Arthur may have been a rogue in many ways, but he never did imprison your mother. You are not his son, no matter what anyone has told you. Anne, here, is the chosen offspring. She is older than you and, on top of being the only heir to the Wessex crown, she is and has already been named Queen of Wessex and Camelot. I doubt you would find a sympathetic ear to your claim in these parts."

"Perhaps not," Peada replied, somberly. "But my father would think otherwise. And he has enough power to make things happen. To make me King of Camelot as well as King of Mercia."

"Puppet king, perhaps." Anne was satisfied to have Merlin do the talking. He knew more than she did about the workings of this era. "You might think you could be king, but you are weak, lad. Penda and Abrecan are very powerful. They would only use you to their advantage. Certainly not to yours."

"Little do you know, you little wizard of nothing." Peada was getting desperate to make his point. And, in his desperation, he was speaking out of line, insultingly. "As long as the metal of my ring remains in your hearth, Abrecan has a link to this castle. To me. He will arrange my rescue. He will make me king."

"I doubt it," Merlin replied. "I removed the gold piece this morning before the hearth was relit. It has been disposed of, its magic removed. How? You might wonder. Well, I might be a weak little wizard, but I do have my ways. The gold piece was sent back to your father and your wizard. They have no means to save you. Not now. We have the upper hand. And so it shall continue to be."

Peada noticeably sizzled where he stood. "I am the rightful King of Camelot," he growled.

Anne unsheathed Excalibur and held it before her, point to the ceiling with the hilt at face level. "If what you say is true, Prince Peada, then you and only you will be able to unsheathe our father's sword, Excalibur, from the rocky earth at our feet." Not waiting for arguments from either side, she quickly turned the sword around, point to the floor and stabbed it deep into the stone flooring. The ground rumbled and shook; sparks flew. The blade continued to sink until it was half buried. Satisfied, Anne glanced at her half-brother. "If you believe you are the rightful king, then unsheathe Excalibur and I will follow you. I will be the first to proclaim you king."

"This is a trick." Peada took a step back until he was right up against the outside wall with nowhere else to go. His eyes darted frantically from Anne to Merlin to Sir Galahad and back to Anne again.

"No trick," Anne assured the boy. "It is a fact that only the one who wields the famous sword Excalibur will lead the knights of the round table of Camelot." She pointed to the sword. "Pull it out and you will be king."

The boy took a step forward, eyes darting around frantically. Another step and he reached out his hands to take the sword. The hilt sparked and he jumped back. "It is a trick."

"No trick," Anne reassured him again.

Taking a deep breath to bolster some modicum of courage, Peada marched toward the sword again, placing his hands on the hilt as sparks sizzled all around him. He screamed in pain but held on and pulled. His face revealed his exertion, while his hands gripped with a ferocity unexpected for one so young. The sword didn't budge. All it did was sparkle and sizzle. "No!" he howled, the pain of failure was evident in his voice as the pain he must be feeling where his hands made contact with the electrified sword hilt. He didn't give up. He continued to pull and tug. To no avail. Until, unexpectedly, a powerful surge up the hilt of the sword jolted along the boy's hands and arms, forcing him to release his hold. Another surge sent him sprawling on the stone floor.

"No!" he shrieked again, forcing himself to his feet. He made a step toward the sword, but another jolt pushed him back. He watched in horror and disbelief as Anne stepped forward and easily pulled the sword from the stone. "No!" he bellowed.

Raising the sword again, point to the ceiling and hilt to her face, Anne said with reverence, "Thank you, Excalibur." And she kissed the hilt. She sheathed the sword at her side and patted the hilt fondly. "Satisfied?" she asked, making eye contact with the startled, angry boy.

"No! Never!" he spat, shaking his head. "That was a trick. He did it. Merlin conjured up something. That probably is not Excalibur anyway." His hands waved frantically in front of his face as he rattled on and on about all the obscure possibilities to explain his failure, but the fact remained. Anne had the sword, the crown and the belief of the people. And that's all that mattered in the end. Peada would never be more than the Saxon prince, and, at the moment, a prisoner of the Queen of camelot.

Merlin made his announcement=. He had not moved since he arrived. "Only the one who can wield Excalibur will rule Camelot. Excalibur has chosen the rightful heir. Anne is Queen of Camelot."

Sir Galahad took over the dialogue. "If you care for better accommodations, Prince, I suggest you show your manners. If you really are a prince, you should know how to behave in front of a lady, especially one who is queen."

Peada merely scowled in response.

"Now, Peada," Anne said as soothingly as her seething temper would allow. "I believe we need to come to some sort of arrangement. A compromise, if you will."

"I will not give in to your demands," the prince snapped before Anne could continue.

"You have not even heard what I have to say," Anne scolded him as she would a little boy. It was amazing how a jump through time and forty-eight hours could change a seventeen-year-old into an adult. *You have to do what you have to do in life.* She could hear her grandmother's words as if she were standing right next to her, talking into her ear. Taking a deep breath to brace herself and control her emotions, the girl-turned-queen continued, "I would like to provide better accommodations for you than this. You will still be under guard, for your safety as well as ours. I am afraid my people would not think twice about removing your head. If you can prove yourself to be reliable and trustworthy, we may be able to lessen your restrictions, in time."

"And what do I have to promise to gain this privilege?" the boy snarled. "Bow to the one who claims royal superiority?"

"For starters," Galahad stormed. "Yes."

Peada glanced nervously at the stormy eyes that faced him. There was no way out. With great reluctance, and considerable grunts and grumbles, the boy knelt on one knee. "My Queen," he said in no more than a whisper.

"Rise, my half-brother, Peada." Anne held out her right hand in a symbol of peace and acceptance. Noticing the boy's surprise as he slowly stood up, she added, "For until someone can prove otherwise, I believe you to be telling the truth. However, you are not King of Camelot and may never be. Why? Because of your Saxon blood and the fact that everyone in my realm hates the Saxons." Anne studied the boy. "You will need some fresh clothes. I will have Grace see to that. She is our half-sister as well. It would appear that our father got around. Who knows how many more would-be kings are out there waiting to claim what they believe is their right and privilege? How old are you?"

"I have seen fifteen winters, my Queen," he quickly added the words of reverence when he noticed Galahad's steely gaze fixed on him with a vengeance.

"Younger than me and younger than Grace, it would appear." Anne took a step back. "We will talk more later, you, Grace and I. I will have you escorted to better quarters where you will find water to wash, clean clothes to wear and food to eat. You will not lack any comforts befitting your rank as prince."

Anne was turning to leave the cell, but stopped abruptly when she heard the boy murmur the words, "Only my freedom."

Glancing over her shoulder, she replied, "For now, Prince Peada. What happens next depends on you."

"And my father." Peada continued to be in an argumentative mood.

"If he lives. The last time I saw him, he was quite dead from the point of Excalibur." She marched out, not waiting for any further confrontation from her half-brother, even though she could hear him calling out, "Abrecan will have remedied that by now, my Queen."

Merlin quickly fell into step beside the queen as they allowed the torches they held to light their passage through the tunnels and up the damp, dark stairs to the main level.

Chapter Twenty-Two

"What are you doing up here?" Anne stood in the doorway to her chambers. Grace was riffling through Anne's bag. "What are you looking for?"

Grace started at the sound of Anne's voice. She obviously wasn't expecting to be interrupted. She dropped the handful of items she had pulled from the queen's bag. Straightening up, she turned to greet Anne with a fake smile plastered on her face. "I was merely collecting your things, my Queen. I understand you are to take over your grandfather's chambers on the main floor. I knew you would want your personal items stored in your new chambers."

Anne knew it was a ruse. Grace was looking for something. What, she didn't know and probably never would know. "I have discarded my personal effects," Anne stated bluntly. It was evident that Grace would need watching. Closely.

"Even your grandmother's journal?"

Ah! So that's what she was looking for.

Anne feigned ignorance. "Journal? What journal?"

"The one you were studying last night," Grace elaborated.

Anne continued the ruse. "I do not know what you are talking about. There is no journal." Anne marched over to her half-sister and collected the items that were strewn all over the bed, stuffing them into the bag. "I shall take care of these myself." Turning to leave, she paused at the door, "Would you like to lay claim to these chambers, Grace?" In the back of her mind, she was thinking that this would be an excellent place to keep her sister under lock and key if need be. Except for the secret passage. One that Grace knew about.

Do not worry about the secret passage, my Queen. Merlin spoke in her head. This ability to speak inside her head was unnerving, especially since Merlin's voice just seemed to pop in at the most unexpected times. Unnerving, yes. But also helpful. Anne had so much to learn and she needed all the guidance available, both inside her head and outside. *Your grandmother knew about Grace and showed you the passage as a ruse to make Grace think she was trusted. The door at the bottom does not lead to my secret cave or to any other era. Grace has her own key, which will open that one door, but no others.*

But where does the door lead?

It is merely a door into a locked cell in the castle's basement prison.

Anne had to bite her tongue to prevent herself from laughing out loud. How fitting! Grace might try to flee, but she would only end up in a prison cell if she did.

"If it would please you, my Queen," Grace answered with forced civility. Obviously, the feigned compassion of the previous day was eroding.

"Yes, it would please me, Grace." Without another word, Anne marched out of the chambers and down the long, winding stairs.

Depositing the bag in her new chambers, she glanced around. *Is there a secret passage here, Merlin?*

Yes. Behind the fireplace as in the other chamber. The door at the bottom of the secret passage is the one you want. It is the one that leads you to a portal to my most secret cave, where you may take refuge if need be, or move to another era to hide for a period of time.

She was about to investigate, but a knock on the door stopped her. "My Queen." It was Sir Galahad. "David informs me that Blackie is ready, and the wagons are hitched and full of empty buckets to carry back the fresh water."

"Very good." She paused to allow her eyes to roam the room once more, taking in every nook and cranny. She studied the door. "Sir Galahad." She ran a hand around the frame.

"Yes, my Queen."

"Does the castle have its own blacksmith?"

"Yes, my Queen." His voice revealed a note of surprise. Anne had to admit her question sounded a bit naïve. Of course, the castle would have its own blacksmith.

"Order the blacksmith to prepare metal slips to hold a draw bar and have a draw bar installed on the inside of this door. Before tonight, please."

Sir Galahad lifted an eyebrow at the request, but he didn't argue. "As my Queen requests, it shall be done." He took a step away from the chambers, then stopped and turned to face her. "Any particular reason, my Queen?"

Anne met his gaze with one of equal intensity. "More security, Sir Galahad. We need to improve the castle's security reinforcements. After all, it was only yesterday that the Saxons entered without any resistance."

"Point taken," the knight nodded. "I will attend to it before we leave the castle."

"When we return will be soon enough," Anne suggested. "We need to make our way to the water source as quickly as possible, in order to have ample time for several trips. Clean water is an essential to a healthy life, Sir Galahad."

The knight bowed his head in response. "Shall we, then?" He pointed toward the grand hall that lead to the courtyard beyond.

Anne beamed in response. "Lead the way, Sir Galahad. We have work to do."

When Anne appeared at the castle entrance, a cheer erupted in the courtyard, "Long live the Queen of Camelot." David proudly held Blackie's bridle, as the horse stomped her feet with growing impatience. Blackie nickered in response to the crowd's enthusiasm, tossing her head with regal pride.

Left hand regally placed on Excalibur's hilt, Anne raised her right hand to acknowledge the people who crammed into the courtyard to meet their new queen. She smiled brightly emanating passion and assurance to all who witnessed the event. Blackie had lost her patience. She was not going to wait any longer. She pulled on the reins until David lost his grip and then trotted up the few steps to the entrance to greet her mistress. The crowd cheered even more.

With a chuckle, Anne rubbed Blackies' muzzle. "You funny munchkin."

She hadn't intended for others to hear, but Galahad obviously had. "Munchkin?" he queried in little more than a whisper, loud enough for Anne's ears alone. "What is a munchkin?"

Anne laughed more heartily, shaking her head in answer to Galahad's query. How could she explain a nickname from the twenty-first century? It didn't matter. She would make it her pet name for Blackie. The mare appeared to be in agreement. She bared her teeth in what might look to some, at least it did to Anne, like a big grin and snorted, stomping her right hoof with feigned impatience. "All right, girl. All right." Anne laughed some more and patted the mare fondly on the neck.

David trotted up the steps and took hold of Blackie's reins. Again. "You will not be escaping me this time, fair mare," he scolded the horse softly. Blackie merely tossed her head in response while Galahad assisted Anne into the saddle.

"Ugh!" the girl groaned as she settled into the hard leather contraption. "We are definitely going to have to make some improvements with these saddles. Could I not ride bareback again?" Her eyes darted between the knight and the wizard. Both were shaking their heads, adamantly opposed to her suggestion.

"You are the queen," Sir Galahad, bowed his head. "You must ride like a queen."

Blackie tossed her head in agreement and, without Anne's direction, made her way carefully down the stone steps into the main courtyard. The people parted and cheered as Blackie trotted grandly through the castle confines toward the main gate. Galahad and Merlin had to hustle to mount their horses and keep pace, with David close behind on his own mount.

The procession grew as Blackie carried Anne with great pride and dignity evident in every stride through the main gate, across the mote and into the scraggly array of dwellings beyond the castle walls. Anne was satisfied to notice the people hard at work, building the great fires she had requested. They paused as she passed, adding to the cheer. Those who weren't otherwise occupied with assigned tasks, joined the growing cavalcade, cheering and jostling each other for a prime position as close to the queen as possible. As much as Anne wanted to nudge Blackie into a gallop and leave the crowds behind, she knew this procession was important. Her 153escrye needed to see her, to cheer her, to touch her if they could.

Finally, the group moved beyond the last dwelling and there was only a vast, open field between them and the line of trees that marked the distant forest. Blackie didn't need any urging. As much as she obviously enjoyed the adulation, she was ready to run. She broke into an easy gallop, Anne laughing with pleasure as the wind whipped her cloaks behind her and frazzled her hair. She tried sinking deeper into her seat to avoid the hard thumps on her rear end when it made contact with the unbearably hard saddle, but to no avail. She conceded defeat and allowed Blackie to have her run. Once they approached the tree line, she pulled on the reins and slowed the horse to a trot, then a walk.

Sir Galahad and Merlin pulled up beside her. "This saddle has to go!" Anne shifted uncomfortably in her seat. "Who designed this monstrosity anyway?"

"All fine ladies have elegant saddles such as this, my Queen," Sir Galahad responded.

"Well I need one finer than this. And more comfortable."

Chapter Twenty-Three

Merlin nudged his mount ahead to take the lead, and the others followed him into the forest. There wasn't much of a path, so the wagons that were slowly catching up had to make their way with care.

"There's a waterfall up ahead." Merlin shifted in his saddle to glance back at Anne and Sir Galahad. "That is where we will find the freshest, cleanest water. You must instruct your people, my Queen, not to use this stream as a dumping place. Like any other fresh water, it would not take much to poison it with human and animal waste."

Anne already had it in mind to post guards to protect the water source.

The gurgling and rippling sounds of falling water intensified as the group closed in on the source. Merlin took instant charge, instructing everyone to tether the horses downstream and allow them to drink there. David and some of the other young lads were tasked with looking after the horses while the others dipped their buckets and water bags at the base of the waterfall. It wasn't a big waterfall, but its flow was significant enough and refreshing. As they worked, they each took a turn sipping from cupped hands and then drizzling the remnants down their faces. There was a general muttering of assent and approval as the fresh water met with welcome lips.

Merlin scolded them. "No washing here. Do that downstream. This location is our source of safe drinking water, and safe water for cooking." He waved the dissidents toward the location where the horses were tethered.

Sir Galahad organized a chain of men to transport the full buckets to the waiting carts, each man handing one bucket to the next, much like in a fire brigade. The task of lining the carts with water-filled buckets, in this organized manner, was completed in considerably less time than Anne had thought it would.

Merlin assigned two men to stay behind, to stand guard of the water source, with strict instructions on what was allowed. He assured the guards they would be relieved later in the day. The return jaunt was a little slower as the carts were now full and sloshing the contents with every rut in the path. Back at the castle, Anne had the men pour the collected water, what was left of it, into the huge caldrons that now sat next to the bonfires ready to be perched over the flames. The last bucket emptied, she sent the men back to the spring to collect more water.

Relinquishing Blackie to David's caring hands, Anne chose one of the caldrons and asked someone to position it over the roaring flames. She reached into her pocket to retrieve the last remnants of her food rations, a bag of oatmeal, and tossed the contents into the water, dropping the bag, which was plastic, a material that wouldn't exist for over a thousand years, into the flames to be obliterated. Picking up a large ladle that was perched nearby, she placed one end in the caldron and started to stir. While she stirred, she told a story, loud enough for those close to hear. Others quickly shouldered their way to within hearing distance.

"A long time ago, there was a town that was starving. They had eaten the last morsels of food and, after a long, soggy summer, during which time nothing grew, they were destitute. The hunting game was sparse as well. There was very little to eat. Fathers and older brothers came home night after night, following a fruitless day of looking for some animal suitable to eat. There was nothing. Even the mice and rats were long gone."

The rhythm of the stirring matched the soothing tone of her voice as she carried on with the story. "One day, a lone man came to town. He was hungry, too. He stopped at each hut as he entered the town, asking for a little morsel to eat. He was met with shaking heads and doors closing before he had moved onto the next hut. Finally, after visiting every hut in the town, he gathered some sticks for kindling and started a fire in the middle of the town. He found a caldron, abandoned next to one of the huts, and filled it with water from his water bag. Then he picked up a large stone and set it at the bottom of the caldron full of water. Placing the caldron over the burning fire, he picked up a stick and started to stir, sniffing the steam that arose with great interest. 'Hmm!' villagers could hear him exclaim. Slowly, one after the other, the people stepped cautiously out of their huts and made their way to the interesting spectacle in the center of the town. 'What are you doing?' a brave, but very hungry boy asked, rubbing a hand over his growling tummy.

"'I am making stone soup,' the man replied, glancing up briefly to award the boy with a warm smile. 'It smells so good. Do you not agree?' The boy stepped closer and sniffed. He was not sure what to make of this man making stone soup. How could stone soup smell so good? But it did. He sniffed and he sniffed. And his stomach grumbled in contented anticipation. One of the town's elders, a lady that had helped so many children come into this world, a healer, walked bravely up to the man carrying one, long, withered potato. 'This is my last one,' she handed it to the man. 'Add it to your stone soup for more sustenance. And here are the last of the herbs from my garden.'

"The man took the offerings and bowed his thanks, adding them to the caldron. Soon everyone was approaching with their own meagre offerings: a carrot here, another potato there, a small turnip. Each item was accepted with grace and thanks before being added to the mix. Finally, after everyone had contributed something, the man announced, 'It is ready. Bring your bowls for there is enough for everyone.' And they did. No one could recall the last time they had eaten so well. The man left the next day, taking the town's hunger with him."

The message was clear: share and everyone will benefit. People were 158escry158y scurrying away to their ramshackle dwellings, returning with what little they had to offer. By now, the men had returned with another load of fresh, clean water. The remaining caldrons were filled and set over the hot, crackling fires. All kinds of food were being added to one caldron or another. A few herbs from the castle kitchens added some flavor. As the people worked together, they talked and developed amongst them a strong bond of community."

"Good story, my Queen," Merlin whispered in Anne's ear as he came to stand next to her. "I do not believe I have heard that story before."

"You have now." Anne gave the wizard her brightest, warmest smile. She sniffed the steam rising from the caldron where she continued to stir. "Mmm! Gather your eating bowls, my people," she called out in a clear, bright voice. "We shall all eat well tonight."

The people cheered and began forming lines at each caldron, ready to accept what fare was offered. People who hadn't shared more than a word or two, were chatting up a storm and becoming close friends. As people congregated around the food, others picked up instruments of one kind or another, all handmade, home-styled folk instruments. There were pan flutes coarsely constructed from reeds or hollow stalks; a few shawms of varying lengths, crudely carved from a single piece of wood that flared at one end into a bell-shape much like a trumpet; several timbres, instruments from the Old Testament, a hoop or wood with metal inserts that clanked and rattled like tinkling bells; early fiddles or rebecs, also crudely carved and strung with four or five strings; lutes and even a bagpipe, crudely made, but clearly functional. There were other instruments, too. If there wasn't one available and a person wanted to join in, two sticks made an ample instrument of percussion. One man led the group, not by official appointment, but because he had a voice that carried and a gift of poetic beauty that transfixed the gathering.

"He's the castle's scop," Sir Galahad whispered in Anne's ear. "He composes poetry and sings them at gatherings such as this. I do believe he's singing a poem about you."

Anne felt warmth flush her cheeks at the handsome knight's suggestion and smile. She turned away, both to distract herself and keep him from seeing her embarrassment. As the older knight caused her jitters to return, she couldn't help but wonder what had happened to the younger knight, the handsome Sir Roderick.

He is close, my Queen. Just waiting your bidding. Would she ever settle and accept Merlin's unexpected inserts through mind speak.

The evening stretched on. Full bellies encouraged camaraderie and good spirits. Singing, dancing and just listening to the music and the stories, while watching the stars light up the clear night.

"Good omen," Merlin announced, loud enough for Anne's ears alone.

"What is?" she asked, glancing at the sky that twinkled with a thousand stars. Or more.

"The clear sky. The stars. We haven't had clear skies in months. This is a good omen on the start of your reign as queen. And the people know it. They are soaking up the scop's words, as if it were nectar to sooth weary souls, and so it is."

It was late when Anne made her way back inside the castle. The sounds of merriment carried on behind her, melting away the uneasiness of entering an almost empty castle. Sir Galahad and Merlin accompanied her, the knight ordering the guards to resume their posts. Grace appeared from the shadows of Anne's newly appointed chambers, ready to help the queen settle for the night. The men bowed in obeisance and left Anne in Grace's care.

Chapter Twenty-Four

Anne was pleased to find her chambers as she had left them. Her order for a draw bar to be installed had been carried out and she was satisfied with the heavy wooden beam.

"What do you need that for?" Grace asked as she helped Anne disrobe and prepare for bed.

"You can never have enough protection, Grace," Anne stated simply. As Grace reached to take Excalibur, still sheathed in the belt, Anne held it back. "I do not think that is wise, Grace. Our half-brother, if that is what he is, had a very shocking experience when trying to handle Excalibur earlier today."

"The Saxon prince?" Anne nodded in response. "You really believe he is our half-brother?"

Anne merely shrugged. "I do not know. And we probably never will know for sure. He claims to be our father's son, and he did have an explosive connection to the sword when he attempted to take it. It might be wise for you to avoid touching it. I would not want your hands burnt by the sparks that flew on his."

"It may not happen, my Queen," Grace pointed out. "Perhaps I do have as much right to touch the sword as you."

Anne had to cough to muffle a gasp of exclamation. "Really? So, you do resent me being Queen?"

Grace stuttered in response. "No, my Queen." She took the handful of robes that she had picked up off the bed and hung them on the peg on the wall, close to the hearth, but not too close as to catch a hot coal and burn. Shaking her head, she turned back to face the queen. "I was just saying," she repeated, but Anne waved off any further comments.

"That will be all for tonight, Grace. Thank you for your assistance."

Grace hesitated slightly, then, noticing the determined look on Anne's face, she curtseyed and walked out of the room, pulling the door closed behind her. Anne tucked the sword under the bed coverings, intending to keep it as close as possible while she slept. She wrapped the sleeping robe around her and made her way to the closed door. She pushed it firmly shut and lifted the beam onto its metal holders, which, Anne was please to notice, were firmly anchored into the wall on either side of the door.

After banking down the fire, Anne retreated to her bed, confident she was safe enough to sleep the night. She had considered checking out the secret passage behind the fireplace, but she was too tired. Exhausted, really. Sliding under the bed covers, she felt the chain around her neck, satisfied that the key was safe and where it should be. Pulling Excalibur close, she slipped into a deep sleep.

She didn't know what caused her to jolt awake. Voices. Familiar voices. Ungodly voices.

"That is her, my friend. The one who claims to be Queen of Camelot."

It couldn't be, could it? Anne forced her eyes open, taking in the darkened confines of the room. This was not her royal chambers in the castle. The walls were stark, the mattress hard, creaking as she moved. She was lying on a cot, with thin blankets, in a room that was not her own.

Cackling laughter attracted her eyes to the source. A door. With a tiny window at the top. "Abrecan!" she yelled. "What have you done?"

More laughter. "Dr. Abrecan to you, my dear Queen." She heard more voices laughing along with Abrecan's. "Our dear, fair Queen Anne of Camelot."

As she watched in horror, the face moved away from the window and a sharp noise accompanied the slick movement of a sliding shield that closed it off and, sadly, the only source of light.

"No!" she screamed. She fought with the heavy weight of fatigue that gripped her entire body, making her feel as if she were tied to the bed, paralyzed in a prone position. Pushing herself into a sitting position, she felt around for Excalibur. It was gone. She clenched her fists, relief washing over her as she felt the bite of the ring inside her fist. Her hands hastily felt around the neck. She exhaled another deep breath of relief, finding comfort in the chain that remained firmly settled around her neck, the key safe. For now. Allowing her hands to fall on her lap, she noticed the thin, cottony texture of the outfit she wore. A hospital gown, no doubt. Not a sixth century outfit, but one from the twenty-first century.

She had to focus. To think. To figure out what was happening to her. How did she get here? What was this place? What was going on? What was the last thing she remembered? So many questions.

She remembered lying in bed with Excalibur tucked closely beside her, one hand loosely grasping its hilt, the ring making a loose connection, while the other hand patted the key where it lay on her chest. She had been tired. Exhausted. Asleep before she was fully settled under her coverings. Nothing was making sense.

A clank startled her from her musings. A lock disengaged and a creak pierced the vacuous tomb. For that was what the room signified. A tomb. Glancing toward the door, she noticed it open. Slowly. Two men, clad head to foot in white, marched into the room. She quickly tucked the key underneath the gown and clutched a fist around the ring, hoping the motion hadn't attracted any attention.

"Let's go, my Queen," one of the men spoke, but both guffawed at the title of 'queen'. "Dr. Abrecan awaits. And he doesn't like to be kept waiting."

The men grabbed Anne underneath her arms and yanked her to her feet. "Where are you taking me?" she shrieked, trying to resist.

"Look, lady." The same man who called her 'queen' gripped her arm more tightly. "We can either do this the easy way or the hard way. Your choice."

There was no point in resisting. She wouldn't find her answers in this tomb. Giving in, she allowed the men to usher her out into the hall. The lights were brighter, but the air was just as stale, just as sanitized. Looking right and left as she trod along with her escorts, she noticed door after door, much like the one she had passed through. Moans and shrieks pervaded the walls from beyond the doors. Other than the sounds, there was nothing to suggest any other human presence. She wasn't even convinced that her escorts were human.

The men's feet clomped along on the hard, linoleum floors; Anne's feet, cushioned inside some sort of slipper, merely scuffled. Everything echoed. Sounds bounced off the walls, the floor and the ceiling. The hall stretched on and on, with no intersections or exits to suggest an escape route or any other route for that matter. It was merely one, very long, very empty hall.

They reached the end. There was a door. Not like the cell doors that she had passed. This one was more official. A larger window than the one that graced her door was labelled with the words: "Dr. Abrecan, Chief Psychiatrist."

The man who spoke knocked.

"Enter."

He turned the knob and pushed the door open, then pushed Anne inside before slamming the door firmly shut behind her. The room was exceedingly bright. More so than the hall. She blinked, keeping her stance where she had been left, allowing her eyes to accustom themselves to the new lighting. When she could see better, she glanced around the room, studying it, taking in every little detail. The men who escorted her were gone. At least, she believed they were. Though it was possible they merely stood on the other side of the door, on guard to prevent her from trying to escape.

She felt very much alone. But she wasn't; not really. A man sat at the large desk at the far end of the room, a room lined with rows of filing cabinets on one side and shelves stocked with peculiar bottles and boxes with syringes sticking out the open ends. It was the bottles and syringes that concerned Anne. Who knew what this mad wizard had in mind for her!

"Come in, Anne." The voice was Abrecan's, only this one had an air of professionalism. Firm, concise, neither warm nor cold. It was the voice she expected to hear from any physician in the twenty-first century.

"Abrecan." Anne refused to move.

"Dr. Abrecan to you, my dear."

"Queen Anne to you, wizard."

He quirked his eyebrow quickly, a glimmer of agitation showing in his eyes like a flash of lightning, brief and then it was gone. "Very well, Queen Anne," he snapped the words with precision. "As you wish. Stand if you must. I would like to ask you some questions. First, do you know what year it is?"

Anne had a feeling she was being tricked. This was not the sixth century. But was it the twenty-first century? And, if so, when? At the time she left it? Taking a chance, she chose the last year she remembered, before she had found the door. "2019."

Abrecan appeared satisfied. "Very good. Now, who is the Queen of England."

Another trick? "Queen Elizabeth II."

"Ah! Good! We are getting somewhere. So, you admit that you are not the Queen of England."

"Not in this era," Anne muttered, then realized she should have remained silent.

"Then, in what era are you queen?" Abrecan wrote something on the pad of paper in front of him before returning his gaze to Anne, tapping the pen on the desk. It hit the surface with an irritating, hypnotic patter. Anne focused hard to avoid its influence.

"You know full well, wizard."

"I am not a wizard. Not here. Not now. I am a very respected doctor in the field of psychiatry. Now answer the question."

It was Anne's turn to snort. "Psychiatrist, my ass."

"Fitting words to come from the mouth of a queen."

Anne grasped her hands tight in a grip. The ring bit into the palm of her right hand. Resisting the urge to study her hand, to look at the precious ring, or to reach inside the neck of her gown to check on the key, Anne glared at her adversary. Her enemy. Her half-brother. Ugh! She hated the idea that she was related to this monster.

Abrecan grinned and returned the girl's stare. "We couldn't remove the ring." He knew what she was thinking. Unsettling. But then again, Merlin always knew, too. A wizard's gift. "And, yes, I can read your thoughts." Nodding at the girl's clenched hand, he continued in a voice barely audible, "I didn't want to cut off the finger. Not yet. But I will need the ring soon. It appears that only you have the power to remove it. Another one of Merlin's tricks, I suppose." Shaking his head as if to clear the cobwebs from his thoughts, Abrecan broke the gaze and studied the notes on the desk in front of him. "Now answer my questions. In what era are you queen?"

He obviously couldn't read all her thoughts, or he would know she had been thinking about the key.

Anne allowed the silence to impregnate the space. She closed her mind to thoughts that might hinder her attempt to take control. If she could take control. She had to believe that this wasn't real, that there was a way to escape this nightmare. Finally, she answered, in a clear, determined voice, with head held high, her gaze every bit the queen that she was. "In your era, Wizard Abrecan. And, if you know what is good for you, then you will get down on bended knee and beg for my forgiveness."

The wizard cackled with laughter. Stilted. Harsh. He slapped a hand on the desk to emphasize his humor and bellowed, "Right. And I suppose you want me to pledge allegiance to you, too. Am I right?"

Anne didn't answer. She waited, allowing the silence to penetrate. Finally, "Of course. But first I demand some answers. Where am I, Abrecan? Where is this place? And what is it?"

"It's a mental asylum, my dear. You have obviously been rather unbalanced for some time and you were brought here to be treated."

"Brought here? Where is here? And treated for what?"

"This is the Rideau Regional Psychiatric Hospital in Grenadier Falls. You are being treated for schizophrenia."

"What? I am not schizophrenic! If anyone is, it is you." And she dramatically pointed a finger at the accusing man.

He merely snorted in response. "Now. Back to my questions. What era, girl? In what era are you queen?"

Anne chose to answer with her own laughter. This one as forced as Abrecan's, only much brighter without a hint of evil. "My dear Abrecan," she ignored his attempt to argue her use of the more personal address. "You may think you have the upper hand, Abrecan, but I am under no obligation to answer any of your questions." She waved her hand as if dismissing him. "Besides, I have already answered that question."

"Very well. Next question. Where is the prince?"

"Which one?"

"The one you kidnapped."

"So, you do admit to my royal status."

"Hardly. I am merely asking you about the prince you continue to mention. What was his name?"

"And I ask you again, Wizard. Which prince?"

"And I tell you again, I am not a wizard!" The man was on his feet, leaning his hands on the desk. Yelling. Froth and spittle dripping and flying from his mouth.

Keep aggravating him, Anne.

Merlin. Where have you been?

It does not matter. I am here now.

"Answer the question!" The man was yelling, now. Insanely so. He punctuated each word with a fist thumping on the desk. Papers ruffled in the air, scattered by his tantrum. For that's what it was: a tantrum. "Where! Is! The! Boy?" More spittle flew, the trajectory powerful enough to splash Anne in the face. She grimaced and blinked, but otherwise didn't move an inch. She would not be cowered by this madman.

"Are you referring to Prince Peada, son of Queen Sunniva and our father, King Arthur?" Noticing the wizard's startled expression, she quickly added, "Oh yes, I know we are related, half-brother. You are the son of King Arthur and his half-sister, Morgawse. Disgusting, I know. But she did trick him."

"She did not!" Abrecan pushed his shoulders back, standing up a little straighter, a modicum of dignity evident in his outrage. "He tricked her. He seduced her, like he did all the other women. Like he did Queen Sunniva. Like he did your mother."

It was Anne's turn to appear startled. Gathering her thoughts, she realized that the conversation had quickly converted from one between a doctor, a psychiatrist, and his patient, to one between two siblings, or half-siblings as it were. Two rivals from the sixth century. Anne was no more in a mad house than Abrecan was. This was a ruse; a ploy to unsettle her and make her speak.

"Now answer my question. Where is Prince Peada?" Abrecan wasn't about to give up.

Anne merely shrugged her shoulders and gave the man a coy look. "As you know very well, I am Queen of Wessex, Queen of Camelot, and soon to be Queen of England? And we are both from the sixth century?"

"Be gone!" Abrecan waved his hands in dismissal, sending the remaining papers on the desk flying across the room. "Guards!" The same two men stepped into the room, taking up position behind her.

"Take her back to the cell." They grabbed Anne's arms and hustled her out of Abrecan's presence. As they marched her down the long, empty hall, retracing their earlier steps, Abrecan's voice echoed in their wake. "And silence that ragtag lot, will you?"

He was referring to the cries, wails and screams that permeating through the bolted doors lining the narrow passageway. As they passed each door, one guard or the other would pound viciously on the door and yell, "Quiet!" Not that it did much good. The wails only started up again once they had progressed a few steps further down the hall. It was an eerie sound that shook Anne to the core. Who were these prisoners? And what fate awaited them at Abrecan's hands? She shuddered at the thought.

As they approached the cell she occupied earlier, Anne heard a familiar voice. "Anne. Anne. Is that you?"

"Mother?" Anne was sure the voice was her mother's. Could it be? Grandmother had insisted her mother had been killed in an accident. Could Grandmother have been wrong? Had her mother been trapped here, as Abrecan's prisoner, all this time? Well! She had to admit, it hadn't been that long since she departed the twenty-first century. Not even a week. However, it seemed like so much longer. So much had happened.

"Anne. Anne." The voice was desperate. Calling for help.

"Mother!" Anne wasn't allowed to stop, to call out again. The hands that gripped her tightened and she was forcibly shoved into her cell and tossed like a rag doll onto the cot. As she scrambled to sit up, she heard the door behind her slamming shut with a resounding crash as the locks were slid into place. If only she knew more magic. If only she had Excalibur in her hand. If only…

"Anne." The voice was faint, barely audible.

Pounding on the door next to hers made the room shudder. "Quiet!" the men yelled in unison, their footsteps fading as they marched away.

Grab the sword. Be quick.

Merlin. My mother.

Yes. I know. You must escape first. Release the locks that bind you to that cell, then we shall rescue her.

So, it is her. She is alive.

It would appear so.

Why did everyone tell me she was dead?

No one really knew for sure. Remember your grandmother was killed by the same thugs that sent you running for your life.

Yes. Did Abrecan kidnap Mother to use her as bait to lure me?

Possibly. Now hurry. There is not much time before the guards return to drag your mother away. You and she must be gone before they return.

But how? I am locked in this cell. I have no way to escape.

Yes, you do. Find the sword. Grab it.

Where?

It is still where you left it. You are sitting next to it.

Anne slid her hand over the bed coverings, making contact with the contoured outline of a sword's hilt. It remained invisible, until she wrapped her right hand around what felt like the hilt and allowed the ring to connect. Excalibur sizzled to life.

I must have shoved it aside in my sleep.

You did. But Excalibur never left your side. It was you, who left it behind.

In my dreams? Is this just a dream? A nightmare?

And it will continue as a nightmare until you unlock the cell door with the key, unlock your mother's cell door, and find your way out of this asylum and back to your own chambers in the sixth century.

Anne didn't need further encouragement. She wanted nothing more than to escape this madhouse. Clutching Excalibur at her side, she walked over to the door. With the tip of the key, a keyhole appeared where one hadn't existed mere moments before. She inserted the key. The door opened, allowing a flash of bright light to wash over her. She blinked her eyes, trying to adjust to the sudden glare. With tentative steps, glancing right and left, she made her way into the hall.

"Anne!" It was her mother's voice. Softer this time. Accompanied by choking sobs.

"I am coming, Mother." Anne followed the voice and found the door that she was sure led to her mother. She inserted the key again and the door opened. The light inside the cell was as dim as it had been in her own cell. She squinted to study the space, noticing a similar cot in the corner and a prone figure curled up in a fetal position. The figure shuffled, raising an arm to shield her eyes from the hallway's glare. What little she could see appeared so familiar. Could it be? "Mother?"

"Anne?" The woman stretched and pushed herself into a sitting position before slowly testing her feet to stand.

"What has he done to you?" Anne rushed to her mother's side, wrapping her free arm around the woman's shoulders.

The door behind her slammed shut. Abrecan's evil cackle could be heard in the hall.

Use the key again, Anne.

Merlin. Help us.

I am trying to. Do as I say. Use the key again. Insert it into the lock on the door. When it opens this time, lead your mother through. You may have to shoulder most of her weight.

I will. Anne tucked her left hand under her mother's arm and half lifted her to her feet. It was difficult, as her other hand was grasping Excalibur, her only line of defense. "Mother. Can you walk?"

"I shall try." She groaned as her feet shuffled forward, leaning heavily on her daughter. "It is painful. He did horrible things to me, Anne. My feet. He burned them."

"No. Mother." Anne grimaced. "Let us get you somewhere safe and perhaps Merlin can heal you. We just have to make it to the door."

"But how? You cannot escape Abrecan. He is evil. A powerful evil."

"And Merlin is more powerful, Mother. And I have some powers, too. I have the key. Grandmother's key."

Mother groaned again. "That blasted key. I see you have Arthur's sword as well. I suppose there was no stopping what was meant to happen. And your grandmother?"

"He killed her, Mother." The women sniffled as they moved forward at a snail's pace. "Come, Mother. A couple more steps." She was within reach. Still grasping her mother, she juggled the sword and the key in her right hand, managing to manoeuvre the key into the keyhole. The click of the key making contact and turning back the locks shattered the silence and the door opened. Not to the institution's hall, but into a cave, a welcoming fire burning in a central hearth. It was much like Merlin's cave, the one he had led her to when she first arrived in the sixth century.

As if conjured to appear, Merlin stepped forward and reached across the chasm, taking Anne's mother's other arm and half lifting her across the threshold. Anne jumped in quickly; the opening slamming shut with a shudder and a yell that rattled the cave's walls like an earthquake.

"No!" It was Abrecan. He had lost his two most valuable prisoners.

"You are safe now." Merlin lifted Mother in his arms and laid her gently on the soft rugs that beckoned beside the hearth.

Having her settled, he turned his attention to Anne. "I will care for her. When she is healed, I will bring her to you. But right now, you must return to Gloucester Castle. It is morning. And Grace will be pounding on your door, demanding entrance. You must be there to greet her. Watch her carefully, Anne. She is one of Abrecan's spies. She truly believes the wizard will make her queen once you have been disposed. She expects to find your chambers empty this morning and you missing. She then hopes to step into your place as queen."

"Why did you insist I trust her?" Anne asked. "Why did Grandmother assure me I could trust her?"

"At the time, we were all trying to believe in Grace's potential to be a good friend and confident," Merlin admitted. "Even if she did show some leanings toward Abrecan. I needed more proof before I could accept that she was caught in his evil web. Now I have it. And now we must expect the worse from her."

"Why is it that all my half-siblings are consumed with greed and the desire for power?" Merlin didn't answer. Crouching next to her mother, Anne took the older woman's hands. "Get better, Mother. We have much to catch up on."

"Go, daughter of mine. Claim your destiny. You were always meant to be queen." She waved her hand in dismissal. "I was wrong to dismiss Mother's teachings. I see it now. You are strong and capable just like your father. I thought by trying to protect you in the twenty-first century, I could keep all the evils of the sixth century far in the past. I was wrong. Grandmother was right. She was always right. I should have listened. You have to claim your father's Camelot. Your Camelot."

Standing up, Anne noticed Merlin had opened another chasm. "You have much to explain, oh wizard of mine." Anne forced a smile that didn't quite reach her eyes as she studied Merlin.

"And explanations you shall have. Later. I must see to your mother first. I must care for Princess Evelyn."

Realization dawned and Anne smiled at the wizard. "You really care for my mother, do you not, Merlin?" He didn't answer. He didn't have to. Anne merely nodded. "Take care of her. Please. She is the only family I have left. The only family I can trust." She diverted her eyes toward the chasm, noticing with clarity that she could see her private chambers beckoning. Would she be lucky enough to catch a few hours sleep before being disturbed? The pounding on the door answered her question.

"My Queen. My Queen." It was Grace. She was sounding frantic. A ploy? If Merlin was right, then it must be. "Please open up. It is morning. It is past time to arise. Is everything all right?"

"Coming, Grace." Anne stepped through the portal, feeling the rush of air as it shuddered shut behind her. She stifled a yawn, sheathed the sword and placing it on the bed ready to strap to her waist once she was dressed and proceeded to unbar the door.

Grace stood on the threshold, a startled look plastered on her face. She was obviously not expecting to find the queen alive, well and still in her chambers.

Chapter Twenty-Five

Dressed and prepared for another full day, Anne emerged from her chambers, pleased to discover that everyone was actively performing the assignments from the previous day. Water was being carted from the fresh spring source; the great caldrons were being cleaned and readied for another day of feeding the general population, the great fires on which the food would cook were being stoked and kindled into action with young boys scattering into the woods to collect the kindling. There were men out hunting and others stalking the land, spying, watching for clues of enemy Saxon invasions.

As Anne stood at the grand entrance to the castle, Sir Galahad sidled up beside her, his brother, David, a few steps behind, leading the Saxon prince.

"I think we should put the lad to work, my Queen," the knight suggested.

Turning, Anne studied the boys. Focusing on David, she addressed the lad. "What do you think, David? Can you keep this prince out of trouble for a day?"

The boy nodded, his face reflecting an eagerness to please and to serve. "Yes, my Queen."

"What tasks do you suggest?"

"Mucking out the stalls, my Queen. They can always use an extra hand or two in the stables."

She ignored Peada's grimace, biting back a smile. "Mucking out the stalls it is, then. Make sure you guard him well."

"And work him hard, brother," Sir Galahad added. "Alongside of you." He quirked an eyebrow. "Doing the same as you."

David muffled a deep sigh. If he had been planning to take it easy, merely standing guard while Peada did all the dirty work, then his hope for a relaxing day were quickly shattered. "Yes, brother." He grabbed the Saxon prince by the arm and led him away. "Come on, Peada."

"You should address me with proper respect," the Saxon prince scolded as he reluctantly followed David.

Their voices faded as they moved away from the front of the castle. The last words Anne heard were David's. "You have to earn my respect first."

It was safe to laugh. She caught the sparkle in Sir Galahad's eyes and the two shared a chuckle.

The day passed much as the previous day, ending with the combined efforts of the community to fill the caldrons with tasty morsels of this and that. Anne was diligently stirring one of the concoctions when a familiar voice appeared at her side.

"I can see that your grandmother has taught you well." It was Mother.

Anne paused from her stirring long enough to glance at the woman standing next to her. Healed, presumably by Merlin's magic potions, she was standing on her own and showing no lingering effects from the ordeal she had undergone as Abrecan's prisoner. "Mother," Anne greeted her. Someone stepped up to claim the ladle that Anne had been using to stir. Relieved of her duty, temporarily, she reached her arms around the woman and the two embraced.

"I have so much to explain," the older woman sniffled into Anne's shoulder. "I have been so angry for so long and I am afraid I have taken it out on both you and Mother. I should have appreciated her more while she was still alive. And now I cannot tell her how much I really did care. Between anger and fear, because yes, I was afraid, I did not know what to do or how to survive, except to work hard, which I did. And that just made me more angry. Here I was a princess and I was cleaning other people's messes. It just was not right. And yet we had to survive somehow. In a very different era than the one in which I was brought up." She sniffled again. "I am not the cold-hearted bitch you must have thought I was. I really did, and do, care."

"I never thought of you as a cold-hearted bitch, Mother," Anne confessed, stepping back so she could study her mother. "I just did not understand." She smiled as she glanced at her mother in her new attire. Dressed in clean robes and standing unaided, her hair tied back in a neat bun, she looked every inch the princess she was. "You look better. Revived. We will eat and rejoice and then retire to my chambers where we can safely share our stories. Until then, you are my mother. Stay by my side. Please." The older woman nodded in response.

Well said, my Queen. Merlin spoke in her head. *She is the best friend you could ask for and probably the only one you will ever be able to fully trust. Except, of course, myself.*

Anne chuckled softly at the wizard's words. *Of course. Probably the best friend you could hope for, too. Am I right, Merlin?*

Perhaps. Anne was startled to hear a response. She hadn't expected Merlin to be so forthcoming. So, the wizard had a soft spot for someone. And that someone was her mother.

Chapter Twenty-Six

The night progressed much like the previous night. Everyone was fed, content and overjoyed to have another princess in attendance. Satisfied that all was well, Anne led her mother into the castle and to the royal chambers.

"Stay with me tonight, Mother. And tomorrow, we shall have you settled in your own chambers." Anne shut the door behind her. She was about to bolt it with the bar, but a voice from the shadows made her jump.

"So, the Princess Evelyn returns." It was Grace. She almost sounded resentful, not like the helpful Grace of the past few days. What had happened? Or was everything else just a ruse?

Anne hesitated, but Evelyn marched to the center of the room, confronting Grace head-on. "And you must be Violet's daughter. Grace, is it?" Studying her carefully, she added, "You look very much like your mother. How is she? Does she miss her best friend as much as I have missed her?"

"I am sure my mother will be pleased to see you again, Princess Evelyn," Grace stated with an air of superiority. "But, mark my words, what has not been done yet, will soon be done and then I shall take Anne's place."

"You really believe Abrecan will allow you to be queen?" Evelyn was blunt and to the point.

"But of course. Who else would rule supreme?"

"You really have no clue who you are dealing with, do you?" Anne's mother uttered with a slight shake of her head. "All he wants is the crown for himself. Do not be delusional. He is using you, Grace. He is using you to get what he wants."

"He is my brother," Grace began to retaliate.

"Half-brother," Anne interrupted. "And you are both my half-siblings as well. Who does he think he is that he can dictate the who is who of the kingdom?"

If Grace's eyes could shoot daggers, they were doing so with great efficiency as she glared at Anne first, then Evelyn. "He is Abrecan. Oldest son of King Arthur. That is who he is."

"And," Evelyn spoke more firmly and with conviction. "As the oldest son, he believes he holds the strongest claim to power."

"So, what is holding him back?" Anne queried. "He has the magic to make it all possible and the heritage to back his claim."

"Greed can be a sticky wicket, Anne," Evelyn used a twenty-first colloquialism that was lost on Grace. "He wants his siblings and rivals under his full control. Then, and only then, will he take what he believes is rightfully his to take."

"The crown," Anne finished the thought. "But can he wield Excalibur? Young Prince Peada could not. Can you, Grace? Can my half-sister, the one who claimed to want friendship only days ago? Can you wield Excalibur?" Anne didn't wait for an answer. She pulled the sword from its sheath, kissed the hilt with reverence and then plunged it through the rushes and into the stone floor beneath.

The women stood frozen, listening to the shrieking and sizzling as the blade ground its way deep into the stone. Releasing the hilt, Anne motioned to Grace. "Pull out Excalibur and wield it high. If you can do so, then I will bow on bended knee and allow you to claim the crown. If that is really what you want."

Grace hesitated. Briefly. Then, with a proud gleam in her eye and a wicked smile stretching across her face, she slowly approached the sword. She knew how to wield a sword. She had been trained by the best swordsmen. Grasping Excalibur's hilt with both hands, she strained to pull it out. The sword sizzled and spat at her, but it would not budge.

"No!" she screamed at the top of her lungs. The sword sizzled more fervently, but Grace wouldn't release her grip. Until, finally, her hands flashed off and she crumpled to the floor, studying the now singed palms as tears dribbled down her cheeks.

"You cannot rule Camelot if you cannot wield Excalibur," Evelyn pointed out as Anne took claim of the sword and pulled it out with ease.

"Abrecan probably has the power to extract it." Grace's fury was evident, her face shining a bright, crimson.

"If he had been able to extract it, do you not think he would have done so by now?" Evelyn challenged the Grace, stepping closer to confront her face to face.

"Perhaps he could not find where it was hidden," she argued in vain.

"He is a wizard, Grace," Anne pointed out, having resheathed Excalibur and taken position next to her mother. "He could find it if he were meant to have it. Given that he could not find it, suggests quite strongly, that he was not meant to have it. That he was not meant to be king."

"No!" Grace clamped her hands on either side of her face, covering the ears. "No!" she screamed. "I will not listen to you. It is all lies. Lies. I will be queen. Just you wait and see." And, scrambling off the floor, she dashed from the room, hands still clamped on her head, tears pooling down her cheeks, yelling at the top of her lungs.

As Anne glanced warily at her mother, the two listened to the shrieks as it retreated and diminished in volume. Merlin entered, with a slight knock on the door that remained ajar after Grace's hasty exit.

"It would appear that you have angered the enemy within," he stated the obvious, pausing briefly to close the door firmly behind him. To ensure no unannounced intrusion, he lifted the bar and placed it on the brackets, barring the door shut.

"We need to talk," Anne said. She walked casually over to the hearth and poked the dying embers before adding some kindling and another log. Satisfied that the fire would catch on, she took the nearest seat, Excalibur still sheathed and the belt firmly clasped around her waist. She motioned the others to find somewhere to sit. There was one other chair. Merlin carried it over to the hearth, allowing Evelyn to sit. Merlin crouched on the floor rushes, sitting cross-legged between the two women.

"I know you have plenty of questions," Evelyn broke the silence that engulfed the trio as they restlessly attempted to settle in their seats, wondering where to start.

Anne nodded. "Lots of questions. And too few answers. Merlin here," she nodded to the wizard, "has been very sparse in his supply of answers."

"For good reason." Merlin held up his hands in feigned defense. "You were being tested."

Anne's eyebrows shot up. "Tested?"

"To ensure that you had not been contaminated and recruited by Abrecan," Merlin answered. "He has a way of taking over the minds of others and controlling their actions."

"Like Grace and Peada?"

Merlin nodded. "You might appear to be sincere in your actions. You did, after all, fight the Saxons with honor and dignity."

"But so did Grace," Anne added.

"Exactly." Merlin stared into the flames intently. "When you first arrived, you told me your mother was dead. I knew otherwise, but I could not say if you really believed she was dead, or you had been brainwashed with the notion that she was dead. I suspected she had been kidnapped by Abrecan and was being held somewhere as his prisoner."

"You are a wizard, Merlin." Anne shook her head in disbelief. "It does not make sense. You must have been able to sense my sincerity. You must have more magic than Abrecan."

"Abrecan has become increasingly more powerful over the years." Merlin continued to stare into the flames as he talked. "He has focused his powers on mind control and illusions. Something I have minimal interest in and thus little ability at best."

"But, Merlin," Anne challenged. "If I had been compromised, my mind taken over by Abrecan, would I still be able to wield Excalibur? The others could not."

"Point taken," Merlin agreed, a tone of reluctance evident. "But I had to be sure. As I said, Abrecan's powers have increased substantially."

"So, I," she quickly corrected herself as she glanced across at her mother, "I mean, Mother and I cannot be safe anywhere or at any time. How do we protect ourselves? And how do we know for sure that you are not Abrecan in disguise? You look and sound like Merlin, but, if what you say is true, then he could masquerade as you, Merlin. And trick us through your image."

"All very true, my Queen." Merlin's head dropped till his chin rested on his chest, a look of remorse evident in his posture and his voice. "I have no means to assure you that I am who I say I am and that I am the genuine Merlin."

"The one and only." Mother spoke up with conviction. "He is Merlin."

"How can you be sure?" Anne wasn't convinced. Not yet. Too many things, unexplainable occurrences, just didn't add up. "How can I be sure?"

"There is one way to prove who I am." Merlin let out a deeply held sigh and allowed his head to lift and his eyes to focus on Anne. "There is only one other person, other than yourself, my Queen, who can lift the sword Excalibur from the stone."

"You?" Both women exclaimed in unison, their gazes riveted on the wizard seated between them.

"I thought only the rightful heir to the crown could lift Excalibur," Anne pondered aloud. "You mean to tell us, that you are also the rightful heir?"

"I am and always have been the rightful heir." Merlin pushed himself off the floor. "But I have always denied my right, my claim, preferring to research my powers and to use my powers for the good of others." He motioned to Excalibur, still firmly sheafed. "Place it in the stone floor and allow me to prove I am Merlin."

"But cannot Abrecan, as the son of Arthur, also have the powers to retrieve the sword?" Anne asked, not totally convinced that this was the only way to prove that Merlin was, in fact, Merlin.

"If he could, he would have done so by now," Merlin explained. "You said so yourself, I believe, when you were arguing with Grace. I was the one who should have carried the sword, so many years ago. I chose not to. I chose to support Arthur, my nephew, and his claim to power."

"Anne," Evelyn spoke softly. "Allow Merlin to prove himself."

With a nod, Anne stood, picked up the sword and plunged it into the stone floor at her feet. Excalibur shivered and sparked, as it had done before. Merlin reached for the hilt. There were no sparks or complaints issued from the sword as it had done with Peada and Grace. The wizard wrapped his hand around the hilt and lifted the sword with ease. Released from its stony grip, the sword sparkled and glistened as Merlin swung it slowly and with care until the point was skyward. As Anne had done on several occasions, he brought the hilt to his lips, kissed it, then reached to hand the sword over to the queen. Anne took it with ease, copying the wizard's motions and reverently kissing the hilt before resheathing it.

"Very well. You have proved yourself." Anne resumed her seat as Merlin crouched back down on the floor. "But am I to repeat this motion every time we meet? There must be a better way to ensure that you are Merlin then to go through this exercise of testing your ability to extract the sword from the stone."

"I agree with Anne." Both women fixed their gazes on the wizard.

Merlin was quiet, pondering the dilemma. When he did speak, it was with a solemn conviction. "Anne. You must pierce me with Excalibur. Here." He pointed to the side of his abdomen. "All the way through."

"What!?!" The women exclaimed in unison. Anne shook her head vehemently.

"You must." Merlin insisted. "I will conjure a spell that only I know. It will heal the wound quickly and the scar it leaves behind will only be visible to the one who bears the sword. By touching the point of Excalibur where you pierced me, the scar will glow. For only your eyes to see."

Anne shuddered at the suggestion. "I cannot."

"You must. Now. Before Abrecan catches on to what we are doing and conjures his own spell to counter mine. Quickly."

Anne took a deep breath and unsheathed Excalibur. Wrapping her hand around the hilt, she instantly felt the connection when the ring made contact. Before she could stop herself, the sword helped her make the decision, leading her hand to plunge the weapon deeply through the side of Merlin's abdomen.

He cried out as blood gushed all over the floor rushes. Anne pulled the sword out, forcing her eyes to look away, to focus on the flames in the hearth. She heard the wizard clamping a hand over the wound and her mother leaving her chair to go to his aid. She couldn't turn around. Not yet. She had just wounded one of the few people she could truly trust. And she wasn't even sure it was the right thing to do.

"You may look, now." Merlin's voice was quiet. "The wound has healed. The only evidence is the blood in the floor rushes which we must sweep into the hearth to clear away any proof of what we have done and to make sure my blood cannot be used to cast a spell against me. Or worse, through me to you."

Anne stepped back from the hearth and glanced down at her mother as she gathered the bloodied floor rushes and dumped them into the hearth. Merlin was right. There was no evidence of the wound. Not even a scar.

"Touch the blade where you pierced me." She did as she was told. As a slick scar appeared on Merlin's skin, she almost jumped back into the hearth. Fortunately, her mother was behind her and saved her from a fiery demise.

"No one else can conjure such a scar, Anne," Merlin assured her. "Not even Abrecan." He allowed his tunic to drop, covering the wound that was and wasn't there.

"Okay. So, you are who you claim to be. This really is not getting us anywhere. And what about Mother?" Anne reclaimed her seat, leaning forward and resting her elbows on her knees. She glanced from one to the other. "I am not going to pierce my Mother."

"You do not have to," Merlin assured her. "There is no blood tie between Evelyn and Abrecan."

"He needs a blood tie to invade us?" Anne asked. "Something like the body snatchers?"

Evelyn coughed.

Merlin appeared confused. "Body snatchers? I have never heard that expression, but I suppose it would suit Abrecan. For that is what he does. Though, it is more the mind that he snatches, as you say, and not so much the body. I believe he can control the minds of those unrelated to him, but those powers are not as strong, nor as lasting, as when he invades a blood relative."

Anne chose not to explain her twenty-first century choice of words. She carried on. "So Mother is who she says she is?"

Merlin nodded. "As far as we can tell. Yes."

"But we, I mean I will never be completely assured?" It was half question, half statement. Merlin merely shrugged his shoulders. With a deep sigh, Anne spoke with determination, "Then, let us carry on. You have much to explain and you have to help me protect myself, especially when I am asleep."

"Perhaps we should start with protection," Merlin pushed himself off the floor, then reached out a hand to each lady. "You both must be on your guard at all times. First, you must inspect your space and make sure it is safe before speaking."

"Why? Are there hidden cameras in the room?"

"I do not know what a camera is," Merlin continued. "But be assured that Abrecan has the ability to spy on you at all times."

"So, he was probably spying on us while we made sure that you really were Merlin?" Anne was becoming increasingly confused.

"We were quick," Merlin explained. "And I had cast a temporary spell to protect our little circle. Now, I must show you what sort of devices he plants to allow himself to watch over you at all times and kidnap you when you are unaware, like in your dreams."

The wizard approached the hearth. He reached up to one of the stone outcroppings and pointed to a small, rough, elongated, black stone. "Schorl." He didn't touch it, merely indicating where it was, almost unnoticeable as its rough shape and dark color allowed it to blend into the stonework.

Evelyn leaned in closer to look. "I would have thought that was black tourmaline."

"It is. Schorl is the more common name," Merlin explained, allowing his hand to drop. "It is Abrecan's signature. If it is in the room, or anywhere nearby, you can be assured that the evil wizard is watching and listening."

Anne gazed upward, studying the stone. She had never been very good at recognizing one stone from another, but this stone was definitely something she wanted to recognize. "It is not very attractive." Stepping back, she cast a look at Merlin. "I would have thought Abrecan used gold as his medium for spying. Peada's ring was gold, was it not?"

"A rare blend of gold." Merlin nodded in agreement. "It is another of his signature stones. But gold is too obvious. If he wants to be inconspicuous, like in your private chambers, then he will use something that blends in with the surroundings."

"And schorl does blend in," Anne noted.

"Exactly."

"Is he observing us now?"

"No," Merlin shook his head. "I have installed a vision of what he might like to see, to mask what is real. It will not last, however. So, we must learn quickly how to protect ourselves."

"Get rid of the schorl?" Anne asked the obvious. "Throw it into the fire like I did the gold ring?"

"And you learned how well that worked." Merlin stepped away from the hearth and repositioned himself on the floor. The ladies reclaimed their seats and waited. "No. If we remove the schorl, he will merely find something else to replace it. Perhaps it is better to let him assume that we have not discovered his ruse."

"Let him think he has managed to spy without our noticing," Anne added.

"Exactly." Merlin slapped his knees as if he were accentuating his statement. "Now. Listen and learn. Before Abrecan finds a means to break through my spell."

"If Abrecan can break through your spells, Merlin," Anne flashed a look of doubt, "what makes you so sure he cannot break through a spell I cast? That is if I really can cast a spell."

"Oh, you can." Merlin sounded so sure of himself. "You have the power. We are related, my dear queen. You are much more powerful than you realize. More powerful than I am. More powerful than Abrecan. And, with the ring, you will be unstoppable. That is what concerns Abrecan the most. All you need is some training, to learn how to garner your powers and combine them with the powers of the ring."

Anne didn't look convinced. Growing up in the twenty-first century, the idea of magical powers was something she only read about in fantasy novels or saw in movies. This was becoming much too real for her to accept, let alone comprehend. "Very well." She let out a deep sigh. "I am not sure how this will empower me, but I am willing to try anything. At least it might gain me a good night's sleep and the peace of mind that I am safe while I sleep."

"Exactly. A very good place to start." Merlin motioned to the girl. "Join me on the floor. You, too, Evelyn. We shall form a tight circle and begin with some simple protection spells."

Anne wasn't sure how long she sat with her mother and the wizard. The hearth had long since burnt itself out, allowing a cold draft to billow through the hole that allowed the smoke to escape. The stone floor was hard and cold, even with the rushes covering it. And she was stiff and sore from sitting cramped for such a long time. Anne shivered.

"Cast it again," Merlin insisted.

Anne repeated the chant, feeling the warmth of the ring in the palm of her clenched hand.

"Yes. That is it. You have done it."

"Can I sleep, now?" Anne yawned.

Merlin chuckled. "Yes, you may. You, too, Evelyn. I will leave you ladies here. You will be safe in this room until the sun rises. Remember, my Queen. Never remove the ring. And keep Excalibur close and safe. Good night, ladies. I shall leave as I often come."

The wizard vanished.

"How does he do that?" Anne asked, glancing at her mother who appeared even more tired than Anne felt. "I do not know if I can ever get used to all this magic."

"It is no different than the twenty-first century, daughter," Evelyn spoke softly. "Only the magic of the future hides under the veil of science and technology. In this era, magic is real and definitely not hidden."

Chapter Twenty-Seven

Having conjured a protection spell, Anne was relieved to open her eyes to sunlight filtering through the slits in the stone walls. After a long, satisfyingly deep sleep, she felt refreshed for the first time in days. She ran her thumb over the ring, content that it was still secure on her hand. Reaching across the bed coverings, she was relieved to find Excalibur close and safe. Her mother slept on, next to her, snoring softly.

Personal needs forced Anne to leave the comfort of sleep. She slid out from under the coverings, trying to move without disturbing her mother who probably needed the sleep more than Anne had. Just as she finished her necessities, a pounding on the door startled Evelyn awake with a shriek. Anne jumped as well, not just from the pounding, but also from her mother's ear-piercing exclamation.

Recovering, Anne called out, "Who is it?"

"David, my Queen. I have fresh water."

"Just a minute." She breathed a sigh of relief. "Is it all right to let him in, Mother?"

She nodded, yawning sleepily. "Yes, by all means."

Making her way to the door, Anne smiled to herself. David was harmless enough. His obvious devotion made him someone useful to have around. It was always beneficial to nurture the devoted ones, or so Merlin claimed. And he was no blood relation, which was reassuring. If Merlin was right, then David shouldn't be so easy to fix under a spell cast by Abrecan. And if he was as devoted to Anne as she believed him to be, she knew a spell had already been cast: her spell.

She opened the door to find not only David, but Sir Galahad. As David bowed and quietly slipped past with his pails full of fresh water, the valiant knight bowed and offered his apologies. "I do apologize, my Queen. But it is imperative that we speak. There has been trouble at the tree line bordering our lands with that of King Penda. There have been sightings of the king himself. It would appear that Abrecan was indeed successful in reviving the king that you had quite obviously killed. We need to act quickly."

"Yes, of course." Anne was unaccustomed to military protocol and strategic battle plans, but she knew a problem when faced with one. King Penda was definitely a problem. "Have my horse saddled and the men armed and ready to ride. You may fill me in as we make our way to confront this Saxon menace. Give me a few minutes to dress and ready myself. I shall meet you in the courtyard."

"Very good, my Queen." Galahad bowed his head.

"David." Anne stopped the boy before he could make a hasty exit with the slop pails. "Where is Grace?"

"No one knows, my Queen," he half whispered, almost afraid to answer. "She slipped out in the dark last night, before the drawbridge was pulled up. No one has seen her this morning. Nor her mother."

"Not surprising," Evelyn muttered from where she continued to lounge in bed, waiting for David to leave so she could begin her morning ritual and dressing for the day.

Anne chose to ignore her mother's remarks. She hadn't met Grace's mother, so she really couldn't judge for herself, but things didn't look very reassuring. Grace was obviously under their half-brother's spell.

"And the prince? Peada? Is he still locked in the cells?"

"No, my Queen. He was moved to better chambers last night, but he has disappeared, too. It would appear the guards were drugged and he slipped out during the night while they slept. Or, he had help from Grace." The boy shifted uneasily from one foot to the other.

"More likely with Grace's assistance." She patted the boy fondly on the shoulder, causing him to blush a deep crimson. "That will be all, David. Oh!" she stopped him again. "Have someone prepare a quick repast for myself and my mother. Something I can eat while we ride. And make sure Blackie is well groomed and ready."

The boy grinned at the final request. "I have already seen to Blackie, my Queen. She is ready." And he slipped into the shadows of the hallway, carrying his pail with care so that it wouldn't slop all over him and the floor rushes.

"Shall I ride with you, Anne?" Evelyn pushed off the covers as she sat up.

"No. I need you here to make sure things run smoothly in my absence. If I do not return, you may have to send out a rescue party." She coughed back a laugh that gurgled at the back of her throat. "If that is what they call it in this era. I must hurry. You may take your time and enjoy a morning repast."

"Let me at least help you with your hair." Evelyn was standing now.

"There is no time." Anne shook her head.

"Well make time. I will not take long." Evelyn made her daughter sit by the hearth, cold now from the long night of not being attended. She efficiently unbraided the long strands and, picking up the comb from the side table, she proceeded to pull it through the tangled mess. It was a soothing action, one that lulled Anne into complacency. Not for long. Another knock on the door ended the pleasant mother-daughter moment.

"Your army awaits, my Queen," David called out, loud and clear. "And so does Blackie."

Evelyn quickly braided the hair, tying the ends with some ribbon. Anne flashed some water on her face, a quick wash being all the time she could afford. She changed into some fresh robes and, with her mother's help, tied everything securely. Finally, with Excalibur in its sheath, belted around her waist, and her trusty knife tucked away, the girl was ready to ride. Ready to battle, too, if the need arose. And, she was afraid that this really would be a day of battle, a day of considerable bloodshed.

Rushing out into the courtyard, Anne called out orders as David held Blackie while she mounted.

"After we leave, bring in the people from outside the walls. They will be safer in here. Make sure there is lots of food and clean water to care for everyone should there be a lengthy siege."

"The rain barrels are full, my Queen," David mentioned. "We had a good rain last night and Merlin told us to collect as much rainwater as we could."

"Continue to do so," Anne instructed. "And pull up the drawbridge after we leave. Lock everything up tight. I trust you, David, to care for things here and to care for my mother."

The queen wasn't sure, but she sensed the boy standing a little bit straighter at the instructions and veiled compliments. He was now a man. At least in the eyes of his queen. And he had been instructed to take charge.

Mounted, Anne took note of the number of armored men, both mounted and on foot, ready to follow her into battle. As she was about to nudge Blackie forward, a young lad, mounted on a slender bay mare, tucked in front of her, a pole balanced on one foot with a colorful flag flapping in the breeze above his head. Anne chuckled softly at the sight. "I have my own banner," she said to no one in particular. With a bold yellow, almost gold, background, black embroidery work marked the images of three crowns, one on top of the other. Black embroidery also formed a decorative framework around the flag, allowing the intensity of the yellow-gold to blaze with glory in the sunlight.

Merlin heard. "Indeed, you do, my Queen. Your father's flag, the royal standard of King Arthur. And now your royal standard."

"Very impressive," she nodded her approval, her confidence in the mission emboldened by the sight of her own standard.

The boy with the flag led the group, then Anne, who was flanked by Merlin and Sir Galahad, with Sir Roderick mere paces behind, through the castle gates and across the mote. More men fell in step behind the horse soldiers, determined to fight for their queen, the very queen who provided food for their empty bellies. This was a woman they respected, even though it had been such a short time since she had arrived. Carrying all manner of weapons, from mere sticks to rusty knives and makeshift swords, the army grew as they made haste toward the tree line border.

"You have quite the army, my Queen," the wizard remarked. "Knowing you were otherwise occupied, I took it upon myself to set a perimeter of protection around the castle."

"Thank you, Merlin," Anne acknowledged the man. "I do not know if I would have enough power in me to do what you have done. So, I sincerely thank you."

"You have the power, my Queen," Merlin pointed out, allowing his horse to keep pace with Blackie. "As long as you have the ring, Excalibur, the willpower and the strength to believe in yourself, you will be unstoppable. Be sure you have cast your own protection spell."

"I appreciate your vote of confidence. And I have done so." She hadn't, but she wasn't ready to admit to Merlin that she had messed up on her magic. Not yet. She muttered the spell under her breath, clenching the ring tightly between her fist and the horse's reins, before shifting her attention to the rider on the opposite side. "Sir Galahad," she asked, infinitely aware that Merlin was pretending not to notice her gaff. "What is the status? How many hurt or worse? How do we know that the Saxons have invaded the tree line?"

The knight allowed his horse to keep pace with Merlin's, the two enveloping the young queen with their presence and support, ready to protect her at all cost. "I have no reports of injuries, my Queen," he responded with his usual calm confidence. "My scouts returned as soon as they knew the status. A few remained within sight of the advancing Saxons, but safe enough. The greatest concern is what you can see on the horizon." He pointed ahead.

Anne looked and gasped. "What have they done? Set fire to the forest?"

"Exactly that, my Queen," Sir Galahad replied. "With the long dry spell and little more than lightning from last night's storm, the forest was an easy target. They will burn the world if they keep this up."

"Well, our world at the very least," Anne said quietly. "Can we stop it, Merlin? Stop the fire?"

"We could try," Merlin surmised, a tone of hesitation evident in his voice. "But I suspect Abrecan has cast a spell to protect the flames and ensure that they continue to intensify and move forward. Move toward us. He intends, by the looks of it, to burn us out."

"Then we must construct a firebreak," Anne insisted.

"A what?" Galahad queried, obviously confused.

"A firebreak to stop the flames from pushing forward," Anne explained. "We clear a path along its course, removing dry brush and grass from wide strips of land. We use the cleared brush and grass to create our own fire, smaller, but one to stall the kindling of the approaching blaze. It is a controlled burn technique to help guard against fire. When Abrecan's roaring blaze reaches ours, the two will clash and burn each other out. In theory, anyway."

"Interesting concept. A fireguard. It is worth a try," Merlin agreed. "I can create a wall of fire that is cast by my spells, one that will break the flow of the invading flames."

"Good. Then let us get closer and do that." Anne shifted again in the saddle to face the knight. "We should send some men around to the rear of the advancing Saxons and their raging inferno and trap them between us and the flames."

"You do have some strange words to express yourself, my Queen," Galahad responded, "but you may have a valid strategy." He pulled back and called several of his men, issuing instructions to circumnavigate the advancing flames from either end to trap the Saxon's without their knowledge.

"That may work, my Queen," Merlin agreed. "With Abrecan focussing his energies on the fires, he may not even notice or be aware of our plans."

"It may work," Anne admitted. "But such a waste."

Galahad returned to her side. "The men are making their way around the approaching menace. Sir Roderick volunteered to lead one group around to the south."

"Very good," Anne commended his actions. "I have not seen much of Sir Roderick."

"Oh! He has been around," Galahad reassured her. "Keeping up with all the tasks you have set in motion at the castle. It was one of his scouts that first sighted the Saxon approach."

"So, he and his men have been on patrol," Anne surmised, with a brief nod. "Very good." Focussing ahead at the approaching wall of fire, she groaned. "Such a waste of trees and wildlife." She nudged Blackie into a gallop, her banner bearer forced to do the same.

As they neared the blaze, the horses became jittery, reluctant to progress further. Anne reined Blackie in and started giving instructions to the mounted men, who, in turn, instructed the footmen to use whatever they carried to clear the brush and build the firebreak. Anne, accompanied by Merlin and Sir Galahad, rode the length of the construction, monitoring the progress as the heat and smoke of the approaching fire caused them all to struggle for air.

"Look!" several voices called out.

Anne moved Blackie closer to the voices and allowed her eyes to trace the direction of their pointing. Two figures were making their way through the blaze. Mounted, but clearly tied to their mounts, the horses galloped with sheer terror, determined to escape the fiery inferno. The flames chased the mounts, catching their manes and tails ablaze, as well as the mounted figures. As they drew closer, Anne gasped.

"Grace. Peada." She started to rush forward, but Galahad and Merlin both grabbed Blackie's reins, preventing her. She struggled against their resistance, anger flashing in her eyes. "We have to help them. They are my half-siblings."

"It is too late, my Queen," Merlin said sadly. "They are dead. Or, at least very close to death. This is another of Abrecan's ruses to drag you out into the open. To place your life in peril."

"But I have to help them," Anne sobbed, shocked at the carnage. Both horses and riders were smoldering as they crumbled to the ground, mere paces from the firebreak.

"They are beyond help, my Queen," Sir Galahad spoke softly, regret evident in his voice.

"Abrecan is a monster!" Anne wailed. "I can't believe he's family."

"Simply put, he had no further use for the two," Merlin stated with a sharp edge to his voice. He obviously was disgusted with what they were all witnessing. "They had failed him. In his eyes, they were useless. Not to mention, a challenge to his reign."

Anne was startled. "I thought he was not interested in being king." She wrinkled her nose as the smell of burning flesh overpowered the smell of burning timber. As far as she knew, Abrecan was her only remaining half-sibling. How could a hero like her father, King Arthur, have such diabolical children? "This makes me sick."

Pull it together, my Queen. Hold your head high and let the people see a queen they can respect and follow to the very gallows of purgatory.

And I thought I had a way with words. Is there any way to kill a wizard? To kill Abrecan?

Only Excalibur can kill a wizard.

Then I and my trusty sword will kill the beastly wizard and rid this world of his menace once and for all.

Cut off his hands first, my Queen. Then plunge the sword deep into his chest, chanting "Abrecan Abrecan Abrecan. From the fires of hell and to hell you must return."

With a nod, Anne took several deep breaths to steady her thoughts. Pushing back her shoulders, she lifted her head high. She unsheathed Excalibur and raised it, point skyward, well above her head. She was no longer waiting for the firebreak to finish its work. It was time to be aggressive, to meet the enemy head on. "Charge!"

"Charge?" Galahad queried, but his voice and his query was lost in the cacophonic roar of swords being unsheathed, rallying cheers, and horses plundering behind the queen as she raced Blackie toward the firebreak, which they jumped with ease, and through Abrecan's sizzling flames. The knight and the wizard struggled to keep abreast of their queen, but the thick smoke clogged their eyes, reducing visibility. As they breached the flames, they were met with another wall, a human wall of Saxon warriors.

Anne nudged her horse right into the thick of the battle, swinging Excalibur left and right, limbs and heads dropped as she plowed through the melee. She saw the king, Penda, mounted at the point where the tree line had once marked the boundary. Where Penda stood, Abrecan couldn't be far away.

"Okay, Blackie." Without a free hand, she couldn't pat the horse's neck as she would have liked. She tried sending her warm, loving thoughts, and used her voice to reveal her compassion and trust. "We have a job to do, Blackie. Take me to that man. Take me to the king who somehow came back to life."

Blackie didn't need any urging. There was a bond between the horse and her rider. It was as if they thought as one. She charged across the terrain that was quickly becoming littered with fallen bodies and severed body parts.

"Penda!" she yelled as she leaned into her ride. "This time you will die." Her eyes were glued to the target. It hadn't moved.

As she came closer, she observed the eyes. They were blank. This man wasn't alive. It didn't matter. Dead or alive, she would remove his head once again. Raising the sword, she took aim. As Blackie galloped up beside the Saxon king's horse, which also stood still as a statue, Anne swung. Penda's head toppled to the ground before the sword made contact. The ground shook. Blackie started, backing up, away from the mounted, headless king. An eerie laugh crackled through the air, sparkling electrical charges like lightning when it struck a valid target. Anne's eyes darted around, looking for her adversary. When she glanced back at her victim, she watched with horror as both king and rider dissolved into dirt and dust and swivelled to the ash-covered earth.

At that moment, Abrecan stepped out of the shadows of smoke, staff in hand, eyes glowing with an intense ungodly power like nothing Anne had ever seen before. Not even in the worst horror movies of her past in the future.

"Abrecan!" she gathered her wits and snarled. "Today you die!"

"I do not think so, child, half-sister of mine. I believe today is the day you either wed me or you die." He took a couple of menacing steps forward. Slowly. Calculatingly. "Our father bedded his half-sister and so shall I. Together we can and shall rule the world."

Anne chose not to argue. Raising her sword, she took aim on the wizard's right arm, the hand that held the staff. Before he could react, before he even realized what she was thinking, what she already knew, she swung Excalibur, shearing both staff and hand from Abrecan's arm. Blood splattered everywhere. Anne wanted to gag, but knew time was of the essence. Her target stumbled, clearly shocked by her quick and precise action. Before he could retaliate or, worse, vanish, she swung Excalibur again, severing the other hand as it reached to retrieve the staff still clutched in the dismembered right hand.

Feeling the surge of power, she plunged the sword deep into the evil man's chest, ignoring the startled yells of "No!" And, as she twisted and dug the sword deeper, she chanted Merlin's words, "Abrecan Abrecan Abrecan. From the fires of hell and to hell you must return."

The wizard shuddered and shrivelled before her eyes. Like the phantom zombie Saxon king, he dissolved into dust and soot, spreading across the charred earth. As his remains scattered, the land beneath Blackie's feet and all around the mounted queen sprung to life. Great trees, mere charged remains at the firebreak behind her, returned to their full glory, creating a lush canopy that surrounded the girl, an arch of honor fit for a queen.

The remaining Saxon warriors dropped their swords in horror and fell to their knees. Anne's brave warriors sounded a cheer that was echoed from beyond the new forest where Sir Roderick and his men had encircled the invading Saxons. The war was over. For now. Abrecan was dead. For now.

It was time to reclaim the land for her people and to build a new Camelot. To build England.

Chapter Twenty-Eight

"Thank you, Merlin," Anne trotted Blackie back and forth along the tree line, her valiant escorts keeping pace.

"For what?" the wizard asked.

"For bringing this all back to life." Anne waved a hand majestically, sweeping across the wide expanse of forest that had re-grown in mere minutes, erasing the scarred land which the roaring fire had left behind.

"I did not do anything," Merlin objected, allowing his eyes to follow the direction of the queen's hand as it moved in a wide semi-circle. "You did it."

"Me?" Anne shook her head, glancing at the older man. "No." She shook her head more vehemently.

"Yes, my Queen," Merlin nodded his head to counter her shaking head. "It was you and Excalibur and the ring. And the chant that I taught you. Once you obliterated Abrecan from this world, smoldering him into nothing, you allowed the earth to rejuvenate itself."

"But I thought that only a wizard could kill another wizard," Anne continued to shake her head in disbelief.

"A wizard or a witch," Merlin corrected. "Remember Abrecan killed his own mother, who was a witch."

"So, I am a witch?" She glared at the man, not sure if she wanted to be known as a witch.

"A good witch," Merlin chuckled. "It is not a bad thing, my Queen."

They were interrupted by approaching horses. Sir Roderick was leading a group of mounted knights through the new forest. He pulled up short in front of Anne and dipped his head with dignity and honor. Before greeting the knight, Anne muttered to

Merlin, "We shall talk more of this." Refocusing her attention, she called out, "What news have you, Sir Roderick?"

"My Queen. We have routed the Saxons and hold them on the other side of this forest which miraculously re-grew to its designated magnificence." The knight swept a hand that encompassed the thick woods around them. "It was amazing. We had managed to close our snare around the enemy and were pushing them into the wall of fire and the flames vanished. Just as quickly, these trees took root again and here we are. My men and your men are truly amazed, my Queen. The Saxons are quite startled and fearful. We have rounded them up and taken their weapons. They are now our prisoners, awaiting their demise at your command." He ducked his head again.

"We should put them to work," Anne spoke with confidence. "They destroyed this land and the people, they should help rebuild it."

"As slaves, my Queen?" Sir Roderick didn't appear too happy with the idea. "Should we not just kill them all and be done with them for good?"

"If they do not prove themselves worthy of our forgiveness, then that will be the final option. We need men to clear the fields, to plant, to bring in fresh water and build trenches to take away the waste water. Our people are weak and hungry. Make these men pay for the damage they have done. If they prove themselves worthy, we may allow them at some later date to reclaim their freedom."

Reluctance evident in the tone of his voice, the knight bowed his head again and declared, "As you command, my Queen."

"What now, my Queen?" Sir Galahad spoke. "Do we return to Gloucester Castle? Or carry on eradicating the Saxon menace?"

Anne was torn, not knowing whether she should return to Gloucester Castle and reassure her mother and the others that all was well. That the Saxons had been routed for good. Or should she carry on? Move forward into unknown Saxon territory? Claim what was once King Penda's?

Merlin solved her dilemma. "There will be time to visit with your mother later. For now, you must ensure that the Saxons are routed once and for all."

Still torn, she exhaled a sigh of frustration. Would she never have the opportunity to get to know her mother better? It was something she wanted more than anything. But, she was now a queen. She had to consider others before herself.

With a nod, she gave Sir Galahad her answer. "We carry on. Arrange for a messenger to take the news of our victory to the good people of Gloucester."

"As you command, my Queen." Sir Galahad pulled his horse back, turning him around to carry out his orders. Sir Roderick took the other knight's place beside the queen.

"Lead the way, Sir Roderick," she gave the order. Sir Roderick nodded and nudged his mount forward. Anne followed and the group moved deeper into the thickness of the newly grown forest. They rode in companionable silence, single file as the thick overgrowth made the passageways too narrow to navigate otherwise. Breaking through a clearing, they all but stumbled on hundreds of men, crouched on the ground, naked from the waist up. They had no weapons, nothing to defend themselves from the multiple lashes and beatings they were being subjected to as her prisoners.

"Stop!" Anne yelled. "Sir Roderick. Put an end to this violence! Now! I will not have the world view me as a heartless queen, one that beats the downtrodden. I am not like these Saxon warriors who are now our prisoners. I will not lower myself to their level of abuse."

Sir Roderick was startled by the queen's tirade. It took him a few minutes to come to attention, before nudging his horse into the melee and yelling at his men to cease.

The damage was done. Blood soaked the earth and the Saxons' backs were drenched with the red substance that oozed from their veins. They neither yelled nor moaned, merely giving the victors a look of defeat, a frighteningly sad look that pierced Anne's heart. She instantly slid from Blackie's back before anyone could stop her. She approached the first Saxon and bent to offer him comfort, tearing a length of fabric from the bottom of her skirt to tend to his wounds. He merely bowed his head, accepting the fate that awaited.

Looking up at her companions, she all but wept as she said, "These men are starving. How could they fight? Why would they fight for someone who cared naught for their well-being?"

As she used one hand to carefully dab the cloth over the seeping wounds on the man's back, she tucked a finger of the other hand under his chin, pulling the head gently upward so she could look into his eyes. "What is your name?"

The man started to talk but coughed instead. While Anne waited, the coughing subsided. In a crackling voice, one that revealed a dry mouth from lack of water and nourishment, he spoke quietly, with a guttural accent that betrayed his native Saxon tongue. "My name is Aethelric. I am the only surviving son of King Penda."

"Which makes you truly a noble ruler as your name suggests," Anne noted as the man allowed his eyes to meet hers briefly before glancing back at the ground. "You need not fear me, Saxon prince. You may never be a king, but you will live and you have the opportunity to earn my respect." Turning to the others, she called in a loud voice, "Water. This man needs water."

Aethelric shook his head. "My men need water before I do. We are all starving and thirsty."

Anne was able to give the man a knowing smile before his eyes darted away again. "You really are noble, Prince Aethelric." She finished her ministrations and stood up to retrieve her own water bag. She uncorked it and held it to the man's lips. "Your men will be given drink, even if I have to do it myself." Satisfied that Aethelric had been allowed some water, she moved onto the next man that lay, crumbled on the ground, almost in a fetal position. His back was bloodied as well. Anne cared for his wounds and lifted his head so he could drink. And then she moved on.

Merlin joined Anne in her healing, caring administrations. Sir Galahad, having rejoined the queen's procession after carrying out his orders, and Sir Roderick, reluctantly, copied their actions. Others joined in when they saw their queen bent before one Saxon after another.

When her water bag was empty, Anne stood and reached for another. Glancing around, she felt content that others were caring for the Saxon prisoners as well. "This is good," she announced to all who worked around her. "These men may be our prisoners, but, if we want them to work for us, they must be fed, given water and clothed. Without the basic necessities of life, these men are useless."

It was dark when the Saxon prisoners had all been cared for. Anne sought comfort with the others around a warm fire. A caldron boiled over the flames and the men made multiple offerings to what everyone now called the queen's stone soup.

"There is plenty of game in these woods, my Queen." One man stood over the caldron, stirring the pot. "It makes plenty of stone soup for all of us. Including the prisoners."

"That is good," Anne agreed. "What is your name?"

"Ceadda, my Queen. It means…"

Anne finished for him, "Warrior. And you are a fine warrior. Thank you Ceadda for caring for the stone soup."

He bowed his head as he continued to stir the pot.

Chapter Twenty-Nine

Sleeping on the hard, cold ground wasn't Anne's idea of a comfortable rest, especially after the strenuous battle the previous day. But who was she to complain? At least she wasn't tied up like the Saxon prisoners. She was never left alone, regrettably. Part of the rituals of being a ruler, always being watched and protected. Even trying to do her necessary rituals was difficult as either Merlin, Sir Galahad or Sir Roderick followed her into the woods to make sure she was safe.

"You could at least turn the other way," she scolded Sir Roderick who had been the one to tag along this time. The knight continued to unnerve her, especially when he was watching her so intently. "It is not as if I am going to vanish in thin air." Perhaps she shouldn't have said that. After all, stranger things had happened since her arrival into this era. Sir Roderick obliged and once turned allowed Anne the privacy she needed. She finished and was washing her hands and face in the cool spring water of the creek, away from the source where they would acquire drinking water, when a vision appeared as a reflection in the water. It was Abrecan.

"You have not rid yourself of me yet, dear queen." As quick as the vision appeared, it vanished, but not before Anne let out a pained shriek that shattered the air and had Sir Roderick running to her rescue, sword drawn. He found the queen still crouched beside the creek, hands dripping water, body frozen in shock. She hadn't bothered to rise and draw her own sword; the shock had been too great.

"My Queen." The knight touched her lightly on the shoulder. She jumped, letting out another shriek.

"Oh! Sir Roderick!" Jumping to her feet she inadvertently fell into his arms, awkward though it was with one of his arms still clutching the hilt of the sword. He was more than ready to do battle, to slay a dragon in his queen's defense, but this offering of warmth and reassuring comfort was foreign to his fighting nature. He reluctantly allowed his free hand to wrap around her shoulders and pat her back gently.

Sobbing into his shoulder, she muttered, "Why can he not leave me alone? I killed him. He should be dead. Where is Merlin?" She pushed back. "I need to speak to Merlin."

Looking a bit dazed, the knight relinquished his hold on the queen and, taking her hand, led her through the trees back to the camp. Somewhere along the way, their hands separated, but not before Anne cast a sidelong glance at her escort and rewarded him with a smile. "Thank you," she whispered. He merely nodded in response as Anne rushed ahead to find Merlin.

"You saw him?" Anne nodded. Merlin didn't have to look up to see the expression on her face. He didn't have to hear her confession. He knew. "He may be able to invade your dreams. For now. But he cannot come back unless you allow him."

Standing with her arms crossed, as much to ward off the morning chill as to look annoyed at something else Merlin had neglected to tell her. "Why would I want to do that? And how?"

"Why? Because he is your half-sibling after all." Merlin pushed himself off the ground where he had been sitting, contemplating, praying, casting chants, Anne couldn't be sure which.

"So!"

"He will most definitely try to play on your sympathies and try to convince you that he has changed. And that he will help you." Merlin took Anne by the shoulders, giving her a gentle shake. "He is evil, Anne. Always has been and always will be. Do not allow him to convince you otherwise."

She nodded. "But, even if I agreed, the question of 'how' remains unanswered."

"There are ways," Merlin stepped back. "He knows them. Remember, he did bring King Penda back from the dead. I have chosen not to learn them as I do not agree with bringing back the dead. But I do know of these ways. Evil. Pure evil!"

"He would teach me that?" She raised an eyebrow to emphasize her question. "In my dreams?"

"He would."

"So, how do I keep him from my dreams?"

"Use the chants I taught you and your mother the other night. It worked once; it should work again."

"And if it does not?"

He left that question unanswered. Just as well. Anne's attention was being drawn away. To the Saxon prince she had assisted the previous day. Prince Aethelric. He was forcing himself toward the queen, in spite of his bindings. Sir Roderick, Sir Galahad and several other knights tried to restrain him, but he shrugged them off.

"Let him approach," Anne commanded. "Prince Aethelric. You wish to speak to me?"

"My Queen," he bowed his head. "I would like to request that I accompany you when you venture into our castle, Tamworth Castle. You have shown compassion to me and my people on the battlefield. I would hope you would show equal compassion when you witness firsthand the sorry state of affairs of our women and children. It is worse than what you have seen here."

"My Queen." It was Ceadda who spoke up. "We need the Saxons to restore the lands between the forest and Gloucester Castle. If we do not get the crops in soon, we will have another year of bad crops and winter starvation."

"He is right," Sir Roderick agreed.

"But surely there are enough Saxons here to tend to both the fields and Tamworth Castle," Anne argued. She was not angry at Ceadda for speaking up. She wanted to hear the opinions of her people. "You do well, Ceadda, to advise me of the situation, but I think we can come to a compromise. Do you not agree?"

"If I might suggest, my Queen." The Saxon prince was struggling to be extra courteous to his captor queen. Anne nodded for him to continue. "I could choose a handful of men to come with me and help at Tamworth. The rest will follow your men here to work in the fields around Gloucester."

Pausing to add emphasis to her words, she was quickly becoming an efficient stateswoman, Anne tapped a finger thoughtfully on her chin. "I agree with Prince Aethelric. Give them mounts. Not theirs, ours. We do not want them on horses familiar with their riders. Tie them securely and attach a lead rope to each horse." She held up her hand to ward off the protest she knew was eminent. "We can move faster on horseback. If we have to lead a string of prisoners on foot, it will take a fortnight to reach Tamworth." She allowed her eyes to travel across the faces of the men before her. "Sir Galahad and Merlin will accompany me. You, too, Sir Roderick. Ceadda, I need you to supervise the men going west to clear the land."

The men nodded in unison, and murmured their agreement, "Yes, my Queen." Anne couldn't tell if their accord was genuine or forced, but it didn't matter. She was in charge and she had to demonstrate her ability to make decisions and to follow them through.

"Prepare the horses. We ride within the hour."

"Yes, my Queen." The men made way to do as instructed. All except Merlin who chose to remain close to Anne.

Ceadda moved forward swiftly and grabbed Aethelric roughly on the shoulder. "Let us go, Prince," he all but spat. "You have had your say, now leave the queen alone."

Shrugging the hand off his shoulder, Aethelric stood tall and proud, lifting his head with dignity. "Thank you, my Queen." He ducked his head and backed slowly away before turning and following Ceadda to collect some men in preparation for the journey.

Chapter Thirty

The camp, a hive of activity when Anne returned from the creek, was all business as people prepared to move out. The cacophony of voices and horses, yelling and snorting, crackled the air with urgency. There wasn't much to gather up as Anne's men only had their mounts (those that had one) and their weapons. The Saxons had nothing but themselves. The fires were carefully doused and stamped to oblivion, making sure nothing was left behind to smolder and cause a reoccurrence of the previous day's destructive fire.

Hardly registering the scene around her, Anne wandered amongst the activity, Merlin beside her, his staff diligently keeping a steady rhythm that matched their pace. They didn't talk. Too many ears. They could mind talk, but Anne's head was in such a jumble, even that option didn't seem plausible. Talking would come later. At least, Anne hoped it would. She had so many questions. She always did these days, it would seem. A young boy led Blackie toward the queen and Merlin helped her mount. He mounted his own horse, adjusted his staff and followed Anne as she moved away from the camp noise. Not too far. Enough that they could talk without yelling and without others listening in.

"Why, Merlin?" It was the all-inclusive question that plagued Anne's mind. "Why?"

"Why what, my Queen?" the wizard answered with gentle patience. He understood Anne was plagued with questions, but this all-inclusive 'why' didn't help him ascertain which 'why' she was addressing at the moment.

"Why all this? What is the purpose? Why does he want to control all of this? Why now? Why me?"

"Too many why's." The two rode in silence, circumnavigating the camp while the others mounted and finished their preparations to depart. The young queen was fuming with questions, mostly unanswered. "One can and will never understand the greed of man, the desire to control all. Magic, my magic, your magic, is a gift, not something to be trifled with. It should be used for the good of all men." Noticing the sharp sideways glance from his queen, he quickly added, "And women."

"What do I do, Merlin? Is he really dead?" Her question was met with silence. "His necromancy power is obvious. But can he really bring himself back from the dead?"

Their question and answer period was cut short as the others approached. The queen's standard was raised and the boy who proudly bore it once again took the lead. Anne and Merlin, with Sir Roderick mere paces behind, fell in behind the standard bearer. The men assigned to her guard fell in behind, many hanging onto ropes that controlled the horses bearing the Saxon prisoners. They marched through the forest at a steady pace, but, once they cleared the tree line, they urged their horses into a trot. Even so, it was no more than a gentle trot, allowing the queen to pursue her conversation, and her questions of course, with Merlin. Everyone else was busy with their assigned tasks of containing the prisoners and watching for traps and ambushes along the way.

"There is so much that does not make any sense, Merlin," Anne pondered aloud. "If he has this much power, why not wipe us all out with a sweep of his staff. He could do it, could he not?"

"Yes, he could," Merlin agreed. "But I suspect Abrecan lives on the drama he creates. He enjoys making a scene. He enjoys watching his power unfold and control others."

"All the world is a stage," Anne paraphrased a fine line from Shakespeare, one that wouldn't be scribed for centuries. "And we are all mere actors on the stage of life."

"Very true, my Queen," Merlin readily agreed.

Anne suddenly pulled Blackie up short with a gasp as a horrid thought invaded her brain. Merlin reached across and took the reins in his hand, making Blackie continue to move forward. "You have an army behind you, my Queen," he scolded her gently. "Do not stop short without warning."

Chastised, but not silenced, she spoke her thoughts out loud. "What if he's mastered the science of cloning? What if he's still alive, in the twenty-first century? What if the Abrecan I killed was his clone? Or one of his clones? What if my own mother is a clone, controlled by Abrecan? What if all of these men and women are clones?"

"I cannot answer questions, my Queen," Merlin was stumbling over his words, "when I am not sure what you are asking. I do not understand this term, cloning. What is a clone? And you also mentioned necromancy. What is that?"

Anne chuckled softly, not because she found anything funny, but because she was, once again, using her knowledge from the future to apply to things in the sixth century that hadn't happened. Yet. She still had a lot to learn about the comprehensive English language of the sixth century. Cloning hadn't been developed until well into the twentieth century. At least, the cloning that she understood, the creating of an identical living creature. Perhaps it did exist earlier. In the form of magic, of course. And necromancy? Well, that went back to ancient times, but it was merely known as magic in many cultures.

Taking a deep breath to bide her time, she started an explanation, hoping she was being as simple as possible. "Terms from the future, in a way, Merlin. Although, I am sure both have been around since the beginning of time. Necromancy is the magical ability to not only talk to the dead, but to bring them back to life. You may know it as nigromantīa or nekromanteía."

"Black magic," Merlin finished for her. "I understand black, or dark magic. It is evil. Ungodly. We know that Abrecan was evil and ungodly to the core. Go on. Explain cloning."

"Some living creatures, both plant and animal, have the ability to recreate themselves without having…" she coughed, unsure of whether or not to say the 's' word.

Merlin said it for her. "Sex."

She cleared her throat again, pivoting her head away from Merlin so he couldn't see the blush that was creeping up her neck and across her face. "Yes. Basically, that is cloning. Creating an identical being from fragments of the original."

"Like using some of a creature's skin or hair to create a duplicate?" Merlin queried. His voice revealed a depth of comprehension and interest. It was the scientist within the magician. "Another form of necromancy, I suppose. But what would someone do with duplicates? Would that not become confusing, even for the original creature, to ascertain which one was which? If that is what Abrecan has done, cloned himself, then how many Abrecans are out there? How powerful are they?"

"Now who is asking all the questions?" Anne laughed, the tension released and the unease of embarrassment drained away with efficiency.

"You may have something in your assumptions, my Queen," Merlin said thoughtfully. "We shall have to be extra cautious. It may well be that the Abrecan you killed was merely a clone, as you call it."

"Perhaps we will know more once we reach Tamworth Castle. Perhaps we will learn more about this monster wizard."

"You believe he has his power center at Tamworth?" Anne could feel Merlin's eyes studying her intently.

"Where else? And there is probably a door there to a more sophisticated laboratory in the future. Probably the Grenadier Falls facility where he held my mother and I captive."

"Laboratory?"

"A place to do experiments and to study things scientifically. Or what you would call, magically. Your caves are your laboratories."

Merlin nodded his head, pensively. "And Grenadier Falls?"

"A community in the future where experiments were performed on people's brains. Very archaic, even for the future."

"You have the key?" It was more of a question than a statement.

"Always." She patted her chest, feeling for assurance that it remained where it had always been.

Merlin merely nodded. After a moment's silence, he muttered under his breath, "There may be doors, to many places unknown. But will your key work? And will the passage be a safe one?"

"We may never know, Merlin," Anne whispered loud enough for his ears alone. "It may be a chance we have to take."

"Or we could return to Gloucester and use the door we know is safe," Merlin pointed out.

"But how safe is Gloucester if we do not know whether or not we can trust Mother? She may be a clone, Merlin. Her mind may appear to be unscathed, but she may be totally under Abrecan's control."

Merlin didn't answer. His silence reflected his doubt. He wanted to believe that Anne's mother was the woman he obviously loved. But was she?

"And you, too, for that matter," Anne interjected into the pregnant silence. "How do I know you are the genuine Merlin?"

"We went through all that the day before last, my Queen. I proved myself."

"But could not a clone, a duplicate of you, have the same ability to extract Excalibur from the stone?" She was on a roll. Argumentative. Unsure of what was real and what wasn't.

"At some point, Anne." He reverted to the more personal address, his whisper emanating a coarseness that revealed his frustration over her ongoing doubts. "At some point," he repeated, "you have to trust."

"But when, Merlin? How?"

Chapter Thirty-One

They came upon a wide stream intersecting the path. Anne pulled up Blackie and dropped the reins, allowing her to drink. Shifting in her saddle, she addressed the Saxon prince, "How much further, Prince Aethelric?" He was close behind. How much had he heard? Was he real or cloned?

Sir Roderick, who was holding the lead to Aethelric's horse, loosened his grip to allow the prince to move closer to Anne. "You really should drop the 'prince', my Queen. For, in my present situation, I am no more than your prisoner."

"Very well, then, Aethelric. How much further?"

"Just over the rise you see ahead," he nodded beyond the stream. Taking a deep breath, possibly to bolster his courage, he added, "I could not help but hear what you said about Abrecan. He does have some sort of space in the castle where he does things. To people. Where he brought my father back to life. Sort of. He was never the same after he was resurrected. Void. Empty. And there is more than one Abrecan. I have seen at least three together in one room. Which one is the real Abrecan? I have no way of knowing. It is pure evil. Frighteningly so. But there was nothing I or any of my Saxon brothers could do, as he appeared to have control over all of us. Most of the time."

Merlin grunted. "Trust the evil wizard to have more tricks and powers than he deserves." He sounded genuine. At least to Anne, he did. But was he? Or was this part of the ploy to make Anne trust him? Merlin had his own magic. Surely, he would have the powers to block Abrecan invading Merlin to create a Merlin clone.

Anne nudged Blackie into the stream, the banner bearer taking his cue and splashing on ahead. It was a soothing sound, listening to the multiple hooves splashing through the water. Refreshing, too, as the water washed away some of the weariness from both horse and rider.

"Was there at least one who remained when you left for battle?" Anne asked Aethelric.

"At least."

"And were there more copies of your father? Or duplicates of anyone else, for that matter?"

Aethelric shifted uneasily in his seat, obviously uncomfortable with having his hands tied while riding and allowing another to lead his horse. His unease indicated more disturbing revelations. "There are many more of all of us, my Queen," he half spoke, half whispered. "Even me."

"How do I know who is the original?" Anne shook her head in disbelief. "Each of the clones will claim they are the original."

"Does it matter?" Merlin asked. "As long as one is trustworthy enough and unaffected by Abrecan's brain control, then we can allow one to live."

"And keep that one as the original," Anne supplemented. "Perhaps, Merlin. But, if what Aethelric says is true, we could be marching into a well-planned ambush, with who knows how many fighting men waiting to surround us."

Merlin pulled up short, reaching over and tugging at Anne's reins. "Then, my Queen. We cannot go into the castle until we know it is safe and secure."

"But my people," Aethelric argued. "They are all starving. My wife and children are in there. Starving."

Struggling with her emotions, an urge to charge in and save the dying Saxon women and children, Anne called out, in as booming a voice as she could muster, "Halt!"

The banner bearer had almost reached the rise in the land, the one separating them from their destination, Tamworth Castle.

Still clutching the reins of Aethelric's horse, Sir Roderick muttered, a little louder than he had planned, "We should have allowed the men to kill every Saxon when we had the chance."

Anne heard. "You may be right, Sir Roderick. But it is too late to live on what we could have done in the past. We must access the current situation and move forward, with a well-planned strategy."

"One not even Abrecan could possibly predict and prepare to prevent," Merlin added.

"We must shield ourselves, Merlin." Turning to the wizard, Anne added with urgency. "He knows we are coming. He knows we are close. We need a shield around us, so he does not listen to our plans. We need a shield now."

Merlin didn't need further urging. Nudging his horse into a trot, then a canter, he progressed around the long stream of followers, chanting vigorously as he moved. He rounded the men into a tight circle as he made his progression around them, not once, not twice, but thrice.

When Merlin finished the third lap, he pulled up next to Anne, who had moved into a circle of her men, the prisoners at the outer perimeter. "Safe, Merlin?" she asked, keeping her voice low, for Merlin's ears alone. She didn't dare mind-speak as she wasn't sure if Abrecan could tap in and listen.

Merlin nodded. "Guard your thoughts as best you can and speak in a very soft voice."

Returning Merlin's nod with one of her own, Anne, suggested in a muted voice, "Can you create a door here, Merlin? Is it possible? Can we take all our men into the castle through that door? Or, can we invade the facility in the future and take down Abrecan at what must be his home base?"

"Not everyone can transverse through the door, my Queen," Merlin answered. "But your idea of confronting the monster in the future might be a good strategy."

"So, you could create a door, a passageway to the future?"

"It is possible."

Reaching over to pat Blackie, more for distraction than anything else, Anne continued, "We could send the men to the castle while you and I," she waved a hand randomly around her, "and whomever else you believe might be able to accompany us, visit Abrecan at the Grenadier Falls facility in the future. I wonder what would happen if we made the clones jealous of each other. Certainly an Abrecan duplicate would have as much ego as the original and each clone would not take kindly to the idea that one of the other clones was superior to him."

"A battle from within." Merlin nodded his approval. "It might just work." Glancing around the gathering, the wizard shuffled in the saddle restlessly. "The protective barrier weakens. Guard your thoughts. Command Sir Galahad to lead the men toward Tamworth. Keep the royal banner at the head of the procession and the castle dwellers will believe that you are amongst the approaching invaders."

Anne nodded. "And Sir Roderick?"

"He and two of his men, well armed, will accompany us. Tell him to choose wisely. There is a cave nearby to hide the horses and for me to create the doorway."

Turning toward her two valiant knights, she gave the orders. Sir Galahad didn't look too happy about leaving the queen in the other knight's care, but he took his orders gallantly, calling the remainder of the king's men, along with the prisoners, to follow the royal banner. It was a ploy to make the target think the queen approached. As they made their way toward the Saxon castle, Aethelric glanced back, several times.

"He is a suspicious one," Merlin muttered.

"I did warn you about trusting the Saxons," Sir Roderick grumbled under his breath. He had chosen two of his most valiant men, whom he introduced: Godwin and Wodan. They appeared strong, sturdy and, if Sir Roderick believed them to be trustworthy, then they must be that as well.

"Shall we, my Queen? Valiant knights at arms?" Merlin glanced at the small gathering. "Our Saxon spies are beyond the line of sight. They will not see whence we go. But we must move quickly. I, and our queen, must have your assurances that whatever happens from hence will be kept between ourselves. It is a magic more powerful than anything you have ever seen before. There is no time for questions. Clear?" The men nodded, slapped fisted right hands against their chest and ducked their heads in acknowledgement.

Chapter Thirty-Two

Merlin continued his instructions. "Your task is to follow the queen's orders and mine, without question, and to keep us all safe. Do not take matters into your own hands. Do not make your own decisions. You are the royal guard. Act as such." This time he didn't wait for a response, nudging his horse into a fast gallop, south toward the tree line that marked a ridge of hills with steep slopes. Anne followed close behind, knowing the wizard knew this land better than anyone else. If he said there was a cave, a safe one, within the rolling hills ahead, then who was she to argue. She had never been to England, not even in the future.

As they reached the base of the first hill, Merlin pulled his horse to a slow, gentle trot, and, finally, a brisk walk. The others copied. The footing became more difficult as the horses trudged up one mound after another, each one progressively steeper than the previous. No one talked, each focussing on the treacherous terrain, the men glancing behind and around for any rogue Saxons. Anne and Merlin were intent on their destination secure in the knowledge Sir Roderick's men were vigilant in their task.

After one particularly steep climb, they reached a slight plateau, a flattened path which hugged the edge. It was a sharp drop on one side and an equally onerous rise on the other. They rode single file, now, the horses hugging the side of the path furthest from the drop, the riders feeling the sharp rise brush against their legs.

Merlin stopped abruptly and dismounted. "Here," he pointed to a thick grove of lush green shrubs. Dropping his horse's reins, he started pulling away the shrubbery. The others dismounted and left the horses to graze while they assisted the wizard. They uncovered an opening and Merlin held up his hand indicating they should remain outside while he surveyed the interior. Staff in hand, he all but slithered through the opening. A few minutes later, he returned and motioned them inside.

"Tether the horses here." He pointed to the large area mere steps within. "Bring them water and nourishment to keep them satisfied while we are elsewhere."

"Can we not take the horses?" Sir Roderick asked. "They would certainly assist in a quick retreat."

"Where we are going, Sir Roderick," Merlin explained in a quiet, but firm voice, "there will be no retreat. We either defeat the monster Abrecan, or die trying. Horses will be of no use. As you will soon find out."

The men busied themselves settling the horses into their makeshift stable. Merlin told them to pull the shrubbery back over the opening to camouflage their cave entrance. Meanwhile, he waved the staff in an all-encompassing motion, twirling it around in the space around the opening. As he did this, he muttered the words of a spell, presumably to seal their secret cave from prying eyes. Tasks completed, he led them further into the cave where he began preparing for their exit to the future.

"You have been here before, have you not, Merlin?" Anne asked. "This is one of your many caves." Merlin merely nodded and continued with the preparations.

Anne and the knights watched, awestruck. No one moved. No one spoke. The spell being cast was intense. The wizard's staff sparkled with light and electrified energy. Overpowering. Even the air crackled with its energy and power.

Finally, Merlin nodded. "We are ready." Pointing to the far wall, he instructed. "Place your ring hand on the wall, my Queen."

Slowly, Anne took one step forward. Then another. She paused when she stood next to Merlin. Glancing into his eyes, she noticed the intensity of the worry she felt mirrored behind a glaze of complacency. "Merlin," she whispered, loud enough for his ears only. She didn't finish. Choosing to mind speak, *What if I am a clone as well?*

Not possible. Merlin's voice, even in her head, sounded so sure. *Your ring would, could never allow such a thing to happen.*

But all Abrecan would need is a stray hair, left behind somewhere I slept.

Still not possible. Believe in the magic, Anne. Believe in your magic.

With a reluctant nod of acceptance, she continued to the far wall as instructed and placed her hand on it. The ring vibrated with energy. The wall grew warm and shuddered, almost with excitement, if it were possible for such an inert thing as a rock wall. Sir Roderick told her later, much later, that her entire body glowed, emanating a bright light from deep within and the wall shone equally bright. Then the wall vanished, replaced by a passage through which Anne and the others saw bright lights, reflecting off shiny surfaces and a hallway leading to no visible vanishing point. Grenadier Falls. More precisely, the Rideau Regional Psychiatric Hospital in Grenadier Falls. The horrors of her nightmare returned unbeckoned.

Merlin. The voice within her head quivered. *Why here?*

I traced Abrecan's whereabouts. Do not question how. I just know he is here. Magic.

She nodded. Understanding, but reluctant nevertheless. This was one place she never wanted to revisit. *I thought your doors led to one place and one place only.* She was delaying the inevitable, grasping for more information. She had thought they'd end up on the thirteenth floor of the Royal York Hotel in Toronto, the place where she had escaped into the sixth century, and then make the journey to the Grenadier Falls facility. Instead they landed right on target. Had it only been days since she first stepped through the portal into the sixth century? It felt like months. Years, in fact.

I have the means to adjust the access points. We do not have time to take detours. Better to take the direct approach before Abrecan realizes our tactics. Sir Galahad should be reaching Tamworth Castle by now. He will surround it, as I instructed him to do, and set fire to it, burning all within.

"No!" Anne stepped back from the portal, pivoting to glare directly at Merlin. "No!" she repeated. "What about all the innocents? The women and children?"

"Aethelric will be instructed to help as many women and children escape as possible. It is the only way, my Queen. We must destroy Abrecan and his power sources. Tamworth is obviously his main portal in the sixth century and this one we are about to enter is his place of operation in the twenty-first century. We must go, my Queen. We must stop what has already been started. Before it is too late and there is no way to prevent his ever-growing power to take over the world. If we fail here, then all the lives lost today will be for nothing."

Anne wasn't too happy. She hadn't realized Merlin would take matters into his own hands and issue orders without her consent and approval. However, she realized the urgency of the situation. It was now or never. Sir Roderick and his men were shuffling their feet nervously at the arch connecting the make-shift stable to this room with the now open portal to the future. They were nervous. Fighting men though they were, fear etched across their faces. They would follow her. She knew it. But with fear and reluctance, the unknown more frightening than anything they had ever before faced on the battlefield.

She nodded at Merlin. "Time to erase Abrecan. All of them." She took one step into the doorway and paused abruptly. "Protection spell cast, Merlin?" she glanced over her shoulder.

"Cast yours as well, my Queen. We may need all the protection we can muster. And valiant knights," he made a sweeping gesture toward Sir Roderick and his men and made them glow with the energy projected from his staff. "Keep close to the queen," he issued orders, "and myself at all times. We must remain together. As a group, we stand a fighting chance of being victorious. Keep a hand on the hilt of your sword ready, but do not draw until you hear our command. And, most important, do not look into Abrecan's eyes. For in that one look, he will take over your mind and control your actions." Without further instructions, he stepped up behind Anne and the two led Sir Roderick and his men through the portal into the asylum of the future. Had Abrecan sensed their presence? Was he reinforcing his defenses as they stepped into his domain? Only time would tell.

Chapter Thirty-Three

With everyone through, Merlin pointed his staff at the portal and it vanished. "Lead on, my Queen. You have been here before. You must know the way."

It was a moment to panic, but she flushed it down with a big gulp, merely nodding in response. She had only been here once and in a dream. Or had it been a dream? She was continuing to question what was real. The place, as she knew it from her studies of such facilities (and yes, Granny had insisted she study everything there was to learn about such facilities; now she knew why, but how had Granny known?), was huge: several floors and multiple long rows of corridors leading past locked doors behind which voices in distress and wails of despair cast an eerie aura, shattering off the pristine walls, well lit ceilings and shiny clean floors.

Merlin told her to lead, so lead she did. Away from the portal, or at least where it had been. Down the long hall they walked, passing one intersecting corridor after another. Her footsteps were muffled as she wore only soft slippers, suitable for a lady of the sixth century. The men's feet clomped behind her, echoing and ricocheting against the floor, walls and ceiling, rattling the windows in the doors they passed. The armor clattered and clanked as well. If their presence hadn't been forewarned, it was hard to miss now with all the noise they were making.

The men were uneasy. Anne heard their whispered queries.

"What is this place?"

"Why is it so bright?"

"And without windows to let in light?"

"Or wall sconces lit with flaming torches?"

"And so quiet."

"Except for your stomping." One knight chided another.

"And yours, too."

"Very eerie."

"Silence, men," Sir Roderick scolded them, forcing his voice low.

They arrived at the end of the hall. There was a door. A light illuminated overhead, marking four letters, "Exit". Anne pushed the door and walked through. It was a staircase. Leading down.

"This must be the top floor," she muttered to herself. There was only one way to go. Down. The group tromped down the stairs to the next landing. There were more stairs descending further, but Anne chose to open the door. The halls beyond appeared the same as the ones above. She waved everyone forward and they marched down the hall.

"We will search this floor before proceeding to the next floor down," she whispered over her shoulder, barely loud enough for the others to hear. They reached the opposite end, their passage blocked by another door. This one didn't have the words 'Exit' illuminated above the door. Instead, a name on the window was highlighted from the glow of the lights beyond: Dr. Abrecan, Chief Psychiatrist.

They had arrived.

"What is a psychiatrist?" Merlin whispered in her ear.

"A magician of sorts who studies the human mind." Taking a deep breath to bolster her courage, she rotated the knob and pushed the door inwards.

"Ah! Anne!" Abrecan stood behind his desk as he had the first time she was in this room. "Or should I say, my Queen?" Looking beyond her, he added, "And Merlin, Sir Roderick and noble knights. To what do I owe this honor?" He certainly didn't appear unnerved by their sudden appearance.

"How many are there?" Anne snapped. "How many of you? And how many others have you cloned?"

Abrecan laughed. It was evil, bone-chilling and cold. Anne clenched her hand around the ring, willing the warmth of its power to sooth and protect her.

"More than you can count." Abrecan puffed his chest with pride. "At least a dozen at Tamworth."

"The one I killed?"

"Another clone."

"How many elsewhere? How many here?"

"Let me see." He tapped his chin thoughtfully, grinning with satisfaction at having the attention he obviously craved. "No others in the sixth century. I have lost count of how many I have here. Would you like to meet them?"

"And who else have you cloned?"

"Never fear, my Queen. I have been unsuccessful in cloning you. Something to do with your ring, I suppose. May I see it?" He gazed eagerly at the girl's clenched hand.

She tightened her grip, tucking it under the folds of her robe in an attempt to conceal it, and stated with firm conviction, "No!"

He merely shrugged his shoulders. "Well, then. Since you are here. All of you. Let us go and meet the others. Shall we?"

"And how do I know you are the original Abrecan?"

"You do not know, my Queen. But trust me, I am the original." He chuckled, "Or at least, I think I am."

Abrecan walked around his desk and elbowed his way past Anne and her protectors. As he reached the door, she muttered, "You, Abrecan? Any of you Abrecans. I will never trust."

The evil wizard paused briefly, then reached for the knob and pulled open the door. "This way," he declared, marching forward. He slapped the palm of his hand on the wall next to his door and all the doors along the hall cranked open. "Abrecan. Abrecan. Come out, Abrecan." His proclamation sounded more like a chant than a command. It had a similar effect. Within minutes the shadow of each doorway was blocked by a figure of a man, all duplicates of Abrecan.

One of the knights gasped. "There must be hundreds of them!"

"Two hundred and fifty to date," the Abrecan from the office voiced with pride evident in his eloquent articulation of each word. "Minus the one already eliminated by our illustrious queen in the sixth century." He pushed back his shoulders and marched down the line of Abrecan look-alikes, or clones, each one standing brightly at attention awaiting the next command.

"But which one is the real Abrecan?" Anne called out in a commanding voice. "Which one is the original?"

"I am," the Abrecan army responded in unison.

The Abrecan from the office laughed heartily. "You see?" Halfway down the hall, he pivoted on his heels. He glanced back at the eerie reflections of himself. "We are all originals."

"That is not possible," Merlin finally spoke with his usual authoritative voice. "Only one can be an original. No magic in this world or the next is powerful enough to make these many originals out of one real original."

"Oh, Merlin. Your sense of magic is so, how can I say it?" he waved his hands in front of his face as if twirling a wand to cast a spell. "Shallow."

"Do not look," Merlin muttered the reminder under his breath, as a wave of magic projected toward them. "Close your eyes if you must, but do not look."

Abrecan from the office laughed heartily, yet again, and dropped his hands. "You are pathetic, Merlin. Pathetic."

"I may not understand your terminology," Merlin began, but Abrecan interrupted him before he could finish his thought.

"I merely mean that you are quite old-fashioned and a little backward in your thinking," the evil wizard explained.

Merlin shrugged, muttered something under his breath, presumably another spell, and continued, "You may perceive me as backward, old-fashioned, but at least I know my place in this world and I do not abuse my magical powers to my own evil gains."

The Abrecan from the office merely shrugged his shoulders, brushing off Merlin's perspective as inconsequential. The Abrecans lining the hall shrugged their shoulders in unison, in cue with their original, whichever one it was.

With a deep breath, Anne moved toward the nearest Abrecan, and addressed him, "What is your name?"

"Abrecan." The reply was curt, abrupt.

"Are you a wizard?"

"Yes."

"Are you the original?"

"Yes."

"Then who is he?" and she pointed to the one who continued to stand halfway down the hall, observing her with keen interest.

She didn't wait for an answer. She moved to the next Abrecan and asked the same questions, receiving the same answers. When she heard the answer to the last question, she stomped her foot and yelled, "No you are not. You are not the original." She pointed the index finger of her left hand in the man's chest, her right hand, still clenching the ring, was wrapped around the hilt of Excalibur. Ready. Waiting.

She returned to the first Abrecan and poked her finger in his chest, as she had for the other. "You are not the original either."

"I am," the two Abrecans argued back, neither one flinching at her prodding, or batting an eyelid at her proclamation.

"NO, YOU ARE NOT!" She yelled and she proceeded to walk down the hall, poking one Abrecan's chest after another. "And neither are you."

They continued to argue, each one in turn as she challenged them. The volume of voices intensified until they could barely hear the queen as she issued her challenges. The Abrecan from the office held up his hands in a motion of dismay, or casting a spell, it was difficult to tell which, and yelled, "QUIET!"

Everyone heard his voice, but the foray of arguments intensified all the more.

Finally, Anne stopped in front of a clone halfway down the hall. "If you are the original Abrecan," she dared, "prove it." She waved her left hand in a sweeping motion to all the other clones. "Command these clones to do your bidding. Make them bow down to you." And she accentuated her words with a repetitive stabbing in the man's chest.

"And you," she left this Abrecan and moved onto the next. "You stake your claim as well. Prove it."

Before the Abrecan from the office could take action, or even realize what Anne was about, the clones broke rank and began brawling amongst themselves. The ones closest to the Abrecan from the office descended upon the real original, if that's what he was.

Anne stepped back as the all-out brawl became violent. One Abrecan after another fell to the ground, knocked out and trampled upon.

Standing next to Merlin again, Anne unsheathed Excalibur, calling to her men, "To arms. Attack." She held up her sword, allowing the energy to spark from tip to hilt and along her arm, igniting her feeling of power. Of control. As Sir Roderick and his men unsheathed their weapons and began the task of beheading one Abrecan after another, she heard Merlin chanting next to her, his energy glowing more powerful than hers.

"The doors to this floor are sealed. There is no escape. And Abrecan, which the original one from the office may or may not be, is too immersed in self defense to be able to render an effective spell to protect himself."

"You hope," Anne muttered under her breath. Spells and incantations, magic at its best, had served her well so far. At least to a point. There was always the unexpected incident potentially marring the magic's effectiveness. She could only hope what they were doing here, at this moment in time, present and past, would eradicate all worlds from Abrecan's unholy magic. But, then again, history did have a way of creating one evil monster after another. So, perhaps ridding themselves of Abrecan was inconsequential in the grand scheme of things.

Sword raised, she plowed down the center of the hall, Merlin close behind. Her target was the Abrecan from the office, the one now totally surrounded by his creations, his clones. They were beating him with such force and intensity that the wizard could barely raise his hands to deflect the blows, let alone cast a spell. Once she felt close enough, she brought Excalibur down in a swirling motion, removing a couple of Abrecan heads in the process, stopping only when the point of the sword was in direct line with the heart of the now prone Abrecan.

"No!" he shrieked, holding his hands higher to shield the blow that he knew would inevitably come. "You will never stop the others without me. There are more. Lots more. I have cloned everyone." As his body crumpled into a heap on the floor, he said, "Except you and Merlin. The only two I could not clone."

"Because we are too powerful for you," Merlin spoke pointedly. "For a backward, old-fashioned wizard, that is."

With a snort, Anne waited no longer. She allowed her mind to direct its energies through the sword, projecting from its tip with an electrical force more powerful than the worst lightning strike of summer. The prone figure of the Abrecan from the office sizzled before her eyes, his pathetic shrieks of "No!" reverberating up and down the hall.

While Anne maintained the surge of energy, the figure sizzled to ashes, the 'no's' fading into oblivion, until the only sound was the repetitive thuds of heads tumbling onto the floor followed by headless bodies. It was a bloodbath, but a job that had to be completed. Who knew if she had successfully eliminated the original Abrecan? She had to eliminate them all to cover her bases, to ensure his extinction.

"He is dead. Save the rest of your powers. We must move quickly, my Queen." Merlin nudged her elbow. "The other floors must have clones as well. We must eliminate them all. And then return to the sixth century to ensure that Sir Galahad has been successful with his task."

"And my mother?" she glanced at the older man.

"We may never be sure," Merlin sighed deeply, his own emotions barely in check. "We can only hope that we choose the right one to keep alive. If we allow any of them to live."

Sniffling ever so slightly, Anne muttered softly, "I do not know if I have it in me to kill my mother. Neither the original nor the clones."

Chapter Thirty-Four

As they approached the door to the stairwell at the opposite end of the hall, Merlin chanted loudly, holding Anne back until he had finished the chant. "The spell has been released. Let us check out the rest of the facility." Merlin pulled the door open and motioned Sir Roderick and his men to proceed. Anne remained behind. "Incinerate them," he commanded. "Like you did the one from the office."

#"You do not believe he is the original, do you?"

Merlin shrugged his shoulders. "I have my suspicions. You have to admit, the battle was a little too easy. Something cannot be right."

Without comment, Anne raised Excalibur again and focussed her mind to send sparks down her arm, along the length of the sword and cascading off its tip. She manoeuvred the energy to encompass the entire hall, marvelling yet again at the instantaneous effect it had on the now prone and headless Abrecan bodies. They all sizzled, some convulsed and then burnt into cinders.

Satisfied the bodies had been obliterated, she directed the sword to Abrecan's office at the far end of the hall. Powerful thoughts and explosive energy whipped down the hall, making contact with the end. The explosion that resulted whipped flames in every direction, a fireball extending itself back down the hall toward the exit door where Anne and Merlin continued to stand. Anne was immersed in her power trajectory, oblivious to her personal danger. Merlin, however, saw it for what it was. He grabbed Anne's shoulder roughly and pushed her through the door, pulling it shut with all the force he could muster, meanwhile chanting up his own storm, barricading the stairwell from the approaching fireball. It hit the door with a thunderous explosion, but Merlin's protective barrier held. The heat of the flames crackled and ignited the door and the wall, heating up the interior of the stairwell, but not penetrating the barrier. They were safe. For now.

"Up or down?" Sir Roderick asked.

Merlin uttered another chant. "The upper floors have been incinerated from the explosive fire on this floor. The Abrecans we encountered are all gone. All that remains is below us."

"Then we go down," Anne stated the obvious. "To the basement, the bottom floor. That is where Abrecan will have his laboratory. Merlin, seal all the other floors as we go down."

"Very good, my Queen," he readily agreed.

The knights led the descent, their heavy footsteps clattering profusely on the concrete structure so foreign to their world in the past. They passed one floor with Merlin chanting ferociously. Banging and exclamations echoed from the halls beyond the barricaded doors.

"The clones have been released," Anne said, more to herself than anyone else.

They passed another floor as Merlin continued his chants. More noise from beyond the door. And, finally, they reached the bottom of the stairwell. There was nowhere further to descend. It was eerily quiet beyond the door. One of Sir Roderick's men took the initiative and pulled it open. While the knight held the door open, Merlin, followed by Anne and Sir Roderick walked through, glancing nervously from side to side, looking for booby traps or, worse, assassins waiting to ambush them.

The noise that greeted them was ominous. A slow hum of engines and feeble lights illuminating parts of the large room that stretched the expanse of what had been long hallways and locked chambers in the floors above. Large machines hummed and beeped. As they moved closer to the center, the humming intensified and the light became more attuned to stage lighting, with powerful beams zeroing in on center stage, where all the action was taking place. This was becoming more and more like a stage production, with Abrecan, the original, directing all the action.

There he was. Not standing in the enclosed circle of humming machines, but inside a glass case partially full of some sort of clear liquid, with tubes pumping sustenance into his body. Anne couldn't be sure, but she thought she saw a glimmer of a smile on the evil wizard's face when her group walked into his viewing range. Why was he encased? Was he the original and all the other Abrecans who had confronted her mere clones? Was this his method of cloning?

There were other glass cases. Lots of them. All with bodies in various stages of creation. All the bodies were adult form, and adult size, but not necessarily Abrecan features. There were others, too, probably at various stages of being cloned. All of the bodies were partially immersed in liquid with tubes attached to various parts of the body. It was like a horror clip from an old sci-fi movie.

Anne knew something about cloning, its use of cell nuclei being injected into an egg whose nucleus had been removed, in order to create a newly fertilized egg. But the clone was born naturally and had to mature into adulthood like any other living creature. It took years before the clone would reach the age and so-called maturity of Abrecan. Abrecan had a completely original form of cloning. He was creating fully formed, adult look-alikes. It was too fantastic to believe. And too horrific as well. It was a dangerous combination of twenty-first century science and sixth century magic.

"Ah! Here she is. The queen herself." The voice was Abrecan's, garbled somewhat from the foaming water within his glass cage. "Come closer, my dear. And have a look. What do you think?" The eyes didn't blink. The mouth didn't move. Where was the voice coming from? "Closer, my dear. You have nothing to fear from me." And the head twitched when a cackle, possibly a laugh, sent waves of bubbles around the wizard's head.

Anne took a step closer. Then another. Gingerly placing one foot before the other. Her eyes darted around, taking in one glass-encased figure after another. She was about a dozen steps from Abrecan's glass case, when she stopped. Froze. Her eyes were glued on one glass case. "Mother?"

"Anne." It was her mother's garbled voice.

"Why? How? And who is that woman at Gloucester Castle"

"Oh, that." Abrecan really did laugh this time. "So much for your ability to test to make sure someone really was who they said they were." He laughed some more, creating a tsunami of bubbles that sizzled to the top of the case. "That was a clone, my dear. Everyone around you is a clone. Did you not know that?" There was a pregnant silence, then he laughed, "Well, perhaps not everyone. But you will go through the remainder of your life wondering who is real and who is not. And you will never know for sure." More laughter. "So, even if you do manage to kill me today, I will have won. For there are so many out there who are mere duplicates. And you will always be questioning their loyalty. Never sure. Never content in the knowledge of trust." More laughter.

Merlin stepped forward. "Enough, Abrecan. Why did you do this? For what purpose?"

"I did it because I can, dear Merlin, old-fashioned wizard that you are." The eyes on the man in the case brightened as they clasped onto those of Merlin's. "And, because of my success in this venture, I really will be the victor and rule the day. Forever."

The noise from above was intensifying. Sir Roderick stepped forward. "I believe the barriers have been breached, Merlin. The clones are coming."

Abrecan let lose a bellow of hoots and crackling howls. "And the end is nigh for all of us."

Glancing around at the contraption, Anne sought the connections to the glass cases. Finding the one for her mother's, she swung Excalibur, which she still clutched ready for battle, and severed the cord. The gurgling inside the case stopped abruptly. Her mother coughed, moving her limbs in a frantic attempt to free herself from a watery doom.

"I am sorry, Mother," Anne wailed. Forcing herself to block the sounds of her mother gasping for air, she swung Excalibur on the cord connecting another case. Sir Roderick and his men followed her cue. As the cords were disconnected, the gasps and gurgling intensified to another level, creating a cacophony of garbled sounds. All the while, Abrecan stood in his glass cocoon, regaling Anne and the others with tales of his marvels and successes.

"My dear queen," he crooned. It was difficult to imagine a grown man, and a sixth century wizard at that, crooning like a witch without moving a face muscle to suggest he was actually talking. However, the voice was Abrecan's and it was definitely crooning. And the bubbles inside his enclosure were gurgling away, adding to the marbled sound effects. "You cannot stop what I have already done. Look around you. There must be hundreds of glass cases containing all manner of men and women. All of these people I have managed to duplicate. Many times, in fact. It is really quite Phenomenal; do you not agree? What I have done with my magic and the marvels of clone research that began with dear little Dolly." He was referring to the first recorded clone, a sheep. It happened in the late 1990s, if Anne remembered correctly. "I helped clone Dolly. Did you know? I was a much-revered scientist on the team at the Roslin Institute in Scotland. Along with British scientists, Drs Wilmut and Campbell. I was one of their key advisors: Dr. Abrecan, geneticist supreme. Well," he chuckled and the bubbles gargled to the surface. "The supreme part is my own personal addition to my title. I like it. What do you think?"

Without pausing to think of an appropriate, educated response, Anne blurted out the first thing that came to mind. "I think you are insane, Abrecan. You are no scientist, geneticist or otherwise. You have some magic, but you only use it to conjure up evil spells to cause havoc in the world." Anne took a step closer to the bottled Abrecan, sword arm poised to attack. For that's all he was now: a bottled original. She felt the momentum move her; she was only just winding up and the words couldn't come out of her mouth fast enough. "Putting yourself into a bottle and creating Abrecan wannabes is not something to be proud of. And yet here you are, boasting with pride at accomplishments that have served no one any good. Not even yourself. And these so-called accomplishments are no more than displays of ego-maniacal wizardry of the worst kind."

The wizard threw back his head, the first movement within his glass case, and laughed heartily. It was all that was needed to spur Anne into action. She slashed Excalibur against the life-cord to the case, as she had done to the other, now dead, glass-encased originals. Caught off-guard, too engrossed in his cackling, Abrecan coughed and sputtered violently. His eyes flashed wide open and he focussed an intense glare on his opponent. But Anne wasn't about to wait for his retaliation. Lifting Excalibur, she pierced it through the glass with a force that sent particles of all sizes flying in many directions, mostly into her face. She could feel the cuts and burns as the sharp edges made contact with the bare skin of her face, neck and arms. She didn't back down. She shoved Excalibur deeper into the now cascading waterfall of fluids, piercing one tube after another before she felt the pressure of its tip crumbling into the wizard's chest. She twisted and turned and made sure there would be considerable pain.

There must have been, for Abrecan shrieked with horror, "No!" drawing out the vowel to a fading emission of garbled sonority.

While Anne had ensured the encased Abrecan's fate, Sir Roderick and his men were copying her motions and taking care of the others. All around her, glass was being shattered, fluids were soaking the floors and original specimen were being bludgeoned, decapacitated and worse, until there was no encased life remaining in Abrecan's specimen. Anne stepped back with satisfaction, watching the final defeat of Abrecan. Or was it? As the cacophony of sounds diminished, an eerie beep permeated the space. It was repetitive, short blasts, concise.

Alarm shot through her veins with a ferocity Anne didn't think possible. She stepped back further, knowing immediately what was happening. "It is a bomb," she yelled. "The whole building is going to blow. In minutes. Abrecan created a fail-safe countdown to obliterate his work. He must have hot-wired the timer to his glass case. By destroying it, and him, I have triggered the timer. Now the device is set to explode. I have no idea how long we have. We must leave! Now!"

Merlin stepped closer. "What do you mean by 'bomb'?"

"No time to explain, Merlin. You have to get us out of here. Now. No time to waste. Can you make a door? Take us somewhere?"

"Not as quickly as you would like," the wizard responded.

Sir Roderick approached, soaked from the knees down and covered with shattered glass. "There is a door at the far end. Perhaps it leads outside."

"But that will not help us escape. As soon as this blows, the police will arrive and they will most likely arrest us." Anne was frantic.

"I do not understand. Police? Arrest?" Merlin asked first and Sir Roderick repeated.

"No time to explain." The beeping had taken on a new pulse. Quickened. Time was running out. "We must exit the building. Then you must create a door, a passage to our time. Away from this place. Far away."

Anne sheathed her sword, calling to the others to do the same. She ran to the door Sir Roderick had mentioned, motioning the others to follow. It was an emergency exit. Pushing the door outwards, it set off another series of alarms. Meanwhile, the beeping sound had accelerated even more.

"Run!" She screamed as she plowed through the door, followed by the others. The knights weren't used to running in retreat, but they were in foreign territory. The sounds were obviously terrifying them. Swords sheathed, they followed their leader without argument, panting more from panic than exertion.

They were no more than a dozen paces from the building when the explosion racked through the complex, sending massive fireballs in every direction. Anne was knocked to the ground, but Merlin managed to tug her back to her feet, not missing a stride in the process. The others stumbled but kept running. With flames at their backs, the group continued to put as much distance between themselves and the doomed building as they could. Another explosion wreaked through the air, sending more plumes of fire, this time knocking them all to the ground. They crawled a few paces then paused briefly, glancing back and watching in horror the faces in the windows that appeared to call out for rescue. Their voices were lost in the cacophony of explosions and roaring fire, but the expressions were definitely horrific, many faces pressed tight against the glass windows, frozen in a poignant scream, as the glass melted from the heat, the flames roared around them and the building crumbled beneath their feet. It was as if everything, living and concrete, was melting.

The flames ripped toward them, but Merlin had set up a protective barrier that held. Barely. The heat certainly penetrated, causing them to sweat excessively. The noise deafened their hearing. The massive power of each explosive force knocked one or all of them to their knees several times.

They pushed themselves off the ground repeatedly and continued their escape.

In the distance, came the unmistakeable wail of sirens.

"What is that wailing?" Sir Roderick gasped, coughed and spat out ashes and dust to clear his throat. "It sounds like a massive heard of wild animals."

Anne didn't answer. How could she explain? There wasn't time. She coughed, too, trying to clear her mouth of the residue of ashes and cinders. "We have to leave, Merlin. We have to leave this time. We need a door. A way out. Now!"

"There are none, my Queen." The group huddled beyond the line of old oak trees marking the long drive to the facility they had left behind. Panting profusely, a couple of the men leaning over with fists on bent knees, they surveyed the quickly deteriorating remains of Abrecan's house of horrors, as Anne was quickly beginning to think of it.

The sirens were louder, getting closer. Lights flashed in the distance.

"What are those things approaching?" one of the knights asked as he struggled to catch his breath.

"Some sort of magical dragon force?" The other knight added his question.

"Magic indeed," Merlin agreed.

Anne didn't bother to answer. There wasn't any point. These men wouldn't understand cars and fire trucks, police and firemen. They wouldn't understand the forces they were about to face. The swords they bore with pride in the sixth century were no match to the weaponry of the twenty-first century: guns and tasers. They had to leave before their fighting prowess was put to the test.

"Merlin!" she turned on the wizard. "I cannot stress enough how important it is to leave. Now." She was trying her best to keep her emotions in check, punctuating each word with forced, slow precision. She knew what might, and probably would, happen once the police rounded them up. They had no way of knowing. Or understanding. "I do not care if there is a door or not. You need to create one. You need to get us out of here. Now!"

The first police car pulled up close and two figures stepped out. "You there," the one who had been the driver called out. "Hold on. We need to take you down to the station for questioning."

The fire trucks had arrived en masse, circling the building and connecting the hoses to douse the flames. Their attempts to extinguish the burning remains backfired. As the water hit the buildings, more explosions erupted.

"The water is contaminated," Anne muttered under her breath. "They must be pouring gasoline on the flames instead of water"

"Gasoline?" Merlin queried.

The police marched toward them, several others, having just arrived, exiting their cars and joining the group that were now encircling Anne's little army.

"Hold on, there," the first officer called out again, holding his hand forward as if to quell any resistance. "Keep your hands where we can see them."

The circle of armed police was tightening its grip. There was nowhere to run.

"Merlin!" Anne muttered sharply. "Now."

The wizard started a chant. He raised the staff to cast his spell, spiralling his staff in a circular motion and twisting around, spinning his body faster and faster.

"Hey there!" the same officer was now yelling. "I said keep your hands where I could see them. Remain where you are." Several officers had pulled out guns. Or tasers. Anne wasn't sure which. There wasn't time to consider which.

"Merlin!" She was frantic.

The wizard kept muttering and chanting. "The tree." He pointed to the grand old oak, the one standing within their range, within the circle of police.

"These warriors have strange looking weapons," Sir Roderick muttered to no one in particular.

Anne overheard and responded, "Much more dangerous than anything you have ever seen."

A pop exploded. One of the police had fired his weapon. A bullet could be seen forming a slow arch as it made its way toward Merlin, the only one of Anne's group who appeared threatening with all his chanting, spiralling, staff rotations, and hand motions.

"It moves too slow," Anne marvelled. "Merlin's magic must be working."

A door flashed open in the trunk of the old tree revealing another lush, forest space, alive with the songs of chirping birds. The police gasped and stepped back, all the weapons now aimed at the armed sixth century group. Pops exploded as guns fired and taser charges sizzled. Everything moved in slow motion.

"Let us depart," Merlin ceased chanting and pointed to the opening.

"Where to?" Anne asked the question that was on everyone's mind.

"Wherever it takes us," he responded vaguely. "Hopefully far away from here."

Chapter Thirty-Five

The vision through the portal revealed a wooded grove, much thicker and denser than the one surrounding the smoldering ruins of the psychiatric hospital. The sun barely cracked a glaze through the overhead canopy of evergreen branches and leaf-laden oaks and maples. The silence which had beckoned with mere bird songs and wildlife crackling through the underbrush, erupted as the group plowed through the door and the vocabulary exploded with swear words from the past and the future.

There was the inevitable, "Ouch!" and other such gasps as one after the other tumbled into a thick growth of thorny brambles.

"What the?" the sentence was left abbreviated as two extra bodies, a man and a woman, appeared through the door. Armed and looking exceedingly dangerous, garbed in the twenty-first century wardrobe. The bullet proof vests, labeled with bold white lettering spelling out the word 'police', the warriors of the future had their weapons drawn, pointing in multiple random directions with no decided purpose except to make a statement of dominance and control. The older male uniformed police had a gun drawn, the younger, presumably a new recruit, female uniformed police held a taser. A crackling radio spat static in a loud mishmash of cackles as there was no signal in this time and place, whenever and wherever it was.

"We have some new recruits," Anne whispered, presumably in the direction she last saw Merlin. It was difficult to tell with everyone falling into thick shrubs and bouncing out of the thorny prison as quickly as possible. She didn't wait for a response, unsheathing Excalibur and hacking her way out. She made a wide circle around the others who were too busy unbinding themselves from the prickly branches to notice her or the others. Stepping up behind the armed police from the future, she pointed the tip of her sword at the taller, older-looking of the two. The sword sizzled and sparked, making the man jump, rubbing his neck in shock.

"What the?"

"Do not even finish that thought," Anne warned in little more than a growl. She was getting good at this. Taking control, managing and manipulating others to do her will. Pleased with herself, she realized, too, this was not the time to gloat. "I would suggest you put those weapons away. Either that or we take them away and discard them. Which I would rather not do, as thousands of years from now archaeologists might be wondering how their dig uncovered twenty-first century weapons from the sixth century."

"The what?" the older policeman made a move to turn on Anne, but she maintained her pose with Excalibur shooting another sizzling spark his way. "All right! All right!" He holstered his gun and nodded to the younger recruit to do the same with her taser.

Satisfied the weapons were safely sheathed, she lowered Excalibur slightly. "Hands where I can see them." They held up their hands.

"Now, could you at least explain what just happened?" the older man requested. "And, where are we?"

"More likely when," Anne corrected him. Glancing around at their surroundings, she pointed to the young oak tree through which they had made entry. "There's the old oak tree," she pointed. "And through the woods is where the grand nuthouse of the future will stand, harbor mental patients and a madman intent on duplicating all that is evil. Until the day we arrive and blow it all to smithereens."

"You're trying to tell me we've jumped back in time." The older policeman wasn't buying into anything Anne was saying.

"I am." She gave him her sweetest smile. Forced, not genuine. "Perhaps we should start again with a few introductions. Let me begin. I am Queen Anne of Camelot, daughter of King Arthur. This is Merlin." The wizard had managed to untangle himself from his bed of brambles and stepped forward to take his place at her side, his trusty staff firmly gripped ready to take action if required. "And Sir Roderick." She motioned to the knight flanking her opposite side. "And over there are his knights."

The older policeman bellowed a raucous laugh. He allowed his hands to drop, slapping them on his thighs. "That's a good one. And I suppose that sword you carry is Excalibur?"

Anne nodded. "It is."

"Right. And I'm the Wizard of Oz and this here," he pointed to the young recruit, "is the Queen of Sheba."

Merlin looked exceedingly confused. "You, sir, are no wizard. Of that I am quite sure. And I know nothing of this place called Oz or Sheba."

More laughter. "Is he serious?" he pointed at Merlin.

"Keep your hands where I can see them," Anne warned, raising the sword again. "And, unless you want me to address you as Oz and her as Sheba, then I suggest you give me your real names."

The woman took charge. "I'm Alicia and this is Chuck. We are members of the Ontario Provincial Police."

"I gathered as much." Anne nodded at the woman. "Thank you for providing us with some names." Turning to Sir Roderick, she gave her orders, "Have your men guard these two, then join Merlin and I while we discuss options."

Out of earshot of the others, Anne asked, quite pointedly, "What happened, Merlin? Where and when are we?"

"When I cannot say, but certainly well into the past." He pointed at the baby oak tree. "You were correct to surmise that this is the grand old oak we used for the doorway. The one we used must have been at least a thousand years old. Doing the math, we have not gone back to the sixth century, but close. And, we are in your Grenadier Falls, which, I believe, is nowhere near Camelot."

"So how do we return to your cave in the sixth century, Merlin?" Anne asked, re-sheathing Excalibur, but keeping her hand poised ready for a quick draw.

"I believe we will need your key, my Queen," Merlin confessed. "Had we used that in the first place, we would have returned to our place of origin."

"Then, why did you not suggest it?" Anne was showing impatience in her stance and tone of voice.

"There was no time, as you recall." Merlin placed a hand on the girl's shoulder. "The time for arguments and accusations is past. Let us more forward. I believe if we position ourselves near where we entered, and I create the door as I did before, you can insert the key to return us to my cave, as you call it."

"And what about those two?" She pointed at the police attachment.

Merlin shrugged. "They will have to accompany us until we find a means to return them to their time and place. If that is what they desire."

"Very well," she nodded sagely. "We had best get started. The light is fading and the day is almost over. We have had a long, tiring day, and I am sure that our knights are as tired and hungry as we are."

Merlin didn't need further incentive. He studied the oak seedling closely, considered the direction of the sunlight, what remained at this time in the afternoon and what little filtered through the thick canopy above, and then began counting paces. As he marched in what appeared to Anne to be an easterly direction, he pushed branches and overgrowth out of his way, marking a path for the others to follow. Which they did, at Anne's insistence.

"Now where are we going?" Chuck muttered his protest in a barely subdued voice. No one answered. One of the knights shoved him forward. He tripped and almost lost his footing, but his partner grabbed his elbow and steadied him before he could crumble to the ground.

"Keep up, Chuck," Alicia whispered sternly. "We have no idea where we are and we are rather at the mercy of these people."

Chuck grunted in response. He was a policeman to the core and not one to give in so easily. The knights pushed them forward again.

The group hacked through the forest, no one really sure where they were headed. They merely followed the lead: Merlin. He appeared to know something. When he stopped, abruptly, Anne, followed by the others plowed into him, so intent they were at keeping their eyes focussed on the footing and manoeuvring through the thick shrubs.

"Here!" he pronounced with firm conviction. "Right here. That tree there will suffice as a door. Anne, have the key ready." He didn't wait for acknowledgement, merely proceeding with his chanting and hand motions until, as before, a door appeared in the trunk of the tree. It glistened and sizzled with energy, causing the police to step back in a mixture of awe and fear.

"What the?" Chuck, once again, didn't finish his exclamation.

"Anne," Merlin commanded. "Now."

While awaiting Merlin's magical incantations, Anne had slipped the key from underneath her tunic. Still safely fastened around her neck, she held the key ready to use. Stepping forward at the wizard's instructions, she inserted the key in the glistening hole that she assumed was the keyhole. And she turned it, opening up a chasm of intense light and energy.

"Let us depart," Merlin waved toward the door. He led the way, followed by Anne and Sir Roderick. The knights had to shove the police through the opening, their protests abundantly loud and clear.

A nicker greeted Anne on the other side. "Blackie!" Tucking the key safely underneath her tunic, she patted her chest, reassured that it was safe, before moving through the cavern. It was lit only by the glare of the open chasm, which instantly disappeared once the others were through and Merlin disconnected the opening. As he called out incantations to light the wall torches, Anne felt her way to the opening to the next cavern where the horses had been secured. And there was Blackie, muzzle ready for a treat and a fond pat. Anne gave her the latter, apologizing for not having a treat handy.

"Later, Blackie," she reassured the mare with affectionate pats and rubs. "I will give you lots of treats when this is all over."

"Where are we?" Chuck snarled. He was obviously a man with little patience. "What kind of nightmare have you brought us to this time?"

"We did not invite you to follow us the first time," Sir Roderick was losing his patience. "Had you stayed where you belonged, you would not be at our mercy now. As it is, you will have to do as you are told and be quiet about it."

Anne returned to the chamber to dispel the growing tension. She was disturbed to find her trusty knight standing nose to nose with the policeman, hand on the hilt of his sword ready for battle.

"Enough!" She stepped between the two and, placing one hand on each chest, pushed them apart. "Tonight we eat and rest. In the morning we head for Tamworth Castle to see how Sir Galahad has fared." She turned to Sir Roderick, "Your men shall take turns watching these two and standing guard outside."

He nodded in response, eyes still glued on Chuck as if the conflict had not been resolved.

"Chuck," Anne stepped away from her knight and motioned for Chuck and Alicia to make themselves as comfortable as possible in the corner farthest from the entrance.

"Where are we?" It was Alicia who asked this time, her voice calmer, but rather shaky.

"Whether you care to believe it or not, you are in the sixth century, in one of Merlin's many caves, just south of what you would know in the twenty-first century as the Thames River and not far from what will one day be England's capital, London." She stood tall and looking every bit as regal as her voice sounded, in spite of her travel weary wardrobe which was displaying a rather saggy complexion of overuse and heavy travels. "I am who I said I was, Queen Anne of Camelot, daughter of King Arthur. And," she patted the hilt of her sword with both respect and affection, "this is the famous sword, Excalibur. Before we entered the facility at Grenadier Falls in your era, we had fought a vicious battle against the Saxons, led by the evil wizard Abrecan, whom we found doing cloning experiments at the facility which exploded prior to your arrival." Noticing the doubt in Chuck's eyes, she shrugged. "Believe what you want, but you are here, under our care and protection, for the time being. Until we can find a way to get you back to your time. If that is what you wish to do. In the meantime, I suggest you make yourselves as comfortable as possible and stay out of mischief."

Alicia cleared her throat. "If I might be so bold." She was clearly unsettled by what she wanted to say. "It has been awhile. And. Um. Where would I find the lady's room in this place?"

Anne had to chuckle. She couldn't hold it back. "Merlin," she coughed to stop the chuckle from becoming a full-blown laugh. "Alicia and I have some personal needs to take care of."

"I shall accompany you," the wizard announced. "To protect you, of course. Never fear," he noticed Alicia's blush of embarrassment. "I will look the other way."

Merlin went a step further. Not only did he find the ideal secluded spot for the ladies to take care of their private needs, but he also provided some lighting. The sun had almost set and the thick tree coverings cast eerie shadows of extended darkness. There was a stream nearby as well, so the ladies were able to wash some of the dust and grime from their travels.

"I will never take a public washroom for granted again." Alicia's comment made Anne laugh. Now that the two were alone, out of earshot of everyone else, the policewoman opened up and became rather chatty. "You don't appear to be from this time," she noted. She was curious. "You talk and dress like you are a sixth century queen, but somehow I think your story spans the centuries, so to speak."

Anne had to chuckle at the last comment. "Yes, I guess I do have a story spanning the centuries. Too long to capsulize. But, basically, I was born and raised in the twenty-first century. Homeschooled, I grew up listening to my grandmother's tales of the Middle Ages. Mother always chastised her for feeding me too many fairy tales. When I was older," she paused and laughed, splashing more water on her face. "That sounds funny, now. Because I have really only been in the sixth century for a little over a week. So much has happened and so quickly. It feels like much longer than a week." Glancing off into the darkness, she lost herself in her thoughts.

Alicia startled her with another question, "So, you came back here. How? And why?"

"Because it was my destiny," Anne spoke softly with both compassion and conviction. "My grandmother was Queen Rosalind, wife of King Ceawlin of Wessex. Times were difficult and dangerous when she was expecting my mother. Merlin sent her through the door to the future. Mother was raised in the twentieth century. When Merlin sent a message that things were safe for their return, Mother was a teenager. At Gloucester Castle, she met and fell in love with King Arthur."

"Your father."

"My father." She chuckled again. "Quite the womanizer. I seem to have quite a few half-siblings scattered across the country. Anyway, my father left abruptly and Mother, traumatized and angry, insisted on returning to the twentieth century. It was the end of the twentieth century. I was born at the cusp of the new century. A millennial as you call us. I was brought up with all the privileges and conveniences of the twenty-first century."

"What happened? Why didn't you stay in the twenty-first century?"

"They found me in the future and I had to escape to the past." Anne leaned over the trickling creek and splashed more water on her face.

"Who found you? And where?"

"We had a small downtown apartment in Toronto. Mother worked odd jobs cleaning other people's homes. To make enough money to keep us housed, warm and fed."

"Why would she work? There must have been priceless treasures you could sell to support yourselves." Alicia studied the young queen crouched next to her.

"That might have attracted unwanted attention and brought the enemy to our doorstep sooner than it did."

"I suppose," Alicia conceded. "But still. Royalty living in a small apartment, in downtown Toronto and cleaning houses for a living. It just doesn't make sense."

"It wouldn't be the first time in history, Alicia. Many of the Romanov's who escaped the Russian revolution were destitute, living in poverty."

"Hmm! You do have a point."

The ladies stood, shaking the water from their hands. They didn't rush to return to the cave. The female camaraderie that had been initiated was a pleasant change from being surrounded by men most of the time. Fighting men, too.

"You know," Alicia broke the silence. "I was just thinking. There was an incident about a week ago. In Toronto. Someone broke into the cordoned off thirteenth floor of the Royal York Hotel. Made quite a mess and then mysteriously disappeared." Turning to face Anne, the two studied each other as best they could in the fading light. Merlin had obviously caused his magical illumination to dim, allowing night to settle in as the sun had long since set. The shadows were creeping up around them. "Was that you?"

Anne gave an almost imperceptible nod but was refrained from answering by Merlin's voice calling through the darkness.

"All done?" he asked.

"Yes," Anne answered. She took Alicia's arm and led her toward the wizard's voice and then followed him into the cave.

Chapter Thirty-Six

How Merlin managed it, Anne wasn't about to ask. He wouldn't tell her anyway. His magic was his power, his secret power. But there was plenty of food for the congregated travelers and the cave warmed up nicely with the heat from the hearth and the body heat from the horses in the outer chamber. It was cozy, though the hard rock surface didn't do much to add comfort to the equation.

Alicia and Chuck were settled in the corner furthest from the opening, Sir Roderick's two knights situated on either side of them. Chuck had the look of a man fuming beneath the surface. Alicia, on the other hand, appeared to be settling into the strange setting with ease.

Crouched uncomfortably next to Merlin while Sir Roderick stood guard at the entrance, Anne whispered, "We need to find them appropriate clothing before venturing off to Tamworth. Either that or send them back."

"We cannot send them back from here, Anne," Merlin noted. "They will have to wait until we return to Gloucester Castle."

"Why?" Anne challenged the wizard. "You managed to take us to the future from this portal, why not send them back from this location."

"It is rather complicated, my Queen." Merlin let out a deep sigh. "Too much magic in one location within such a short time frame can affect the transference from one place to another. It would be best and safer to take them to Gloucester and transfer them from your portal at the castle."

"Abrecan has managed multiple passages through portals, or so it would seem," Anne argued.

"And look what it's done to him and his power," Merlin pointed out. "Not a safe idea at best. The other option would be the cave where you first arrived. Which is a little out of the way and might slow our progress."

"Yes, it would. Then we must dress them appropriately. And find them a couple of mounts. Do you think they know how to ride?"

Sir Roderick ventured into the conversation. "Well, if they do not, they will learn quickly. We ride at sunup. And I believe Merlin has rounded up a couple of extra mounts for our guests."

"Is that true, Merlin?"

"Yes, my Queen. I do have my ways. There are plenty of horses in these hills. All I had to do was call them and they came."

Anne laughed softly. "You make it sound so simple."

Merlin quirked an eyebrow. "But it is simple, my Queen. Very simple. Now get some rest. Tomorrow we head for Tamworth, to survey Sir Galahad's progress."

"And the wardrobe?"

"Already taken care of," he half-smirked, "though I doubt it will be an easy task convincing Chuck over there to change his attire."

"Probably not," Anne agreed. "Perhaps Alicia will convince him."

"A task for the morrow. Now sleep."

Anne didn't think it was possible. So many thoughts were whirling through her mind. Was Abrecan really dead? For good? What awaited them at Tamworth? And, for that matter, at Gloucester? Was the mother she left behind aware that she was a clone? Or was she? How would she ever know for sure? The women in the glass-encased tomb of Abrecan's nightmare facility in Grenadier Falls certainly looked real enough. Was that a ploy? Another one of Abrecan's many deceptions? Or had Mother managed to deceive Abrecan before he could store her in the living tomb and create multiple reproductions? So many questions. So few answers.

She was startled from a deep sleep by a raucous outside. The horses were stamping their feet in protest as sounds of scuffling and yelling permeated the space.

"What have you done with my gun?" It was Chuck.

"I do not know what a gun is." One of Sir Roderick's knights stated in defense.

"The weapon I carried in my holster."

The others in the cave stirred at the disturbance. Alicia broke the startled silence within the cave. "What is he arguing about now?" She spoke with a voice that betrayed her frustration with being shackled with such a man as her superior. "And what has happened to my taser?" She slapped her hands around her, checking her holster several times. "It's gone. Who took it?"

Merlin spoke. "I have what you call weapons. I have stored them safely so you cannot catch us unawares and use the weapons to our disadvantage. You do not know what you are dealing with in this time and place and your weapons will be more of a nuisance than a help."

"But how do we defend ourselves?" Alicia challenged the wizard.

"Like the rest of us." Merlin was standing up now, back to the entrance, facing down the lone female police. "Can you wield a sword? Shoot an arrow?"

"I can do both," Alicia responded, pushing herself off the ground so her eyes could meet the wizards at the same level. "Though I am better with a sword than bow and arrows."

"Then sword it shall be," Merlin nodded with approval. "But, should you turn your sword on one of us, your head will quickly leave your body. We are, all of us here, much better trained than you are."

"Perhaps." Alicia was not one to stand down. She glued her gaze on Merlin, meeting his stern expression with one of her own, almost equal in its intensity.

Chuck stomped back into the chamber, breaking the staring war between Alicia and Merlin. "Give it back, Merlin, if that's who you say you are." He held out his hand in a defensive challenge. "Now."

"I am not one of your underlings from your time and place, Chuck." Merlin would not be cowed. "I do not take orders from the likes of you. You had best learn your place here if you wish to live long enough to return to your time and place."

Sir Roderick stepped up behind Chuck and shoved him roughly into the chamber. "You need to watch your mouth!" He snapped at the policeman. "Sit!"

"I don't take orders from you either," Chuck resisted. Turning to face his adversary, he pushed back. He raised his right hand in a fist and aimed it at the knight's jaw. It never made contact. One of Sir Roderick's men stepped up behind and grabbed Chuck's wrists, forcing them behind the man's back. It wasn't easy. Chuck was strong, obviously used to fighting and holding his own in hand-to-hand combat. Hands out of commission, he didn't stop. Using his feet, he balanced on one leg and quickly manipulated the other behind the man restraining him. With a backward shove, the knight tripped over Chuck's foot and the two landed with a thud on the stone floor. The action loosened the man's grip and Chuck, lying on top, rolled off, shook his hands free, and bounced to his feet, resuming a defensive pose.

"Chuck!" Alicia took a few tentative steps forward. "No. Stop. This is neither the time nor the place. These people have done nothing to ignite your anger. You must realize that." Chuck wasn't listening. He bounced around like a boxer in the ring circling his opponent. Alicia didn't give up. "Chuck!" She reached across the chasm and placed a hand on her superior's shoulder. He shrugged it off and jumped out of range. "Chuck!" she was yelling, trying to rein in her own anger and frustration. "You have to listen to me. You have to listen to them. We are in their world, now. Their time. We have to go along with what they tell us until such time as we can return to our own time and place."

"You really believe the lies they are spewing at us?" Chuck spat on the ground at his feet and maintained his hopping, shuffling from one foot to another, sporadically pumping one fist or another in front of his face. Sir Roderick and his men circled the bouncing policeman, eyeing him cautiously without intervening. Anne took shelter in the corner, taking in the early morning action.

Alicia, giving up the attempt to stop her boss, sidled up beside her. "He's a kickboxing champion with a vile temper. Don't know how he ever made it into the police force." She shrugged her shoulders. "I tried."

Anne nodded in response. "Do not worry. Sir Roderick and his men are well trained in battle moves. They may not be champions in a fighting ring, but they do know how to fight."

The ladies huddled together in silence, watching the battle play out before them, the tiny space of the cavern seeming all the smaller for hitting, punching, jumping and grunting as each man struggled to gain the upper hand in combat. No one noticed the wizard and his antics. Merlin was chanting, waving his staff in the air above his head. A swirl of energy sparkled around him and then spun out like a lasso before landing with both grace and targeted finesse over the bouncing policeman, pulling the man off-balance before he could deliver another blow to one of the knights. The constraints spread like netting and encompassed the man from shoulders to feet, making any type of attack moves impossible.

"What the?" before Chuck could finish his explicative, Merlin tightened the enchanted lasso and tossed the end of what now appeared to be a tight rope to Sir Roderick. Chuck was spitting out every curse word he could think of, but he was no longer bouncing and his hands were pinned tightly to his chest.

Merlin stepped up to the man. "If you persist with these comments, we will have to gag you as well."

Chuck spat in response. "Take that, wizard." He snarled.

"Very well." Merlin waved his staff again, chanting. Waves of fabric wove through the air and spun around Chuck's head, tight and snug. His eyes popped wide, but the only sound he could utter was a grunt.

"Until you can learn some manners and respect," Merlin ceased his incantations, "you will be bound and gagged." Turning to Sir Roderick, he said, "Put him in the corner. We must prepare for the day." To the ladies, "Perhaps you two would care to refresh yourselves again at the stream." They nodded and followed him out of the cave, Anne managing a friendly pat on Blackie's rump as she passed by.

Huddled between the shrubs and the stream, the ladies went about their business, chatting softly.

"It's so peaceful here," Alicia let out a sigh of contentment. "No mad rush of traffic and noise. Just nature at its best." Allowing her hands to hang over the stream, dripping with fresh water, the young woman breathed deeply. "I think I could spend a lifetime here."

"But your life in the future?" Anne glanced sideways at the young policewoman. "Your career as a police officer?"

"I can keep the peace wherever I am." She shook her hands to release the remaining drips of water and stood up, allowing her eyes to roam the comfortable natural enclosure.

"Why did you join the police?" Anne asked, shaking the residue water off her hands, but allowing herself time to gaze at the reflection in the water.

"To keep the peace," Alicia answered simply. "I come from a long line of police enforcers. As a teenager, I rebelled and allowed myself to be attracted to the other side of the law, shall we say. I had a choice: join the police and do good or join the criminals and end up behind bars. I spent a week in a youth detention facility in Grenadier Falls, my hometown. There wasn't much to do in the small town, so it was easy to get caught up with the excitement and drama of drugs, alcohol and misdemeanors. Once released, I watched in horror as my best friend was molested and beaten unconscious. I was to be next, but the police had honed in on our location and arrived in time. I decided then and there to join the police and work on the side of good."

"Chuck knows of your past, does he not?" Anne asked, taking her time to stand up and face the other woman.

Alicia nodded. "And he uses his knowledge against me whenever he can." She ran a hand through her hair, pulling the fingers through the tangles. "Thank heavens for short hair at a time like this," she chuckled softly.

"You could stay here, Alicia. But what about your family? Your parents? Siblings?"

"No siblings. Father was killed in the line of duty about five years ago. Mother died of cancer a year later. No other extended family. No special someone. I'm on my own. Completely."

"As am I."

Alicia glanced at Anne in surprise. "I thought your mother was alive. I heard Merlin mention something about her."

"I am not sure it is my mother," Anne said, remorse barely hidden in her voice. "The mother I left behind at Gloucester Castle may just be another one of Abrecan's clones."

Shaking her head as if trying to wrestle free of cobwebs in the brain, Alicia held up her hands in feigned shock. "Whoa. Wait a minute. That facility you bombed in Grenadier Falls?"

This time Anne held up her hands, shaking her head. "No. No. We did not destroy the facility. Abrecan had a self destruct code built into his computers. He blew himself up and all the clones in the facility with him."

"We'd been suspicious of the goings-on there for some time," Alicia shook her head again, disbelief evident in her expression. "But cloning? Are you sure?" Anne merely nodded, a faint grimace marking her expression. "And this Abrecan, what is he to you and this era?"

"He is my half-brother, so I have been led to understand." Anne started pacing. "Though I hate to connect myself to him, we did share a father, King Arthur. His mother was Morgawse or Morgan le Fay, Arthur's half-sister."

"The witch who seduced her half-brother and, I believe if I remember the legends, seduced Merlin as well, learning all his deep, dark, magical secrets." She reached out a hand and placed it gently on Anne's shoulders to stop her pacing. "So, the legends are true?"

Anne nodded. "Abrecan learned from his mother then killed her. Only a witch or wizard can kill another of his or her kind. Abrecan's power grew with each new conquest. How he managed to learn about cloning, I will never fully understand. But he did. And he took the science to a whole new level by creating a duplicate adult from the original. And not just one, but many. The castle we ride to today, Tamworth, is the former Saxon stronghold and Abrecan's base in this era. We have defeated the Saxons, at least for now, I hope, and the captive Saxons informed us of the many duplicates roaming the castle grounds. What Abrecan did was pure evil. He starved his clones and, when they died of starvation, he replaced them with duplicates. With clones. At least, that is how I have come to analyze things. We shall see when we get there if my suppositions are correct."

The ladies stood in silence, allowing the gentle gurgles of the stream and the quiet birdcalls to soothe their thoughts. "I could stay here forever," Alicia said again, softly. "In this place. Right here." She breathed deeply.

"You are welcome to stay," Anne admitted. She was starting to like this woman and enjoy her company. Perhaps here was someone she could truly trust. A soulmate. She shook herself as if shuddering off residual water after a shower. She wouldn't jump to that conclusion yet. Merlin had warned her and she would heed his warning, to be careful of whom she trusted.

Chapter Thirty-Seven

"Ladies," Merlin called from beyond the line of trees and shrubs that served as a privacy barrier. "We must leave. Soon. May I enter?"

"Yes," Anne called out.

Merlin emerged through the overgrowth and motioned them to follow him to higher ground. Curiosity had them climbing through brambles and other prickly shrubs that clung to the hillside, all without question. At a level outcropping, the wizard stopped and pointed at the gentle waterfall. "There is a small cave behind the water," he explained. "You will find clean garments. Change quickly. Alicia, you must leave behind all your items from the twenty-first century. They will be safely stored until such time as you decide to return to your era. Should you decide to stay, I will destroy them so that there is no evidence of people from the future venturing into this time."

The ladies merely nodded in response, Alicia looking more confused than Anne. "Come," Anne held out her hand. Alicia took it and they scrambled up the rocky incline to the base of the waterfall. Finding a path that led behind, they ducked under the cascading waters and into the cave Merlin had told them about. It was dark, but enough light filtered from beyond the waterfall to help them find the items of clothing. They helped each other disrobe and adorn the clean garments.

"Wow!" Alicia exclaimed, once attired like a sixth century lady. "So soft. Loose-fitting and comfortable."

Anne handed her a belt and demonstrated how to fasten it snuggly so the sword, once sheathed, wouldn't loosen its grip. "I hope you can ride."

"In this?" Alicia laughed. "Seriously?"

Anne joined in the laughter. "Seriously. You will get the hang of it. I am sure Merlin has chosen the perfect mount for you. He did for me when I first arrived."

Alicia was silent. Thoughtful. "The incident in Toronto. At the Royal York Hotel. Something about a vacant floor. You never did fill me in."

"The thirteenth floor," Anne interjected. "That was the location of the portal. For me. I am not sure if the portal at the Royal York is still there." She shrugged her shoulders. "Merlin has opened a few new portals in various places. And Abrecan? Well, he seemed to have a knack of creating a portal just about anywhere by merely snapping his fingers."

"Scary stuff."

"Yes. It is. We shall have to work on your language skills. If you want to remain here, you will have to speak like the rest of us. Start with avoiding contractions and acronyms. That is what Merlin made me do."

"So, that explains your very formal vocabulary." Alicia laughed softly. "I shall try."

After bundling up the police uniform and other effects, the ladies emerged from the cave. Merlin was waiting where he had left them. He nodded with satisfaction at the sight of the two ladies approaching. Anne already had Excalibur sheathed. The wizard held out another sword, hilt forward. Alicia took it and gazed at it with reverence. "Use it wisely and only in the service of our queen." She nodded somberly in response and sheathed the weapon.

"Now, let us go." Merlin didn't pause any longer, turning to pick his way back down the incline. "The men and horses await. Though, I must say, your partner is being rather difficult."

"I am not surprised," Alicia murmured as they carefully picked their way downhill.

"He refused to disrobe and discard his clothing from the future. The best we could do was throw a cloak around his shoulders to cover most of what he was wearing. It makes him look like a plump monk." He shrugged his shoulders. The ladies shared a giggle.

The horses were ready at the cave entrance, stomping their hooves, impatient to burn off some pent-up energy. Merlin assisted Alicia with her mount while Anne snuggled with Blackie, rubbing behind her ears affectionately.

"May I be of assistance," Sir Roderick came gallantly to her aid. He flashed a bright, warm smile and held out his hand. She took it but glanced away shyly in a vain attempt to halt a blush she could feel creeping up her cheeks. She was beginning to warm up to this man, this valiant knight. He had a strong impact on her, his kind eyes connecting with hers with an emotion she had never before experienced.

"Thank you, Sir Roderick," she murmured once mounted, focussing her attention on settling her skirts around her legs and draping the cape over Blackie's rump.

"Anything for my Queen," the knight gave a bow and stepped back, keeping his eyes focussed on Anne until she happened to glance his way. Then he winked and was rewarded with a faint smile and the ever-glowing blush before turning to mount his own horse.

"We must make haste," Merlin insisted. "There is a storm coming. Do not let this warm sunshine fool you. Winter has not fully given up its icy grip."

Anne shuddered at the thought of riding through a winter storm. Winter was her least favorite time of the year.

"I hate winter," Alicia muttered as she brought her horse up alongside Anne's.

"Me, too," Anne agreed, nudging Blackie forward, allowing Alicia to pull in behind her.

They rode single file down the narrow path. Once the ground leveled and the path widened, Alicia once again rode abreast of Anne, Sir Roderick and Merlin in the lead, the other knights and the angry policeman bringing up the rear. They urged their horses into a steady gallop and managed to cover significant ground before the skies clouded over and a chilly wind picked up, blowing in from the north. By the time they reached the spot where they had parted ways with Sir Galahad, drops of sharp, icy pellets dribbled around them, the sharp nip of the cold and ice biting into the exposed skin of their faces. Even the horses fidgeted with disgust.

Merlin kept them at a steady pace. With the ground becoming increasingly more treacherous and the footing slippery, he cautiously slowed the pace to a trot. They crested the final hill, the one Prince Aethelric said would provide them with a good view of Tamworth, pausing at the top.

"Oh my!" Anne gasped as she mounted the hill, pulling up Blackie so she could survey the path of destruction beyond. Smoke billowed into the air with blackened ferocity and blew with the cold, wintery wind across the chasm and into their faces. They all coughed, struggling to cover their mouths.

"Is that Tamworth?" Alicia asked.

"I suppose what is left of it," Anne spoke through a spasm of coughing. She was shocked at the vast expanse of destruction that stretched below. The castle must have been large, considerably larger than Gloucester. The charred remains covered acres, as far as the eye could see.

They could see figures moving about, where presumably the castle had once stood. A hand raised to beckon them, a banner was swung back and forth. Sir Roderick answered with a wave. "It is your banner, my Queen, the one that led the men to this castle and the battle they must have endured."

"I hope it is our men waving the banner," Merlin muttered as he nudged his horse forward, following Sir Roderick's lead as he made his way carefully down the steep embankment. The others followed, taking equal care on the steep descent. At the bottom, they splashed through the rushing waters, blackened by the soot of the now demolished castle. Though angry in its rush to cascade the rocks, the water wasn't deep. The others followed and, all soaked to the skin, made their ascent on the opposite side. Sir Roderick displayed caution, placing his hand on the sword's hilt ready for action. The others copied. Merlin's staff, perched as before on his foot, glowed with reserved energy, ready to strike at the wizard's command.

There was a collective gasp amongst Anne's group when they reined in at the riverbank. What lay before them was a blackened depression in the ground covering an area slightly larger than the layout of Gloucester Castle. There was nothing left of Tamworth, only charred, smoldering remains and this eerie looking hole in the ground.

"Oh my!" Anne sidled up to Merlin. "What do you suppose happened?"

"Probably the same thing that happened at Grenadier Falls," Merlin responded blandly.

"A failsafe trip wire that affected both places and both eras?" Anne asked no one in particular. "What kind of magic did this wizard possess?"

"Very unholy, foul magic, my Queen," Merlin growled under his breath. "Very evil."

Chapter Thirty-Eight

Anne's group remained rooted at the top of the rise, gawking at the demolition, for lack of a better word. They could see people and horses milling about, all around an immense cavity of destruction. A few riders 279escry279hed at a gallop. Anne noticed Sir Roderick tightening his grip on the sword, always prepared for anything. As the riders approached, Anne felt a surge of relief.

"It is Sir Galahad," she breathed more evenly and allowed herself to smile.

"You mean the famous Sir Galahad from King Arthur's knights of the round table?" Alicia asked, no longer trying to mask her tone of amazement.

"One and the same," Anne allowed herself a soft chuckle.

"Wow," was all Alicia said in response.

Anne wasn't sure if the woman beside her was remarking on the fact that this was a knight of the round table, or he was merely a very good-looking knight of the round table. She let it go. For now.

Sir Galahad pulled up short and ducked his head toward Anne. "My Queen," he greeted her. "Merlin. Sir Roderick. And," his eyes rested on Alicia, a smile broadening across his face. "Others?" He quirked an eyebrow, something he did frequently when pondering an unanswered question, especially a question he hadn't yet asked.

"This is the Lady Alicia," Anne took the initiative to introduce the former policewoman. Alicia glanced sideways at Anne at the reference to 'Lady'. Chuck could be heard snorting behind them, his disgust and disbelief obvious.

"And the gentleman between Sir Roderick's knights?" Galahad asked.

"We are still investigating his identity," Merlin answered this time, his response causing a smile of amusement on both lady's faces. Anne coughed to hide a chuckle gurgling at the base of in her throat. "It would appear we have arrived too late to see Tamworth at its finest," Merlin continued.

Sir Galahad allowed his gaze to follow the others. "That would be an understatement, Merlin. We were evacuating the common folk and all of a sudden everything erupted. Like some sort of magic consumed the space, the building and any living thing within a measured distance from the perimeter of the once grand castle. It was a nightmare, really. Burning, rotting flesh. Body parts strewn all over the place. Not a pleasant sight."

The ladies cringed at the 280escryiption, Anne taking a deep gulp and breathing deeply to stall the growing nausea in her gut. It didn't help. The deeper her breath intake, the more she could smell. Between the explosion at the Grenadier Falls facility and the demise of Tamworth Castle and its occupants, Anne was convinced that she would never be able to rid herself of the smell of burning flesh, burning buildings, burning equipment – basically the burning smell of everything. And this mess continued to smolder.

"How deep?" she asked. She hadn't meant to ask. The smoke above the charred remains was dense and it was difficult to ascertain the depth of the cavern. If there was even a bottom to it. If she couldn't see the bottom, she was sure no one else could either.

"Hard to say, my Queen," Sir Galahad answered, his voice bland, devoid of expression. "We tossed some rocks into the mess, but didn't hear anything crumble or crash as it landed. Perhaps it is now a bottomless pit."

"I believe it is," Merlin interjected his opinion. Pulling his horse around so he faced the queen, he added, "I do believe it has become an open portal to the Grenadier Falls facility."

"Can we traverse it?" Anne asked. "Or, better yet, seal it to prevent movement between the two eras?"

Before Merlin could answer either question, Chuck exclaimed with exuberance, "Yes," high-five pumping his hands in the air. He was ignored. No one knew what he was doing with his hands anyway. That is, no one except Anne and Alicia. "Let me pass. I want to return."

Although he tried to nudge his horse forward, the knights held him back. "Let me go," he yelled, grasping as best he could one knight's hand then the other in a faint attempt to free himself. "I want to return to my time and place. This," and he waved his hands around frantically, "is a world full of madmen and madwomen." His eyes darted at each one of the men and women, unsettling them and making them fidget restlessly on their mounts.

"Who is he?" Sir Galahad demanded.

"Someone who does not belong here," Merlin stated simply.

"Why not let him go?" Alicia asked. "He will never be happy here."

"We do not know what will happen on the other side," Merlin explained. "Or, if there is another side. He might be stepping into a fiery inferno for all we know."

"Perhaps it is where he belongs," the young policewoman muttered under her breath. Anne had to bite her upper lip.

Chuck wasn't about to give them any choice. With an intense kick in the horse's sides, he managed to break free of his captors.

"Wait. Stop." The knights nudged their horses to follow, but Merlin stopped them.

"Let him go," the wizard commanded. "We can do nothing for him here."

As the knights reined in their horses, Chuck continued to kick his horse forward. Everyone watched in horror as the horse and rider galloped toward the pit. In spite of its reluctance to approach the burning ruins, Chuck pushed him on. Until, at the last moment, before charging into the charred remains, the horse stopped abruptly, skidding across the now slick ground as it sent its rider in a head spin, deep into the center of the cavern. Chuck's yell could be heard echoing against the acoustical odds of a void chamber. As he plummeted, the sound diminished exponentially. Then he was neither visible nor audible.

The group was too stunned to speak at first. Alicia was the first to break the silence. "Do you think he made it to the other side?" she asked in barely more than a whisper.

"We will never know," Merlin responded.

The cold wind from the north bit into the sombre group, the assault of spiked ice pellets intensified with vigor. Sir Galahad led the group cautiously down the slope, mindful of the now slippery footing and the cavernous void that awaited them at the base of the hill. He angled his direction to the west, descending while at the same time navigating the group around the charred remains of Tamworth. "We are in for some nasty weather. Late winter type of weather. These ice pellets are nothing compared to what's coming. I can feel it in my bones."

Anne chuckled, remarking in a teasing voice, "You are not old enough to feel the weather in your bones, Sir Galahad."

"He might not be," Merlin added, his usual serious tone of voice challenging anyone who would beg to differ. "But I am. And I agree. We must seek shelter and warmth for a long night of late winter's worst."

"And," Sir Galahad continued to explain his reasoning as the group approached a sheltered forest grove, away from the castle remnants. "With the wind coming from the north, we did not want to continually receive the brunt of the smoke and fumes from the burning rubble."

The ladies shuddered as they studied the so-called sheltered area. With no building for shelter, no warm hearth for light and heat and nothing soothing to eat or drink, it was roughing it at its most miserable.

Those who didn't huddle, kept bustling around the space, creating shelters as best they could using branches collected from the nearby woods. Several fires roared its warmth, sending a deep gust of grey smoke upwards to collect with the trailing smoke of the smoldering ruins. The refugee families, despondent and looking helpless, shuffled as close to the warmth as they could, their sparse garments offering little comfort, let alone warmth.

The ladies shivered. It was getting cold. The temperature was dropping quickly.

Several boys rushed forward to collect the horses. Anne dismounted and took a good look around her. Many of the people she recognized, the men who had followed her into battle only days before. There were others, though. Saxon men, women and children. They were clearly recognizable: gaunt faces that indicated days, perhaps weeks and months of starvation, tattered clothing and hollow eyes. They worked slowly to set up the shelters, their lack of interest or concern symptomatic of their condition.

Alicia stated the obvious, in little more than a mutter, loud enough for Anne's ears alone. "Who are these people? They are starving."

Anne merely nodded. She was too intent on taking in the severity of the situation. At first glance, Anne didn't realize how many there were. As she followed Sir Galahad and walked through the crowded confines, she witnessed with a growing sense of unease, the vast number of Saxon refuges, not to mention her own people.

"Sir Galahad." She tugged on the knight's arm to garner his attention. "Are all these people from Tamworth Castle?"

He didn't break his stride, nodding in response. "We tried to evacuate as many as we could. We sent Prince Aethelric in to raise the alarm and get people outside. This is all we could rescue."

"You mean there were more?" Anne gasped.

The knight nodded again. "A lot more, from what the prince told us."

"And where is Prince Aethelric?"

"We have not seen him since the castle disappeared in a cloud of flames. We kept sending him back into the castle to rescue more people." The knight sniffled. "I am sorry, my Queen. I was actually starting to like the man. He was brave to the end. Determined to save as many of his people as he could. A real hero."

"I cannot believe the number you did rescue," Anne exclaimed, allowing herself to glance around yet again, more slowly this time, all while keeping pace with Sir Galahad. "Are there any duplicates?" she asked for lack of a better word to describe something so totally alien to the sixth century as cloning.

"Lots."

"What do we do with everyone?" She ran her hand along Excalibur's hilt, not for protection, but for reassurance. There was no need to draw her sword. She noticed Alicia doing the same, the young woman's eyes darting nervously around the cramped space. "And can we trust them?" Her voice was loud enough for Sir Galahad to hear, but it was marked with unease. "There are more of them than us," she stated the obvious.

The knight merely shrugged his shoulders. "We can only hope that they are all too weakened by hunger to be a threat." He paused briefly to face his queen. "We could turn them out, but, with the bad weather coming, it would not be looked upon with kindness."

Merlin stepped forward. "He is right. We must have some faith that these people will be more grateful to us. We are, after all, providing them with food and relative shelter."

"Is there enough to feed them?" Alicia took the initiative to ask. "There are a lot of hungry mouths to fill."

"The forests are teaming with wildlife," Sir Galahad explained. "My men, and those Saxons healthy enough to assist, have spent most of the day hunting. We have done a little better than our queen's stone soup. We will manage."

"Stone soup?" Alicia quirked an eyebrow in Anne's direction.

"I will explain later."

Sir Galahad and Merlin had moved ahead and the ladies thought it best to catch up. The hungry eyes that followed were unsettling.

At the far end, the knight stopped, pointing to the collection of makeshift shelters that had already been erected. "The largest one over there will be for the ladies," Sir Galahad announced. "Merlin, Sir Roderick and I will inhabit the ones on either side and post regular guards to ensure safety."

Anne and Alicia pondered the scene before them. The ramshackle dwellings, made of branches and gatherings from the forest all around, had the appearance of a multitude of beaver dams, only not as efficiently constructed. With a large fire being tended between the shelters, there was a sense of warmth, a feeling of being cocooned. But would it be enough for the weather that was quickly approaching. The ladies shivered noticeably as a brisk, cold wind swarmed the group and whipped their cloaks astray. The flames from the fires smoldered slightly and sent up plumes of smoke, making everyone cough and choke as the air fought to clear.

Chapter Thirty-Nine

The hot gruel warmed their insides and the well tended fires provided marginal heat, but only when the wind let up briefly and ceased blowing the smoke in their faces. As the flakes and icy pellets started its uncaring descent, the ladies retreated to their assigned shelter, such as it was.

"I do not mean to sound too brash." Alicia shivered as she spoke. Crawling along the cold ground, barely covered with a thin carpet of leaves that didn't do much to offer warmth. "But, if we were to share our body heat, it might offer us some modicum of comfort to get through this storm and the night ahead."

Anne's teeth were chattering as she shivered uncontrollably. "I agree." The ladies snuggled together and wrapped their combined robes around them. There were no other creature comforts available. They would have to make do and shiver together through the night.

The wind whistled and wailed outside the shelter, ruffling the twigs and branches that encompassed the space. The ladies snuggled in closer and wrapped their robes more tightly around them. The swords added to the discomfort of the cold hard ground beneath them, but not knowing how safe they were, neither one dared think of removing the weapons, rather keeping them close at hand should the need arise to defend themselves in the middle of the night.

Uncomfortable and cold, sleep held off despite their gnawing fatigue. Alicia broke the silence first. She spoke in a whisper, "Are you awake, my Queen?" she asked, using the formal greeting she had picked up from the others.

"Call me Anne," was the response. "At least when we are alone."

"It is too cold to sleep," Alicia stated the obvious, her body convulsing in shivers setting off Anne's body in an imitation that needed no encouragement. "Perhaps if we talk, we shall block out the discomforts."

"I agree. It is worth a try. What do you want to talk about?"

"You," was the instant response. "And me. But first you. Why did your mother and grandmother bring you up in Toronto? And in the twenty-first century?"

"Well, they could not very well bring me up in Toronto in the sixth century," Anne attempted a dash of light humor.

"Very funny," Alicia poked the queen gently in the ribs.

"I do not know how they chose the safest time and place," Anne admitted. "Perhaps it was Merlin's doing."

"The exit point was Merlin's doing," Alicia noted in a serious tone of voice. "So, I guess it makes sense that he chose the time and place as well. But he really does not know much about the future, does he?"

"He knows enough," Anne admitted. "As for being sent to the future, it was a ploy to deceive those who meant us harm in the sixth century."

"Abrecan."

"And others."

"But they found you and you had to escape to the past."

"Yes, they did," Anne admitted. "At least, Abrecan found me. And sent his minions in to take charge, killing Grandmother and kidnapping Mother. Though, at the time I believed Mother had been killed, not kidnapped."

The shivers were lessening as the conversation added its own dash of warmth to the space around them. They were quiet for a few minutes, then Anne spoke again. "Now. What about you? You told me something of your background, but are you happy with your choice of being a policewoman?"

"Sometimes I am," Alicia responded. "It is a job. One to be proud of. But that Chuck is a piece of work. He hates me. I am sure of it. He hates being saddled with a female rookie with a record, even if, as a juvie, it is sealed."

"I somehow get the impression that Chuck hates everyone and everything."

"I believe you are right." They were silent, each caught up in their own thoughts. "Do you think he made it back?"

"No way to know, really," Anne pondered the question. "You could ask Merlin. Or, you could go back to see for yourself. But is that what you want? To return to the twentieth-first century?"

"I really do not know," Alicia let out a deep sigh. "I thought it was what I wanted. But now I am not so sure."

"Meeting a certain dashing knight from Arthur's round table would not have anything to do with your indecision, now would it?" Anne teased gently.

If Alicia was blushing, it was too dark to notice. She did manage a nervous cough and decided to tease back. "And what about your dashing knight? Sir Roderick certainly has eyes for no one else but you."

"And who else would he have eyes for?" It was Anne's turn to nudge Alicia. "You are still considered a prisoner. And the other women are emancipated Saxons. And probably clones at that."

"And that is probably all Sir Galahad sees in me."

"Oh. I do not know," Anne chuckled softly. "His eyes did light up a few notches when he first met you." She didn't add the memory of her first meeting with the gallant knight. She had thought then that he was something special. For her. But then along came Sir Roderick. And Alicia.

"Hmm!" She sighed deeply and allowed the silence to mellow. "So. Are you going to tell me about Sir Roderick or not?"

"What about him?"

"Who is he?"

"He is Sir Roderick of Dumnonii." Her statement received no response, so she continued. "You know Dumnonii as Cornwall.

Sir Roderick is technically King of Cornwall, which is an ally to Wessex, my grandfather's territory and now mine."

"So, a marriage to Sir Roderick would be a politically correct move on your part," Alicia said lightly, a note of humor evident in her voice.

Anne nudged her and quickly changed the subject. "Seriously, Alicia. Do you want to stay?"

"And if I did?"

"I think we could be great friends." There was a hopeful edge to Anne's voice. "I need someone I can trust."

"But how do you know for sure you can trust me?" Alicia shuffled uncomfortably. "I could be another one of Abrecan's cloned spies."

"Sure. You could. But there are times when one has to take a chance and just trust. We all need a friend. Do you have many friends in the twenty-first century?"

"Not really." Alicia's head made a rustling sound as she shook it to accentuate her answer. "In fact, none that I can think of."

"Would you like to stay? Be my confidant, my trusted friend? And, perhaps something more to a certain knight?"

Alicia chuckled softly. "You certainly do know how to sell your point. I shall sleep on it." She yawned deeply. "Perhaps we can sleep now."

The noise of the storm continued to rage around them outside their shelter. Although the cold and discomfort didn't help, the conversation had warmed the ladies marginally and fatigue finally took over. They both fell into a restless sleep.

Chapter Forty

It was a dull silence that wakened the ladies much later. The wailing wind had stopped, the crackling fires had ceased. It was as if they were suddenly in a vacuum. A vacuum, however, that was peppered with incessant snores from the compound beyond.

Anne moved away from the cocoon the two ladies had created and peaked through the makeshift opening to the ramshackle shelter of sticks. It was still dark, the fires had smoldered to mere embers. Alicia's head poked around behind Anne's seeking a look at the world beyond. "It is so quiet."

"Except for the snoring," Anne chuckled softly.

"I thought there were guards posted."

"Over there," Anne pointed to a slumped shadow next to their shelter. "I guess fatigue settled in for the guards as well."

"Or they were drugged," Alicia suggested.

"Ever the suspicious mind," Anne whispered back. "No wonder you went into law enforcement."

"Are you ladies all right?" The man's voice startled the two and they bumped heads trying to extract their bodies from the cramped shelter.

Sir Galahad crouched down in front of the shelter. "Sorry to have startled you." He chuckled softly. He reached out a hand and helped the ladies, one at a time, crawl out.

The ladies shook their legs and rubbed their arms to restore circulation. Lying on a cold, hard surface all night did wonders for cramps. "We were merely taking in the surroundings and noted that our guards were asleep," Alicia stuttered an awkward response.

"Other than the snores," Anne added, "it was so quiet, we did not expect to come in contact with anyone."

"I took over the watch a few hours ago," the knight explained. "The storm passed quickly, but it left behind a thin layer of snow on the ground. With any luck, the sun will soon be up to melt it all away." It was already starting to look lighter indicating that morning was approaching. "Perhaps you ladies would like to refresh yourselves?"

Anne responded. "Yes, we would. Where can we find some privacy?"

"This way."

They were led to a quietly moving stream, one that merely gurgled and slapped its way across the stony surface, slurping along the shore. The spot was ideal, cocooned with a thick canopy of trees all around. Nice and private.

"I will wait in the bushes," Sir Galahad announced. "Call if you need me."

The ladies knew they could trust a knight of the round table to be honorable. They were safe from prying eyes. The idea of a refreshing wash and the relief of the morning ritual didn't hold them back. However, the water was exceedingly cold. They projected a collective gasp as they ducked their hands into its depth and then splashed it on their faces.

"Are you sure there is nothing you would miss from the twenty-first century?" Anne teased as she continued to wash and allow the cold, clear water to wake up every cell in her body.

"Maybe a hot shower or two," Alicia chuckled.

Anne watched the other woman out of the corner of her eye, as she ran a finger over the surface of her teeth in a futile attempt to clean them. "How about a toothbrush and some toothpaste?"

"Yes." This time the two women shared a hearty chuckle.

"Actually," Anne confessed. "I burned my toothbrush back at Gloucester Castle. It would not last forever, anyway, and it would take some explaining, should someone from this era find it. But, you are quite right, it would sure be nice to freshen the teeth while the supply lasts."

"So, when do we head to Gloucester?" Alicia shook her wet hands over the water and then wiped them on her robe as she pushed herself off the ground.

"Soon, I hope," Anne admitted, copying the other woman's actions. "We have to scout out the area and make sure there are no Saxon clones lurking around every hedge and hidden crevice. I also want to establish a central location for the castle I intend to build. My castle."

"A new Camelot?"

"Not quite," Anne made her way toward the tree line where Sir Galahad waited for them. "Camelot was my father's ideal. Not mine. I want a castle that will make a statement on who I am and what my country, what my people mean to me. Somewhere near the old Roman walled city of Londinium along the grand River Tamesis."

"London!" Alicia exclaimed. "On the Thames River. You plan to build the city of London well before its time. What a grand idea!"

"Actually," Anne pointed out. "It already exists. Well, sort of. The Romans built Londinium around the year 43 AD. Then they abandoned it, though it still exists. The Saxons have a settlement slightly west of the old Roman city, which they call Lundenwic. I want to rebuild on the Roman site, use some of its infrastructure and make it a safe place to live for centuries to come. No more black plague because everyone dumped refuse in the Thames and then used it as a source of drinking water and for cleaning purposes. And, it is a prominent location. I want to prevent the Viking invasions which, in the history we learned, happens in the next couple hundred years. I want my country, my people, to prosper and to be safe from invasion."

"Noble thoughts, my Queen." The ladies jumped at Sir Galahad's voice.

"How long have you been listening in?" Anne asked, shooting a half-hearted look of accusation at the knight.

"Long enough to know some of your intentions, my Queen." He pointed in the general direction of the encampment and started to lead them off through the forest. "Let us gather the others, have some refreshment, and then we can ride off to Londinium to assess the situation. Should be a good day's ride. Perhaps longer if we encounter resistance."

Around the fires that were now sizzling with flames and much appreciated warmth, with pots stewing whatever contents it could conjure, Anne shared her ideas with Merlin and Sir Roderick, while Sir Galahad and Alicia listened in, adding some suggestions to what they had already heard.

"I think your idea is sound and well thought out," Merlin nodded his approval. "You are indeed your father's daughter. And what do you plan to call your new grand capital city?"

"Not Camelot," Anne said for the second time that morning. "My grand castle, my capital city, will be called London, a name that will stand proud and secure for centuries to come."

Chapter Forty-One

It took longer than a day to reach Lundenwic. The Thames was roaring high from recent record amounts of rainfall. Traversing the waters, even at the source, long before the river widened considerably, was a challenge at best. Once they managed to cross, they were able to follow its meandering route as the second longest river in England made its way to their destination.

They had to make camp in the trees lining the riverbank. The nights were cold, but not as wintery cold as the night they spent shivering near Tamworth. Riding all day made them tired enough to sleep, in spite of the rugged, uncomfortable conditions.

"They call it the River Isis," Sir Roderick announced as they plodded along over the uneven shoreline, day three of their excursion weighing heavily on the weary travelers. "At least at this point it is known as Isis."

"Not a name one would want to hear where I come from," Alicia muttered under her breath. Anne bit the corners of her lips. She knew Alicia was referring to one of the many militant groups that terrorized much of the world in the twenty-first century.

"Roman goddess of magic," Anne spoke before the knight could interrogate Alicia further regarding her comment.

"The what?" he asked.

"It is a mighty river," Anne continued to share her knowledge of the mythology behind the Thames River. "A mighty river which brings together two tributaries, Thama and Ysa. Male and female deities, Ysa, or Isis, being a benefactress of rivers. We may even find some effigies of Isis at Lundenwic, left behind by the Romans."

"Hmm!" Sir Roderick pondered. "And why would some people object to the use of the name Isis?" So, he hadn't forgotten Alicia's earlier comment.

"People throughout time have always found a way to transform something good into something evil," Anne explained simply.

"Like Abrecan?" he asked.

Anne nodded in response but was prevented from commenting further by a call at the head of the procession. The scout, who had been sent ahead to secure the path had returned.

"Armed Saxons ahead," he announced, loud enough for everyone to hear. "They must have been warned of our approach."

Swords were unsheathed and the knights around Anne and Alicia tightened its rank. Battle ready, they moved forward with greater caution.

Merlin held up his hand and they halted. "Wait," he commanded. "They are not making any aggressive movements. I think they want to talk."

Anne observed the line of Saxons that blocked their passage. She had to agree with Merlin, they didn't look at all aggressive. As if to prove the point, three of the Saxons nudged their mounts into a steady walk, leaving the rest behind.

"Come, my Queen," Merlin called over his shoulder. "I believe it is time to demonstrate some diplomacy."

As Merlin's horse moved forward, Anne pulled Blackie up next to him with Alicia, Sir Galahad, and Sir Roderick trailing behind.

"Valiant knights," the wizard called over his shoulder. "Keep your distance." And the two knights held back while the ladies accompanied Merlin the final few paces to meet their Saxon counterparts.

The horses paused, head-to-head, snorting at their counterparts. The Saxons studied Merlin and the ladies with glaring intensity. As the eyes raked across the ladies, Anne felt a rankling of unease, noticing out of the corner of her eye that Alicia was straightening her shoulders in defiance, her eyes staring down the Saxon who faced her.

"Greetings." Merlin broke the silence.

There was a collective muttering amongst the Saxons, then, the one in the center, presumably their leader spoke up, his voice edged with disdain. "Who sent you?"

"No one sent us," Merlin replied, keeping his voice calm, almost soothing.

"Was it Abrecan who sent you?" A deviation on the same question.

"Like I said." Merlin's voice reflected an edge that wasn't there before. "No one has sent us. Besides, Abrecan is dead." He paused to let his words sink in. The Saxons glanced nervously amongst themselves, disbelief evident in their expressions and the tone of their voices as they muttered amongst themselves.

"It cannot be!" the Saxon leader's voice exploded with venom and spittle splashed over his mount's head. "Abrecan is a wizard and he cannot be killed."

"But he is dead," Merlin repeated, still remaining calm in the face of adversity. "And wizards can be killed, by someone of equal or more power than they possess. I am Merlin. I am a wizard. And these things I know." He motioned to Anne. "My Queen, here, Queen Anne of Camelot, daughter of King Arthur, with her own magic, killed the evil wizard. I was there and I saw it happen. We have come from Tamworth, or, I should say, what is left of it. There is nothing left of Tamworth but a smoldering hole in the ground, which we will have to cover when we return. It was too much of a fiery chasm to deal with before we left. And there is nothing left of Abrecan and his evil creations."

More muttering amongst the Saxons. The leader spoke again. "You say you are Merlin and that this is Queen Anne of

Camelot, daughter of King Arthur. How do we know what you are saying is true?"

Anne drew her sword slowly. Noticing the Saxons reach for their weapons in self defense, Merlin held up his hand as a peace offering. With Excalibur drawn, she raised the sword high, allowing it to glitter in the sunlight, its energy sparking laser shards in every direction, its warmth trickling down her arm and throughout her body. She could feel herself glow along with the sword.

The Saxons gasped, some pulling their mounts back in fear. The leader slid from his horse and slowly approached Anne, bowing on bended knee. He obviously knew what the sword was. He recognized the evidence presented. "My Queen," he paid homage to Anne. The others copied their leader, leaving the horses to trail over to the river's edge for a quick drink.

Anne dismounted and approached the Saxon. "Your name, sir," Anne commanded in a regal voice.

"Prince Aethelweard, my Queen. First born son of King Penda's cousin, King Aethelric, King of Guthrium," he answered solemnly, head still bent in reverence.

Anne dubbed the Saxon prince with the tip of Excalibur, first one shoulder, then the other. "I dub you a revered knight of the kingdom of Queen Anne of the new Camelot, soon to be known as the mighty kingdom of England. Rise, Prince Aethelweard."

The prince stood up and faced the queen. "Is my uncle dead as well?" he asked.

Anne nodded. "And his son, Prince Peada."

"A useless wimp," Aethelweard muttered under his breath. "My father, King Aethelric, is also dead. Killed by the invaders who beached their longboats on the shore many days ago."

"Vikings," Anne exclaimed, eyes widening. First one problem, then another. She recalled her studies of this era. There were a large number of Viking invasions, including the takeover of Lundenwic. "How many lives lost?" she asked gravely.

"Too many," the prince replied, "The women were kept to be used. Slaves. Any of our soldiers they captured were beheaded."

"Not so different to what the Saxons do when they conquer," Anne noted.

"Very true, my Queen."

"So, is this all who remain from Lundenwic?" she nodded to his gathered men at arms.

"We have more in the camp nearby," Aethelweard replied. "We had hoped you were bringing Abrecan and his magic to scourge the invading plague from our land."

"We have Merlin," Anne nodded toward the wizard, who remained mounted and ever vigilant. "He is more powerful than Abrecan and his magic is a good magic. Safe."

"Then you have come to help us," was the satisfied response. "I will lead you to our camp and we can plan strategies for erasing these invading raiders, or Vikings, as you call them, from our land."

Chapter Forty-Two

The encampment was well concealed, surrounded by thick forests all around. Close to the amenities the river and its nearby feeding streams, the Saxons, now coupled with the queen's men, could hide out for days if not weeks. The invaders would have to thrash their way through the thick growth of old trees and thorny shrubs to find this place.

"If we are this close to Lundenwic," Alicia whispered in Anne's ear, "then we must be somewhere near Hyde Park."

"At least before the riding trails were constructed and the nobility used it on a daily basis to parade around either on foot or on horseback," Anne chuckled softly.

"Or in an elaborate carriage," Alicia added.

"You may be right," Anne agreed. "But it will certainly be some time before London's park becomes part of the city landscape."

Having stretched their legs and allowed themselves a few minutes privacy to take care of necessities, they settled in with the others, sitting cross-legged on the ground around a gently smoldering fire.

"Will not the smoke from the fire alert the invaders that we are here?" Alicia spoke up. Glares flashed her way and, in spite of her police training, she shriveled marginally, leaning in to Anne for moral support.

Anne reached an arm around the woman and patted the shoulder softly. "I have to agree with Alicia," she announced with authority. The glares lessened. "Smoke is either a result of careless tragedy like a forest fire or human presence."

Merlin interjected. "I have cast a spell, my Queen," he assured the ladies. "It will mask the smoke. The invaders you call Vikings will not find us here due to the smoke trail."

The ladies nodded, reassured.

"Now," Merlin took control of the meeting. "To the task at hand. Aethelweard, perhaps you could give us some idea of the layout of Lundenwic, so we can make plans."

Picking up a stick, the prince proceeded to trace the outline of the settlement. "There is no castle, therefore, no moat. There is, however, a large stone building in the center where the king and his court resides. Not specifically a castle, but it serves as such. The entire settlement is surrounded by a stone wall, except along the river and here," he pointed to the furthest corner from the river. "This is where the forest encroaches on the settlement. No one has seen a need to clear away the thick growth of old trees and shrubs merely to erect a wall."

"And no one would think it possible for invaders to sneak in through the forest," Merlin added.

Aethelweard nodded in agreement. "The guards will be positioned along the wall to watch for possible attacks." He pointed again to the forest protected corner. "There will be no guards here. Some locals believe the woods to be haunted and I am sure they have shared the stories with the invaders." He shook his head. "No. Very unlikely that they would expect and be prepared for an attack here." He tapped the ground with the stick to emphasize his point.

"Then that is where we enter," Merlin announced. "I shall set the stage with a good storm to mask any commotion. We slip through the forest and into the settlement and take up positions around the castle that is not a castle and at various other points in the settlement."

The Saxons glanced around with nervous energy. Speaking for his men, the prince offered his concern. "And what about our women who are still in the settlement. Still being used. My wife is one of them."

With a deep sigh, Merlin spoke in a conciliatory tone. "I understand your grief and your concern. And your anger." He held up a hand to stop interruptions which he sensed coming. "We will rescue the ones we can. But it is paramount that we attack quickly and without hesitation."

"What about the longboats?" Alicia asked, pointing out something Merlin hadn't mentioned in his plan. "Should they not be destroyed as well? We do not want the invaders to escape only to invade again at a later date and with a larger group of invaders."

The wizard nodded. "We shall send men to sneak aboard the boats and set them aflame. But we must orchestrate our actions, so the alarm is never raised and the invaders are caught totally unaware."

"And what about the queen and I?" Alicia asked.

The question was met with silence. All eyes made contact with Merlin, who merely rubbed his chin thoughtfully.

"Perhaps we could be used as bait," Anne broke the silence. "Since these Viking invaders obviously enjoy using women, seeing two women, unused and alone, in the middle of their compound, might be enough to pull them out into the open."

"Into a trap," Aethelweard finished the thought.

"I think we call it an ambush," Alicia added. "And it just might work."

"Dangerous," Sir Roderick and Sir Galahad spoke at once, their concern obvious.

"You will be putting your lives at risk," Merlin agreed. "And I am not sure we want to risk the queen's life."

"But I am dispensable," Alicia noted, grimacing. "Especially since I am what some might call an uninvited guest."

"I agree with Alicia's suggestion." Anne held up her hands to ward off further protest. "Alicia and I are both well trained to defend ourselves. And," she patted the hilt of her sword fondly, "I do have Excalibur handy."

Merlin nodded, reluctantly. "I can provide a protection spell. How much effect it will have at the hands of an army of plunderers, I really do not know. But it might help."

"And, I will have my fighting knights and brave Saxons all around me," Anne gave a bright, confidant smile, as her eyes roamed around the circle of me."

"It just might work," Sir Galahad agreed with the same intensity of reluctance as Merlin.

"It might," Sir Roderick added his word of approval.

"How do we sneak them in?" Aethelweard asked the obvious.

"Through your back forest entry." Alicia picked up her own stick and pointed to the far corner that Aethelweard had described as merely forest protected. "We come in with our fighting men. As you take up position, so do we. And so do the men who will set the longboats aflame. A whistle will suffice to set the battle in motion. And, when we hear the whistle, we shall call out in our most feminine, alluring voices." Anne chuckled at Alicia's suggestion. "We shall have the invaders melting at our feet and all in a disarray. Easy for your men to cut down."

"When?"

"Between sunset and the rising of the moon," Merlin instructed. "The darkest part of the night. I will conjure up a storm."

He wasn't allowed to finish the suggestion. Sir Roderick interrupted with a resounding, "No," which was echoed by Sir Galahad and several others.

"Too obvious," Anne pointed out. "They probably have their own wizards and conjurors who will recognize a spell-induced storm and set the alarm."

"And," Alicia added. "We would be just as much at a disadvantage in a storm as they would."

There was nodding heads all around the circle. It was decided. The plot was ready to set into motion. Without the storm.

"Tonight it is," they all agreed.

Chapter Forty-Three

As they tread carefully through the thick woods, Anne couldn't get the classic lines, *it was a dark and stormy night,* out of her mind. It wasn't exactly stormy; Merlin had acquiesced and refrained from casting a spell to bring them stormy weather. But it was pitch black. As opening lines go, the most mocked, overworked-line-from-the-future suited their current situation. Anne couldn't see more than two inches in front her nose and, with everyone moving with stealth, it was difficult to trust the ears to provide safe passage.

She dared not speak, though she desperately wanted to. Any voice would be better than this void of sight and sound. It was like a vacuum. There were no bird sounds, no wildlife evening chatter. Even the air was still, almost stagnant. Eerie was the only word that came to mind. And the classic punch line, *it was a dark…*

She wasn't allowed to think through the remainder of the phrase as they had broken through the thick woods and were entering a vast open space. Glittering light from smoldering fires provided marginal visibility, casting shadows from the nearby buildings. They were inside Lundenwic. Everyone scurried to their assigned posts. Alicia grabbed Anne's arm and the two ladies made their way around the outlying buildings, keeping to the shadows as they followed the description Aethelweard provided. After weaving through several dark corridors between buildings, they noticed a larger structure just ahead.

"The main building," Alicia whispered. She didn't get to say any more.

"And th-what have we here?" A figure stumbled toward the ladies, his slurred speech, heavily accented, and unsteady gait evidence to his recent drinking binge.

"He speaks English," Alicia exclaimed, reaching for her sword.

Anne stopped her. "Not yet," she whispered. "We should play along. Make him think we are helpless and unarmed."

"Th-what you say, missie," the man was closer, his breath wreaking with his recent consumption, his words projecting spittle at his feet, some barely missing the ladies. "Come to get more, have you?"

He reached for Anne and dragged her toward him. Alicia launched at him and pummeled his back. "Let her go," she demanded.

"Oh! So you's jealous, eh? Want me for ye-self?" He dropped Anne's wrist and grabbed at Alicia, but she stepped back quickly and the man lost his balance, falling face first into the hard dirt.

"Come," Alicia pulled Anne along. "Let us get into position before the whistle blows."

"Or he comes to his senses and realizes he has been dumped," Anne added.

Alicia snickered softly. "Was that a pun, my Queen?" she asked.

Anne didn't answer. They had more important fish to fry than a solitary drunken Viking, currently lying flat on his face in the dirt.

They scurried around the main building and were making their way to the center of what might be termed a courtyard, when the whistle reached their ears. It was time.

"Hello," Alicia called out in her most feminine voice.

"Hello," Anne echoed.

Faces appeared at the door. Large, gruesome, deeply shadowed faces, backlit with the minimal light provided from the hearths within. Voices grunted and hooted in an unfamiliar language. Then, another figure elbowed his way through the congregation at the door and marched toward the ladies, his identifiable horned helmet somewhat askew.

"And what have we here?" he growled. "Two untested treats?"

The ladies forced smiles upon their faces and batted their eyelids, not sure if their efforts were obvious in the dim light.

"They are so tall," Alicia groaned, keeping her voice just loud enough for Anne to hear. "Legends are right."

"And those helmets they wear with the horns," Anne added, "make them even taller."

"And more gruesome."

Trust in Excalibur. Merlin's voice echoed in Anne's head. *Have faith in your powers and your sword.*

That is easy enough for you to say, Merlin. You are not here to face these demons. Anne replied in her thoughts.

Have faith.

Taking a deep breath, Anne braced herself, forcing her body to stand as tall as possible. The man approached, the ground reverberating the impact of each footstep.

"Two fine treats to keep me warm tonight," he sneered.

"I am so glad you speak our language," Alicia kept up the dialogue. "It would appear that we are lost. We need a safe place to spend the night."

"Safe and warm," Anne added, finally finding her voice. She didn't like this coy act. But the intent was to keep the men interested in their presence and not conscious of the impending danger closing in on them. So far, it was working. At least until the shouts reached their ears and the men looked in the general direction of the commotion.

"The boats!" several yelled. Some of the explicatives were in a foreign language, but, as they dropped whatever they held and started running toward the river, it was obvious they were cursing about their fleet of longboats lighting up the night sky with ferocious flames.

The man who had approached, turned his back on the ladies to utter commands. His mistake. No sooner was his back turned, then Excalibur was unsheathed and the man's head was separated from the lower part of his body, horned helmet and all. Anne wasn't sure how it happened. She didn't recall standing on her tiptoes to wave the sword at the level of his neck. It happened. Quick. Swift. Efficient.

Others approached. Alicia had her sword unsheathed. The ladies positioned themselves, back-to-back. "Time to send these Vikings to never-never land in their burning boats."

Anne had to chuckle as she allowed the sword to take aim at another victim. The tall Norsemen were losing their heads, helmets and all, to the mighty Excalibur. Anne couldn't have done it without the sword's magic, a magic that connected to her entire body, that sparked energy between the ring and the sword's hilt. It was an awesome feeling, but not a power she ever wanted to abuse. Not like her half-brother, Abrecan. She cringed at the memory of the evil wizard.

The Vikings swarmed out of the buildings around the compound, like angry bees protecting the hive. Anne and Alicia held their ground, reassured to note that her men and the Saxons were doing their part.

The swarming ceased. Silence consumed the space, and the air stank of freshly drawn blood and burning timber from the longboats. Heads rolled through the blood-soaked ground, bodies strewn everywhere. Although she had been an active part of the carnage, Anne couldn't squelch the screech that she expressed when a head rolled toward her, bumping her ankles. She jumped and almost tripped on another head. She would have, too, if Alicia hadn't grabbed her elbow.

"It is over, my Queen," the former policewoman announced, maintaining a comforting grip on Anne's elbow.

Aethelweard appeared before them, almost as if he had walked through a dense fog and suddenly took shape. He bowed. "We have been victorious," he announced, his voice sounding grim, rather than jubilant over the victory. "Lundenwic is ours. Or" he quickly corrected himself, "I should say, Lundenwic is yours."

Pulling herself together, Anne nodded in response. "See to these bodies," she commanded, her voice still a little shaky, but firm. "Burn them as we planned. As the Vikings like to be sent to the world beyond. Alicia and I will inspect the buildings and see if any of the women and children survived."

"I shall accompany you," Merlin appeared at Anne's side.

Anne merely nodded and led the way to the entrance of the main building. She walked through the opening, standing briefly at the precipice to allow her eyes to adjust. Flames burned in the hearth at the far end, but other than that, there was no light. The disarray and the stench were impalpable. The floor was littered with remnants of clothing and food. Rats scurried hither and thither, their movement causing a slithering sound that sent shivers up and down Anne's spine. That wasn't the only sound from within. There was also whimpering and sobbing.

As Anne's eyes adjusted, she noticed figures huddled in groups in the far, darkened corners. She approached cautiously, but stopped abruptly when she saw them huddle more closely together, frightened by her appearance.

"I will not harm you," she spoke in a calm, soothing voice. "I am here to help." She gasped when she was close enough to one group to notice that they were all women and they were stark naked. "Oh my!" she exclaimed. A few more steps and she crouched down to be at eye level with the group. A little girl, not more than ten, sat in the center of the huddle. Anne focussed her attention on the girl, shocked that one so young could be used so violently and unspeakably. "What is your name, little one?"

she asked. Receiving no answer, she glanced around the sea of faces. "Does anyone understand what I am saying?"

"I do," a timid voice spoke. It was the woman whose arm was wrapped around the child.

"And you are?"

"Aelflaed. Wife of Prince Aethelweard. And this child is Bletsung."

"The prince is outside," Anne mentioned. "Shall I fetch him?"

Aelflaed shuddered and slithered further into the corner, tugging Bletsung with her. "No," she exclaimed. "He cannot see us like this. We have been used. He will not want anything to do with me or our child."

Merlin touched Anne's shoulder before she could respond. *Clothe them and take them away from this place of horror. They may never be the same again. They may never want to step foot in this place after what they endured here.*

Anne nodded. Glancing at the group of women, she asked softly, "Where can we find some clothes?"

Her question was met with stunned expressions. Aelflaed finally answered. "We do not know what they did with our clothes. They said we were their instruments of pleasure, and we did not deserve to wear anything. They took our robes. Perhaps they burned them, like they burn everything else."

"They are gone, Aelflaed. We have killed them all. We will find clothes for you and we will take you from this place. We will care for you."

"It is too late for that," the Saxon woman replied with a sharp cold edge to her voice. "Too late."

Anne stood up and backed away. She noticed Alicia trying to talk with another group of huddled women. Turning to Merlin, she asked, "Where can I find some clothes?"

"I noticed a pile of what might be clothing behind the building," he answered. "Perhaps the Vikings were planning to burn everything."

"We had better take a look before the others use it as kindling to burn the dead bodies."

She motioned to Alicia and the two women left the building, Merlin close behind. They made their way around to the back and found the pile Merlin had mentioned. The women quickly picked up one item after another, until their arms were full. They returned to the building, carrying the clothes. Placing them inside, in the center, Anne announced, "Find something to wear. We shall return with more robes."

It took several trips, both women working quickly, in silence. They were too shocked to speak. The Saxon women moved slowly from their haven in the corners.

"After what they have been through," Alicia commented in a low voice as they collected another bundle of robes and garments from the diminishing pile outside, "it will take them a long time to trust again. If they ever do."

"Have you witnessed this before? In your work?" Anne asked, concern evident in her voice.

"I have," was the response, the tone as sombre as Anne's if not more so. "We broke up a human trafficking ring about a year ago." She shuddered noticeably, despite the darkness of night that continued to engulf them. "It was not a pretty sight. I still have nightmares."

"How can we help them?" Anne's compassionate plea was sincere.

"We give them time and space and a listening ear," Alicia responded. "And hope for the best. There is no easy answer. Some never recover."

"I do not know who I ache for the most," Anne admitted, "the women or the child. I cannot believe anyone so despicable as to abuse a child."

"It happens," Alicia admitted, resignation obvious in her tone of voice. "All too often, sadly."

They gathered the last bundle and headed back to the front of the building. Aethelweard stopped them as they were about to round the last corner. "Did you find them? Did you find my wife, Aelflaed, and daughter, Bletsung?"

Anne nodded. Noticing the prince's move toward the entrance, she loosened the grip of the robes she carried and grabbed the prince's arm. "You cannot go in there."

"Why not? I must see them." He was very insistent.

Anne shook her head. "They will come out when they are ready. You must be kind and patient. As you forewarned us, they have been used, and they are suffering from the experience. They will need time."

"They abused my daughter?" He exclaimed. "She is so young. Too young for this." He shrugged off Anne's hold. "I must see them. I must hug them and tell them they are safe now."

Alicia broke in. "You might want to refrain from physical contact for awhile," she suggested. "The wounds they suffer are not visible, but they are deep. Give them time. That is the best thing you can offer them right now. Time."

The big Saxon prince sniffled. It was not something Anne expected from a fierce warrior. "I cannot believe this has happened."

"Why not?" Alicia didn't hold back. "Have you not done the same when you were victorious over other groups of people?"

Anne gasped. "Alicia," she was shocked. She had thought the same thing herself but refrained from expressing her opinions.

"That is different!" Aethelweard was indignant.

"Really? How so?" Alicia didn't wait for an answer. She stomped the remaining steps to the entrance and slipped inside.

Anne followed her, not wishing to confront the angry Saxon prince any further. Alicia was right. Aethelweard had obviously done the same thing to other women in a conquered village, the same horrible 'using' the Vikings had done to his wife and child and all the other women in Lundenwic.

The women and children had managed to assemble some semblance of an appropriate wardrobe and were sufficiently covered. A few were already busying themselves tidying up the mess left behind by the invaders. Aelflaed was one of the women who decided to put her hands to work.

Anne approached her. "Your husband wishes to see you."

"He lives?" she glanced warily at the queen who merely nodded in response. "I do not wish to see him. Not now. Perhaps never."

"You need time," Anne agreed, reaching to lay a reassuring hand on the woman's shoulder. Aelflaed cringed and shuffled away from the touch.

"I need more than just time," the woman responded with a touch of bitterness. "What they did to me, to the others, to my child, is unspeakable. And I know that our men do the same thing when they conquer others, when they are the invaders. It is not right."

"You are correct, Aelflaed." Anne allowed her hand to drop to her side. "I will find a safe place for you and the other women and children. Somewhere to recover. Then you may choose whether you wish to return to your husbands. If they still live."

"We have no choice," Aelflaed sniffled, turning away from the queen. "We are only women. And so are you. How can you, one woman, dictate what those men want to do?"

"I am a queen, Aelflaed. Queen Anne of Camelot, daughter of King Arthur. I will see to it that you are treated well. With respect. With care. With compassion. You deserve that much."

Anne didn't wait for a response, turning away from the troubling scene and making her way outside. The bonfires were set and the smell of burning flesh permeated the air. The longboats had long since sizzled to oblivion. She knew it would take more than a few fires to erase the horrors that had befallen this community. Particularly the women and children.

Chapter Forty-Four

It took several days to clean up the settlement. The Saxon women and children were taken to the camp, away from the evil memories. Anne thought it might be best to move them to Gloucester Castle. The further away, the better. She hadn't consulted anyone yet about her idea.

She walked around the enclosed area, intently observing all the activity. She hadn't seen Alicia since the early morning and was pleased to find her monitoring some work at the far end, near the wooded area where they had snuck inside and ambushed the Vikings.

"Alicia," she greeted the woman as she approached.

"My Queen," Alicia honored her new friend with a smile. "We are repairing what the Saxons must have considered adequate plumbing. It has been flowing into the river at the same point that drinking water was being bailed. Not good. Very unhealthy."

"I agree."

"I have devised a system, much like the septic system country residents in our era use." She pointed beyond the wall and into the forest. "The channels will lead the liquid waste away from the settlement, into weeping beds over there."

"And what do we do when the settlement expands?" Anne asked the obvious.

"Then we expand as well," Alicia explained. "Until we have the sanitation systems they have in the future, we will have to make do with what we have." She gave Anne a conspiratorial wink, and added, "I might even be able to devise some sort of indoor plumbing. At least for the main building. I would make it simple enough, building on the already existing infrastructure set down by the Romans, so as not to change the future in matters of plumbing."

Anne had to laugh at her friend's enthusiasm. It wasn't all that long ago that Alicia had followed them into this time, leaving behind a career in police enforcement. She was adjusting well. "So how is it you know so much about plumbing?" She had to ask.

"Reform school," Alicia confessed. "They taught us quite a few practical skills. In the hopes of preparing us with a skill to use as a career in the outside world."

"A valued skill, indeed." Anne patted Alicia's shoulder fondly. "I will not hold you back, then. I have some things to discuss when you have a few minutes."

"Soon," Alicia returned to her supervision. "I will not be long here. Just have to make sure the men understand what I am asking them to do."

Sir Galahad rode into the courtyard as Anne made her way across the compound. There were others with him, a woman, by the looks of it. The sun was bright, and Anne had to shield her eyes to make out who was amongst the riders. As they approached, her face lit up.

"Mother!" she exclaimed, a smile spreading across her face. She hadn't expected her mother to arrive so soon, but, with Merlin and his magic, she supposed she shouldn't be too surprised. Anne was about to dash forward to greet the riders, but held back, doubts plaguing her mind. Instead, she glanced at the knight who was dismounting mere feet away. "Sir Galahad. You return. I wondered where you had gone."

"My Queen," he ducked his head in a half bow after handing the reins to a waiting lad. "On Merlin's orders, I went to Gloucester to fetch your mother."

"Is she my mother?" the queen pondered aloud.

"You do not believe otherwise, do you?" The knight appeared confused by the queen's outburst.

Shrugging off the query, she asked, "And young David?"

"He wanted to come, my Queen," Sir Galahad approached her. "But I convinced him he was needed at Gloucester Castle. He is maturing into a fine lad, one who will make a hearty, trustworthy knight for your round table, if you so choose to follow in your father's footsteps."

"Yes," Anne agreed. "I had already thought of knighting him."

Merlin appeared at Princess Eveline's side and assisted her in dismounting. He wrapped an arm around her and led her toward Anne. "She is your mother, my Queen."

"How can I be sure?" Anne wasn't convinced. Not after all the Abrecan clones they had eliminated. Not after seeing and destroying a woman encased in fluids and a glass enclosure being milked for the purposes of cloning.

"It is I, Anne." Eveline approached her daughter. "My Queen, my daughter. I befriended one of my clones and between us, we managed to trick Abrecan into believing the clone was the real me. She so wanted to be real. I could not refuse her the opportunity."

"Then why were you imprisoned?"

"Abrecan started to suspect. Unsure, he locked me up."

"I know it is the real Princess Eveline, my Queen," Merlin repeated his conviction. "I have my ways. I know these things."

Reluctantly, Anne wrapped her arms around her mother and exchanged a hug. She wasn't sure how long it would take before she could trust this woman. So much had happened, her trust shattered.

"Very well." She stepped back. "For now, I shall believe you are my real mother and not a clone. Should you make me suspect otherwise, I will act swiftly."

She was rewarded with a smile. "I would not expect less," her mother responded. Were the response and the smile genuine? Only time would tell.

"Any news, Sir Galahad?" Anne reverted her attention to the knight in charge.

"I am pleased to report, all is peaceful between here and Gloucester Castle, my Queen," was his steady response. "The people are hard at work tilling the fields. And, should this weather cooperate, we will have a good harvest late summer, providing enough food to get all of us through the winter."

"Very good." Anne was satisfied. She changed her focus again. "Merlin. We need to relocate the Saxon women and children. They will never heal their inner wounds, their spirit, while they live close to the place that scourged their faith in life."

"I agree, my Queen," Merlin nodded his approval. "What would you suggest?"

"Moving them to Gloucester Castle," Anne explained. "They can work alongside our people to rebuild and sow the fields."

"An admirable plan," Merlin agreed.

"No!" Prince Aethelweard had sidled up to listen into the conversation. "My family. Our families. Stay here with us. They belong to us. Not you." He was angry. Almost spitting with venom.

Alicia spoke before anyone else could respond. "They do not belong to you, Prince Aethelweard." Her voice was as stern and uncompromising as the prince's. "No one belongs to another person. And these women and children have been abused beyond tolerance. You must give them time and space to heal. Perhaps at a later time, you may join them at Gloucester Castle. But for now, you need to let them go."

"Well said, Alicia," Anne agreed, a tone of surprise barely masked. She hadn't expected anyone to speak for her, to speak what was on her mind. But Alicia had done just that. And very effectively.

"But what about us?" Aethelweard drummed a finger into his chest. "What about our needs?"

"Oh! Get over yourself!" Alicia spat a twenty-first century expression.

Anne intervened. "Allow them to heal, Prince Aethelweard." She spoke with as much respect as she could muster, given the topic. "You will be too busy over the next few months to have any other needs."

Sir Galahad coughed lightly to muffle a chuckle. The prince stomped with rage and stormed off. "I will keep an eye on him," the knight suggested. "He may have plans to escape with the women and children before you can relocate them."

The knight moved to issue orders, but Merlin stopped him. "Let them go, then. We can only do so much."

Anne interjected. "I will talk to his wife, Aelflaed. Perhaps I can sneak some or all the women away before Aethelweard and his men take matters into their own hands."

"If she and the other women want to leave," Alicia pointed out bluntly. "Sometimes their guilt over what has happened makes them determined to do what others tell them to do. Like, in this case, their husbands."

"But they should not feel guilty," Anne argued. "It was not their fault."

"Who is to blame is not the issue," Alicia said, her experience in these matters evident in her resigned tone. "The guilt complex is very real and very difficult to deal with. Both for the victims and those trying to help them recover."

"It is not right," Anne admitted, giving into Alicia's firm revelation. "I will speak with Aethelweard's wife again. And the other women. Perhaps they will choose to stay with their husbands. It's their choice to make, after all."

"All you can do is try, my Queen," Merlin assured her. "Now. Another issue we must address. The doors."

Everyone looked confused. Anne was the first to realize Merlin's reference. "You mean the portals to the future," she spoke in a low voice, one that only Alicia, her mother, and Merlin would hear. Merlin nodded. "What about them?"

"I think it might be best to close those doors," he said gravely. "Permanently."

"All right," Anne was hesitant. "But may I ask why?"

"A safeguard," Merlin confessed. "There are too many, thanks to Abrecan. And we will never be assured that he is gone. At least gone from our time. We must seal the entryways to protect our people in our time." He moved to face Alicia. "But first, I must ask you to make a decision, Alicia. Do you wish to stay here? Or return to your time in the future? It is a decision you must make quickly, as I feel the need to seal the doors is rather urgent. And, once you decide, the doors will be sealed. All of them. Permanently. I can re-open them if needed, but I would prefer not to do so. Consequently, once the doors are sealed, you will not be able to change your mind."

"As much as I would like to visit the future one more time," Alicia spoke with care. "To make sure Chuck made it back safely, there is nothing there for me. And, even if I was reassured, he was safely in his allotted time, there is nothing I can do for him or say to him." She glanced at Sir Galahad. "I think I have found my place here."

Anne hadn't realized she'd been holding her breath. She let it out with a whoosh of air and impulsively wrapped her arms around Alicia. "I am so glad you chose to stay, my friend, my Lady Alicia."

"As am I," Sir Galahad spoke with care.

Chapter Forty-Five

Standing at the river's edge, Anne took in the bustle of activity all around her. The Viking longboats were gone, but other vessels plied the waters, some with fishermen intent on a good catch to market in the growing community behind her, others ferrying passengers and cargo up and down the river. The reconstruction of Lundenwic was well underway, the trenches dug for Alicia's elaborate scheme to improve on the Roman method of plumbing. The buildings not deemed worthy, demolished and new buildings were being constructed. They had all summer to make the town habitable for everyone.

Her pride and joy, though, was the large building along the water's edge. It wouldn't be quite the same as the construction she and Alicia had read about in the twenty-first century, but it would be something to tide the hazards of time and provide a number of tasty stories along the way. She called it her Tower, her very own royal residence and, with a fortified wall surrounding the complete complex, it was indeed a fortress and a community within the community. With the official renaming of Lundenwic as London, her Tower would soon be known as the Tower of London.

She was assured parts of the Tower would be complete before winter set in. She would be spending the cold winter nights holding court within the Tower's walls, safe, secure and hopefully warm.

She was startled when she felt a presence step up beside her. She wasn't totally surprised as she had requested Sir Roderick join her by the river. They had both been too occupied since the occupation of Lundenwic to seek out the other except in an official capacity. Sir Galahad was off on yet another mission,accompanying the Saxon women and children who requested they be relocated. Alicia had requested she join him on the mission, wanting to help the women adjust and heal. Anne couldn't hold her back. Her mother was away, too, off somewhere with Merlin, assisting in the closing of all the portals, or so they claimed. She was alone and she felt the empty void left behind when the others left. But she had her own work to do, and she was determined to bring her noble plans to fruition.

The fingers of her left hand touched the key that still hung around her neck. She wouldn't be needing it now. Not with the doors being closed and sealed. Would she continue to wear it? As a talisman? A good luck charm? Or would she find some place safe inside her new tower to hide it away for future generations to discover? Her right hand moved the ring around on the finger it had claimed not so long ago. She felt the surge of energy in the sword that was strapped to her side. Excalibur. Hopefully she would be able to release her bond to the sword, to allow herself the luxury of walking around unarmed. She would find a safe place, in the tower, and a good sturdy stone to hold the prized possession until it was needed again. If it ever was.

She didn't have to look at the knight to know his dominating features: his height, his hair color, his kind eyes. Especially the eyes. She felt a flush warm her cheeks.

"My Queen," Sir Roderick broke the silence, clearing the air. "Work progresses well on your Tower."

"It could be our Tower, Sir Roderick," she half whispered.

He didn't answer, merely waiting for what was to come.

"We make a good team," she continued. "You and I. Do you not think so?"

He cleared his throat again. "My Queen. I do not know what to say."

"Tell me what you are feeling, Roderick." She allowed the title to be dropped, using a more personal approach.

Gently placing his hands on Anne's shoulders, he manoeuvred her so they were facing each other. He tucked a finger under her chin, lifting her face so her eyes could meet his. "Are you sure, my Queen?"

Emily-Jane Hills Orford has fond memories and lots of stories that evolved from a childhood growing up in a haunted Victorian mansion. Told she had a 'vivid imagination', the author used this talent to create stories in her head to pass tedious hours while sick, waiting in a doctor's office, listening to a teacher drone on about something she already knew, or enduring the long, stuffy family car rides.

The author lived her stories in her head, allowing her imagination to lead her into a different world, one of her own making. As the author grew up, these stories, imaginings and fantasies took to the written form and, over the years, she developed a reputation for telling a good story. Emily-Jane can now boast that she is an award-winning author of several books, including *Queen Mary's Daughter* (Clean Reads 2018), *Gerlinda* (CFA 2016) which received an Honorable Mention in the 2016 Readers' Favorite Book Awards, *To Be a Duke* (CFA 2014) which was named Finalist and Silver Medalist in the 2015 Next

Generation Indie Book Awards and received an Honorable Mention in the 2015 Readers' Favorite Book Awards and several other books.

A retired teacher of music and creative writing, she writes about the extraordinary in life and the fantasies of dreams combined with memories. For more information on the author, check out her website at: http://emilyjanebooks.ca

9 781952 020339